MATTHEW FRANK

The Killer Inside

PENGUIN BOOKS

PENGUIN BOOKS

UK | USA | Canada | Ireland | Australia
India | New Zealand | South Africa

Penguin Books is part of the Penguin Random House group of companies
whose addresses can be found at global.penguinrandomhouse.com.

First published 2021

001

Copyright © Matthew Frank, 2021

The moral right of the author has been asserted

Set in 9.25/12.5 pt Sabon LT Std
Typeset by Jouve (UK), Milton Keynes
Printed and bound in Great Britain by Clays Ltd, Elcograf S.p.A.

Epigraph quotation 'Lineage', from *Crow: From the Life and Songs of the Crow*
by Ted Hughes © 1970, reproduced by kind permission of Faber and Faber.

The authorized representative in the EEA is Penguin Random House Ireland,
Morrison Chambers, 32 Nassau Street, Dublin D02 YH68

A CIP catalogue record for this book is available from the British Library

ISBN: 978-0-718-18719-4

www.greenpenguin.co.uk

*For Sam, Luke and Jamie, my heart's blessing
and gift to this world*

In the beginning was Scream
Who begat Blood
Who begat Eye
Who begat Fear ...
... Who begat Never
Never Never Never
Who begat Crow ...

Excerpts from Lineage, a poem by Ted Hughes,
first published 1970 in *Crow: From the Life*
and Songs of the Crow

Prologue

Harper surveyed the corpse with a bitter expression and one-word summary – '*Bastard.*'

Fran had known her fellow detective sergeant just long enough to know she didn't like him all that much and generally agreed with him even less, but in this instance he'd pretty much nailed it.

Three bodies in as many weeks. Girls in their late teens or twenties; slim, pretty and dead. Neck twisted tight with grey electrical cable. Drugged, raped, strangled, cleaned with chemicals inside and out, wrapped in translucent blue plastic and dumped. More expedience than ritual. Utter horror.

And this made four.

Same sick MO. Same geographic area. One suspect. No evidence worth a damn.

Not quite the gentle introduction to genteel Greenwich she'd been hoping for in transferring from war-zone Croydon.

'Let's hope he's slipped up this time.' Detective Chief Inspector Groombridge didn't look or sound like he expected that to be the case. Julian Sinclair, if he *was* the killer, had thus far been too careful. Groombridge glanced at Fran. 'They all do, eventually.'

Eventually.

Fran was allergic to waiting. Murders were usually easy. If the killer wasn't standing over the body with a weapon, it was just a case of knocking heads together until someone coughed up a name, and then piling on the pressure till they screwed up or cracked. But this . . . wasn't usual.

By the classic definition – a person who murders at least three people in service of psychological gratification over more than a month with a cooling-off period between each – this was a serial killer.

Contrary to films, TV and books, a very rare event indeed even in gun-crazy America, let alone genteel Greenwich.

The local rag had already given the bastard a nickname – 'The Greenwich Strangler'.

Pretty much said it all, without saying the half of it.

The lack of detail made available to them hadn't stopped the news media having a field day, broadcasting every twist and turn. They were setting up on the perimeter cordon now, preparing for their latest factless speculations. One called out to DCI Groombridge, who ignored him, staring instead at Paige Talbot with a grim expression.

Sixteen years old. Reported missing three days ago. Now found.

She almost looked like she was sleeping peacefully beneath the stars, her skin appearing pale blue from the moonlight rather than from cyanosis or bleach burns. Except for the dark bruising and welts around her mouth and neck and elsewhere.

The killer liked it rough.

Fran wondered how many bodies Groombridge had seen, how many cases, usual or unusual, solved or unsolved. He was the second reason she'd transferred here, the first being a strong desire to be away from her old DI. Groombridge had given her a mauling during the interview and then offered her the job just as she was about to tell him to poke it where the sun didn't shine. He'd been no less hard on her since, but for all his sharp edges, her esteem for him grew daily. She could trust him. It was implicit. He was copper to the core.

Harper, on the other hand, rang hollow.

It didn't take a genius to put this on Sinclair, though.

Two of the girls were taken on their way home from bars he'd regularly haunted, one on a night that door CCTV had him there. The third girl had worked at the dental surgery he attended, and surely it was only a matter of time before a connection to Paige Talbot was uncovered.

Thirty-six, an accountant by training, Sinclair had served some time in tax planning before segueing into financial consultancy and angel investment. No dirt, so far. A generous income with occasional windfalls. Enough for a swanky modern flat on the river, healthy accounts, exclusive gym membership, sharp clothes and a flash car, everything the modern player needed on the pull. But so far, his very proximity was his defence. He was a player, with dozens of one-night conquests, a regular predator stalking the local bars, unabashed and unafraid. He didn't come across as the usual cocksure shit you'd picture, given his success ratio, but perhaps that worked in his favour – playing the decent-guy angle. The theory was he targeted girls that turned him down. He had no real alibis for the somewhat approximate times the girls were taken, killed or dumped. He lived alone with no one to vouch for him. But he knew enough to play dumb. He'd been in for questioning three times and given them nothing but polite bafflement while the press lapped it all up – Sinclair's face splashed everywhere, painted as monster and innocent in equally appalling headlines.

Or maybe it wasn't him.

Fran had spent the last three weeks desperately trying to find anyone else they could point the finger at, but every lead came up short.

What if Groombridge was wrong? What if the killer didn't slip up? How many more girls . . . ?

No. Not on her first case here. Fran was determined. If Julian Sinclair *was* doing this, she would stop him.

PART I
Three Years Later

I

FRIDAY, 1 APRIL

Stark smiled, sipping his single malt while the girl laughed at her
own joke.

Megan. Solicitor. Likes triathlon, mojitos and talking for two.
And, with a bit of luck, inviting home quiet ex-soldiers with scars. So
far, thankfully, she didn't seem to have recognized him from his
most recent bout of unwanted fame. She'd slipped in beside him at
the bar twenty minutes ago and opened with a smile, the way only
beauty can. Stark preferred it when they made the first move.

His most recent brush with death had, his shrink insisted, proved
more flirtation than embrace. He'd clung to the light, in her words,
to life. A commitment to recovery – from depression towards acceptance, the soldier giving way to the policeman, to a new Stark, master
of his PTSD instead of slave to it. He could consider it a rebirth, she
insisted. He'd changed before, so he could again. That's what real
people did, or could do. Or so she said. This may not be what she had
in mind, but baby steps were still steps. Within sensible, self-imposed
restrictions, his life might be enjoyably overlapped with others', so
long as everyone read the minefield warning signs. His ex, Kelly, had
strayed too close. He'd not let that happen again. And Megan looked
like she could read well enough.

Her friends hovered a little way off, gossiping and glancing, fend-
ing off or fishing for attention of their own.

She leant in to hear his response over the heart-thudding bass and
laughed, touching his hand, perfect white teeth glowing in the UV
light, her perfume blissful against the background fog of sweat and
booze.

Raucous laughter broke the spell momentarily, and he glanced over to see a group of young lads swaying out of sync with the music, the disconnected dance of the one-too-many. They'd surrounded a girl in a skimpy sequin number, leering and laughing. Lads on it, like so many; letting off steam or building up a head of it – like squaddies on a pass.

The object of their attentions seemed happy enough, bouncing between them, as, if not more, inebriated.

Megan touched his hand again, leaning in to regain his attention, but Stark was no longer listening. Surrounded Sequin Girl had his full concentration.

Marianne Pensol. Fellow police constable. Almost unrecognizable with her childlike ponytail and fringe replaced with a severe crop.

He'd not seen her since the tragic day that had spun them both out on convalescent leave. A coward with a rifle and police blood on the street – one dead, three wounded including Stark and Pensol, despite his over-publicized efforts. He'd returned on light duties a week ago. Pensol was still off, and from the look of it, coping in a not dissimilar fashion.

One of the pack indulged himself in a grope. She slapped his hand away but carried on grinding to the beat. The lad tried his luck again, spooning her from behind in time with her moves, hands reaching round for chest and groin. She wriggled free but her dancing did little to dissuade him.

'Hey, Earth calling,' Megan tried over the music, patting his hand.

Stark looked back into her ridiculously lovely face and sighed deeply. 'Excuse me a mo . . .'

Perplexed, she watched him slip away from the bar, and her. Stark didn't hold out much hope that he'd get to conclude their conversation. What he was about to attempt had sub-optimal prospects of ending peaceably.

'Annie!' he said loudly, slipping between two of the lads. 'Mind if I cut in?' He smiled at them but avoided eye contact, slipping an arm around Pensol and swinging her in a wide ballroom-style twirl to spread the hyenas out.

They would mind. Now it was just a question of how much.

'Hey,' called the groper. Leader, Stark guessed, not the biggest but the most sure. Lean. Fit. Possible martial artist from the way he stood.

He gripped Pensol as she rocked on her heels, her initial amusement giving way to vaguely vocalized protest. 'You okay, Annie?' he asked, upbeat, holding her hand and guiding her a few steps further from the pack. Her mascara had run. She'd been crying as she danced.

'Oi!' called the leader, re-closing the distance, three henchmen at his shoulder.

'S'all right . . . I'm just her friend,' lied Stark. 'Come to tell her the taxi's here.'

She looked at him, confused. Then smiled in recognition, flung her arms around his neck and landed a big wet kiss, which he only just managed to catch on the cheek instead of the lips. Even so, if a tipping point was needed, that was probably it.

The leader shoved Stark's shoulder, causing Pensol to topple, gripping Stark for balance.

Surrounding dancers had already parted, sensing trouble. Stark glanced around, hoping for bouncers. He caught a glimpse of Megan at the edge of the dance floor, frowning, and cursed any and all gods.

'Sorry, mate,' he tried. 'I promised her I'd get her home and the taxi's here. No harm done.'

Eyes on the lads, Stark felt Pensol regain her balance, but failed to notice as she fetched him a full-on haymaker slap round the face. She stood there swaying, a look of fascinated horror on her face. The henchmen howled with laughter, but the leader had had enough.

Stark saw the punch coming, swayed aside and thrust a palm into the back of his attacker's shoulder to redirect the momentum, sending the lad sliding face first across the dance floor.

The henchmen stared in shock, then at Stark, uncertain how much they fancied stepping in.

Stark readied himself.

A heavy hand grasped his shoulder.

He gripped it as he twisted and swept the legs from his unseen assailant, stepping back to keep the original quartet in his eyeline and Pensol behind him.

Everyone stared. At Stark, and the twenty-stone bouncer he'd just felled, visibly the most shocked of all.

Stark took Pensol's unresisting hand and led her from the club before the Red or Green forces regrouped to stop him, two other bouncers stepping aside, content to watch him leave, Megan and her friends staring at him like he'd just stepped off a flying saucer.

The cold air barely registered as he waved to the first cab idling in the rank outside.

Pensol keeled over and puked.

The cabbie pulled away and drove past them, shaking his head.

Stark sighed and waved a bank note at the next in line.

Pensol's clutch bag furnished her driving licence, address and keys. He ignored the condoms, thinking instead of the doe-eyed rookie he'd met just a few months back, giggling with her cohort and stealing timid glances.

Twenty minutes later he was guiding her into the bedroom of her ground-floor flat. She made another play at kissing him, but he held her at bay and tilted her on to the bed.

He fetched a flannel from the bathroom to clean her face and returned to find her passed out. The sick was all down her dress too, so he unzipped it and peeled it off her, trying to ignore the fact that she had nothing on beneath but a cotton thong with polka-dot love-hearts.

She was quite beautiful; a slender elfin goddess, her skin aglow in the soft bedside light, like an artist's muse captured in alabaster, with one hyper-realist twist – the bullet wound and surgical scars in her ribcage. Healing well. She was lucky – the bullet removed from her lung had taken a deflection en route, slowed enough to prevent an explosive exit wound.

She'd left the hospital before him. By the time he'd come out of his personal bunker, she'd retreated into her own and he'd left her to grieve in her own way – put her from his mind, in all honesty. He wasn't family or friend; it wasn't his place to look out for her. A mistake, perhaps. There were few rights or wrongs in such matters, but he knew from bitter experience the rabbit hole of depression such events could lead down.

Rolling her into the recovery position, he tugged the duvet over her pale form, shifted a pile of clothes from the papasan chair in the corner, kicked off his shoes and settled into it with a sigh.

Not quite the night's end he'd hoped for.

Waiting until he was satisfied that she was breathing peacefully, he closed his eyes.

Recollections of the deadly day that had brought the occupants of this room to this point flashed unwelcome to mind, chasing and snapping in the long dark . . .

FEEEEEEEAR!

A mocking scream high above, where a tiny shadow circled lazily though the blinding sun.

Crow.

Portent.

Watching.

Waiting, with Death's own patience.

Hungry.

Hands blistered and charred with black tiger stripes. Blood-matted, singed fur. Always bloody. Pinky finger there but not . . . Side torn with shrapnel, leg . . . useless. Breath ragged. Blood soaking into the desiccated red dust. Life leaching. Pain. Fury. Control . . . control . . . fight! Relax, breathe, aim, hold, fire! Rifle barking percussive death, defiant . . .

Relax, breathe, aim, hold, *fire!*

Death. All around. Bodies in the street.

Laughter. Contempt. Spit . . . Desperate fingers slipping from bloody hand, falling, falling. Victory. Red in tooth and claw.

The crow froze in the sun and stooped like a bullet . . . *NEVER NEVER NEVER!*

Stark woke with a start, heart scudding, mind lurching in disorientation . . . eyes struggling to adjust from desert blind to cold pre-dawn light, leaking in around unfamiliar, ill-fitting curtains . . .

Phone, vibrating in his jacket pocket . . .

Hands trembling, he squinted at the caller ID with a resigned certainty.

Fran – detective sergeant and general bane of his life. The only person he knew with no qualms whatsoever about calling at ungodly hours.

'Sarge,' he croaked, dry-mouthed and sore-headed.

'You sound like shit,' she announced, over-loudly. 'Where are you?'

'Hell.'

'Just deserts. How soon can you get here?'

Stark groaned inside, wondering if she'd ever tire of phoning on his days off to ask him that. 'Why?'

'It's today.'

He sat up, then curled up as his head announced that pounding was merely a prelude to the main percussion piece.

'Did you hear me?' demanded Fran.

Stark remembered the date. April 1st . . . April Fool's Day. 'Is this a wind-up?'

'Does it *sound* like I'm joking? Sodding CPS withdrew their appeal, just like I said they would. Sinclair walks this morning.'

2

He left Pensol sleeping, crept from the room and silently closed the door.

As he was pulling on his shoes, the smell of coffee turned his head.

A girl in baggy pyjamas leant in the kitchen doorway, eyeing him disapprovingly over a steaming mug. 'Did you even leave a note?'

Stark tried not to look guilty. 'I just helped her home. Nothing happened.' The girl – a flatmate, Stark assumed, seeing the open door to the second bedroom – looked unconvinced. 'We just work together. I'm –'

'I know who you are,' she interrupted. 'That's what makes this worse.'

Stark didn't know what to say to that. He'd hoped that Pensol's unrequited crush on him had been forgotten in the subsequent turmoil.

The flatmate took a slurp of coffee. 'She's been hurt enough.'

'Then hopefully she won't even remember I was here.'

'And if she does?'

'Tell her I hope she's okay.'

The flatmate's expression indicated deep dissatisfaction.

Stark fished a card from his jacket and handed it to her. 'Look . . . Keep this tucked away for . . . I don't know . . . for emergencies, I guess. Has she said when she's coming back to work?'

The flatmate took the card, lips pursed. 'She's in a bad way. I don't know if she will go back.'

Stark knew that state, but there was little he could add. Nodding, he left and set off on the mile-plus penitent limp home without the walking cane he'd left at home to improve his chances of pulling the likes of Megan the triathlete, telling himself this wasn't a real walk-of-shame but feeling it was all the same.

Fran saw his car pull up and stepped back from the window. Forty-five minutes. To get home from whatever den of iniquity she'd roused him from, clean himself up and drive to hers, shiny as a new pin. She never ceased to be amazed. Or irritated. She hated lateness, in others at least, but Stark wore wordless punctuality like a prize rosette. Or a medal. And he had quite enough of those already.

She looked at her watch again.

'Muttering darkly to oneself is considered a poor reflection of mental stability,' said a voice behind her.

Fran turned to glare at Marcus, who smiled amiably back over his espresso. Bless him, he needn't have got up too. But they were still in the early days of whatever this was, and his gentleman genes probably still thought it rude to let a lady skip breakfast alone, or to hang around in her flat without her. 'Are you calling me unstable?'

'Most data contain outliers,' he conceded, retreating behind science.

'So now I'm abnormal?'

'Unique,' he suggested, trying not to laugh. 'Not to mention formidable, kind-hearted and did I mention beautiful in the mornings?'

'And the rest of the time?' she demanded.

'Positively radiant, like the sun.'

'Watch you don't get burned,' she replied, pulling on her coat and picking up her phone as it buzzed with Stark's text saying he was outside.

Marcus leant over to peck her on the lips. 'Good luck.'

'Thanks.'

'Try not to immolate anyone.'

She harrumphed, letting the door slam shut behind her.

Stark's pin looked more shined than new for once, she observed, settling into the passenger seat. 'Heavy night?'

'The usual battlefield of debauchery,' he countered, guiding the car out into traffic. He never gave much away.

Fran didn't like being driven, least of all by Stark, who drove like an old lady. But she was still locked in a battle of wills with Central Procurement, who'd been trying to fob her off with some tiny piece of shit as if it were somehow her fault that her previous unmarked car had been inconveniently riddled with bullets three months ago. And she was stubbornly refusing to sign out a car from the borough pool in case CP decided that was good enough.

It wasn't Stark's fault either, really, but she was making him drive her around in penance all the same. For reasons she'd more or less had to force out of him, he was better driving than being driven too – more a reflection of his combat PTSD than her more 'assertive' driving style, she was determined to believe. The car pool had furnished him with an automatic on open-ended loan since his recent triumphant return, to take the load off his injured leg – after she'd let them know their hero was stubbornly limping to work.

Hard to believe that it was only three months since she'd paced up and down outside the operating theatre not knowing whether he was alive or dead, like that idiot philosopher with the cat in the box. Stark had explained that one to her once but it just made her cross. *Thought experiment . . . ?* Just open the sodding box and *look*! But of course, the surgical staff wouldn't *let* her look. On TV the hero gets shot through the leg and two minutes later they're hobbling after the bad guy. In real life the hero bleeds to death; and Stark *was* a hero, with medals and scars to prove it. More medals due, if the press had their way. Not that he'd talk about that, or any of it.

He'd given her the scare of her life, and then just folded himself away, refusing to see anyone he knew after his surgery. Formal debriefs and statements had been taken by the Mass Incident Team from HQ. Fran, Groombridge and the rest of the MIT were too close, the whole station, witnesses instead of investigators. Such a mess. It was weeks before he got in touch. No apologies, just an email to say he was out of hospital and down at his mother's place in Gosport.

It was the dreaded exams that broke the ice.

How's the revision going? he'd asked as a postscript.

Non-existent, she'd replied. *Too busy clearing up your mess.*

Nothing for several hours, making her think she'd offended him. Emails were a misunderstanding minefield. But then a reply, with a web-link to the Inspectors' Exam study notes login page, and – *need some help?*

No doubt he'd already memorized every page of his Sergeants' Exam notes and was bored.

It was another week before they actually spoke by phone. He'd seemed hesitant. Not a word she would normally associate with him. And then, of all things, an apology. For not being in touch sooner. For not checking in to see if she was okay. For scaring her, taking risks and leaving everyone else to clear up the mess. He hoped the team and the wider station were recovering as well as could be expected.

She'd been joking in her email, she insisted. He'd stopped a madman at ridiculous personal risk and paid a high price.

They'd all paid a high price, he'd replied.

They hadn't talked about it since.

And he'd returned to work in better shape, limp aside. Better shape in his head. More of the old spark. Some kind of corner turned.

The walking stick was back, though. A legacy from his old army injuries, returned with police injuries. The secret sting in its tail was something both she and DCI Groombridge were having to ignore again for now. A sword-cane was hardly authorized police issue, but it had been given to Stark by high royalty. His old limp had all but faded before the idiot took a fresh bullet. She knew he hated relying on a stick and would shed it again as soon as he could, and they could all relax.

'Where to?' he asked.

'Belmarsh.' The prison service had played a shell game with the press, shifting Sinclair between prisons and sending out decoy vans and misinformation, but he would walk out the gate of Belmarsh maximum security prison in half an hour, the place he'd called home for the last two years, and the place Fran firmly believed he should rot in for the rest of his hateful days.

Sodding barrister! Sodding appeal judges and CPS! Sodding, fucking lab techs!

She realized she was muttering under her breath again, and stopped. Stark made no mention of it, as usual. She silently cursed him, and Marcus too.

God, it was good to have Stark back.

Especially today. She needed his counterweight, today more than ever. A man of few words; of action and dark capabilities. If she'd possessed his skill set she might well do harm today. Instead, he brought the detachment she could not. Uninvolved in the original case, he had no motivation to let her throttle Sinclair the moment the filthy shit breathed free air.

Fran had six motivations. Six names she'd like to carve into Sinclair's eyeballs: Karen Gillespie, Magda Janowski, Teresa Leman, Paige Talbot, Leah Willoughby and Sara Brompton.

3

Pink ripples hung in the indigo sky while the sun dragged its heels somewhere below the artificial horizon of London's urban sprawl. Pink sky in the morning – coppers' warning.

They'd have a name, that kind of cloud. Stark would know it, so she wasn't going to ask him.

Even in this light, Her Majesty's Prison Belmarsh wasn't pretty. Fran derived some satisfaction from its content but the edifice itself was not the eighth wonder of Thamesmead, let alone the Royal London Borough of Greenwich or wider world. The wide, empty car park, sheltered from the main road by trees, gave it an off-season theme-park gloom.

She sipped her coffee, forgetting its dregs were long cold. Swallowing with great reluctance and an apology to her protesting stomach, she opened the car window and poured the remnants on the pavement – lest she forget again. It wasn't like her to let a coffee go cold. She wasn't feeling herself today. She felt achy and tired, like she was coming down with flu. To hell with that, though, with Sinclair walking free. She could be ill later.

Stark shifted in his seat, adjusting the rear-view mirror to peer at something. 'What?' she demanded irritably.

'White van. In the bus stop, through the trees.'

Fran shook her head. 'Stop being paranoid.'

One last decoy transport van with armed escort had emerged five minutes ago, just in case any press paps had decided to bet on the outside chance, but the coast appeared clear. Even Sinclair's detestable barrister had been sent to the wrong prison, through a regrettable and entirely deniable administrative oversight that Fran had taken great pains over. Hopefully the spiteful cow was standing outside HMP Wandsworth at this very moment with a phalanx of TV reporters, and about to look as foolish as she delighted in making everyone else look.

'You sure you want to do this?' asked Stark, not for the first time. It wasn't like him to be cautious. That in itself should sound a warning note, so Fran ignored him. 'The Guv'nor would have a fit if he knew we were here.'

'The Guv'nor would be here himself if he wasn't . . .' She trailed off. Stark shifted in his seat again.

If he wasn't tainted by this shitstorm, Fran concluded silently. DCI Groombridge was taking all the flak. Protecting his team. Protecting Fran. This mess was her fault. Misplaced forensics wouldn't have mattered if she hadn't screwed up their only witness.

A prison officer appeared from the portcullis-styled door, a man beside him. Sinclair? He looked smaller. The prisoner extended a hand – a farewell. The officer ignored it. The prisoner shook his head and the door closed behind him – a prisoner no longer, not even an ex-con officially.

Julian Sinclair: rapist, murderer, free man. Conviction quashed on a forensic technicality. Exonerated.

Fran placed her hand on the door handle.

'Seriously,' said Stark. 'This isn't a good idea.'

'Just shut up.'

'You know I'm right.'

'That's why I want you to shut up.' She glanced at him. 'Stop smiling.'

'Just a poorly executed grimace, Sarge. Let's just go for breakfast, my shout.'

'There's no way that motherfucker is walking free without me staring him in the eye,' said Fran, bitterly angry. 'He has to know we're not done.' To know they would never stop watching him; that he wouldn't get away with it again, even removed from the Sex Offenders' Register as he would be from today. Whatever rock he slid under next they would make sure the local force knew exactly what he was.

She climbed out, leaving Stark to decide if he'd follow.

He did, of course.

Sinclair was looking around, no doubt for his bitch barrister and adoring press. *Too bad, arsehole.* He'd courted, pouted and pranced for the cameras quite enough. Now he'd have to go back inside and beg for a taxi or wait at the bus stop like any other jailbird.

He saw her approach and hesitated.

Fran waited for the smile. Sinclair was snake and charmer rolled into one. Sexual predator and smug shit; casually evading their budget-limited surveillance to carry on taking girls even after becoming prime suspect, named in all the papers. *Six* victims by the time they finally had enough to arrest him, that they knew of, five dead, one survivor. Young women, raped and throttled, cleaned and dumped. He was careful, methodical, calculated and cold-blooded. And he smiled. All through his arrest, trial, conviction, failed appeal, and now this sodding referral by the Criminal Cases Review Commission, he'd smiled and diffidently proclaimed his innocence.

He wasn't smiling now. Prison had done him no favours. He looked older, thinner, almost frail, eyes wary. On the record, he'd taken one beating inside before being taken out of the general population, but his bitch barrister had claimed continuous physical and psychological abuse and a blind-eye policy from prison officers. Even if half of it was true, Fran could find little sympathy. The fact that he could make her feel that way, made her stomach turn.

Now came the smile, or a weak imitation of it, though he was wise enough not to proffer a hand to her. Fran fought the temptation to claw his serpentine face.

His gaze shifted to Stark with a flicker of recognition – mirror opposites of celebrity.

Fran opened her mouth to deliver her message, but the sound of screeching tyres cut her off.

A white van skidded to a halt behind them.

Two men jumped out of the sliding side door, sporting blue overalls, hoods and hockey masks.

'*Get in the van!*' the first man bellowed, pointing a pistol at them.

Stark stepped into Fran's eyeline, arms out sideways, keeping her and Sinclair behind him.

'*Get in the* fucking *van!*' screamed the man, voice distorting around the thick plastic mask.

Stark put his hands up, capitulant, stepping forward . . . but the gun went off.

Fran's entire body shook with the shock of it.

Stark's movements changed in an instant; shifting sideways, thrusting the gunman's arm upwards, delivering a vicious blow to the mask and twisting the weapon free in one smooth action.

In the blink of an eye the gunman was sprawled on the ground groaning with Stark brandishing the pistol over him in a double-handed grip.

But in another blink, Stark collapsed to the floor like a rag doll.

Behind him the second assailant stood with a crackling electric stun baton.

Fran felt for her bag and the CS spray and ASP baton she'd taken to carrying since the recent shootings, but it was in the car.

The first assailant struggled to his knees, groped for the dropped pistol and climbed up into an off-balance sway, blood leaking through the hockey-mask holes, pistol arm coming up but waving around drunkenly.

Fran flinched backward, tripped over something and sprawled on her arse, cracking both elbows.

It took her a second to realize it was Sinclair; prone, still and bleeding. *Shot.*

The guy with the stun baton stood looking around, seemingly uncertain what to do next.

'*Gotta go!*' screamed the driver through the open window, his face covered in an identical mask. '*COME ON!*'

As if to punctuate his words, the prison alarm siren went off, signalling that officers inside had heard the shot – and Belmarsh had its own dedicated CO19 firearms team. These fuckwits had chosen a dumb place to attempt a kidnap.

The stun-baton guy grabbed the dizzy pistol guy, dragging him into the van.

With a cloud of smoke, it wheel-spun out the car park and away.

4

'Little point asking why you were there,' DCI Groombridge muttered darkly. 'After we agreed it was a terrible idea.'

Fran winced, glad he wasn't there to give her that look which always made her feel ten years old and never failed to get her back up. She bit her tongue. 'Guv.'

'Anything hurt?'

Fran opted not to mention her bruised elbows and backside. Or the nausea of having a gun pointed at her, again, added to stomach backflips at yet another coffee-breakfast and generally feeling like crap. As if the smell of hospitals wasn't bad enough, a porter's trolley of disgusting patient breakfasts had just been wheeled past, and the so-called food on offer in the canteen downstairs was below contempt. 'Just my pride.'

'Well, that could use a dent or two,' he replied tartly, but Fran recognized the current of amusement beneath and allowed herself a rueful smile in the privacy of her own end of the phone call. He never remained angry with her for longer than necessary to make his point. 'Well that's the ticking off dealt with. How's that shithead Sinclair?'

'Flesh wound, but they won't let me near him yet. Bullet through the trapezius muscle – top of the shoulder by the neck, close to the jugular – inch over and it might've done us and the world a favour.'

'Normally that would be a sentiment deserving of another ticking off,' mused Groombridge, 'but in this instance . . . We'll have no shortage of suspects.'

'We've got to start with the Talbots for this, surely, Guv.'

'Agreed. But there's a long line behind them that would love to get their hands on Sinclair just as much.'

But few with form like the Talbots. Paige Talbot, victim number four, had a broad extended family, but it was her brothers that fit this frame. Three – like this morning's crew. They were big enough, bad enough and dumb enough to pull a stunt like this. The eldest, Dean, had served four-out-of-seven for violent assault, and was still on licence. The younger two, Troy and Blake, were little better, with youth records as long as your arm, minor convictions and reputations for violence, robbery and car theft. And the matriarch, Rhonda Talbot, had been ejected from Sinclair's trial for shouting death threats; threats Dean later repeated for the TV cameras outside.

'How's Stark?'

'Stoic.'

Groombridge huffed a laugh. 'The two words share etymological roots in Old English, I believe.'

'He's got a grump on 'cos the second perp zapped him, I think.'

'Ahh,' said Groombridge sagely. 'Not exactly light duties. Well, perhaps his pride could use a dent too. Any chance we can keep his name out of this?'

'Well, there was no press there . . .'

'But?'

'But, for a second it looked like Sinclair recognized him.'

'Great. And if there was anyone more inclined to spin the press . . .' said Groombridge, his tone reminding her that it was her fault Stark was there at all. The last thing this mess needed was something else for the media to sink their fangs into, and Joe Stark was national news all by himself.

Stark rolled his shoulder with a wince, its perennial ache exacerbated by his earlier fall. God, he hated being tasered. Twice in special forces selection, now twice in the police. He'd banged his head pretty hard too. The paramedic had declared him more lucky than concussed but, all things considered, he'd far rather be waking hung-over from mojitos next to Megan, the solicitor-triathlete, right now. Some headaches were more worth it than others.

Fran had left him behind to assist the scenes of crime officers and speak to the prison officials.

The only blood on the ground was Sinclair's. There was a small spot on Stark's cuff, but this was as likely to be from his own split knuckles punching a hard-plastic mask as from the perp behind it. Hardly anything to be proud of. Taking the gun had been an instinctive reaction to it being fired, but failing to turn it on the second perp in time had been unforgivable. He was lucky it had been a stun baton and not another gun or a blade. His only consolation, the fact that the would-be kidnappers had fled without their prize.

No tracking devices had been found on his car – a long shot anyway – but somehow the perps had known where and when to strike. Surely they hadn't just followed him? The army drummed threat assessment in hard and experience burned it in harder.

The van had been caught on the prison's CCTV. DCs Williams, Hammed and Dixon were working with the traffic camera team back at the station to trace it, starting from the one near the prison bus stop, but nothing had come over the radio since the description was broadcast.

The SOCOs had already found the bullet, impacted in the prison's brick façade after passing through Sinclair's flesh. Fired from a Glock 17 or 19, Stark was sure from his brief time with it. He clenched his fists to stop his hands trembling. Adrenaline comedown, anger and more. If he closed his eyes for more than a blink the barrel flickered in his vision with its deathly whisper – *Next time, next time. If not you, them . . .*

'Constable Stark?'

Turning, he found a solid woman in her fifties eyeing him quizzically.

'Eleanor Grainger,' she smiled, extending a hand.

Disconcerted, Stark shook it. 'Governor Grainger . . .' He glanced down at his bandaged knuckles and the SOCO T-shirt and high-vis jacket he'd cadged from the Crime Scene Manager. His jacket and shirt were in an evidence bag. 'I . . .'

'Wasn't expecting the organ grinder?' she suggested.

'Well, no. You really needn't have.'

'Happy to,' she smiled. 'You rather saved the day, I'm told. A habit of yours. Figured you deserved the VIP tour.'

'I'd hardly call what happened here –'

'Never look a gift horse in the mouth, Sergeant.'

'Oh no, I'm just a Detective Constable,' Stark insisted, trying not to think about the upcoming Sergeants' Exam he'd been corralled into by Groombridge.

Grainger shook her head. 'You can take the sergeant out of the army, but not out of the man, I've always found. Speaking of which . . .' She stood to attention and snapped off a salute. 'Colonel Grainger, at your service,' she smiled. 'And a pleasure it is to meet you, Sergeant Stark VC.'

He should've recognized her demeanour at once. Perhaps he'd hit his head harder than he thought. Being saluted by officers was something the NCO in him would never get used to, but the little bronze medal locked away in his bank deposit box demanded it. The Victoria Cross. Her Majesty's highest award for military valour, or in his case for allowing anger to overcome self-preservation. He forced a smile and saluted back.

'Red Caps,' she explained. Royal Military Police. Monkeys, as they were unaffectionately known in the ranks – short for Monkey Hangers – after an infamous incident in Hartlepool during the Napoleonic wars. 'Twenty-five years in. Still on the books if they ever need me.' She sounded like she missed it.

Technically Stark was still a reservist too. The fact that he'd never pass fit again seemed less important to the army than his PR potential. The damned medal again. He'd long since given up asking for his discharge. Perhaps when his MoD handler got back from her sunshine holiday in Helmand . . .

'Used to find them, like you,' said Grainger. 'Now I guard them.'

'And the bit in the middle?' asked Stark, who'd seen the system incarcerate the good and now free the bad.

'Not our job.'

'But if we don't care, who will?'

She smiled diplomatically, gesturing toward the prison. 'Shall we?'

'My client will allow you to speak with him just as soon as he feels well enough,' chirped the Bitch Barrister brightly, enjoying every second. Miranda Moncrieff, QC, clearly still ruffle-feathered from the morning's shenanigans.

'His doctors tell us he's well enough now,' said Fran evenly, muzzling her frustration, if not her dislike. This woman had torn her and her star witness apart on the stand two years ago. And now she'd succeeded in tearing apart the forensic evidence to get her monstrous client released.

'I think Mr Sinclair should be the judge, don't you?' said the BB chippily.

Fran had little faith in judges today. 'Mr Sinclair may have information pertinent –'

'So what now?' demanded Moncrieff. 'You'll arrest him for impeding an investigation? You just can't seem to help yourselves, can you? This is moving beyond harassment into persecution. I promise you questions will be asked about this morning's debacle. One might call the lack of protection offered to my client, innocent in the eyes of the law, wilful, were it not so obviously vindictive.' Fran suspected she was being rehearsed upon, and this speech would be trotted out for the cameras before long. Getting Sinclair off would be the making of this amoral witch's career, and she'd milk it for every penny. 'My client –'

'Didn't he stop being your client this morning?' Fran interrupted curtly. A barrister's work ended at the courthouse steps, but this one wasn't about to be cheated out of her limelight. 'Or does he anticipate rearrest?'

Moncrieff was too cool to bite back. 'The only arrests you should be concerned with are the Talbot family and whoever in your so-called organization tipped them off.'

'Unlike *some*, the police don't spout wild accusations without evidence, such as witness statements,' Fran smiled thinly. 'So, since you seem to be doubling up as his solicitor, perhaps you'd tell Julian that I'll be back for *his* first thing tomorrow morning. It'll be in his interest to cooperate, for once. And in the meantime, I'm sure he'll be happy to have two burly uniforms guarding his door.'

Fran left before the ice queen could get a riposte in, feeling pleased with herself. She wondered if she'd hate the barrister quite so much if the bitch wasn't so slim, pretty, self-assured and successful; and decided she would.

5

'Death threats by the dozen,' reported Stark to the team, after privately changing into a spare shirt from his desk drawer. Grainger had provided digital scans of all of Sinclair's mail, which the prison service had the right to inspect, legal correspondence aside. 'And a worrying amount of fan mail.'

'Sick saddos,' added DC Williams, a reliable bellwether for the general sentiment.

'Focus on the hate mail for now,' said Fran. Stark silently wondered if they'd find any from her.

'Do the Talbots even know how to read and write?' huffed Williams. He could usually be relied upon to ease the darker moments, too. He reminded Stark of some of the better corporals he'd served with. The other two DCs were privates through and through. The next in years was Hammed, experienced but prone to miss things, and Dixon, dependable but unconfident. Stark liked all three well enough, but they'd been together longer and even after two years he still felt like the outsider. His fault, not theirs, and he didn't mind. He'd always felt that way – in school, the army and the police. Of the three, only Hammed appeared to harbour any discontent that Stark had leapfrogged them to the Sergeants' Exam, but they all seemed to accept it. His injury-truncated army career had ended with sergeant's stripes. Perhaps it was that. Certainly that was how DCI Groombridge put it privately to Stark – a natural re-levelling.

'There was a rumour the Talbots might use prison contacts to come at Sinclair by proxy, but nothing came of it,' said Stark. 'And they're not in here, apparently,' he added, waving the memory stick Grainger's team had given him.

'They made explicit threats on his life at the time,' said Fran. 'And there's three of them.'

'I agree,' said Groombridge, fresh from HQ. 'And Dean served time in Belmarsh – he could have bought or extorted the time and location from a guard, directly or indirectly. Find and talk to them. They'll have alibis ready, I'm sure, so get details, times, places, associates. The more information they give us, the more edges we have to unpick their lies . . . if it's them.'

'DNA should cut through the crap,' said Fran. 'We've got all three brothers on the offenders' database.'

'If the blood sample DC Stark so kindly obtained doesn't turn out to be his own,' agreed Groombridge. 'At least there should be enough heat on this to get testing approved.'

'I'll go through these for other candidates anyway,' suggested Stark, knowing it was the kind of tedious task that his reputation for borderline-OCD thoroughness inevitably landed on his desk anyway. 'And we shouldn't discount the Jersey connection.'

As the only member of the team not involved in the original case, Stark had reviewed the prosecution files at Fran's behest months ago when the fresh appeal and case review was little more than disturbing rumour. The team and the CPS had looked hard at Sinclair's business dealings for something they could use but found nothing. His customers, from architects to undertakers, even those whose businesses had ultimately gone belly up, had used their praise for his professionalism to emphasize their astonishment at the charges he faced. Until the offshore side of his dealings became public knowledge.

Whether or not you believed Sinclair was a serial killer, he was, by any respectable measure, a scumbag. He'd made money whether the companies he advised were on the up or on the rocks, advising the latter on disposal of assets, including properties, often at knockdown prices to a development company based in Jersey – which he also invoiced. Mutual back-scratching. Sinclair's consultancy had a 'London office', his home, but a 'headquarters' registered to a rent-an-address service in St Helier, Jersey – code for offshore tax avoidance and the squirrelling away of ill-gotten gains. All invoices were paid to the HQ, which then 'loaned' him a monthly sum tax-free. There was, of course, no record of any interest or repayments, nor would there be. And he'd even tried his own hand – picking up the flat above an undertaker's for a pittance and flipping it for a profit when the unsavoury business downstairs foundered soon after despite following his sage business advice. The trial had exposed that aspect of his predatory nature to past and future clientele, but no illegality could be demonstrated.

'Fraud Squad sieved for dirt and found nothing,' replied Fran dismissively. 'Picking off cheap real estate from his client's carcasses and squirrelling the profits offshore wasn't connected to the murders, apparently.'

'Nice little nest egg waiting for the bastard now he's loose to fly south, though,' said Williams, who supported a family of six on police wages. Any prisoner released on licence had their passport withheld, but Sinclair was exonerated and free to skip the country with his barely-well-gotten gains any time he chose.

'Tax avoidance – not *evasion*,' Fran clarified. 'At the end of the day, that's what the Channel Islands are for, they said.'

'Aside from annoying the French,' added Williams dryly.

'But no chance of an Al Capone conviction,' concluded Fran. 'Believe me, I'd happily go for that right now, if only to wipe the slimy smile off his face.'

'I'm just saying people lost money, lost businesses,' said Stark. 'It's not just the families with a grudge against Sinclair.' They all saw the suspect list stretching into the distance, and he pre-empted her next words. 'I'll go through the Fraud Squad report again, too.'

Groombridge nodded. 'What about the van?'

'Nothing yet,' said Williams. 'A first-generation Citroën Dispatch. Fake plates, predictably; duplicated from a written-off Mazda. Cameras show it out on Western Way, heading west, but we lose it after a minute. Traffic are helping us expand the circle.'

'Okay,' Groombridge sighed. 'The politics of this mean I have to concentrate more than usual on keeping the brown stuff from raining down on us, so DS Millhaven takes the lead with DC Stark as bagman. Might as well get used to it, pending their no-doubt-stellar performance in their upcoming exams. We're in a corner here. But I know I can rely on you all.'

Voices in the corridor turned their heads as Superintendent Cox ushered in a senior uniform.

Deputy Assistant Commissioner Stevens – a man with few friends in Royal Hill Police Station and an axe to grind. His recently failed plot to boost his power base by merging the Greenwich force with neighbouring Lewisham had derailed with the bloodbath outside, but he'd milked the PR fallout for every ounce of self-promotion he could.

'Right,' he said, without preamble. 'You'd better tell me how you plan to clear up this clusterfuck.' He didn't go so far as to cast blame, but you could bet he'd be whispering poison higher up.

Groombridge directed Fran to take it from the top. Stevens listened impatiently, occasionally casting an unimpressed glance Stark's way.

'Well,' he said sourly. 'I don't need to tell you what a field day the press will have with all this. Sinclair's legal team were already building a damages claim. They'll be adding zeros as we speak. Find out how this happened. Find the perpetrators. You can't disappear in a vehicle in London in broad daylight. You'll have all the resources you need.' A meaningless statement in austere times, but another whip to lash them with if they failed, thought Stark. 'Try not to fuck this up any more. If I find out one of you leaked the time and location of Sinclair's release, don't rely on the Commissioner's office to close ranks – I'll throw you to the wolves myself. And if you wouldn't mind, I think the press might like to know we're redoubling our efforts to find the *real* Greenwich Strangler.'

The press. Not the victims' families or even potential future victims. Stevens' priorities laid bare, thought Stark as the DAC strode out with Cox in his wake.

'And fuck you very much,' muttered Williams darkly.

6

The Talbot brothers weren't hard to find.

The sign over their yard declared them trustworthy car mechanics, removers of dents and scratches, and provided them with ample cover for disappearing vehicles of the stolen variety should the fancy take them, which they denied it ever did.

The yard was chock-a-block with damaged or down-at-heel motors stripped for parts, ageing luxury marques and boyish rides pimped on the cheap.

Fran recalled the first time she'd come here, the morning after finding Paige's body. Come to tell three brothers their sister was dead, and worse. Each of the bereaved families lived on with their grief, but the Talbots had the profile to act on it. If the nightmares Fran suffered on this case were a tenth of theirs, few could blame them for going after Paige's killer. Sometimes the warrant card in her pocket felt like a galactic black hole sucking in all available light, with Fran stretched forever on the event horizon; another Stark explanation she'd found deeply unsatisfactory. Relativism, in her opinion, was for lawyers.

The same three Rottweilers lolled, chained to a tyre filled with concrete that they were easily large enough to drag around should they take a dislike to you, and stared at her as she weaved between the hulks as if trying to recall why they'd not eaten her last time.

They weren't the most dangerous animals here.

Not for the first time, Fran wished she had Stark beside her. Williams could probably handle himself as well as most coppers, but Stark could handle anything. He had a capability for violence beyond anything Fran had seen before, which while frightening, was damn reassuring sometimes.

Music blared from somewhere inside, talked over by a jabbering DJ using London patois and semi-intelligible hyperbole. Probably not the kind of station that ran regular news updates.

One of the dogs gave a single, booming bark.

'Fuck me,' drawled a gruff voice, 'if it isn't Detective Sergeant Millstone.' Troy Talbot; middle brother; greasy, longer stubble around his jowly face than his pate, emerging into the light wiping oily hands on an oily rag. 'Come to tell us how sorry you are you fucked up and let that cunt Sinclair off the hook?' asked Troy.

If he'd been even slightly less repulsive, she might've considered it. But even were she not severely allergic to apologizing, ever since the criminal case review kicked off, the edict from the lawyers at HQ was 'admit no liability – ever'.

Blake, the youngest, emerged behind Troy. Neither showed signs of injury. There was a good chance Stark had broken the gunman's nose earlier. He'd also suggested that he might have broken the man's trigger finger when he'd taken the gun, depending on the efficacy of the pre-emptive face strike. He said these things like they were normal.

'Is Dean here too?' she asked.

Troy shook his head. 'Meeting with our stockbroker.'

'How's his nose?' Fran fished.

Troy frowned. 'Crooked as ever. Ugly bastard. Got his looks from his dad.' Although they shared a mother, Rhonda, their looks backed up the rumour that each of the Talbot brothers could claim a different father, though not name them. 'Why?'

'What can you tell me about this van?' asked Fran, holding up a still of the Citroën.

Troy peered at it. 'Piece of shit. Yours?'

'Have you ever seen or worked on it? Given it a bit of a boost?' Rumour had it they weren't above supplying the occasional getaway car too.

Troy looked over at Blake but they both shook their heads.

'Mind if we flip through your paperwork, just to be sure?'

Both brothers chuckled. 'Dean ain't much of a one for record-keeping.'

'Mind if we look inside, all the same?' asked Williams.

The two brothers looked uncertain. 'That depends on whether you got a warrant, Officer Millstone.'

'We can get one.'

Now they both looked distinctly uncomfortable. Troy frowned deeply. 'What's this about?'

'They looked as much pleased as surprised,' reported Fran.

Groombridge pursed his lips thoughtfully. 'Alibis?'

'All-night poker with pals. We're following up.'

'And Dean?'

'I left a card with them for him to call me. He wasn't at his home, or his gym. Uniform have his description and Dixon is checking with the hospitals, walk-in clinics and local doctors to see if he turned up anywhere with a sore nose or broken finger.'

'But they let you look around inside?'

Fran nodded. 'Williams photographed some VIN numbers to check, but they obviously didn't have anything stolen there at the time. Or our van. Their yard's CCTV cameras are fakes for show. We didn't spot any on the surrounding streets in or out. Any chance I can sit an unmarked outside?'

Groombridge didn't even bother to laugh. So much for DAC Stevens' promise of all the resources they needed. 'The important thing is to find Dean Talbot. What about his car?'

'A blacked-out Range Rover Sport,' said Fran. 'Parked outside his house. But the Brothers Dim said they often just use whichever car is nearest the gate.'

'All right,' sighed Groombridge. 'Start from the bottom and work up.'

Code for, *we've got nothing*, thought Fran. Same-old same-old.

There was a knock on the door and Hammed poked his head around. 'Sorry, Guv. But Brigade just finished putting out a vehicle fire in Woolwich. White Citroën Dispatch.'

7

The smoke had gone but the acrid smell lingered. Angry car owners remonstrated with police uniforms on the perimeter, demanding to know when they'd be allowed to retrieve their rides. Fran could still feel the heat emanating from the three most irretrievable. The next two out would need new paint at the least. The one in the centre was melted – the source of the conflagration.

Not even a loving mother could recognize these remains but the SOCO officers insisted it was a Citroën Dispatch and pointed to a piece of surviving paintwork inside what was left of the rear cab, clearly blue, but with signs of white spray paint.

So the van had been resprayed for the job. If they could lift the exact chemical composition, they could search the Talbots' workshop for a corresponding tin. She'd seen hundreds there. But the connection would be circumstantial at best, and if they were spraying a vehicle for their own illegal use, even the Talbots had enough nous to toss that paint after.

'Anything inside?' she asked the Crime Scene Manager, one of the juniors for a scene without a body.

'Anything in mind?'

'Plastic hockey masks, times three? Pistol? Cattle prod? Locks of hair and fireproof signed confessions?'

He shook his head ruefully. 'If only.'

'VIN?' The vehicle identification number would be stamped into the engine block and discreet locations inside the bodywork.

'I'll let you know once it's cooled down.'

Fran rubbed her forehead, looking around. A tucked away side street with no parking restrictions, rare gold in London. But no cameras. A car thief's paradise, as the regular dustings of broken glass testified. Not to mention muggers. She made a mental note to check for usual suspects arrested in the area – just in case the perps had been spotted by the kind of citizen that faded away at the first sound of a siren.

None of the current gawpers had noticed the fire start or three men switching vehicles, and the police incident signs were a lottery at best. If Fran had her way they'd read – *If you saw something, please fulfil your civic duty rather than sticking your head in the sand like everything wrong in this world is someone else's problem, or wasting our time with lies, fantasies or mis-rememberings.*

So they were back to scanning local cameras and checking nearby car parks and public transport to see if they could pick up three men travelling together in a conspicuous manner.

Long shots.

Fran cursed under her breath.

Aside from their idiotic choice of kidnap location, so far the perps seemed to know what they were doing. Criminal knowledge with an element of stupidity – the Talbot brothers to a tee. But they all slip up eventually, as a certain DCI was so fond of saying.

Someone had slipped up badly, thought Groombridge, watching the TV, and ice-cool Miranda Moncrieff QC was making hay.

'Questions will be asked,' she stated with cold assurance, 'into why the Metropolitan Police Service fed false details of Julian's release to his legal representatives and family, only for the true time and place to somehow be leaked to would-be assassins.'

In the world of barristers, big reputations attracted lucrative briefs. She'd been cheated out of her prison-release press conference, but this was a hundred times better. The fact that Sinclair's parents had given him up as a lost cause years ago, and no member of his family had shown up for his trial or spoken one word in his defence, did not feature in her proclamations. Instead, words such as harassment, persecution, wilful, vindictive and failures took prominence. A photograph of Sinclair, post-surgery, popped up in the corner of the screen while she painted a masterpiece of the victimized and vindicated saint.

Moncrieff was of the newest breed, first to claim the spotlight since the lifting of the prohibition on barristers talking to the media, unencumbered by the old professional reticence and expert in stirring up a storm. Whip-smart and ruthless, she'd progressed quickly through getting professional footballers off drink-driving charges to getting them off sexual assault charges, and then the big league – a serial-killer rapist with national press attention.

'Instead of walking to long overdue freedom, to begin rebuilding the life ruinously and unjustly stolen from him, he's clinging to life in hospital. Callously thrown to the wolves,' she added, cracking her whip for the media circus lions. 'While the Metropolitan Police seem uninterested in arresting the most obvious suspects in this morning's shooting or unearthing whoever in their so-called organization conspired to leak the details of his release.'

Not for the first time, Groombridge watched her performance with something akin to fascination. It was one thing to hide personal disgust and investigative suspicions behind a mask of professional neutrality in the interview room and for the cameras, as he'd had to many times, quite another to take sides purely according to brief, to debate guilt or innocence regardless of what you knew. He'd seen barristers argue with all their power for conviction for harsh charges on the thinnest evidence, and seen them move heaven and earth for accused they *knew* to be guilty. Thus it must be, of course. Justice demanded advocacy. But when sleep came hard to the honest copper, Groombridge wondered whether barristers slept like babes.

And she was still arguing. Her job finished with acquittal. She'd won, but she was still going. It was the solicitor's job to build the lawsuit against the police now, not hers. Perhaps she'd negotiated an illicit cut.

As she reached her crescendo, icily incisive, another part of Groombridge's brain sensed a more worrying explanation for her performance beyond the cold clarion and self-congratulation . . . she seemed *convinced*.

A less cynical soul might even suspect that she *believed* her client was innocent. A convicted serial killer rapist. She'd seen all the evidence, circumstantial as much of it was, and meticulously torn it apart. Could you do that, especially as a woman, unless you really thought he was innocent? What did she see in Julian Sinclair that Groombridge could not? And, when push came to shove, which of them saw more clearly?

He took a sip of his tea but it had cooled, and the disaster playing out on the news left a bitter taste.

DAC Stevens would be lapping this up. A vindication of his own. The worse Moncrieff painted the police investigation the greater Stevens' case that the Greenwich force was shambolic and ripe for takeover by Lewisham, as he'd advocated in his failed bid for power. A self-serving empire builder, so far from the values of policing it was hard to believe he'd ever worn a uniform without pips. Nothing but the commissioner's stave on his epaulettes was ever going to satisfy the man, and maybe not even that . . .

Moncrieff had finished. The talking heads were having their go now. The faces of the victims were displayed with names beneath followed by live footage of the SOCO enclosure outside the prison and old footage of the Talbot brothers and their mother, spitting death threats at the courthouse, with obvious speculation and claims about police denials to questions Groombridge was unaware of being asked.

No mention of Stark at least, so far. Either Sinclair hadn't recognized him after all or the memory had been wiped by the shooting and surgery . . . or Moncrieff and the lawyers were saving that petrol bomb for when the media flames waned.

Trial by fire. Fran would curse her luck, and him for choosing this moment and this case to push her front and centre. Though he suspected he might have little choice soon enough. She'd have to step up and front this show like the DI-in-all-but-name she had been for years now. He'd rehearsed her long enough that he could withdraw into the wings, ready to prompt when she needed help with her lines. But she'd still hate it.

Groombridge turned off the TV just as his phone rang – an old colleague topping up his pension years advising the Independent

Police Complaints Commission. Too old a friend to beat around the bush. 'I'm sorry, Mike, and you didn't hear this from me, but you should probably start talking to your union rep.'

Stark knocked back a pair of headache pills with some strong coffee, wishing mind-numbing boredom could actually numb a head, while even the vitriol contained within Sinclair's hate mail wasn't enough to make this any less soporific after a night out.

Most were anonymous; the worst ones. There was an almost comical spread of spelling, grammar, handwriting or print quality. Some were simple *shame-on-yous*. Some predicted eternal damnation with varying degrees of pitchfork and brimstone glee. Then there were the personal ones, a small few even pasted together from jumbled newspaper and magazine typescript like cheap movie props, calling Sinclair a monster, asking how he could live with himself and promising comeuppance, mostly of the castration kind while lamenting the abolition of capital punishment. One of these homemade art projects stood above the rest for outright nastiness.

You're not safe. Not anywhere. Not even sleeping in your cell. You'll get what's coming. I'll see you smile choking on your own cock and balls and your asshole split with a shiv!!!

'Charming,' said Williams, reading over Stark's shoulder.

'Shiv . . .' Stark pointed at the word. Prison slang for a fashioned blade or spike.

'Think that one's from Dean Talbot?' Williams asked.

'No way of telling, unless Sinclair kept the originals.' The thing about collage hate mail was that they were very hard to produce without leaving fingerprints or DNA in the glue – much more informative than handwriting analysis, but all Stark had were scans. 'None of this lot was logged in his personal effects on the prison discharge.'

'He might've passed them to his barrister or solicitor, to help ramp up the wrongful conviction suit,' offered Williams. 'Fat chance of cooperation from that lot.' He'd every right to sound disgruntled. He and others had been part of this case, slogged their guts out to bring a killer to justice, only to have it all thrown in their face. 'You look like shit, if you don't mind me saying so,' he yawned at Stark. 'Lucky lady?'

From her parting expression, triathlete Megan doubtless considered last night a lucky escape. 'I wish.'

Williams smiled. The team's only happily married member, he found perverse amusement in the romantic failures around him and seemed to have picked up on Stark's recent sorties back into the fray. Patting Stark on the shoulder, he wandered off back to the CCTV suite where they were having exactly no luck so far, leaving Stark to his sick pile.

Worse than the hate mail, was the fan mail. Despite Fran's edict, Stark felt compelled to review those too. Most were along the lines of sympathy for the obvious miscarriage of justice, wrongful incarceration and general persecution by the corrupt police, fascist state, or just *The Man*. Aside from ambulance-chasing legal offers, most were anonymous. Most bore UK postmarks, but not all. Darker ones included email addresses, inviting VPN-anonymized correspondence. There was no record of Sinclair communicating back, but communications could be smuggled out via lawyers, corrupt guards, freed convicts or, most commonly, illicit smart phones.

One of the UK offerings stood out. Positively chilling, it praised Sinclair's actions, listing the author's opinion on each of the victims and their personal attributes, how much he would have liked to have watched while they got what they deserved, everything the writer would like to have done themselves – graphic, creative and appalling – saving the worst vitriol for Leah Willoughby, the only survivor. The prison service had passed that one to CID but the author could not be traced. The flies and carrion of battle might turn the stomach, but they at least had legitimate purpose. The self-congratulatory sickness of this letter made Stark's skin crawl, long after he'd closed the folder.

8

'Celebrating? Or drowning your sorrows?' asked Fran.

Dean Talbot looked up from his pint, his surprise to see her quickly replaced with a practised twist of distaste. No doubt his brothers had been straight on the phone after her visit this morning, but Dean had conspicuously failed to contact her. 'Not sure I follow you, DS Millstone.'

Fran sat on the opposite stool at the corner table in the dingy pub that Dean had been spotted entering. In the three years she'd been at the station she'd got to know a few of her uniform brethren, but none closely. She found most standoffish. Nothing at all to do with her abrasive demeanour and reputational impatience, she was sure. DC Williams, with his easy-going rapport, had been her usual conduit below stairs when she needed one, but it was Stark who had put her on to Sergeant Ptolemy and his sidekick Constable Peters as the most useful people to know in uniform. Fran always got the impression that Peters was quietly laughing at her behind her smiles, but Ptolemy was a pleasure and the pair paid dividends. A list of possible Talbot haunts and a posse of keen-eyed patrols had located Dean surprisingly quickly. And with a bruised face and cut nose. 'Well . . . some might applaud the shooting of Britain's most hated rapist murderer, while others might lament failing to kill the loathsome shit,' she offered.

Dean shifted in his seat. The best looking of the three brothers, if you liked low-rent wide-boy posturing. 'Can't say I was sorry to hear what happened. Didn't take you lot long to feed our names to the

37

press, I hear, but it's nothing to do with me, Troy or Blake. Plenty of people would like Sinclair dead. Which hospital is he at?'

'When did you get that face?' asked Fran. The cut on the bridge of Dean's nose was scabbed but fresh, with darkness spreading to both eyes. Both hands too, more so on his right, though he didn't appear to have a broken finger.

'Oi, Trev. How'd I get this face?'

The landlord looked over. 'Minor disagreement with some hairy biker after closing time last night. Can't tell who won. You was both ugly fuckers before you started.'

'In here?' asked Fran.

Trevor shook his head demurely. 'I encourage my clientele to take their disagreements outside.'

'Can anyone corroborate?'

'One or two,' said Dean. 'I can give you names.'

'Please.' Fran noted down the two names, both bosom buddies of Dean who'd be called the moment she left. 'And the biker?'

'Never seen 'im before,' said Trevor.

'And he won't be back in a hurry,' grinned Dean.

'Where were you at six-seventeen this morning?'

Dean was well prepared for this one. 'Asleep. With my girlfriend. Want her number too?' He smiled nastily. 'You're not her type.'

'Oh, I don't know.' Fran smiled sweetly. 'I'm sure she'd look on any *Homo sapiens* as a step up.'

'Or *Homo erectus*,' guffawed Trevor, until a glare from Dean set him back to polishing glasses with more diligence than Fran suspected was the norm. At least he didn't use spit.

Ptolemy and Peters had also tapped up a local miscreant, known to occasionally find valuables just lying about inside locked cars in the area where the van had met its fiery end, but with predictably blank-faced results.

And, as predicted, the alibis of all three Talbot brothers checked out, on the surface. Tomorrow would begin the deeper testing, as well as broadening the scope to all the other people who'd willingly spit on Sinclair's grave, while the press calls for arrests grew louder.

One reporter had managed to corner Dean Talbot and now the TV was full of him denying but cheerfully endorsing the attempt on Sinclair's life. Reviewing the fraud squad report hadn't helped, adding a tier of people with a fiscal grievance below those with obvious familial grief. All of which would have to be investigated.

That, of course, was not all tomorrow would bring. Finding out who took a potshot at Sinclair would now run parallel with officially reopening the serial killer investigation . . . trying to put aside the obvious candidate, Sinclair. The people who'd written to him believing he was innocent were in a minority, and there didn't seem to be anyone in Royal Hill Police Station that believed he should be breathing free air, but the media were all over this now.

Stark stood on the station stoop and sucked in a lungful, cool in the early evening dark. As common of late, a day begun with a longing to be back in bed and never imbibe again had flipped to the exact opposite. Nearly getting killed could have that effect too. Grateful for the cane for once, he clicked his way into town in search of a drink.

He'd turned a few corners before something sent a shiver down his spine, setting his teeth on edge. The all too familiar sensation of being watched, followed, in enemy crosshairs, that something malignant was already in motion that you were powerless to prevent. He ignored it, trying not to get angry. Why his fractured mind played these tricks on him at night was doubly nonsensical. Daytime was the soldier's enemy, for patrolling and being seen to, when any Taliban tit with an ancient Kalashnikov could take potshots from a half-mile off, and snipers smiled. Night was the soldier's friend, for targeted ops, where the enemy was the one to be afraid. And yet, these fears most often seized him after dark.

Unable to shake off the creeps, he hunched his shoulders and ducked into the first pub he came to, determined to shun past terrors and present company alike.

9

Morning followed too quickly, and forcing himself through his physio routine paid him back for all the recently misspent nights and missed mornings with pain on top of penitence. With all they had ahead of them, he wasn't the only one to look less than cheerful as the morning meeting coalesced at 8:00 a.m., though it was good to see DCI Groombridge present. Stark had served under enough poor officers to cherish the good ones, and Groombridge was exemplary. One would like to think this might inure him from the potential fall-out of Sinclair's release, but the headsman's axe was as callous as the battlefield bullet. Seeing his mannerisms and rhythms in Fran's call to order and initial summations was little reassurance, and before she got into her stride, everyone's day got a whole lot worse . . .

This can't be happening again, thought Stark.

Deputy Assistant Commissioner Stevens barging in would, in itself, ruin any day, but on this particular day he brought on his heels Stark's least favourite Detective Inspector, and quite the poorest officer he'd ever had the displeasure to serve under.

Stevens' intent was clear before he said a word. And it was equally apparent from the look on both Groombridge and Fran's faces, that this time they'd not been warned in advance.

'Right,' Stevens announced without preamble, 'there hasn't been time to disseminate this through the usual channels, so apologies for trampled toes . . .' His tone was anything but apologetic. 'But with DCI Groombridge facing investigation for the overturned conviction of Julian Sinclair,' he continued, to palpable shock in his audience, 'and no DI beneath him, I've asked DI Harper to step in once again until matters are concluded one way or another.'

'Morning everyone,' nodded Harper, a forced half-smile masking his discomfort. There was none of the brashness displayed when he'd last been forcibly inserted up the team's fundament just a few months earlier. He'd left Royal Hill Station a year and a half ago for a regional post after failing his DI exam, frustrated and resentful, seeing both Fran and Stark as threats, but had obtained DI rank on his second try and then been temporarily seconded back here by Stevens, to disastrous result.

Only four people in this world, other than Harper himself, knew the depth to which his unprofessionalism might've triggered the bloodbath that concluded *that* case, and three of them were staring at him now. Harper only knew about Groombridge for sure, but he must surely guess there were more. Groombridge had asked Fran and Stark to keep it to themselves; the withheld ammunition he needed to quietly end Harper's last secondment had to be kept dry. The fourth was Pensol. All four knew surreptitious threats by Harper may have helped tip an unstable suspect into mass murder. Lives had been lost; others, like Pensol's, scarred.

Even if no one else in the station knew, enough suspected Harper as Stevens' spy in the ranks for him to be universally unpopular. There were still enough freemasons in the force for it to be known that Stevens had sponsored Harper's membership. Was Harper still so desperate for Groombridge's office that he could overlook all that ill feeling, or was Stevens forcing him into this – the poisoned olive branch? The undeserving would be all the more in Stevens' pocket for his bestowal of favour. How many people did he own thus? And how deep did his grudge go? Stark could hardly credit the senior officer's gall. To be trying this again after it had blown up in his face last time, and with his own hands far from bloodless; to swan in here wielding the same blunt weapon . . .

'Did I miss a memo?' asked Superintendent Cox, entering at a brisk pace, tipped off about the DAC's unannounced arrival. 'Sir,' he added with perfect timing to both cause offence and deny it. Stark might have been proud of him, were this whole situation not playing out like a slow-motion repeat car crash.

'You did not,' replied Stevens, with barely concealed disdain. 'But I'm sure you will be just as pleased as your finest troops here, to welcome back DI Harper to be a firm hand at the tiller.'

Implying the ship was veering, or worse, listing. The only thing Stevens allegedly cared for almost as much as power, was his yacht. He probably had a captain's hat with gold trim. And Stark hadn't missed Stevens' eyes lingering on him at the word *troops*.

Cox hardly blinked. 'We'd most certainly welcome DI Harper's help, and any other additional personnel that can be spared.'

Stark had to suppress a smile at Cox's surprising backbone, though Groombridge had always insisted one was there, hidden beneath the moustache-puffing bluster.

Stevens' crocodile smile tightened, but he was too wily to be dragged into any genuine commitment to deliver the resourses he'd promised only yesterday. 'Right then, I'll leave you in Owen's capable hands. A word with both of you . . .' he said to Cox and Groombridge, and stalked out of the room expecting them to scurry in his wake.

Groombridge followed, without haste, but Cox paused just long enough, staring at Harper, for Stark to wonder if Groombridge had shared Harper's secret with a fifth person.

Harper waited until the senior men were out of the room before attempting another smile. '*Surprise . . . !*'

'So the IPCC have decided to investigate?' asked Cox.

'It's surely a matter of when, not if,' replied Stevens.

'But as it stands, your pronouncement downstairs seems premature, sir.'

Stevens shot him a sharp look. 'I think it's high time you got *ahead* of events rather than lagging abominably, don't you? You will of course make your office available to DI Harper again,' he added to Groombridge. 'Appearances count. DI Harper needs the full respect of his team.'

'Of course, sir,' replied Groombridge, deadpan. 'Respect is a fragile thing in this job.'

'And *with* respect, sir,' added Cox, 'DS Millhaven is a DI in all but name and already *has* the respect of this team. For all DI Harper's perceived qualities, he does not command the same. Surely at this delicate time –'

'While I'm sure Millhaven is a capable enough sergeant,' interrupted Stevens, 'she is hardly less tainted by this shambles than DCI Groombridge here, no offence intended.'

Much taken, thought Groombridge. 'Owen Harper was as much a part of that investigation as anyone.'

'But not of its recent collapse. And even if Millhaven scrapes through her exam, we can hardly put someone like her in front of the cameras.'

'Like her, how?' asked Groombridge, more sharply than was wise. *A short, mixed-race woman?*

'Hopelessly under-qualified and inexperienced,' said Stevens, outwardly resenting the inference. 'This case requires a commanding presence to face the press, and that cannot be any less than an *actual* inspector. The Commissioner's office cannot ignore the concerns being voiced –'

'Voiced by whom?' interrupted Cox pointedly.

Stevens' eyes narrowed. 'There is understandable *political* pressure, and concerns over your office's capability to clear up this mess.'

'*Capacity*, sir, surely,' replied Cox. 'My team's *abilities* are beyond reproach.'

'Hardly,' scoffed Stevens. 'Legal Services are all over this like a rash. The IPCC will be right behind. And if your team doesn't pull its damn socks up, the entire case may be taken from you.' A grim threat. Cox would not survive such a vote of no confidence. Groombridge's fate before the IPCC would be sealed. Greenwich Murder Squad would be in the crosshairs, and perhaps the whole station back in danger of being subsumed into its neighbour. Stevens would leverage this to resurrect his power-grab merger plans and bid for the next Deputy Commissioner slot.

'The Sinclair conviction collapsed on a forensic technicality, nothing *whatsoever* to do with my officers,' insisted Cox. He knew he was wasting his breath, but men like Stevens saw a man of his age still at station-level as a failure. Cox might yearn for one more promotion, but he was rightly proud of his patch and disliked threats.

'Exposing an unforgivably weak investigative case,' riposted Stevens icily. 'You blew your only witness and failed to offer anything above coincidence and conjecture. And to make matters worse, you failed to keep Sinclair's release under wraps and let someone shoot him. You're a laughing stock. You've bungled this case from start to finish and I'm putting someone I can trust in to bat.'

Someone *you* can trust, thought Groombridge, and the rest of us can't.

Groombridge ignored the sideways looks from the troops as Fran made a second attempt at the morning meeting, radiating resentment. She ran through the first of the two case boards, starting with yesterday's shooting. Her matter-of-fact efficiency was doubtless a deliberate challenge to the interloper, Harper, to keep up or catch up in his own time, but she occasionally glanced at Groombridge as if he should be stepping in to spare her this ignominy. As if this were any less humiliating for him. And the way things stood, she'd have to get used to working without his safety net a lot sooner than he'd planned.

In recent months, someone had thought it humorous to stick up a notice saying, *'YOU DON'T HAVE TO BE MAD TO WORK HERE BUT IT MAY HELP YOUR DEFENCE WHEN BROUGHT TO TRIAL'.*

Not so funny now, with a looming investigation into his handling of the original case and HQ's directive that he *'maintain the lightest possible touch on the fresh investigation'* – in other words, quarantine.

Bad press had consequences.

And so close to Fran and Stark sitting their exams, this was potentially disastrous. If Owen got his feet under the desk this time, all Groombridge's succession planning would be ruined. Fran could qualify as a DI just in time to find no vacancy to fill and be forced to look elsewhere, leaving Stark a newly qualified DS beneath Owen Harper of all people.

Fran moved on to the second board – Greenwich's very own serial killer.

Photographs of all six women, alive and well, smiling, oblivious to the horrors ahead. Alongside each, key details in Fran's neatest marker-pen hand, and a photo of said horror; the one survivor, Leah Willoughby, pink, purple and bloody among the bleach-scarred cyanotic blues of the rest. A gratuitous reminder perhaps, but no one in this room should lose focus on what this was all about.

'A manhunt and cold case combined,' she summarized. 'Our priority is to review all the available evidence and find out what we missed. Witness re-interviews, camera footage, phone records, forensics. Everything that can be, gets re-tested. All the case files are on their way back from our fearless colleagues at the Crown Prosecution Service as I speak, so we'll see what we've got and divvy it up accordingly. I'll draw up a work roster, but don't expect much rest this week. I won't sleep easy until I see Julian Sinclair back behind bars where he belongs.'

Owen cleared his throat, gliding to his feet from where he'd been perched against a desk. 'Thanks, Fran. Listen . . . I know I've got some catching up to do, and this isn't what any of you want to hear, but as I see it, part of my remit here is to keep us all squeaky. So I have to add that whilst circumstantial evidence still points to Sinclair, the failure to maintain a conviction behoves us to investigate *all* avenues with equal diligence, not least the possibility that some other person, or persons, were responsible.'

Groombridge feared that how Owen saw things was how he'd been told to, and the primary people he would seek to keep squeaky clean would be himself and his overlord.

Fran stared at him like he'd stepped in to her called her stupid and asked her to thank him for it. 'Of course. All options are on the table.'

Owen nodded, point made.

'Until such time as we get Sinclair's lawyers off our backs by nailing him to the wall,' she added firmly. She tapped the board with her marker to continue. 'Six victims – identical modus operandi –'

'Not identical,' interrupted Owen. 'Paige Talbot was younger than the rest and wasn't gagged or drugged. She was *manually* strangled and the electrical cord was tightened round her neck post-mortem, along with the whip marks.'

'All details that were kept from the press,' Fran commented.

'Unless you're suggesting she was the victim of a copycat killer *copper*? Paige was a crime of opportunity and haste but the hallmarks were unmistakable. She looked older than she was and left the club drunk. Her attacker didn't need to spike her drink or sedate her; she'd done it herself.'

'So we all assumed. But we have to be careful to avoid sounding like we blame her.'

Fran blinked in shock. 'We, or me?'

Groombridge winced. Owen could hardly have said anything more incendiary. Not exactly an auspicious new beginning.

Owen held up his palms, 'I said we.'

'*We* stood over that poor girl's naked corpse, cold in a field at one in the morning, knowing what had been done to her. We were there when her family were told. But *I* was there when the pathologist weighed her organs and combed her bleach-ruined hair, and when they lowered her into the ground.' *Where were you?* she didn't have to add. Owen had missed the funeral, attending his poor wife's latest alcoholic meltdown.

'Exactly,' he replied tersely. 'And we owe it to her to get this right, once and for all.'

'That's right,' interjected Groombridge before things got ugly. Owen thought a leader had to stamp his authority on people, rather than earn it from them. 'We're all on the same page.' He looked at Fran as he said this, knowing she'd be busy pencilling his name in beneath Owen's atop her list of people she'd gladly slap right now.

'Okay,' Fran smiled tightly. 'Then let's not forget a key witness who swore Sinclair was her attacker.'

'A witness torn to shreds in court,' countered Owen, knowing full well that Fran blamed herself for exposing the poor girl's frailties to merciless cross-examination.

'And not *one* reoccurrence since Sinclair went inside.'

'And no forensic evidence,' said Owen.

'We *had* forensics.'

'And now we just have the *reports* based on *lost* samples,' countered Owen. ' "*Suspiciously unverifiable.*" ' The very words Moncrieff so enjoyed repeating to the press. He may have been parachuted in here, but he'd followed the case. It was his too, after all, and whatever tarnish he'd accrued, there was still copper beneath, there had to be. The look on Fran's face said she did not agree. 'Believe me, I'd be delighted to prove he did it,' insisted Owen, 'but for the sake of the people in this room, not to mention the wider public, Julian Sinclair must be treated as *a* suspect, not the *only* suspect.'

Fran radiated disgust.

'Thank you, Owen,' said Groombridge. 'Timely advice. I expect you all to heed it.' He looked around the room. A lot of effort had been put into trying to prove Julian Sinclair guilty, but their job was to serve and protect. You didn't do that by ignoring even the smallest doubts.

'Should we sit a car on Leah Willoughby's place, then, Guv?' asked Dixon. 'In case Sinclair really isn't the Strangler and she's a threat to whoever is?'

'She's living in Camden now,' said Fran. 'Spoke to them already, but the best we could get them to agree to was adding her road to their patrols.'

Groombridge's phone beeped, and he scannned the email from Cox with dismay.

Stark looked at him, sensing something amiss.

I I

If there was one recurring lesson in Stark's life, it might be to expect the unexpected. As a classic example, the last thing he might've expected today was to be sitting alone in a car with Owen Harper, who was perhaps the nearest thing to an open enemy Stark had known since combat deployment. Another might be that he should never have expected to keep his name out of this case.

The furore following his near-fatal wounding in the shootings three months ago had fanned the smouldering embers of the fame ignited by his earlier award of the Victoria Cross, and only died down after he'd finally consented to a one-off interview. But his past seemed set to dog his steps.

Sinclair had both recognized and remembered him.

And now, sufficiently recovered to make a statement, the man's law-yers said he would speak only with Stark – the only officer involved, according to their summons, 'who is untainted by the historic persecu-tion, or possibly worthy of the oath to protect'.

'Classic psychopath, latching on to anything to boost their ego,' Fran had insisted, for Harper's ears as much as Stark's after the for-mer had insisted on accompanying Stark *without* Fran. That she had no desire to spend another second of her life with Julian Sinclair until he was firmly back behind bars didn't stop her showing her annoyance. 'Let him do the talking. Give nothing away, professional or personal. And don't screw up.'

Stark nodded. 'Listen to what he has to say in case he says some-thing he wishes he hadn't.'

Williams had given him an encouraging pat on the shoulder, adding, 'And try not to punch him if anyone's watching.'

Dixon's smile had its usual rather-you-than-me quality. Hammed's was somewhat tighter. Stark still had some bridge-building to do there after Groombridge's reminder of the developing hierarchy, but right now he had bigger worries. It was only a matter of time before his face was all over the news again and the whole excruciating fame circus would start over, just as the man who resented Stark for it to the point of pathology was back.

Keeping one hand on the wheel, Harper expertly fished out a cigarette and placed it between his lips, stabbing the electric lighter in to heat up. 'You mind?' he asked as an afterthought.

Stark shook his head. Second-hand smoke was a soldier's code for being safe-ish back inside the base or APC, post-patrol, as familiar as the adrenaline shakes and sudden, complete exhaustion. The lighter clicked out and Harper lit up, cracking the window. He took a deep drag and blew it from the corner of his mouth towards the window to leave a contrail of smoke curling behind. He seemed to be foregoing his gloating this time, so far, but was probably just keeping his true colours folded while he worked out who knew what about his recent mistakes.

Harper made his way through the cigarette in long drags and flicked the glowing butt out the window with no apparent thought for pollution or illegality. 'We need to keep this low-profile, if we can,' he said. 'You, I mean.' He glanced at Stark as he drove. 'The case has enough attention already.'

Did he think the cat wouldn't escape the bag, now Sinclair had remembered what was inside? 'He'll use it.'

'Maybe. But we can play it down, so long as it's just words. Steer clear of cameras.'

A rare moment of agreement, if divergent motivation. At the epicentre of Harper's historic antipathy towards him was the caustic delusion that Stark existed solely to steal his thunder. From the beginning he seemed to resent the fame that the Victoria Cross had hung around Stark's neck and consequently anything Stark said or did. Goldenballs, he'd taken to calling Stark, and it doubtless wouldn't be long before he fell back into that tiresome rut.

As if to seal the point, there was a TV news van outside the front of the hospital, so Stark led the way in through the A&E entrance to slip in unnoticed, but his head chose this daytime moment to hiss that he was in someone's sights again. Furious for capitulating, he scanned the terrain, but the only person who even glanced their way as they crossed the main atrium was a bearded guy in a long coat and cap, pacing up and down, otherwise lost in his smart-phone screen – just another poor friend or relative waiting in hospital limbo for news. Stark had spent too much time on the other end of that equation in this very hospital and others; mother, sister and others worrying about him. Enough to set in him as deep a loathing for medical incarceration as he had for his seemingly unshakable post-combat paranoia.

Given his notoriety, Sinclair had been tucked away in the hospital's discreet private ward. He could afford it, but the expense would doubtless deplete the public purse after the sharks bit. Sergeant Dearing was on guard duty with an awkward-looking rookie and hid any surprise he might have felt to be approached by DI Harper, simply greeting them with a nod. If ever there was a job requiring intimidating deterrent, Dearing – the six-eight stalwart of the Met Police rugby team second row – was your man. Groombridge had managed to get a CO19 armed response vehicle parked outside, but the hospital management were fidgety about guns and Sinclair had rejected armed guards on his door. Standing guard on a hospital room door was below Dearing's pay grade, but the rookie beside him evened things out.

Life in the TA, deployed ad hoc into regular units in strange, hot places and harm's way, had taught Stark the value of quickly attaching names to faces, but this kid must've arrived while Stark was off convalescing. Dearing was teaching what he knew – solidity, politeness and patience.

By all accounts, Stark would need all three himself in the coming minutes. Behind the door waited Julian Sinclair, the man he'd heard and read so much about, but never met – yesterday's brief encounter notwithstanding.

Dearing offered his clipboard. 'Visitors, sir.' He lowered his voice. 'Just the sharks.'

'You can expect a formal complaint about that in short order,' said a brusque male voice behind them. The sharks, circling to take pound-sign bites of police flesh. Stark turned to see a grey-haired man in his late fifties wearing a sharp suit and the barrister, Moncrieff, from the TV – the way things stood right now, in contention with Harper for Fran's least favourite person – a long and prestigious list that Stark guessed frequently included his name. And an attractive woman in her early twenties and a severe skirt-suit who immediately drew Harper's eyes as he introduced himself with his warrant card.

'And DC Stark . . . ?' asked Moncrieff, carefully inspecting both cards, though she probably had a file on him already. 'This is Duncan Bosch, Mr Sinclair's legal representative and his paralegal, Emily Thornton. They will be present at any and all interviews and interactions between Mr Sinclair and the police services, and all correspondence and communication will be addressed through them. Understood?'

Stark made her settle for a nod.

He caught a wry smile from Dearing. The rookie looked happy not to be Stark.

'Mr Bosch has been advising me that his client should be entitled to full and complete privacy during this convalescence,' explained Dearing with the unwavering equanimity of a man to whom spurious complaint was water off a duck's back. 'I tried explaining how helpful it is when would-be-assassins write their names down for us on the way in.'

'We're his *legal representatives*,' Bosch insisted irritably.

'Perhaps you feel your client's recovery might be disturbed by the noise of the pen?' asked Harper. 'Or have you got RSI in that wrist?'

'Have a care, Detective Inspector,' bristled Bosch. 'I recognize your name, and a promotion won't absolve you of your historic part in this mess. I'd be careful of letting DCI Groombridge hide behind you – there's more than enough shit coming to take you down with him.'

'Is that him?' called a voice from inside the door. 'Send him in.'

'Mr Sinclair will see you now,' said Bosch.

'What are you, his PA?' scoffed Harper, reaching for the handle.

'Just Constable Stark,' replied Bosch, smiling tightly. 'You wait out here.'

Harper scowled, but Stark spoke first. 'This is official police business, not a personal call. If your client has something to add to our investigation he can speak to my inspector. But if he's more interested in stoking his ego than helping us find the men that shot him, he can piss off and stop wasting our time.'

Bosch blinked in shock. 'I suggest you adopt a more respectful tone, young man. From everything I've heard, it could easily have been your gung-ho intervention that got my client shot. We'll be demanding that your superiors hand over footage of the incident forthwith.'

'And I suggest you hop to it before we head back to the station and turn our attention back to re-proving your client is a serial homicidal rapist with no right whatsoever to compensation.'

Bosch's face darkened. Clearly he was unused to the kind of blank intransigence only military service could teach.

Stark glanced meaningfully at his watch.

Huffing in annoyance, Bosch knocked perfunctorily, entered and closed the door behind him. The paralegal, Emily, tried to keep up a stern front on his behalf but Stark sensed she was masking a smile. Moncrieff was not. Hers was the brutal beauty of the mountain peak, standing coldly indifferent to foolhardy approach. Emily was sunray through cloud.

Harper stared at Stark, with a modicum of amused approval, whispering, 'What happened to politely listening to what he has to say?'

Part of that was testing how much he wanted to say it. Harper knew that. 'He was rude.'

The door re-opened and Bosch waved them in sourly.

'Thank you,' smiled Harper. 'Perhaps you could rustle up some tea and biscuits too.'

Stark took a deep breath, steadying himself to meet his first serial killer face-to-face.

12

The private room was noticeably more salubrious than the superbug-isolation room where Stark had been hidden away from the public and press during his last spell in this edifice of misery, but in ways which felt aimed more at distinguishing it from NHS rooms than adding any genuine comfort. Bland pastel patterns, inoffensive watercolour securely screwed to the wall, a plastic vase stuffed with plastic tulips, a TV mounted on the wall rather than an articulated arm and not requiring exorbitant pre-payment cards from the vending machine out in the corridor. It still felt crowded with five people standing around Sinclair's bed.

The man himself shifted with a wince of pain, or displeasure. 'Sergeant *Harper*? Long time no see . . .'

'It's Detective Inspector now,' said Harper. 'And I wasn't expecting to see your face again either.'

'Lady Justice spoke up, belatedly,' replied Sinclair dryly. 'An inspector when I only asked for a constable. Should I feel honoured, or do I detect a touch of desperation?' There were copies of all the main nationals on his bed. Most, if not all, had his picture on the front, several raising hackles in the station that morning with accounts of Sinclair's *terrible wounding, suffered bravely confronting would-be kidnappers, no thanks to Greenwich Police and their vindictive and misguided crusade against him* – to paraphrase.

'And the famous Detective Constable Stark, VC no less,' he continued, finding a faint smile. 'I wish we were meeting under pleasanter circumstances.' A calm voice with affected eloquence masking a faint South London accent that Stark knew well from television and police interview tapes, though the man himself appeared considerably reduced. Aged, thinner, drawn and tired, and not just from injury and surgery. The baffled smile he'd worn throughout his trial was a thin thing now. There was an undercurrent of uncertainty in his eyes, like a cornered animal unsure if it should roll over or snarl. Perhaps this was what prison had been like for him – constant fear and posturing.

It was hardly the face of a monster that you might expect, the face of a man who'd raped and strangled a string of young women, but then what *did* one expect – demonic horns? 'Yesterday doesn't really count, I suppose,' Stark agreed.

'No. But I should thank you for doing your best.' It wasn't hard to infer a silent dig lurking beneath his words and Stark had to remind himself not to pre-judge. Sinclair's smile widened and he shook his head slowly. 'I can't believe it's really *you*. I mean, I recognized you yesterday, but . . . lying here after, I half-doubted myself. But here you are . . .' He looked to his three legals, inviting them to share his wonder.

Whatever Stark had expected, entering this lion's den, it hadn't been some kind of fan. 'How are you feeling?' Sinclair's left arm was in a sling. He'd been lucky. Stark had seen far worse.

'Unloved.' Sinclair winced theatrically. 'Bloody hurts, getting shot. How many times is it for you now?'

One through the leg three months ago, still aching. One through the chest before that, preceded by the IED shrapnel that removed his little finger and pinned his helmet to his head and the RPG that peppered his left side and left him with little option but to prop himself up on one knee and return fire . . . *relax, breathe, aim, hold, fire, breathe, bleed . . . breathe, bleed, fire . . . the air stifling, deafening . . . enemy bullets pecking in a line towards him . . .* He shuddered and blinked, dragging in a breath to remind himself that he could, that his chest wasn't choking with blood, that nearly three years had passed.

Sinclair was staring intently. 'I'm sorry, I didn't mean to stir . . . painful memories.'

'We're not here to talk about me.' Stark fumed at his slip. So much for giving nothing away. If Fran was right, Sinclair preyed on titbits. An imagined brother-in-arms relationship might stoke his ego, but pain inflamed his darker passion. If she was right.

'The things the press misrepresent.' Sinclair nodded. 'To them it's all heroes and villains.'

'I only care about the truth.' The words sounded trite even as he said them.

'And what if our truth differs from theirs?' Sinclair mused.

Our? Theirs? 'Truth isn't subjective.'

'Isn't it?'

Stark wasn't about to be drawn on that.

'When in doubt,' said Harper, producing the office's battered Dictaphone. 'If you don't mind?'

'We don't if you don't,' said Bosch, as his paralegal produced their own sleek model. 'No offence, but trustworthiness has been somewhat lacking from your side so far.'

'We're all on the same side today,' said Harper. 'Catching your client's assailants is our shared priority.'

'I doubt that,' scoffed Moncrieff. 'Covering your arses is highest on your agenda and you know it. Why haven't the Talbot brothers been arrested?'

'Because if we charged them, some clever barrister would rip into us for lack of evidence.' It was rare for Harper to converse with a beautiful woman without his eyes taking a tour, but perhaps he'd seen too much of her during the original prosecution.

'That's enough,' snapped Sinclair, wincing again, almost pleading. 'Look where all this prejudice has got me. Somewhere out there are three men trying to kill me, not to mention the *real* Greenwich Strangler. I never thought I'd say this, but *Inspector* Harper is right; it's time we started working together.'

'So . . . ?' demanded Fran.

'Zero intel added,' replied Stark, stiffly removing his jacket. 'Barring their helpful suggestion that we lock up the Talbot brothers. Waste of time.'

As she'd predicted. 'What did you make of him?'

'Hard to say.'

'Try.'

Stark thought about it. 'Careful, bitter, exasperated, but I suppose that's to be expected. But also beaten down, fragile.'

'An act,' scoffed Fran. 'That or the biggest egos are the most brittle. Don't be fooled by his poor-me bullshit. What else?'

'What do you mean?'

'You've just been in a room with the Greenwich Strangler.'

'Assuming it's him.'

She gave that the eye-roll it deserved. 'How did he make you feel?'

'You my shrink now?'

Fran had met Stark's shrink, firmly adding Doctor Haughty McDonald to her list of slap candidates. Stark knew that. 'You're avoiding the question.'

'To be honest, the most disconcerting thing about him was how chuffed he seemed to meet me.'

Fran felt that one sink in. For all his imperviousness, the one thing Stark seemed ill-equipped for was the fame that dogged his exploits. But this . . . 'Hardly what you want from a serial killer. The profiler said psychopaths see people as things, in three categories – irrelevancies, threats and treats.' And the only safety in the first type lay in numbers.

'Comforting.'

He looked more tired than afraid. Reprobate. She strongly suspected that he was getting over his most recent trauma, and his ex, Kelly, with a string of boozy one-night-stands; which despite being pretty much what she'd suggested to snap him out of his love-sick moping, she still managed to disapprove of in a rather enjoyable way. At least until this shitstorm had taken the fun out of everything.

'And our other deeply suspect . . . ?' she asked, eyes darting to Harper through the glass of Groombridge's office, the senior man having just scooped his scant possessions into a filing box for the trip upstairs to the small, windowless storeroom that had hosted him when Harper had last borrowed his office. The would-be-usurper had even apologetically offered to carry the box upstairs, like he wasn't slavering to seize the throne. Revenge for last year's dark deal. Did he think their current troubles freed his hand?

Stark followed her glare. 'Zero intel added.'

Entirely fair and un-harsh. Harper's promotion to DI ranked among her highest gripes with the universe. A man like Harper; least but not last – placed in her world to cause maximum irritation. Fran's hand itched to march in there and slap him. How dare he even show his face here after last time. 'Okay, back up the recording and leave a copy on my desk. Full transcript too. Then help with that lot,' she nodded to the stack of case note boxes in the corner and spread around various desks as the others delved and sifted.

It was going to be a long day.

13

The team had already begun calling victims' families – the mortifyingly offensive process of re-checking the whereabouts and alibis of people whose suffering must already seem unending. Fran took the lead, hating every second, the number atop her list the one she least relished.

Gritting her teeth, she tried it again, listening to it ring, imagining Leah Willoughby sitting in her flat trying to ignore the world outside. A couple of uniforms from Camden had knocked on her door to see if she was all right and been sent away in a tirade of expletives. There were probably reporters trying to get hold of her too. She wouldn't want to talk to anyone right now, especially Fran. It went to answerphone again and she left a second message with no more expectation of response than the first.

'Our van, Sarge,' said Hammed, handing her a printout. Theft sheet for a blue Citroën Dispatch. 'SOCO managed to pull the VIN off the burnt remains. Stolen in Stratford two weeks ago. Local force say they have a few usual suspects, but no leads. And none with links to the Talbot brothers.'

'Sure?' Fran flipped through the sheets. Two weeks; just about the time the likelihood of Sinclair's exoneration hit the news.

'Got them to double-check,' replied Hammed. A habit she was trying to instil in him.

'Good work. Keep in touch with Stratford, see if they'll prioritize this one now – chat to their usuals – you never know. And get the original plates into the camera search and plate recognition records just in case.'

Fran returned to her list. Victims and their families, in order of tragedy.

She almost felt like she'd known them in life rather than just in death – their faces alive from photographs and video, not the squalid pallor of death, bruising, lacerations, bleach-burns and post-mortems. And in the darkest night, she could picture all too clearly the violence and horror of their last hours, like a Hollywood B-movie sick-fest playing out on the inside of her eyeballs, the worst details supplied by the only survivor, Leah Willoughby, and the sheer wall of grief from the families, compounded with each new victim. No training or sodding exams could prepare you for that.

It still hardly seemed credible, two years on. You heard about this sort of thing in the news but it was the stuff of fiction. If it had to happen in real life, it happened far away, somewhere inherently weird like Los Angeles, or Lancashire. Not south London. Not the leafy Royal Borough of Greenwich. And not with you stuck right in the bloody middle, baffled and appalled.

A *serial killer*, for God's sake . . .

Not that they knew that when the first body showed up.

Karen Gillespie, twenty-one. Stunning. There was no other word for it. The universe allocated its gifts with scant regard for fairness. Some it left dumpy, irascible and suspicious – suited for little else than policework; some it blessed with the kind of beauty that meant dull sweetness was more than sufficient in the personality depart-ment. Such was Karen. Blithely smiling through life, doing no intentional harm, turning heads and breaking hearts wherever she went – until she met her killer. Unless she already knew him. It was quickly clear that some of her closest friends disliked her boyfriend, Richard Hardacre, finding him jealous and controlling. His thin alibi did little to deflect the possibility that he'd killed her in some fit of rage, or to collect on the life insurance to pay off the mortgage on the house they'd scraped together a deposit for earlier that year.

The second body had derailed that line of investigation.

Magda Janowski, twenty-three. Wastefully over-qualified Polish cleaner with a heart of gold. Married to her childhood sweetheart from her home village, now an over-qualified London construction labourer. The couple had emigrated to the UK together in search of a better life to start a family. Eight weeks pregnant at the time of her murder, waiting for the twelve-week scan all-clear before telling their family back home. Disappeared from a friend's hen night. CCTV behind the bar had Sinclair buying two drinks in the same club, but he was just one of hundreds. The husband, Roman, had made it through the trial and Sinclair's conviction, then hung himself in the bedroom of their tiny rented flat.

Then Teresa Leman, twenty. Dental practice receptionist. Beautiful, vivacious, flirtatious. Liked to party. String of ex-boyfriends. Liked clubbing, alcopops, ecstasy and drunken snogs with hot boys and occasional girls for laughs. A butterfly, flitting from flower to flower and just too colourful a morsel for a predator to ignore. Kissed a prince and got pond-life instead, perhaps. Julian Sinclair's name on the register of dental patients made the case's first connection, though he of course claimed coincidence.

Fourth, Paige Talbot, just sweet sixteen. Younger than the rest but like most teens, acting and dressing above her age; perhaps paying the price for it that all parents feared. But that didn't make it her fault, even in this bullshit patriarchy. Anyone, regardless of gender, should be free to dress and drink as they wished, without fear; however unrealistic that might be. It was never, *never* the victim's fault. Paige's was a blank page of a life, waiting to be written. Coddled and spoiled by her mother and over-protective brothers, just beginning to venture out into the world and making up for lost time with early forays into clubland. Heart of a child, face of an angel, starting to realize her looks could open doors and reap rewards. Might've become a proper handful, given the chance. In need of a guiding hand. She reminded Fran of her eldest niece, which perhaps explained why it was Paige that really haunted her. Perhaps because Fran had promised herself that her niece's transition into adulthood should bear none of the insecurity and anguish of Fran's own, and why she took this all too personally.

Next came Leah Willoughby, the only survivor. Twenty-two at the time. Disappeared outside a nightclub. Abducted, drugged, violently raped, but somehow she'd escaped and fled, naked and bleeding. She'd been found cowering in Vauxhall Pleasure Gardens – a small public park in this instance horribly misnamed – the following morning suffering from exposure and with little notion of what had happened to her, how far she'd travelled or for how long. Among her fractured recollections, the monstrous face of Julian Sinclair with his charming mask removed, literally. Dismissed by the barrister, judge and jury as the confused recollections of a drunken floozie, consciously or unconsciously imprinted with Sinclair's face after he was identified in the press as a person of interest, with or without the collusion of the over-zealous police. Fran could still picture the pleading look Leah cast her way as the Bitch Barrister, Moncrieff, flayed her alive, the jurors' eyes cooling from sympathy to contempt – still feel the burning guilt.

And finally, Sara Brompton, twenty-four, taken, raped and killed the day after Leah's escape. A hungry monster, cheated of its prey, rushing out to replace it. Sara was almost a spitting image of Leah. Fitness instructor at a local chain gym, just embarking on a fresh relationship with a fitness-magazine-ad co-worker, who'd done the decent thing and waited a full four weeks before finding a new hot babe to adorn his muscle-bound arm. In possession of a watertight alibi, sadly.

But then that didn't matter, because a swab from Leah's rape-kit came back with a high-percentage DNA match for Julian Sinclair, exposing all his obsequious denials as lies. Arrest, charge, trial, conviction – life sentence. And even Leah's evisceration on the stand could be put behind, if never forgiven.

Until that precious swab was lost in the move – literally. Government cuts had closed the Forensic Science Service, and somehow in dividing the work up into a bunfight of smaller 'competitive providers', the sample had been misplaced. Meanwhile, two big cases had floundered in scientific debate about DNA sample size validity and accusations around historical lab-procedure irregularities come to light, gifting defence barristers the spectre of cross-contamination.

All Moncrieff had to do was question the validity of the original results that could no longer be re-tested and kick up enough stink. Inadmissible forensics, discredited witness, circumstantial evidence, conviction overturned . . . So here they were.

Fran could picture each victim, universe-blessed and cursed. All six faces blurred in the bitter cusps of dreams that had made this all the more personal to Fran at the time, and returned in full force since the sickening possibility of Sinclair's release had gained momentum. Leah's living agony and devastation played out against the beauty of the others and the innocent youth of Paige – all screaming in the darkness of Fran's fitful sleeps.

All six women, young, slender, pretty, but otherwise diverse in height, hair and eye colour and ethnicity. An equal opportunity killer, so long as you weren't dumpy or plain, thought Fran, who knew herself to be a little of both. Driven by ego as much as desire, according to the Met profiler. Only taking women good enough for him, but to show them they only qualified under his terms, when and how he dictated, and at the price he set. Poor at handling rejection. Perhaps unlucky in early love. Possible experimentation with prostitutes. Possible porn addict. Vain. Functioning sociopath. Active psychopath. Practised at hiding both. Average intelligence or above, probably considers himself a genius.

Or none of the above. Profilers loved to appear confident, but always hedged under pressure. Fran preferred to stare the suspect in the eye and judge for herself. Of course, her history with men cast doubt on her judgement of male character. Until now, perhaps.

She considered firing off a playfully offensive text to Marcus, but the mood escaped her.

And against all this, the sodding Inspectors' Exam could hardly seem less important or Fran less qualified. Groombridge insisted she was ready, but she'd failed Leah, and either failed to prove Sinclair's guilt or worse, failed to spot his innocence . . .

And now, the list. And strict instructions not to admit fault.

She picked up the phone and tried Leah again.

14

'So this is real?' asked Groombridge, settling into the chair. This meeting was taking place on neutral ground, away from prying eyes.

'Not officially, yet,' said the legal. A superintendent. The Directorate of Legal Services were taking this seriously. He hadn't caught her name. She'd said it, but he'd not listened. He was rattled. Drawing fire from the team was part of his job, but this was far more dangerous than the usual crap and flak. This mess could cost him his warrant card, leaving Fran and the team exposed to fire from without and within. Even exonerated, he might end up quietly promoted sideways, somewhere out of the way. Pride said he'd resign. Alice would support his decision, but clinging to detective rank at the expense of promotion offers hadn't boosted his pension or paid off the mortgage. He'd have to seek work in the private sector. The very thought twisted his stomach.

'But a complaint has been lodged?' asked the union rep, whose belligerence Groombridge had always disliked.

'This interview is simply to begin establishing the essentials of the case from your perspective.' Meaning yes.

'A fishing expedition,' bristled the rep, puffing himself up.

She didn't react. 'Standard procedure, nothing more.'

Precious time wasted justifying every twist and turn of a two-year-old case and current investigation to those whose primary interest lay in mitigating against undesirable political fallout, bad press or legal actions, thought Groombridge, perhaps unfairly.

'The membership won't take kindly to scapegoat-ism,' stated the rep squarely.

The legal stared at him a moment, then transferred her gaze to Groombridge with every intention, he suspected, of ignoring the rep from now on. 'It's in your interest to cooperate.'

'So long as my interests align with yours.' If they diverged, they'd turn on him in a heartbeat and leave the IPCC to pick over his bones.

'We're on the same side here, Detective Chief Inspector.'

Groombridge tried to size her up, but she had a pretty solid poker face. Time to place cards down. 'I'm here to preserve Her Majesty's peace. Some might say you're here to preserve face.'

She shook her head faintly. 'The Met can only preserve Her Majesty's peace by holding itself to the highest standards, unflinchingly, without fear or favour. Your record is unblemished in this regard. I honestly hope it remains so. Nevertheless, the investigation you ran led to the arrest of a man who was subsequently exonerated.'

'Freed,' replied Groombridge levelly. Not exonerated.

'Let's agree on *conviction quashed*.' She studied him. 'And with the CPS shy of retrial, I advise you stick to the facts and avoid undue commentary.'

She was right, of course; obstinacy would hardly prove helpful to his cause with Sinclair's sharks circling, the press sensing blood and Stevens too ... Groombridge held her gaze a long moment and nodded.

'She likely to let us in?' asked Stark. 'If she's there?' Leah hadn't answered the phone and he wasn't convinced about Fran's door-stepping plan, which he suspected had more to do with getting away from Harper than it did sense. 'You didn't part as friends.'

'We were on the same page. We both wanted Sinclair stopped, punished.' Fran left it at that. She'd got too close, she'd admitted with rare contrition. Leah hadn't trusted herself, her memory, but trusting Fran, she'd agreed to testify. It hadn't gone well.

'Her memory is unlikely to have grown more reliable, two bitter years on,' said Stark, taking a left on the advice of the silk-voiced satnav. Leah had relocated north of the river after the court case, trying to escape the fallout.

'Hardly her fault her testimony appeared weak. That's the effect of the roofie,' Fran insisted. Delivering disorientation, suggestibility and memory loss, Rohypnol was the date-rapist spike-drug of choice. 'But he must've under-dosed her, slipped up – that's how she escaped. She recalled other snippets too, not just his face. Words, phrases, the kind of things Sinclair would say.'

'Speculative.' The weight of circumstantial evidence was strong and the forensics undeniable, or so they'd thought. Leah's testimony was to be the cherry on top. Greed. Fran had been too desperate. The barrister, Moncrieff, had made mincemeat of the poor girl. A history of drunken one-night stands, provocative dress and behaviour, erratic job history and a 'sealed' record of juvenile larceny had been trawled up and thrown in her face. Moncrieff even managed to squeeze in a reference to a teenaged abortion before the judge reined her in. Leah was painted as a slut and a liar, a desperate attention seeker willing to sell herself nightly for a few free drinks and compliments, making a play for fifteen minutes of tabloid fame and a tell-all salacious exclusive for sale – utterly outgunned by a professional word-slinger and shit-raker, discredited, maligned and reduced to wordless tears.

And now, predictably, there was a photographer sat astride a motorbike outside her flat. Jeans and leather jacket that owed more to fashion than protection. More incognito than the all-weather gear of the hardcore wait-outside-for-days class, but just as long on lens and short on conscience.

Stark had little time for their sort. His own image had peppered the papers too many times – his ideal being none. The commotion after the recent shootings had been inescapable, even when he'd escaped from hospital back to his mother's tiny house in Gosport. His inherently bubbly and good-natured mother had become quite adept at telling paps to fuck off.

Just when he thought his TV interview had doused the flames, his return to work – as well as being tempered by everything from overt acclaim and spontaneous hugs from colleagues he hardly knew to awkward nods of approval, handshakes and pats on the back – had been widely reported, and tabloid calls for him to receive the George

Cross gained renewed vigour. *'First to do The Double!'* they cried, every time.

No one had ever received both the Victoria and George Crosses; not least because the actions deemed worthy of either so frequently proved fatal, as had nearly been the case with Stark on both occasions. He had heard nothing from the Ministry or Palace, and his contact, Major Pierson, was still off fighting in Helmand. She at least might know better than to inflict it upon him, but the politicians would have no such qualms.

Stark got straight out to go on the offensive.

'Stark,' called Fran, too late.

Visor up on his black helmet, the pap's eyes lit up with pound signs in recognition, but before the camera rose Stark held up a hand and calmly explained that he and his colleague expressly did *not* give permission for their image to be published or sold on and that if this happened he would personally sue for invasion of privacy and arrest the photographer for witness intimidation and impeding a criminal investigation – videoing the whole encounter on his phone, including the man's freelance press credentials and bike licence plate. Then he turned off the phone and told the pap to fuck off before he required a proctologist to retrieve his camera.

Today, this worked. Sometimes it didn't. Stark had smashed three very expensive cameras in the last few months. The one advantage of the public profile these parasites had given him was that any picture of him doing this, any negative report or complaint, would reflect far worse on them than on him. Rightly or wrongly, the people loved Joe Stark VC.

The biker revved away.

Turning, Stark found Fran a few feet away, fixing him with a dark scowl. 'Making friends?'

'Wit and charm, Sarge, just like you taught me.'

'That wasn't smart. We need to keep your face out of this. You attract too much attention.'

Tell me about it, thought Stark.

Fran rolled her eyes. 'Come on . . . let's get this over with.'

67

15

'*Go away.*' The door entry intercom lent Leah's voice added harshness.

'Leah, it's me, Detective Sergeant Millhaven, Fran . . .'

'*I know.*'

'We need to talk.'

'*You need to talk. I need you to go away.*'

'We still want the same thing, Leah,' tried Fran. 'Sinclair behind bars.'

'*You had him behind bars and you let him go. And someone shot him. You should've let them kill him.*'

'That's not what we do, Leah.'

'*Who's that with you?*'

Stark held up his warrant card to the beady black lens above the intercom and introduced himself.

'*The one that used to be a soldier, with the medal?*'

'The very same,' said Stark, suppressing a sigh.

Another pause. Then the door release buzzed.

Fran pushed it open before Leah changed her mind.

Leah's flat was on the first floor, facing the busy road to the front and level with the railway behind as if, with all that had happened to her, she'd not have enough trouble sleeping. All she could afford on benefits. Employment was hard to come by with a sullied reputation and frayed nerves. Leah was in the process of changing her name by deed poll.

The door opened. On a chain. One half of a face, one eye, red, tearful, angry and suspicious. 'Not you,' said the face to Fran. 'You wait outside.'

'Leah, we just want a word –'

'I'll give you two; fuck off.'

Stark bristled. 'I understand your anger, Ms Willoughby –'

It was the wrong thing to say and Leah reacted instantly. 'If you're going to say you understand what it feels like to have your face plastered all over the papers,' she interrupted, 'don't waste your breath. They only said *nice* things about *you*.' Her eye turned on Fran. 'And if this cheap trick was her idea, she's an even bigger bitch than –'

'I was going to say,' interrupted Stark right back, 'that I understand your anger, but it's both misdirected and rude. If you just want to hide in there feeling sorry for yourself, that's up to you, but if you want justice, then like it or not we're your only hope.' It came out harsher than intended, but no one called his sergeant a bitch within his earshot.

'Okay, let's just start again,' said Fran, stepping into the unfamiliar role of calm arbitrator. 'Then Leah can hear what we have to say and we can be on our way?'

'And what have you got to say? That I should lock my door at night, keep off the street, stay away from bars, wear less provocative clothing?' scoffed Leah bitterly. 'I see his face when I dream. I feel him . . .' The door closed enough for her to remove the chain and reveal her whole face. 'And whenever I look in the mirror I still see Sara Brompton,' she circled her face with a finger, 'knowing she paid the price for my so-called escape.'

Seeing her full face poured shame on Stark's harsh words. A different person to the photos in the file, detailing her injuries, but also from the beautiful, happy-go-lucky smiles of the photos taken before. This Leah was harder, razor-edged and brittle like knapped flint, dark circles beneath red eyes – kept awake by the memories that haunted her sleep. Stark recognized the look instantly, and all too well; that post-patrol look, after things had gone bad. The look in his bathroom mirror. Soldiers chose the risk, thinking it wouldn't happen to them but knowing it could. All this girl had chosen was the wrong bar at the wrong time. Seeing Leah in person suddenly made all the horror in the files leap off the page. That someone, Sinclair, should choose to do this, to steal the innocence from this girl, and the others . . . He tried to keep his fury from showing but felt his jaw tighten, fists curling . . . digging his nails into his palms, fighting for control as his shrink, Doc Hazel, had tried to teach him. Trigger recognition. Anger management. The best he ever managed was to deflect what he could into the abyss within, hoping it was as bottomless as it seemed.

Leah eyed him, perhaps sensing his turmoil. 'Or did you come here to ask if I shot him?' She stared, eyes defiant. 'I wish to God I had. I would, if I ever got a chance, gladly,' she declared. 'I'd pay someone to do it for me if I had any money, but there was no compensation for *me*, only for *him* now, right? So don't come here looking for forgiveness. I don't have any.'

'Where were you yesterday morning around six?' asked Fran, sensing their time was up.

'Here. Asleep. Alone.' So saying, Leah slammed the door. And that was that – a wasted journey. Worse, Leah stayed on the suspect list and would be even less inclined to help them or accept any protection.

'Well,' Fran sighed wryly. 'We might have to work on your wit and charm lessons.'

'Got more out of her than I ever have,' said a voice behind them. There was an old man, creaking down the stairwell like a squaddie trying out prosthetic legs.

'Need a hand?' asked Stark.

'Too late now, I'm almost there. Lift's buggered again. Landlord doesn't listen. Doctor says stairs are good for me, anyway. New hips. You lot coppers?'

'Yes. Do you know Miss Willoughby?'

'*Miss*, is it? I could call her some other names,' declared the newcomer, sizing them both up and finding little to his liking. 'Plain rude she is. Never says hello. Glowers at me for offering the time of day. They're all the same, the young. Bloke below's just as bad, with his metal music. And don't get me started on the lot above – coming and going all hours. A dozen of them in there at least. Sub-let. Not that the landlord cares so long as he gets his money.'

'Well thanks for that, Mr . . . ?'

'Baxter.'

'Well, you're obviously a good man on the lookout, Mr Baxter,' Stark said, handing the curmudgeon a card. 'If you see any suspicious characters loitering or asking for Miss Willoughby, please let me know.'

Baxter set off down the lower stairs, muttering to himself, along the lines of being too busy to do other people's jobs for them.

'Wit and charm,' muttered Fran outside, watching him shuffle away down the street.

'Cheer up, Sarge. If he tosses that card in the gutter you can nick him for littering.'

16

The return journey was made in near silence, and Fran's mood took a distinctive downturn as Harper intercepted them coming out of the lift. 'You went to see Leah Willoughby?'

Fran played innocent. 'Is that a question?'

Harper looked suitably vexed but swallowed it, nodding at Stark to give them privacy and watching him go before lowering his voice. 'The next time you stroll off to interview a key witness, I must be notified.'

'Why? So you can make sure I don't dig this hole any deeper?'

'This is serious.'

' "Admit no liability",' scoffed Fran. 'I got the memo.'

'You think this is a joke?'

'Hardly.'

Frustration crept into Harper's voice. 'Look, I know I'm probably not the help you wanted, but I'm on this case now. We're not going to see eye to eye on everything, but can we at least agree that working together has to be better than fighting? We may be the only thing standing between this team and disaster. If this goes south, the buck won't stop at Cox or Groombridge.'

Fran defaulted to offence despite his attempted conciliatory tone. '*Superintendent* Cox and *DCI* Groombridge are above reproach, and the most likely way this could "go south" is if other people put politics before policing.'

'Or blindly mistake a helping hand for a slap in the face,' countered Harper. 'I know you don't trust Stevens but I'm not him, and I've only ever done what I thought best for the job, for the case. You can trust me on that.'

She didn't. There was way too much water under that bridge. And the last thing this case needed was a crass egotist sticking his bloody great oar in, whatever motivation he hid behind.

Harper's shoulders slumped, reading her expression with evident disappointment. 'Cutting me out won't help anyone. Give me a chance. Maybe I'll surprise you.'

Fran watched him lumber away, angry at him for trying to make her feel guilty and furious with herself that he'd succeeded. A dent in her convictions, however minor, was as unwelcome as Harper's slappable face.

Progress in the office did nothing to cheer her.

Of those victim family members that had been spoken with so far, most took predictable offence. All made their opinions known on the overturning of Sinclair's conviction and several, the dads mostly, declared willingness to kill him themselves with as much fervour as Leah had done. And most, given the timing of the shooting, could claim no better alibi than being tucked up in bed with or without shaky spousal corroboration.

Working the list was disheartening, made even worse by Harper hovering like a bad smell. He knew enough to steer clear of her mood during such tasks, but lacked Groombridge's knack for not worsening them with glances.

As far as Fran was concerned, Sinclair had killed those girls and the Talbot brothers had tried to kill him, and if she was anything but copper she'd cheer them on herself. The sooner they excluded all other lines of enquiry the better.

Unfortunately, if the perps couldn't have picked a worse location for the kidnapping, they couldn't have picked a better one for the switch. The traffic camera search had identified a few vehicles they might've switched into from the van, but so far none had checked out. Public transport cameras had to be checked too, though if they'd been trying to kidnap Sinclair to force a confession from him – the working theory – then they had to have intended to switch to another van or car. Unless their plan had been to burn the van with Sinclair in it.

'Right. Where the bloody hell is my bullet forensics?'

'Two days, Sarge,' said Dixon, pulling a face.

'From yesterday, or now?'

His wince deepened. 'Sorry, Sarge; best they can do, they said. Apparently brass are insisting on senior analysts only on all forensics relating to this case, and he's off till Monday.'

'Brass who?', she snapped, steam rising.

'Wouldn't say, Sarge.'

'Same story with the blood DNA, Sarge,' said Williams, who always had more of an eye for comic timing than self-preservation. 'Instructions from on high – no corners cut or queues jumped.'

'Is that so?' simmered Fran.

National press on the worsening performance of forensics services since privatization had resulted in official prioritization of 'tier-one' cases – those involving terror, missing kids and serial killers preying on pretty young women – basically anything that became embarrassingly newsworthy; and sod all the poor coppers trying to solve less photogenic crimes like the epidemic of poor ethnic-minority teenagers stabbing each other outside chip shops. The attempt on Sinclair's life cleared the embarrassment bar by a mile, but it looked like someone had found a way to stymie them anyway.

Try not to immolate anyone, Marcus had said. But that was yesterday. And he only said *try*.

'Guv. How's it going?'

Groombridge stared at the tea and sandwich before him, trying to persuade his stomach that it would feel better full. 'Hours of fascinating fact-checking. I haven't had this much fun since I was a trainee detective.' Which seemed so long ago he could hardly remember it, or the flash of years in between that had dumped him here. But Fran calling to ask how he was doing was usually a prelude to her complaining about how *she* was. 'What do you need?'

Fran explained in her version of calm tones that they were being hobbled and which 'brass-knob' she believed responsible. 'We've got suspects coming out of our ears, a drop of blood and one bullet. How the hell are we supposed to narrow this down with DAC

Shitface clogging up the forensics to keep his nose clean and sod the rest of us?'

'We can't know that for sure.' But they probably could. This had DAC Stevens' fingerprints all over it. A perfect way to look like he was protecting their interests while slowing down the investigation to make them look bad. He'd pop up on the news before long, spouting more empty pledges.

Groombridge had met loathsome characters enough during his career, but most had been on the other side of the law. Stevens had manoeuvred against Greenwich for no other reason than to expand his own power base of cronies and support in his bid for higher office, and although that stock had taken a blow in the aftermath of the recent shootings, the way he'd hijacked the subsequent funerals and debate to showboat in front of the press made Groombridge's skin crawl. It wasn't so much a question of wondering whether there were no depths to which the man would not sink to satisfy his ambition and petty revenges, more of wondering when and where he'd stoop next.

And with his hands tied for slaughter, there was no way Groombridge could push back – even if he had leverage to try.

'What about a call to Marcus?' he asked innocently. 'See if he could call in any favours.'

17

Williams held out Fran's desk phone receiver to her as she re-entered. 'Richard Hardacre, on hold,' he said, face apologetic.

Fran grimaced. Boyfriend to the first victim, Karen Gillespie, and brief suspect, Hardacre had gone on to be quite the pain in the arse – setting up and running the imaginatively titled *Greenwich Strangler Victims Group* web forum for family and friends of the victims; with the notable exception of Leah Willoughby, who'd refused to have anything to do with it.

'Richard. My team have been trying to get hold of you.'

'Some of us have jobs we actually take seriously.'

Fran let that slide. Hardacre was more trouble than he was worth. 'Still, thanks for calling.'

'Did you seriously think I wouldn't? What the bloody hell do you think you're doing? Sinclair walks free and you're straight back to hassling the victims. *Innocent bereaved families.* I'm getting calls left, right and centre. It's bad enough you can't keep Sinclair behind bars – you let someone shoot him and then start pointing fingers at *us.*'

'With honest reluctance, I assure you.'

'Since when has that ever stopped you?'

'Never,' replied Fran, patience slipping. 'Nor ever will. That's the job, asking the questions that need to be asked without fear or favour. I'm sorry.'

'You're *sorry*,' he scoffed. 'If you'd done your job right you might've caught him after Karen, before he killed again and again, but instead you wasted time interrogating me and others. If you'd done your job right he'd still be in prison!'

'As I said, I am sorry –'

'Not as sorry as the families,' interrupted Hardacre. 'And now you're doing it all again. Putting them through it all again. Doing all you've ever done . . . Pointing the finger at whoever's nearest, flinging shit all around in the hope some sticks, instead of *investigating*.'

All too often that was what investigation boiled down to. The fewer the clues the more the suspects. Shaking the tree, Groombridge called it, but flinging shit wasn't far wrong.

'Well, if you want to know where I was at six yesterday morning,' he continued, 'I was asleep, alone, in the bed I bought with Karen when we moved in, in the house I still can't afford on my own but can't bear to sell. And no, no one can corroborate. So you might as well stick me on your squalid list like everyone else whose life Sinclair shattered.'

Fran listened to the dial tone for several seconds before hanging up with a weary sigh.

They needed to get out of this hole. She decided to set Stark on the Talbots. A fresh pair of eyes might help; and she'd seen enough of them. The three brothers' alibis and the various persons providing them would all need deeper scrutiny. But first, she suggested, the mother, Rhonda – in the Royal Marsden Hospital in Chelsea with advanced lung cancer; incapable of any attempt on Sinclair's life but with three willing sons to direct. Stark's wit and charm might be just the thing.

'Same shit, different day,' offered Williams cheerfully as Stark guided the car west into the Saturday afternoon snarl-ups.

Of the three DCs, Williams had been the most fulsome with his congratulations on Stark's propulsion towards the Sergeants' Exam. Glad it wasn't him. He had the years but no ambition, happy as he was and good at his job. All that, and genuinely pleased for Stark. And since Stark's return, he'd already shifted demeanour, slotting in beside Stark like a good corporal to his sergeant. There was no equivalent rank in the police, but that's what Williams was – NATO OR-3, through and through. Stark had shifted too. Perhaps it was studying for the exam, or perhaps just the army in him. His last day of active service, in harm's way, had been as acting sergeant, the official third stripe coming later. And here he was again.

To plug the ensuing silence, Williams filled him in on the kind of details about the Talbots that didn't make it into the files – sealed juvenile records, local haunts and affiliations, the suspicion that the middle bother, Troy, was in fierce denial about his sexuality, and rumours that Paige might not actually be their sister. Stark frowned at that one.

'No, seriously,' said Williams. 'I heard it from a fella used to work in uniform – took voluntary redundancy last year in the cuts – that Paige was the product of some underage distant cousin or some-such, and bloke-unknown.'

'Wasn't that investigated?'

'It was just a rumour,' Williams shrugged. 'And with all the crime scene forensics, there wasn't enough budget to go comparing more DNA. Family insisted it was just the usual nastiness. Rhonda and her offspring weren't the most popular family on the block. And Paige was victim four. We had our prime suspect by that time. Bang to rights, or should've been.'

Hard to argue with the past. And today, Stark's job was to find out which three idiots in hockey masks thought it okay to take pot-shots at perps and zap policemen with 40,000 volts; and that was the kind of incentive a copper could work with.

The transition from uniform to CID was a difficult one for many. Groombridge, he knew, would've stayed uniform his whole career like his father before him, had his old sergeant not quietly pulled levers. In uniform you could still hope to *prevent* crime, not just investigate it. Hanging up your uniform was the decision to work bigger cases, though possibly at a greater personal cost. But today, despite the resentments of the families, Stark felt the righteous thrill. A chance to prevent tragedy instead of just seeking justice. To stop Sinclair ripping apart any more lives, and perhaps prevent the Talbots from throwing away what was left of theirs.

They had parked and were walking into the Royal Marsden Hospital in Chelsea when Stark's phone vibrated, displaying an unknown caller, though the number looked familiar. He answered, gesturing to Williams that he'd catch up with him inside. 'Hello?'

'Joe?'

The voice, hesitant, familiar, heart-stopping.

18

'Kelly?'

'Yeah, hi Joe. How are you?'

Stark was too stunned to answer.

'Look,' she pressed on. 'I . . . I know we promised not to call –'

'Yes,' he interrupted without meaning to. A promise he'd elicited after their break-up seven months ago. She'd attempted to see him in the hospital after the shootings three months ago, but he'd been in no condition to see anyone. There was no keeping his mother out, and he knew that she and Kelly had sat down in the hospital cafeteria to share their worry over coffee. His mother still thought him a fool and regularly told him so. He suspected the two remained in touch.

Kelly sighed, hurt by his silence as ever. 'Look, this isn't easy, I know, but I need to see you, to talk. Please, Joe . . .'

Stark dry-swallowed, shocked by the power she still held to render him useless. 'What is it you're asking?'

'Just a drink, or a bite if you like? Princess of Wales?' The pub on Blackheath where their first date had been cut short by one of Fran's very first *where-the-bloody-hell-are-you-never-mind-the-fact-that-you're-off-duty* calls. Kelly's local. Kelly's ground. He'd not been back since the break-up. 'Or wherever you like . . . I just need to speak with you. Catch up. No strings.'

There was an urgency in her voice. What had brought this on? And why now? He'd been clear, and as honest as he could, short of harm. A fool, as his mother thought, but for the right reasons. The hardest decision of his life. The best, in the clear light of day, and during the long nights, the worst.

'Joe?'

'Why?'

'Can't we just talk?'

Stark couldn't order his thoughts enough to list the reasons why they couldn't. Why they shouldn't. 'I'm in the middle of a case.'

'I'm going away. Just a holiday. I wanted to see you before I went. Next Saturday.'

Reprieve. 'Let me see. I'll text you.'

A brief silence. 'Okay. But please, Joe, it's important.'

She obviously wasn't prepared to say why over the phone. 'I have to go.'

Another sigh. 'Okay.' She hung up.

Stark felt an instant pang of regret, and then guilt at the regret. His ache to know what she wanted filled him with a hollow, gut-churning uncertainty. There was only one word for it, squatting at the back, peering from the darkness, unexpected, uninvited and shameful . . . hope.

HOPE!

A barking, mocking caw . . . Pointed, death-black tongue rattling in gaping, razor-sharp beak . . . pitch-black, oil-gleaming feathers . . . turning its head, fixing him with its pitiless, abyssal eyes. Stark's head spun, pulse accelerating towards impact . . .

'Joe . . . ? You okay?'

Williams. Standing beneath the hospital entrance canopy staring, concerned.

Stark looked around for the crow, just in case, but there was nothing there.

It was raining.

Fat droplets, thudding into the ground like bullets. Into him. He'd neither heard, seen nor felt them begin. If you'd told him he'd been standing here in a trance this last hour, he could hardly have denied it. A dissociative state akin to the flashbacks, but different, and all too familiar.

Or *his* familiar.

Corvus corone, the carrion crow. Guardian angel or personal demon; Stark believed in neither. Regular visitor to his dreams now, both sleeping and waking. A portent of death, or a longing . . . No, not that. Just guilt giving form to the darkness. Just another trick of the light.

'Something wrong?' asked Williams, as Stark joined him beneath the shelter as the heavens really opened.

'Wrong number,' replied Stark. Half-lie, half-truth.

They found Rhonda Talbot hooked up to machines, her breaths misting a clear plastic oxygen mask. Beyond skinny and unwell, the striking bleach-blonde spikes of the old file photos gone, she reminded Stark of one of those wretched hairless cats bred for no better reason than heartless amusement, and with much the same defiant stare.

'The fuck you want?' she demanded without removing the mask, voice muffled if not the contempt.

No one, it seemed, would be happy to see them today. Perhaps Kelly had called just to arrange a suitable time to slap him. 'Good afternoon, Mrs Talbot.'

'*Ms*,' Rhonda all but hissed. 'Ain't never married none of them wankers.' This outburst caused a bout of coughing, which only made her glare at them all the harder, daring them to think her weak. 'Come to ask me if I sent my boys to kill that monster?' she managed, sneering. 'You bet I did. Told them if they ever laid hands on him to rip his fucking balls off and choke him with 'em. Make him pay for what he done to our angel girl. And they will, if they get the chance.' Her vicious glee at the prospect cost her half a minute's gasping. 'Best you can do is stand aside. *Least* you could do. Should've let them take care of him in prison. Should've let them finish him off yesterday.'

'Them who?' asked Stark, inspecting the get well cards – one from each son, but no flowers. 'Your angel boys?'

Rhonda shook her head. Her skin seemed so thin it might split as it moved. How long had she got? Long enough to see this through? To see Sinclair re-convicted? Or to see her three sons imprisoned for attempted kidnapping, attempted murder; her tragedy compounded?

Murder made victims of all – high or low, good or bad.

'You see it, don't you?' said Rhonda, eyeing him keenly. 'You see I'm right. Bring back the hangman. If we still had the stomach, he'd be dead already.'

Stark nodded, though he didn't agree. Would she so willingly watch her sons swing for murder? Then again, had some monster reached into Stark's life to snatch a loved one from him, to commit the horrors inflicted upon Paige Talbot and the others, was there any telling where he might stop? He could only hope the likes of Williams, Fran or Groombridge would intervene. Biological gossip aside, Paige was Rhonda's daughter and there was no mistaking the grief in those watery, hate-fuelled eyes.

'She was my *angel*,' hissed Rhonda. 'Everyone loved her. And you let him . . .' She ran out of breath and had to wait while piteously gasping in enough oxygen to continue, '. . . take her. *You let him!*'

A bleeping alarm brought a nurse running and the two police were shooed out.

Fran made a point of not reacting until she'd achieved minimum astonishment distance.

Two calls in short order.

First, a lab tech, telling Williams that a supervisor had materialized and DNA analysis on the blood sample was underway. Then ballistics, telling Dixon that a senior analyst had miraculously turned up to oversee testing.

Fran cursed the empty corridor.

She'd take the forensics, gladly, but as a short, dumpy, policewoman of colour with four older brothers, experience had taught her to scrutinize gift horses from every angle for the skittish, bitey, shitty, kicky things they so often proved to be.

Groombridge hadn't developed mind control powers. And Stevens hadn't been persuaded by Ghosts of Policing Past, Present and Future that life would be better if he stopped being a steaming pile of spite. But she had called Marcus. More to vent and unfairly blame him than in any expectation of roadblocks actually evaporating. But he was an affable man, with old-chum forensic, medical and military connections. The world shouldn't function on favours. He would infuriatingly refuse to accept she owed him one, or indeed two, but it didn't take much to set a mind like Groombridge's to wondering quite what influence *she'd* brought to bear . . .

'Of course, there's a fifty-fifty chance all this is a waste of time,' mused Williams. 'If the blood DNA gives us a match . . .' No resentment. Just simple statement. Williams had the years to know legwork was often a waste of shoe leather, but if you didn't find the dead ends you couldn't find the true paths. Resentment was the only waste of time.

Every soldier knew it too. 'But in the meantime, we knock on doors,' agreed Stark. One of Fran's favoured sayings; though she frequently altered it to *kick* down doors or knock heads together.

'Dean Talbot's girlfriend, Tanya,' Williams nodded, smiling. 'You'll like her.'

Stark was already confident he would not. Tanya Donnelly: nails specialist. Manicures. And pedicures. Self-employed. Mobile. Uncooperative. What had started as a welcoming sales voice had sharpened as soon as Stark introduced himself over the phone. She'd refused to say where they could meet her. Not a problem, said Stark evenly. If she could just let them know when she'd be home, he would arrange a uniform car to bring her into the station.

Twenty minutes later they were face-to-face outside a modern low-rise at the western edge of Lewisham as she bustled out from her latest digital ministration or nail emergency looking flustered and far from happy.

'I already told you lot, Dean was home with me all night. He didn't have nothing to do with what happened.'

Stark didn't bother highlighting the double negative. Tanya appeared to be largely self-correcting, in her way. Peroxide hair and teeth, carotene tan, bling-plastic nails so long Stark wondered how it was possible to get anything practical done. 'Forgive me for saying so, Tanya, but didn't you say as much after Dean was arrested for assault, for which he was later convicted?'

'That was all bullshit. And so's this.'

'You were charged with perjury.'

'That was bullshit too.'

'You only avoided a conviction later by saying you must have mixed up your dates and apologizing to the court in tears. You won't get away with that again. Little call for pretty nails in prison, but I'm sure you'd be popular in other ways.' Stark knew he'd get nowhere with this, but she had to know what they thought of her alibi. 'You're what legal minds call *unreliable*.'

Tanya's orange face pinched. 'I ain't the one that let a serial rapist snatch up sweet little Paige and kill her though, am I? That's on you lot. You knew it was him and you did nothing. How many more girls did he kill? And when you did finally get him, you've let him go. If anyone's *unreliable* here, it's *you*.'

So saying, she tottered off on her six-inch heels, stowed her equipment in the passenger seat of her pink, brand-emblazoned Fiat 500 and peeled away, flipping them the uber-manicured bird. Tanya Donnelly: finger specialist. Liar on demand.

'You have a genuine talent for pissing people off,' chuckled Williams. 'Who shall we do next?'

19

Brothers two and three, Troy and Blake, did not have cohabitant partners to provide alibis, but had, they claimed conveniently, had three friends round for a late-night poker game, two of whom had crashed on the sofas and seen both Troy and Blake rise in the morning well after seven. All three had willingly corroborated over the phone and were only too happy to reaffirm now in person to Stark, and Williams, swearing hand-on-heart.

Their stories were tight. Each confirmed they'd started out with Five-Card-Draw, then shifted into Texas Hold'em as the night got boozier. A right piss-up, they'd all confirmed. A regular mates-only game. Cash, cigars and booze. Pocket money: the buy-in was fifty pounds and the maximum anyone could lose before sitting out was two-fifty. All five had played to the end, past 4 a.m., with one ahead on cash but no early departures.

Details, details, as Groombridge had said, were the key to exposing lies. But if they were lying, they were good at it. Few if any nervous tell-tale embellishments.

The next step was to give Troy and Blake themselves another try. It was entirely possible a game had taken place. Whether it was that night was another thing. Or whether Troy and Blake had actually been there.

'Here we go again,' muttered Troy as they threaded their way between the cars in the yard. Three dogs looked up from their chains with interest, or hunger. 'Who's your new friend?'

Williams made the introductions.

Troy stared at Stark. 'The one from the news?'

Stark nodded. 'Your brothers around?

'No. Why?'

'We'd like to ask you some more questions about the night before last, if that's okay.'

'And if it's not?'

'It's just routine. The more detail we have for our report, the quicker we can definitively rule you out of the attempt on Sinclair's life.'

'Bring him here and you can rule me back in.'

He meant it too. A mother's son. A sister's brother. 'And the night before last . . . ?'

Troy made an impatient face 'You already know where we were. Bazzer and the others backed us up.'

'We have to be thorough, that's all.'

'So why're you here now, not Millstone?'

'He's more polite,' smiled Williams.

'Unless he politely throws me off a building,' smirked Troy, referring somewhat unfairly to the news footage of the shootings, still gaining hits online, while looking Stark up and down, perhaps weighing his odds.

Stark smiled thinly. 'Do you normally hold late-night card games on a Thursday night?'

'Why not?'

'Don't you have work in the morning?'

Troy shrugged. 'We're all big boys.'

Car mechanics, a plumber, a mini-cab driver and an electrician. All self-employed, working as and when they pleased, willing to lose two hundred and fifty pounds and call it pocket money. Illicit forms of supplementary income were likely involved if the Talbots' reputations were anything to go by. Not exactly a watertight alibi. 'What time did you and Blake leave for work?'

'About eight.'

'How did you get here?'

'Walked. Apparently one can still be over the drink-driving limit the morning after, officer.'

A telegraphed lie. 'Your boss doesn't mind you working after a boozy night?'

Troy frowned. 'I don't have a boss.'

'Dean?'

'Dean ain't my boss.' A nerve touched.

Stark shrugged. 'He was at home with Tanya. Do you or Blake have girlfriends?'

Troy bristled. 'What's it to you?'

'We just need to know if there's anyone else we can talk to about the frequency and timing of your poker games.'

'You think we did it, don't you?'

'It's too soon for us to draw conclusions, Mr Talbot. But the attack yesterday morning was carried out by three masked men, and you and your family have made no secret of wanting Sinclair dead. Maybe you're glad he's free, so you can keep trying.'

The dogs began growling, sensing trouble. Stark levelled a stare at them and they shut up, heads dropping, which seemed to make Troy even more cross. *'Fucking right.'*

'It's more than a talent,' grinned Williams. 'It must also be a lifetime's diligent practice.'

'Not quite a confession,' shrugged Stark, 'but hardly a denial.'

Troy and Blake shared a flat not far from the yard. Adjoining residents had already stated that the brothers were nuisance neighbours, too often noisy for any particular night to stand out.

Blake beckoned them inside with a wordless jerk of the head, clearly expecting them. Policing in the digital age – your suspects could conspire quicker than you could question.

The flat stank. Stale booze, stale sweat, stale smoke, dope and unwashed laundry. The big coffee table in the lounge, along with much of the floor, was littered with empty cans, takeaway packaging, DVD boxes both closed and open with discs adrift, lads' mags and porn, torn up Rizla packets and three ashtrays overflowing with cigarette and joint butts.

A games console was hooked up to the massive TV, *Call of Duty* paused mid-explosion.

'Cleaner's day off,' muttered Blake, clearly a little stoned.

'Better call her round before we come back,' said Williams,

pinching a small clear bag between thumb and forefinger – skunk, mostly empty, but not completely.

'Yeah,' Blake smiled, eyes thin and dopey. 'She really shouldn't leave her shit lying around here. Can't get the staff these days.' The brothers clearly didn't care. Probably wise enough to keep any quantities above 'personal consumption' limits off the premises.

'Do they bring their own biohazard suits?' asked Stark, opening a window.

'Pig five-oh,' Blake muttered under his breath. He was cocky for nineteen, a bad habit learned from older brothers.

Stark had disrespected his elders and betters often enough, but the army and police had taught him to channel it into something useful. Most of the time, anyway. 'Mind your manners or I'll feed you the contents of that ashtray,' he said evenly.

Blake's sneer vanished, eyes flashing like a child blaming the world for reprimanding him. 'I'd like to see you try.'

'No,' replied Stark. 'You wouldn't.'

'He can't threaten me,' the boy protested to Williams.

Williams shrugged. 'Haven't you heard? He throws people off buildings.'

Blake frowned, clearly not a news follower. 'Why're you here?'

Questions were asked and answered, Williams scribbled down the key points, but the story remained tight. 'Why wasn't Dean invited?'

Blake shrugged. 'Doesn't play so much since he shacked up with Tanya. Pussy-whipped, if you ask me.' He pronounced ask, *axe*, like some LA gang-banger or three-year-old – an ever more common affectation that never failed to set Stark's teeth on edge.

'Whose is the third bedroom?' asked Stark, nodding up the narrow corridor. 'At the time of Paige's disappearance, Dean lived here too. Do you sublet now?'

'Dean uses it sometimes.' Blake was looking less and less interested in the conversation by the minute, starting from a low point. 'When he and Tanya have a barney, or . . .'

'Or what?' Or Dean wanted to entertain a different lady friend, Stark suspected.

'Or we have guests to stay,' replied Blake, effecting an upper-class accent. 'And talking of outstaying your welcome . . .' he added pointedly.

'Tell us about Paige,' Williams said.

'Tell *what* about Paige?' asked Blake, boredom giving way to irritation. 'You know all there is to know.'

'Tell *him*,' said Williams, indicating Stark.

Blake let his frustration show. 'She was a spoilt little princess. Wrapped Mum, Dean and Troy round her little finger. Me too, half the time. Got whatever she wanted.'

Stark was surprised. 'Sounds like you didn't like her very much.'

'I *loved* her,' he said, suddenly fierce. 'She was a brat. But she was my *sister*. If you're looking for whoever tried to kill Sinclair, you're looking in the wrong place; but I wouldn't help you even if I could. Hope they have better luck next time. But if you're looking for whoever killed Paige, you don't need my help; you already know where to find him.' Blake's foggy eyes darkened. 'Give me five minutes with the *fucker* and I'll have the confession you lot were too shit to squeeze out of him!'

They left the fetid den with little thanks on either side.

'I wonder if there's anyone who *doesn't* wish Sinclair dead,' mused Williams.

Yet barring a few minor discrepancies, the poker-night alibi looked pretty impenetrable for now. As did any reason for Kelly's call.

Stark sighed. 'Perhaps we're barking up the wrong tree.'

20

Fran noticed a distant look on Stark's face as they entered. Preoccupation. He even checked his phone – something he normally did with the fastidious infrequency of a very private man with no social media footprint and next to no social life, until recently at least. There was no way he'd use a dating app, and in the balance of life Fran would predict it far less likely that he'd be the one left wistfully phone-checking rather than the jetsam of girls in his wake.

Despite the likelihood that he was probably partying slightly too hard, she couldn't fault his commitment since his return to work. Light duties completed without complaint, laudable concentration and forbearance with her frustrations about the Sinclair case bordering on sainthood. Better still, a return of the long-absent spark, the unspoken agreement that he was laughing at you inside, as you were welcome to laugh at him.

She needed that. God help her, if she passed this sodding Inspectors' Exam she'd need it all the more. But Harper's return could extinguish that spark along with all hope. Austerity had denuded Greenwich MIT, leaving the DI slot unfunded. Groombridge had fought tooth and nail for her to fill it with Stark moving from DC to DS beneath her, but there'd be no money for two DIs if Harper clung on.

'Anything?' She could already tell from Williams' semi-smile that their afternoon had been fruitless. A summary of their various conversations confirmed it.

'To be expected,' said Harper, hovering in the doorway of his purloined office like a poor facsimile of its proper occupant. 'Talbots wouldn't confess to shit if we caught them wiping their arses.'

'Anything on the van or assailants?' asked Stark.

Hammed shook his head. 'We've ruled out a few of the victims' friends and families, but the dawn timing makes alibis thin. No sign of where the van spent the time between its theft and reappearance, or where it was re-sprayed.'

'It's the key, nonetheless,' said Harper. 'Got the list?'

Fran plucked it from her desk and he scanned it in silence, rubbing pensively at the evening stubble shadowing his chin. All the people who knew the true time and place of Sinclair's release. Largely orchestrated by a senior prison service official, but the police had been notified, high up with details passed down through those who needed to know all the way to Fran. Stark had already quizzed the prison governor about her people. She could vouch for most of her staff but, she admitted, not all. Try as you might, any group of people in daily contact with the prison population were inevitably exposed to corruption and threats. It only took one or two to see a prison full of contraband with a spike in prisoner-on-prisoner violence or outright insurrection.

And in this instance, when even the most incorruptible must look on the release of a monster with horror, the list of people who may have been willing to leak the information would rise. They may not have planned harm. If anyone had tipped off the press, there would've been cameras, but someone might just have been spouting off frustration aloud in the pub, or over the dinner table, or let slip to a prisoner. Grainger had made enquiries, but the usual prison snitches were either in the dark or keeping schtum.

How the information had made it to the assailants in time for them to mount an attack was another key. 'They must've been ready,' mused Harper. 'This was planned.'

'A release was likely, from a week ago or more. And possibly for even longer,' Fran agreed.

'It's not that hard,' said Stark. The quiet voice he used when he was speaking up despite wishing he could remain silent. 'A street snatch usually includes people on the ground to follow and distract the target as the vehicle pulls up, but otherwise . . . The planning is all in the vehicles. Infiltration. Exfiltration. Then it's a waiting game.

The timing and location remain fluid as long as everything else is in place.' He stood there, blinking, unshrinking from the discomfort of having all eyes on him.

'This isn't some cheap spy movie,' scoffed Harper. 'Any idiot with a day or two could've come up with the same plan.'

'That's my point really. They just bungled the fluid bit, the unpredictable bit, because they didn't put boots on the ground.'

'But they got the vehicles right,' said Dixon, he and Hammed having spent their afternoon tracing suspect vehicles to no avail.

'What's that?' asked Fran, pointing to a traffic photo on Dixon's screen – a white van, at a distance.

'Looks like a Ford Transit,' explained Dixon. 'Coming out of Best Street, about half a mile from the burnt-out Citroën, around the time the Brigade were called. One of a number of vehicles we can't trace. This is our only shot of it, side on, no plates visible, no discernible livery. We don't see it on any other camera, but there's dozens of streets it could've taken without showing up, and once it's gone it's gone.'

'Another white van in a city full,' nodded Harper. The perfect getaway vehicle. 'We could clear up half the crime rate if we were allowed to pull over and search all white vans on sight.'

Why not get on to your sugar daddy, Deputy Assistant Commissioner Stevens, and pitch for the funding, thought Fran.

'Even if we did catch the plates, they only have to pull over in a quiet street and change them,' said Williams, saying what they all thought. Dead end.

Harper glanced at his watch. 'What about Sinclair?'

That had been Fran's job, but scanning through the case files had offered nothing more than it had the last hundred times. The circumstantial evidence still pointed to Sinclair, but the lost rape-kit was their only tangible link. And with the original trail now two years colder, their hope of finding something they'd somehow missed would be laughable if it didn't make her want to cry. 'Nothing new, yet.'

'So . . . bright ideas?'

A sea of silence.

Even Stark.

Great.

'Sarge . . .' Williams was looking at his emails. 'Ballistics. You're copied in.'

Fran clicked open the email on her own screen. 'Newport? Where the hell is Newport?'

Newport, she was informed, was a small port city in South Wales, near Cardiff. And this, apparently, was where the gun was from. At least, it had been used there, according to the NABIS (National Ballistics Intelligence Service) database – a convenience store hold-up where a round had been discharged into the ceiling to scare the cashier over a year ago. No one hurt, but the bullet markings matched that recovered from the wall of Belmarsh Prison.

So now they'd have to cross-reference the files with Newport to see if any of their long list of suspects might have any Welsh dragon in their blood.

21

'Cheers, John,' muttered Stark, as a steaming coffee materialized beside him.

'You're supposed to be on light duties,' commented Dixon.

'Best laid plans.'

'You know, I wasn't sure you'd come back at all, after . . .'

Dixon was more perceptive than people gave him credit, though Stark's doubts went back much further than his latest bullet wound. 'Glutton for punishment.'

'Ready for the Sergeants' Exam?'

'Assuming there's time.' Groombridge had ordered him to apply for sergeant, but if Groombridge didn't survive this . . .

'*Bollocks*. You're *going*. Fran too. I'm not sticking around with DI Owen-will-he-finally-harp-*off* in charge,' Dixon said with feeling – possibly the first negative thing Stark could recall him ever saying about anyone.

Somewhere beneath the files he'd been reading, Stark's phone saved him from trying to come up with something diplomatic or reassuring. He'd re-saved Kelly's number to avoid being caught on the hop again, but this was number unknown. 'Stark.'

'Hi. This is Callie. Annie's flatmate.'

'Sorry, who?'

'Annie's flatmate. Marianne . . . Pensol? You gave me your card in case of emergencies.'

'And is there one?'

'She hasn't come home. She went out clubbing last night, didn't say where. Normally she turns up in the morning, but it's evening now, and her phone just goes straight to voicemail.'

'I haven't seen her. Have you called anyone else?'

'You're last on my list.' Disapproval lingered behind the worry.

'Okay, I'll try her colleagues, Sergeant –'

'Ptolemy and Constable Peters,' interrupted Callie – exasperation now. 'They were *first* on my list, after family. No one's seen her. Her mum's having kittens.'

'Okay, keep trying her number. The battery is probably just dead but let me know if you get through. I'll speak with Ptolemy. If she doesn't show, I'll maybe drop by the club from the other night when it opens.'

'Just let me know if you hear anything, okay?' And with that Callie hung up.

Sergeant Ptolemy was by nature calm and competent. His constant sidekick Constable Peters was equally unflappable in her own way, more usually involving playful teasing or full-on piss-taking.

Neither were smiling now, as Stark felt compelled to explain how the flatmate of their fledgling rookie had come by his card. Omitting details, such as the removal of sicked-upon clothing and sleeping in the same bedroom, only left them more gaps to fill for themselves, but such questions were on hold. Officially Ptolemy's hands were tied – a missing person report could not be filed until forty-eight hours post-sighting. Unofficially, he'd already had Maggie, doyenne of the station control room, put out a call to all patrols. Pensol was known and, following her recent shooting-in-the-line, cherished.

'She's a big girl,' said Ptolemy, to himself as much as Stark or Peters.

'Big girls do cry,' said Stark. 'How much did you know?'

'That she was in a bad place?' said Peters. 'She seemed okay when we spoke.'

They all shared the same look. *Why didn't we do more?* Particularly Stark, who'd done sod-all.

Guilt dogged his steps back upstairs to the office. Williams was just hanging up a call and beckoning to Fran. 'Good news or bad news, Sarge?'

Fran rolled her eyes. 'Both.'

'DNA comparison is back from the labs and we have a match.'

Fran waited. 'And the bad news?'

Williams sighed, looking at Stark. 'That *was* both.'

'Congratulations, Numpty. Half our testing budget to prove you collected your own blood.'

Fran's words rang in his ears as he limped home to mull over their lack of progress, walking cane clicking on the pavement like metronomic tuts. Stark took them on the chin. It had always been a possibility. But right now, they could've used better news. The team meeting at 08:00 would be a shadowless room.

And then there was Kelly: the unknown reason for her invitation, awareness that he needed to answer and guilt at his failure to do so immediately or since. Weakness.

The only other thought that he could fit in his head was worry about Pensol – as with so many things in his life, not necessarily his fault, but somehow his responsibility. With a bit of luck she'd turn up safe and sound-ish before he had to start trawling late-night bars and clubs. His own adventures over recent weeks had fixed a firm map in his head of likely pick-up spots, but he was hardly in the mood in which he'd normally haunt them.

It was only as he left behind the busier streets and neared his own that the sudden, discomforting chill descended on him. Some sight, sound or sixth sense had him checking corners, reflections, straining his ears for footfalls, keeping to shadows and bracing himself as vehicles passed, scanning drivers. The familiarity of it only made it worse.

Until one reflection showed someone keeping pace behind on the other side of the street.

Stark paused to pat his pockets, pulling out his phone but watching the reflection from the corner of his eye. The figure didn't break step. Stark waited for them to manifest from the darkness and pass. A man, hunched in his coat; face shadowed beneath baseball cap, hands in coat pockets against the chill, or gripping a weapon. The madness thinking. This whole thing was beyond ridicule. Starting up, he watched until the man took the next left and melted slowly into the night.

Shaking his head, Stark walked on.

It was only as he neared his own flats, that paranoia coalesced into alarm.

Beside the entrance doorway, almost imperceptible among the shadows, a figure crouched . . .

22

Without breaking stride, Stark slipped automatically into the shadow of a tree and froze, one with the darkness, scanning carefully, feeling foolish but slave to training.

The would-be ambusher could be alone, but the unseen enemy was the one to fear. This might be the man from five minutes ago, or an accomplice.

Somewhere behind instinct, logic insisted this was far more likely to be a reporter with a camera than an insurgent with an AK-47. It wouldn't be the first time, and his recent propulsion back into the limelight had painted a fresh target on his back for the hacks. If they'd connected him to the attack on Sinclair it would be hunting season all over again.

But something wasn't right . . . The ambusher wasn't so much coiled as slumped . . .

He covered the last distance at a hobbling run and found his suspicion confirmed.

Pensol.

Lipstick smeared, mascara run down both cheeks, hair dishevelled, minuscule skirt and sparkly top borderline indecent. Curled, hugging knees against the cold before passing out.

She looked deathly pale, skin cold, but her carotid offered a steady if slow pulse.

No clutch bag on or around her. No phone, keys, cash or cards. Robbed or lost. Perhaps some 'gentleman friend' would take the time to return them, or bar manager, or both combined.

A gentle shake and name-check elicited only a faint moan of protest.

Stark sighed. Unlocked the door to the flats, propped it open with a fire extinguisher and scooped the unconscious girl up off the ground.

A fireman's lift was the best way to carry a casualty, but it was also a sure-fire way to get a drunk to vomit down your back – though it smelt like she might have rejected her last drinks already. Stark went for the movie marriage-threshold-carry instead, walking cane dangling from his fingers, assorted old injuries protesting, despite Pensol's slight frame. She was an easy lift compared to a squaddie in battle gear, but under the circumstances he allowed himself a ride in the lift up to his flat instead of physio stair-penance.

For the second time he found himself removing her sick-soiled garments, this time dismayed to find not even a love-heart thong beneath, rolling her into the recovery position and covering her with a duvet.

Icy extremities meant her lack of shivering could be bad news. Arctic training body-warmth sharing was hardly appropriate, so he filled the hot water bottle Kelly had given him to alternate with cold packs after physio and slipped it in behind Pensol's kidneys.

Once satisfied she was warming, he texted Ptolemy and Peters and called her flatmate.

'What do you mean, she's there?' demanded Callie, relief tainted with distrust, before demanding his address so she could collect her friend. Stark said she was welcome to, but suggested the patient was best left to sleep it off, and Callie reluctantly agreed to leave her in Stark's care overnight.

'Just . . . Be kind. Please.'

Stark felt a swell of affection for her. 'I promise.'

Returning to Pensol, he was pleased to find her colour returning. He sat on the edge of the bed until he was confident that she'd slipped from unconsciousness into sleep.

Then the whimpering and twitching began.

He could imagine all too well what torment of bullets and blood she was enduring. It was strange to be on the outside looking in, to know something of Kelly's helpless heart, to know there was nothing he could do but stroke the poor girl's hair and whisper lies of comfort until she eventually quietened.

As familiar as the sofa was to him as a bed, sleep proved a predictably hesitant ally. Kelly's call had perturbed his new equilibrium and the thought of discussing it with his shrink was almost as bad. And now there was a girl in his bed for all the wrong reasons, and all efforts to calm his mind as Doc Hazel had taught him fell apart. He was about to give up and have a drink when Fran called.

'Where are you?'

Stark almost laughed. 'Everest base camp.'

'Sober?'

'Lamentably so.'

'Good,' she said. 'Cos I've had a second glass of Chardonnay, and I need you to drive me north of the river.'

'I thought John was on tonight?'

'Just do that thing when you get ready unreasonably quickly and pick me up.'

'It's not exactly convenient.'

'When is it ever?'

'That was going to be my next line.'

'Poor you. Wait . . . You're lowering your voice,' she said suspiciously.

Stark could hardly point out that she was too without bursting her little bubble of relationship denial. 'Like I said . . .'

'I don't want to know. Whoever she is, let her sleep or put her in a cab. Meanwhile in the real world, Tower Hamlets think they just found the supplier of our stolen Citroën van with a terminal and some might say *inconvenient* case of lead poisoning.'

23

The smell of a ripe body after two or three days is not something one gets used to. Even hardened coppers relied on competitive professional detachment to maintain outward cool; something DC John Dixon, for all his many good points, simply couldn't summon. To begin with Fran felt it her duty to treat this vocational weakness with exposure therapy, and when that didn't work had slowly grown to find his dauntless sensitivity to death endearing, even something to cherish in this hard, cynical world.

And in such a world, Fran was content to believe this was the reason she'd left Dixon at his desk and roused Stark instead, and nothing at all to do with a desire to know what was going on with him today. Although now she thought he'd left some poor girl in his bed, her curiosity was somewhat conflicted, as it so often was with Stark.

Something had shifted, though. There was something he wasn't saying, though that was just about always true. The incident with Sinclair's would-be killers was enough to leave anyone a bit off, but he'd seemed okay until earlier today – or was it yesterday? she thought, realizing midnight had come and gone. And something later had sent him scurrying downstairs to his pals, Ptolemy and Peters . . .

Certainly, her jibe about the DNA testing had raised no retort. He'd left for the evening with something weighing on him, and hours later it was still there, she sensed, or worse. The girl in his bed? There was always a blur of contradictions competing for space behind his eyes, but she'd learned through considered observation that when something serious dropped into his gears it manifested outwardly as a faint terseness to his responses and a kind of rigid tension – hard to discern from his usual quiet stillness, but more akin to something vibrating so hard that it appeared still while in silent danger of shaking itself apart. She felt proud of this observation. Reading people was essential in this job, and he was all but indecipherable.

She could ask him directly. Sometimes he'd drop a truth-bomb just to derail more questions. But they both had to be in the right mood and his silence on the drive north had stultified further enquiry.

The tragedy of this was his break-up with Kelly. She'd stabilized him, counterbalanced whatever weighed on his fractured brain. He never talked about her now, of course, and it had been months. Cause of death of that relationship remained unsolved, though the suspect pool was singular – idiot meets girl-far-too-good-for-him and screws it up.

COD of the corpse on the floor of this small workshop, on the other hand, was evident – four bullets to the chest, plus an exit wound. 'One in the back first,' postulated Fran aloud. 'Victim spins to the ground, tries to shuffle away. Killer finishes him off.'

'Four times,' said Stark. 'Uneven dispersal. Sloppy overkill. Panic. Amateur.'

'A crime of betrayal and ineptitude,' agreed the local Detective Sergeant, Hobson, left behind by his DI to oversee the evidence-gathering and liaise with the foreigners from south of the river.

'First-time killing, maybe,' Fran said. 'This lot will tell us more.'

Local SOCO were still swarming like bees. The north London forensic pathologist was working with the photographer before bagging the unfortunate – Damien Castor, known car thief and broad-spectrum ne'er-do-well. All the gear for hastily respraying a blue van white was here, including paint and maskings, but it didn't look like vehicle disguise was a regular activity – more a one-off. The step up from thief to getaway vehicle supplier had proved a dangerous one.

'Convictions for taking without consent, possession of stolen goods and driving without insurance whilst disqualified,' listed Hobson. From the theft-sheet, the Citroën van was stolen in nearby Stratford. A link to the Sinclair shooting had earned extra man-hours for the mundane theft, and a keen-eyed uniform had spotted a previously overlooked CCTV camera, which, as luck would have it, had captured the dodgy-departed Damien Castor in the act. Armed with this evidence and a righteous cause, the local CID had gone to feel his collar, only to find someone had taken serious umbrage with him first. That left his murder in the hands of Tower Hamlets, yet of undeniable interest to Greenwich.

Jurisdictional issues were inevitable with nine million residents, discounting tourists, and thirty-two separate borough forces crammed into a city less than twenty miles across. Criminals appeared to have scant respect for borough borders. The Brass did their best to encourage cooperation but local rivalries were exacerbated when budget restrictions stretched the blue line ever thinner, threatening station closures and mergers. Fortunately, Hobson didn't seem the possessive type. 'Suspected of a good deal more,' he continued, 'including supply of class A drugs and unlicensed firearms.'

'Any known connection to South Wales?' asked Stark.

Hobson looked at him curiously. 'And why do you ask that . . . ?'

'If he supplied our perps with the van, he might've supplied the gun too. Glock 17 or 19, last used in Newport.'

'Hmm,' Hobson mused. 'The gun trade is a paperless trail, but as it happens, this stain arrived in our fair capital from that very place. Someone there will want to take a look. Though perhaps the more pressing question is why the likes of your Talbot brothers would need some low-level scrote north of the river to steal them a car?'

'They wouldn't,' Fran admitted. Dean was smart enough to keep this in the family. 'Maybe the gun?'

Hobson stared down as Castor was zipped up. 'Might serve him right if he was killed with an illegal pistol he'd just sold.'

That was the tiredness talking, thought Fran, giving him the benefit of the doubt on the grounds that she'd thought the exact same thing.

Hobson yawned. 'Well, we haven't found a mobile phone, so whoever did this probably wanted to cover their tracks. Come on,' he sighed, 'I'll treat you both to a cuppa in our excuse for a canteen, and we can compare known associates.'

*

DCI Groombridge listened to Fran's telephone update with all the patience he could summon. For the second time in a matter of months he found himself all but sidelined from a major investigation. Last time had been a rearguard action to ward off threatened merger. This time it was politics and PR. Both times stirred by the Machiavellian manoeuvrings of Deputy Assistant Commissioner Stevens who seemed willing to sacrifice anyone and anything to his ambition. The hefty backfire he'd received last time, largely as a result of Royal Hill Station and in particular, Stark, seemed only to have personalized his willingness to trample them in his reach for the next rung of the ladder.

So be it. Groombridge would find whatever leverage necessary to protect his team and keep them free to work.

At least they had a new line of enquiry.

Alice's arm flopped gently on to his as he slipped back into bed in the dark. Her usual silent message – *the call is over; stop stewing and get your head down.* It was strange how effective it so often proved. He cupped her hand with his, thanked his blessed stars and closed his eyes.

HATE!

Crow wings clattered and folded still like a detonation in reverse, leaving the creature staring at him from atop a stone marker protruding from the cracked red earth. A milestone, or signpost, lettering blasted illegible by shrapnel and frost, at the centre of a crossroads, concentric paths shattered with smoking shell craters. No landmarks visible, just the pock-marked land rising all around and disappearing from view.

In the centre, the crow perched like a black, bleak hole in the burning desert shimmer and called out its barking laugh, mocking his carrion stupidity, waiting to see if he would die of it.

He spun in a circle, trying to see what he was missing, unsure if the crow was trying to warn him, until he realized with horror that he was standing dead centre of one vast crater, and the stone, carved not with lettering but the shattered outline of a tiger, marked only a grave.

A viper curled around its base, tasting the air.

The crow pierced him with one baleful black eye and cawed again – *WHO BEGAT BLOOD!*

Stark shuddered awake in a blinding flash, heart-stopping explosive concussion knocking him flat, rebounding ... clammy skin peeling from the sofa leather, neck cricked from awkward sleep.

Seeing his flat around him and the low morning sun cutting horizontally into his eyes, he flopped back, feeling any grasp of intangible portents slip through his fingers.

The crow was gone and silence pervaded the space. Creaking upright, he peeped in to see Pensol still coddled in the blissful deep sleep before the hangover, as she'd been when he'd finally made it home in the early hours.

Showering and dressing stealthily in clothes he'd got out the night before just in case, he crept out again for the early morning meeting, leaving an explanatory note, his number and headache pills.

Dixon greeted him with a motherly enquiry into his quantity of sleep, but had little to add to their night excursion. The Tower Hamlets incident hotline had started generating the usual trickle of spurious sightings and ill-informed opinions, but nothing of use. Their team would prioritize known associates of their dead car thief and fire over questions to see if the spider web connected any threads to the Greenwich investigations. They'd chase down the more obvious low lifes, while their uniform brethren began the local door-to-door trawl for witnesses.

In Greenwich, Stark and his fellow DCs would soon be inundated with follow-up checks, alibi testing and general desk legwork – if that wasn't an oxymoron. None of which made it any easier right now to ignore the text on his mobile from Kelly – *How about that drink?*

How about an explanation? he thought. Know the enemy's number, dispositions and intent before committing to battle. War and love. Love and war.

'Joe ... You should see this ...' Dixon's grave face suggested Stark might *not* want to. He nodded to his screen, popping out the headphone jack so Stark could hear.

24

Guessing what was coming didn't lessen the blow.

'How the hell did they get that . . . ?' he muttered. A photo of him leaving the hospital mortuary entrance with Harper yesterday after speaking with Sinclair, while the news anchor reported 'eye-witness' claims that far from simply being just *part* of the police investigation, Stark himself had 'single-handedly fought off the gunmen' outside the prison, 'saving Julian Sinclair's life'.

Inevitable images followed – Stark in uniform, receiving his VC, the viral video of his ignominious descent from the clocktower roof after the more recent shootings and a clip from his subsequent and sole TV interview.

Of course the eye witness could be any of the prison service or ambulance personnel, but sat in the centre of this suspect-web was Sinclair himself. As if this case, *or* Stark, needed more press attention.

His phone interrupted one distraction with another, the caller both unexpected and predictable, and not to be taken here in front of others. 'Gwen?' he answered quietly, ducking out. 'To what do I owe the pleasure?'

'Funny you should ask,' she countered. 'I'm feeling a little unloved.'

'And there was me thinking our personal lives were off limits.'

'While there was me thinking I'd earned a little *professional* trust.'

Up to a point, though trust had perhaps come as something of a surprise to them both, starting as it had with her stalking him for a scoop. A freelance reporter, Gwen Maddox had proven herself different to her ilk when her brother's death in combat which initially focused her attention on Stark eventually led to her spiking the story. The empathy of grief. So, after the more recent shootings and endless press punditry on his silence and Hazel's therapeutic prodding, he'd offered Gwen an exclusive. Speak in your own words, on your own terms, Hazel's advice. Feed the fire but define the fuel, take the heat, and hope it burns out before you do. His one and only interview, recorded on video amid the clutter of her flat, and Gwen's springboard from print obscurity to industry name and regular pieces on the hottest online news-feed site. She'd taken a few liberties with the edit but not with his words, and that was enough of a win on both sides. 'And if I ever feel the need to bare my soul to the world again, you'll be the first to know.'

'Not even a heads-up?' she protested. 'I get to read about you in someone else's piece?'

'Which part of *I won't talk about police matters* was unclear?' His refusal to discuss the shootings case in any detail had made his one-and-only media interview awkward, not least for driving her to personal questions he wouldn't answer either.

'Victoria Cross recipient fights off gunmen, barehanded, saving Julian Sinclair's *life*. You didn't think that would make it into the public sphere?'

'No comment.'

'Didn't take us long to get back to that,' she huffed.

'No.'

'Credibility's thin ice in my game. People expect me to have the inside line.'

To him. And if she came out with another exclusive, that's exactly what they'd assume. 'You want people to love you, try being police.'

'I hate you.'

'You're not alone.'

'My lot are coming for you, you know that, right?' And there it was: conscience – the underlying reason for her call, and the reason he trusted her above her kind, despite Fran's bafflement. Significant women in Stark's life tended to settle in the Venn diagram overlap between anger and concern – one reason at least for his recent preference for strangers. 'What happened to keeping a low profile from now on?'

'Karma.' The price of his past.

'Or you're just a pathological twit.'

'Equally plausible.'

'You haven't heard the last of me.'

'I embrace fortune's blessings as they come.'

She sighed. 'Take care, Joe. And if you *do* ever want to unburden yourself . . .'

He chuckled. 'I'll call my shrink.'

His smile didn't last long as he re-entered the office.

'So much for steering clear of cameras,' said Harper, propped in the doorway. 'I've been back *one day* and you're on the news again.'

Stark resisted the urge to point out that Harper was in the pictures too.

The big DI rolled his eyes. 'The sharks just called. Sinclair wants to talk to his favourite hero-crush again. Claiming someone threatened him. *If* you can avoid the cameras this time.'

A wish Stark fervently shared. There was a killer on the loose and the public had every right to be afraid. But whether or not anyone still thought that killer was Sinclair, press pressure and political point-scoring didn't always translate into increased resources with the likes of DAC Stevens in charge. Leaving Sinclair himself holding the real power with the press, and Stark starting to feel like a fly in his web.

Gwen's 'lot' wasted no time in confirming her prediction.

Stark had to lie below window level covering his face with a borrowed cap as they edged out of the station car park through the markedly swollen press contingent, and now sat in the back wishing he wasn't there.

If spending time alone with Owen Harper in a car had been low on Stark's list of things to do yesterday, spending time alone with both Harper and Fran got its own parabola on the discomfort scale. Only in Stark's world would this little jaunt require all three of them. Stark summoned, Harper too egotistical to delegate and Fran too stubborn to be left behind again. Listening to her shooting down Harper's conversational gambits might have been amusing, were it not like waiting for the next mortar round to drop. Harper didn't smoke. Respect for Fran, or some desire for hers.

The big man glanced in his rear-view mirror. 'You find out whether you're getting another medal yet?'

The threatened George Cross. 'Trying to keep my head down,' replied Stark, earning a dark chuckle from Harper.

'How's that going?'

Even Fran smiled. 'There has to be a word for people who repeatedly court danger.'

Stark could summon several, probably no more complimentary than the ones that Fran and Harper were thinking.

There were more press outside the hospital today. He kept his face hidden while directing Harper to the rear. There was no sign of paparazzi around the mortuary bay, but he led them in through a service level maintenance entrance all the same.

Sergeant Dearing was on duty with his awkward rookie again, looking a little less patient than the day before as Bosch and his paralegal materialized, and handing over his clipboard with a sheepish grimace. 'The man who threatened Sinclair was Patrick Burgess. This lot vouched for him. Now they're saying he had a gun.'

'An acquaintance of our client.' Bosch bristled defensively. 'Or so he claimed. He called at my offices earlier today saying he needed to see Julian urgently with information that could prove his innocence. When he refused to divulge this to me, I contacted Julian, who confirmed he knew him.'

'Burgess . . . ?' Stark frowned at the accompanying signature. 'Why do I know that name . . . ?' And then remembered. 'The prison records. Burgess was on the visitor log.'

'There you go then,' said Bosch.

'An *acquaintance* whose name appears nowhere in the original case files . . .' noted Harper.

Bosch sneered. 'The same *comprehensive* case files that ultimately amounted to nothing more than malicious speculation and vindictive prosecution.'

'Did you come up with that yourself or did Miranda help you with the more tricky words?' smiled Fran, in what Stark recognized as her last line of diplomacy before resorting to other means.

'Perhaps we can go in and hear what's happened,' Harper suggested dryly. 'Unless you're just here to string out your billable hours?'

Bosch looked at each of them in distaste and knocked on the door, the paralegal behind him careful to meet no one's eyes.

Inside, there was something immediately different about Sinclair. Hospital gown replaced with designer-branded PJs but arm still slung and day-two morphine reduction clearly fraying his edges, he appeared far from happy to see Fran – but there was no hint that he'd just been threatened. Instead, there was a strange look of excitement radiating from him. 'Thanks for coming, Joe,' he said, not greeting the others.

Stark didn't bite at the informality. 'We have a duty to respond.'

'And to protect him,' added Bosch. 'A duty you repeatedly fail in.'

'Perhaps from now on we'll instigate strip'n'cavity searches on all visitors, vouched for or not,' said Fran. 'You first?'

'You're all missing the point,' interjected Sinclair. 'He didn't just threaten me. He told me who killed all those poor girls.'

25

'*He* did?' Fran made no effort to withhold her incredulity. 'Patrick Burgess?'

Sinclair nodded earnestly, looking to his legal team for the belief that neither Fran nor Harper were demonstrating.

'Burgess visited you in prison,' said Harper. 'How many times? How did you know him?'

'Once. And I didn't.'

'You didn't know him?'

Sinclair's excitement dimmed. 'Believe it or not, Detective Inspector, I wasn't exactly overwhelmed with visitors after you put me inside. My family still won't talk to me. So-called friends, either. So when Burgess wrote to Miranda, my barrister, offering moral support and requesting a visit, I was glad of the company. Or so I thought.'

Harper's face was heavy with scepticism. 'And?'

'At first he just seemed harmless. Saying he felt sorry for me. He believed I was innocent. Said he was praying for me. That the police had made a scandalous mistake.'

'So he was delusional,' scoffed Fran.

Sinclair rolled his eyes in irritation. 'He seemed kind. I needed a friend. But then . . . he switched. He started talking about poor Leah, Leah Willoughby; calling her names. Nasty stuff. Slut and bitch, that sort of thing. Prancing whore.'

Stark looked up sharply, but when Fran glanced at him to explain he shook his head.

'You have to believe me,' Sinclair insisted. 'I told him to get out and never come back, but I didn't know what he really was. The prison will verify, he never visited again. But when he turned up this morning, saying he could prove me innocent once and for all . . . I had to hear him out.'

'So what did he say?' Harper was gruff-voiced, losing patience.

'To start with it was niceties . . . Was I feeling better? When was I getting out? To be honest, he still creeped me out, so I told him my arm was fine and I was going home today; I didn't want him visiting again. I asked him *how* he could prove my innocence and he sort of laughed . . . strangely. Then he just said it was *him*. All along. He started talking about retribution, angelic voices telling him to do it all, but now I was free he wanted me to know he was sorry for letting me take the blame.'

'And you can verify this?' Harper asked Bosch.

'No. He would only talk to Julian.'

Harper huffed. 'So some nutcase walks in here and proves you innocent by confessing to your crimes to you and you alone?'

'He knew stuff,' protested Sinclair. 'Details . . . from the trial. Stuff that wasn't in the papers.'

'So get him back in here and he can tell us too.'

'He left no means of contacting him,' said Bosch, with his closest approximation of regret.

'Why didn't you call out to my colleagues outside, to detain him?'

'He showed me his gun,' explained Sinclair as if it should be obvious. 'Said he'd kill me if I called out, and your colleagues too.' He saw Fran and Harper's expressions and tried appealing to Stark instead, initial cheer trampled into desperation. 'I know *they* won't believe me, but you . . . you're new, you're less invested . . .' *in my continued stitch-up*, he didn't quite need to add. '*Please*. I'm telling the *truth*,' he pleaded, near to tears.

Fran had insisted he was a practised liar and the evidence, circumstantial or otherwise, still pointed strongly to him. But if this was a performance, it was a good one. 'Can you describe the gun?'

Sinclair looked incredulous. '*Black?*'

'A pistol?'

'Yes.'

'If I showed you images, might you recognize one?'

'Maybe. I don't know. Why does it matter?'

'Everything matters,' said Harper impatiently.

'So you'll investigate, fully?' Bosch demanded.

Harper paused. For all his deficiencies, he had gravitas. 'Rest assured, we'll give this all the attention it deserves.'

'We can't ignore it,' said Stark once they were outside.

'Well of course we can't,' snapped Fran. 'That's why he *said* it!'

'He's playing us,' agreed Harper.

'Maybe,' Stark conceded. 'Didn't seem like that, though.'

Fran gave him a hard look. 'Say that again when you've spent as much time with him as we have. It didn't *seem* like that, but it never does. He's a liar and a psychopath, and if he can turn on the waterworks it's because he's practised in a mirror.'

'Sarge.' Stark gave her his noncommittal blank face.

For a man who'd been blown up and shot more than once, he retained a disturbing faith in his fellow man. 'So what was it made your ears prick up in there that you didn't want to say?' she asked.

'Prancing whore,' he explained. 'That phrase was used in one of his fan mails.'

Fran huffed. 'He's a clever one, I'll give him that. Trying to sow plausible doubt, painting this Burgess patsy. He's probably got them all in a scrapbook.'

'Or passed them straight to his sharks for litigation ammunition,' muttered Harper.

'Not this one,' said Stark. 'The nastiest offering. Original sin misogyny, holy retribution, the works. Sinclair only got a copy. Original was passed to National Crime but Forensics came up blank – simply styled on generic paper with a common printer, and no DNA to trace the author. But now we have a name.'

Fran rolled her eyes, but sighed. 'Okay, let's get a face. Check the hospital CCTV.'

'He was wearing a cap,' said Dearing, shaking his head bitterly. 'He didn't have any ID but Bosch insisted Sinclair knew him.' The normally implacable sergeant glanced at his rookie, embarrassed and angry with himself at not searching for weapons. And so he should be.

Harper ignored him, stepping away to dial his phone. 'John. It's Owen. I need you to run a name ... Patrick Burgess. Early to late thirties, Caucasian, sub-six foot, brown hair, brown eyes, brown beard ... Check if we have anything on him.'

'I'll call HMP Belmarsh too,' said Stark. 'See if they have photo ID for him.'

'And CCTV, if they store footage long enough,' said Fran. 'I'm sure your new BFF, Governor Grainger, will be only too happy to let you rummage through her drawers.'

'Technically, army reservist *Colonel* Grainger could still order me to run parade ground laps in my boxers.'

'I don't know which mental image scars me more.'

'Don't worry, Sarge, I only take orders from you.'

'If only that were half true. You *take* orders – it's what you do with them afterward that bothers me.'

26

First a name, and now a face, albeit of poor quality, lighting and angle – the best still Stark had been able to pull from the hospital cameras.

Beard. Glasses. Baseball cap. Enough to look conspicuous, especially indoors; more than enough to disguise one's features from cameras. Bulky coat to disguise physique. The photofit tech was en route. With luck, Sinclair, Dearing and the rookie would add details this image lacked.

'He was stocky.' The paralegal, Emily, had volunteered to stick around to help Stark pick out Burgess, and probably under orders to make sure her client's new ploy to deflect blame was given due credence. 'The baggy clothes mask it, but he looked strong,' she added helpfully, though *who* she was helping wasn't really in doubt.

But she was right. Stark could picture him, the pacing screen-slave who'd glanced his way as he'd skirted past the press into the hospital to see Sinclair that first day after the prison shooting . . . Stark had seen him, dismissed him as just another anxious relative.

Stark's phone sounded loud in the small room. Not Kelly, thank goodness. His home landline. Pensol. 'Excuse me,' he smiled to Emily, stepping outside the suite. 'Hello.'

'Hi . . . is that . . . ?'

'Yeah, it's me, how are you feeling?'

She hesitated. 'I don't know how I got here.' There was a question hiding there. The *did we?* question.

'I found you on the doorstep and helped you inside. No drama.

I'm always happy on the sofa.' He'd deliberately left the blanket and pillow there as evidence. 'You found my note then? I'm sorry, I looked around but you didn't seem to have your phone or purse.'

Another pause. 'I don't remember much.'

'We've all had nights like that,' Stark kept it upbeat. She sounded pretty glum, but the hangover from a two-night bender could do that. 'I left some clothes out for you. I washed your clothes – they had sick on, sorry – but the labels said don't tumble dry. They're hanging up on the radiator.' What there is of them, he thought, but who was he to judge?

'Thanks. I . . .'

'Have you eaten anything?' His note invited her to help herself.

'No. I woke earlier, but I felt like death and went back to sleep. I thought I was at home.' She still sounded dazed.

'There's various things in the fridge, but I left you some cash and a set of keys in case you needed anything. There's a shop just round the corner, and takeaway deliveries. Though I should warn you the press might show up outside – my face is in the news again, with a case.'

'Okay . . .' She probably didn't know how to digest that one. A recent victim herself, she would've had to fend off her own share of press intrusion. He'd never thought much past his own problems. 'I don't really feel up to facing the world anyway.'

'Have you spoken to Callie?' He'd left her flatmate's number on the note.

'She'll be cross with me.'

'That's what mates are for.'

'Are you cross with me?' There was resignation in her voice, as if all the world should be.

'No. I've been where you are.'

She was silent for a few seconds. 'Does it get better?'

'Yes.' *With time, effort and help*, he didn't add.

'I . . . I don't want to go home.'

Stark knew that feeling too; the need to be elsewhere, to draw a circle around you and imagine it a wall. 'Stay as long as you like. I'll call Callie and let her know, ask her to pack you some clothes and toiletries. I can pick it up later. Is there anyone else I should call?'

'I . . . don't have anyone's numbers.'

'We'll get it sorted, don't worry. Callie called your mum last night.'

Another silence. Stark guessed she was trying not to cry. 'Thanks.'

'No bother. Get some food and rest and make yourself at home. Not sure what time I'll be back.'

Emily looked up from typing into her own phone as he re-entered, reporting to her masters. 'Girlfriend?'

A rather direct question. Loaded too, perhaps. 'Just a friend.'

Emily nodded, then looked back at the image on the screen. 'Would you like me to work with your artist too?'

'Perhaps,' replied Stark. 'We'll let you know.'

'You might have better luck at the prison.'

'My next stop.'

'I should come along,' she smiled. Perhaps Bosch used her as a sweetener. He would be a fool not to.

Stark smiled back automatically. 'Thank you, but that won't be necessary.'

'But you'll keep us informed of progress?'

'Within the confines of what we're at liberty to divulge during an active investigation.'

The door opened as Fran entered with her usual presumption that anyone standing in her way would realize their mistake, and Emily's amusement was instantly replaced with cool professionalism. 'Of course. If there's anything we can do to help,' she said, handing him a business card and nodding farewell to them both.

Fran watched her leave with cold dislike.

Stark glanced at the card, and noticed there was a mobile number written on the back, with the words – *Call me x.*

He tucked it away, hoping Fran hadn't noticed, but the hint of disapproval told him she had. 'Wit and charm?'

More shock and awe, thought Stark, but on the receiving end. 'Just sipping char with the locals, Sarge.'

She didn't smile. 'Working out friend from foe?' She held up her phone, open on Reuters News website:

WRONG ALL ALONG?

Metropolitan Police actively investigating

NEW SUSPECT in the GREENWICH STRANGLER killings!

*

'Moncrieff?' asked Cox, peeping through his office blinds at the TV vans gathering outside. 'Or this lawyer, Bosch?'

'Together, most likely,' replied Groombridge, watching the Superintendent stew.

'They tip off the press about Stark's involvement too?'

'Fair to assume.'

'At least they had the sense not to release Burgess's name.'

'They might just be saving that for the evening news.'

Cox winced. 'Let's try to find him first, eh?'

DAC Stevens had wasted no time phoning to demand an explanation while refusing to hear one. This wasn't the first time Royal Hill station had proved porous, he'd stated with stratospheric gall, and Cox had better get his house in order before HQ stepped in once and for all.

Groombridge had the discomfort of witnessing the call and pretending not to hear every word of Stevens' raised delivery as Cox had held the earpiece away with stoic patience until the line went dead.

'You'll help Harper prep for the press parade?'

'Oh, I think he can cope just fine without my interference.'

Cox shook his head, displeased. 'You should've said something last year, if you didn't think he was up to the job. You let loyalty stay your hand.'

More than you know, thought Groombridge. Their relationship had long since settled into Cox trusting that anything in need of his attention would be brought to it, but this one fell right on the cusp. His evidence of Owen's historic mistakes was more reputation than career threatening. Quietly dissuading Owen from extending his last secondment here had been best all round, though it still sat no easier than keeping Cox in the dark about the whole sorry business. Whatever the rights and wrongs, a deal had been struck, and now broken. *Not his idea*, Owen had insisted as Groombridge relocated his personal effects again, blaming Stevens.

Or perhaps you're just getting cynical in your old age, thought Groombridge. Let he who is without blame cast the first stone. Everyone made mistakes, and ambition wasn't a crime. 'I still think he could be a decent DI. Just preferably not here.'

Cox eyed him shrewdly. 'I can tell when there are things you're not telling me, you know.'

'Glad to hear it, sir.'

'His own Super rates him highly.'

'Indeed.' Sometimes a tactic for offloading the unwanted. Owen's Super had been willing to loan him out twice in short succession.

'So, he swims or he sinks.'

'It's out of my hands. DAC Stevens was quite clear.'

'While you keep things quietly afloat through DS Millhaven,' Cox stated.

'Fran can swim without my help.'

Cox harrumphed at the non-denial. 'Well, with a bit of luck the IPCC will spit out Stevens' poison and get you back behind your desk where you belong.' His PA, Lucille, hovered at his door with something for Cox to sign and a look for Groombridge reserved for any person who upset other people's carefully balanced diaries.

Cox waved her away. 'I have a meeting at HQ. And the Sinclair shooting?'

'Nothing new. CCTV and traffic cameras are a bust. We're working with Tower Hamlets to find a link.'

Cox rubbed his generous moustache pensively. 'How can we be two days out from a shooting and have nothing?'

'How indeed, with "*all the resources we need*"?'

Cox nodded. Being set up to fail didn't made it any more palatable.

'Not sure my DI and yours are destined to be best buds,' said Hobson evenly. Sergeant code for my DI thinks yours is a cock.

You don't know the half of it, Fran wanted to scream, but couldn't. It was too ingrained – you didn't air your grubby laundry, even when it came to stubborn stains like Harper. For all his faults, he wasn't a dirty cop, just an arsehole. 'Thank heaven for sergeants, keeping the wheels turning.'

'Indeed, well, it turns out our Damien Castor had links to a suspect in the Newport convenience store robbery, so our Welsh comrades have made an arrest,' said Hobson. 'But more interesting to us is that Ballistics just confirmed your bullets match mine. Our car thief's bullets have barrel striations matching the bullet that passed through your Julian Sinclair to lodge in Belmarsh Prison's wall, and the recovered nine-mil shell casings all have matching hammer strike impressions.'

'Our multi-nefarious Glock? That was quick,' said Fran. Even though the ballistics request was submitted by Tower Hamlets, Fran half expected the related Greenwich case numbers to flag up Stevens' forensic roadblocks again.

'Friend in high places,' joked Hobson.

'Careful what you wish for.' Fran left it at that. If Harper was a stain, Stevens was a massive effluent spillage.

Hobson chuckled politely. 'Well, let's see if we can't help our collective betters to the right conclusions.'

27

Governor Grainger's office was, like the woman herself, compact and neat as a pin. You could take the colonel out of the army but never the army out of the colonel.

She stood to salute. 'Sergeant Stark, VC. Twice in a week. I'm honoured.'

'Colonel Grainger,' Stark returned the gesture. 'If I swear not to tell anyone, could we do away with the salutes?'

'And fly in the face of a hundred and fifty years of tradition?'

'We're more or less civilians now.'

Grainger's smile was wistful. 'Do you miss it as much as I do?'

'Sometimes.'

'Yes,' she nodded soberly. 'Some parts more than others. Have you got the log?'

Stark held up his phone. Hammed had scanned through the prison visitors' log on Stark's computer and emailed him the relevant page. 'Patrick Burgess.'

'Right. I'll show you to the security suite.'

'I shouldn't like to take up your time.'

'No bother for a brother.'

– *In arms*. Stark hadn't heard the phrase for a while, and smiled.

'You had any scran?' she asked, looking him up and down suspiciously. Stark realized lunchtime had somehow come and gone. 'Typical NCO; last to eat. Well, the food here's no worse than you're used to.'

The security suite, reached via a labyrinthine march, was as he'd left it two days earlier. The camera footage of the Sinclair shooting hadn't been a fun watch; seeing the two-on-one go badly wrong still stung his pride. You're never in control when they have the gun, but still . . .

'Right, you horrible lot, remember Detective Constable Stark . . .' announced Grainger to the team within. 'Give him everything he needs, starting with a hot drink and half-decent sandwich. Hop to it. Time for a brew and chinwag after?' this last directed to Stark.

Stark gave an apologetic gesture. 'If wishing made it so.'

'In happier times, then. You can pretend I'm saluting you now.'

'Likewise.'

Grainger's security team looked a little nonplussed, probably unused to seeing their boss smile.

They were, however, used to doing as she said. Coffee and an egg sandwich materialized in minutes. Finding Patrick Burgess took longer.

The log directed them to the correct data file, but the visiting reception camera was crowded with people. Stark was beginning to wonder if the log time was wrong when a figure emerged at the front of the queue and removed or was told to remove his cap. The hair and beard were shorter. Burgess. A better image. The pretty paralegal, Emily, had been right. Burgess looked stockier in his coat. Stark felt at the card in his pocket and wondered whether, after the investigation, it would be okay to call her. If Fran had her way, there'd be an arrest and trial in the way too. All things considered, perhaps that was for the best. Pity though.

As he was watching, Burgess got out some paperwork. He hit pause. 'That's him. I need an ID.'

It took a few minutes, but soon Stark had a scan of Burgess's photo driver licence, with address.

Harper glanced at *Goldenballs* on caller ID, and turned off his phone to avoid interference with the microphones. Whatever Stark had to say could wait. From the elevation of the station stoop, he surveyed the assembled press with the familiar thrill swelling his chest even more than usual. There was shuffling at the back as the various camera crews tried not to trip over each other. An appreciably bigger audience than he'd ever enjoyed before – even one or two *international* networks. Uniform had closed off the road to allow for the TV vans. Stark's national-bloody-hero fame had its uses after all.

This was what it was all about: A high-profile case. High stakes. High rewards.

DAC Stevens had bet against Greenwich and Royal Hill months ago and lost. As a lowly betting chip in that game, Harper's reputation had been gambled away too. Make no mistake, this had never been about Masonic fraternity; Stevens had seen him as entirely expendable then, and still did. He was a first-class shit, but as long as he had a use for Harper, Harper would make himself useful, and who knew where it might lead if he played his cards right: promotion, a seat at HQ, on some prize taskforce? Stevens had more than hinted in order to get him on board again.

Just not here, if Harper could help it.

He still didn't know who knew what.

Go quietly or else . . . his deal with Groombridge, ending his last disastrous secondment here – bow out, and the evidence of your collusion with DAC Stevens and role in triggering a madman both go in a drawer. The DCI hadn't been nasty about it and was a man of his word. Better still, he seemed to have accepted Harper's reappearance without spilling the beans, so far. His own fall from grace was perhaps keeping him from it – dumping Harper in it now would only wound the station's reputation further. But he'd never said who else knew. Fran got her nose into everything, and Goldenballs Stark always knew too much and was far too pally below-stairs. Now Harper was back, through no fault of his own, it felt like half the station was looking at him sideways, whispering behind his back . . . blood on the streets, on his hands. Probably his imagination, but how could he be sure?

So be it. He didn't need them anyway. He didn't need any of them. His conscience was clear, and this case could be the making of his career. Now Jess was back on the rails, sober a full twelve months and looking solid, he could concentrate on rebuilding the life they'd had . . . before IVF, the miscarriages, and her descent into booze.

A life without children.

It had all but crushed her. Him too, inside. Weird how it crept up on you. But they'd been happy before, together. They could be happy again. And perhaps he could look himself in the mirror again.

'Detective Inspector! Can you confirm that Detective Constable Joseph Stark, formerly army Sergeant Stark, winner of the Victoria Cross and hero of the Greenwich Clocktower Shootings, was responsible for fighting off the three armed assailants in the attempt on Julian Sinclair's life outside Belmarsh Prison on Friday morning?'

'That's an operational matter and I can't comment.'

'Was Stark injured in the incident?'

'Julian Sinclair's was the only significant injury.'

'What of Joe Stark's medal chances? Is this not yet another reason he should be awarded the George Cross too?'

Harper shook his head and held up a hand until he had silence. The simple power of it thrilled, however irritated he was by the line of questioning. 'Constable Stark is a low-ranking member of the Major Incident Team here in Greenwich, and as such has a *small* part to play in this investigation, nothing more, and that's all I'll say on that matter.'

'Are you any closer to identifying the three masked men?'

'We're pursuing all lines of enquiry in this multifaceted investigation, with diligence and confidence.'

'And why are you here?' asked a cool voice from the back, a hot blonde in red that he thought he recognized but couldn't place. 'Scarlet Jennings, Capital-Cast,' she announced unbidden – a London-centric digital news platform of mounting popularity. 'Is Detective Chief Inspector Groombridge being replaced, following the failings in the Greenwich Strangler investigation and wrongful prosecution of Julian Sinclair?'

'Again, if we could stick to the matter in hand . . .'

'Okay, then what can you tell us about your new suspect in the Greenwich Strangler case? Are Greenwich Police now preparing to admit you were wrong all along? Is Julian Sinclair innocent?'

No. He's bloody not, thought Harper, remembering each corpse, each face . . . *And I'm going to prove it.* He'd won the lead role in a hit show just as it moved to the West End, and it was time to cash in. He took a deep breath, set his face to stern professional and delivered his finest official statement.

28

'Shit-face,' muttered Fran, watching the TV screen in the canteen. Declaratory Harper in his best phrase-book DI patois, playing to the crowd. It wouldn't irk so much if he wasn't so much better at it than she would ever be. If there was ever a better reason *not* to sit her upcoming Inspectors' Exam, it was not having to face the press in this kind of super-heated atmosphere.

'Hardly the respect due his rank,' said a voice just behind her.

She winced as Groombridge slid into the next seat. 'Guv.'

'It's only temporary.'

'You said that last time.'

'And it was. And this time we know he'd never dare get comfy.'

'Not even if the IPCC smear you? Your office is going to look mighty inviting.'

'If that happens, my office will very soon have *you* in it,' he replied, pinning her with his eyes. 'All set for Thursday, I assume.' Her exam. He knew her too well. Knew she'd gladly use the case as an excuse to skip the damn test, and took her hesitation as confirmation. 'I would've thought Owen's reappearance would've made you doubly determined to pass with flying colours. Indeed, his taking the lead could hardly have come at a better time, freeing you, as I *insist* it does, for a few hours to sit the exam.'

If the case allows, she thought, but he could always read silent dissent in her eyes.

'Stark too,' Groombridge nodded. The Sergeants' Exam was on the same morning. 'I put a lot of work into this. I won't see it wasted. This case is important, but so is this team. The only way we can fend off the likes of Owen Harper is to have you and Stark take your rightful places. That's an order, Detective Sergeant.'

She shifted in discomfort. Stark's offer to help her revise had had the exact effect the calculated sod doubtless intended – prodding her to log in and learn alone for no better reason than the certainty that the dirty little swat had learnt all his sergeant stuff and would gobble up the inspector syllabus out of boredom. What he found easy, she found torture, and the thought of sitting down to demonstrate her ignorance made her stomach flip anew. Perhaps this nagging flu-ache would worsen and confine her to bed . . .

'I don't pull rank often, Fran,' Groombridge said, 'but if these are my last days in charge here, let them count for something.'

'Don't say that, Guv. This is *your* team.'

'And I'll make damn sure I leave it in good hands.' He stood, nodded, his gaze fierce. 'Just make sure you do your part.'

Fran watched him go, trying to work out how cross she should be, before another unwelcome voice turned her head back to the TV. Richard *Bloody* Hardacre, reviving his Greenwich Strangler Victims Group song and dance, giving his fulsome opinion on the merits of Greenwich Police over the phone with a stock photo of him from the time of the trial – equally critical that they might've been chasing the wrong man all along or that anyone but Sinclair could possibly be suspected. He'd have half the families up in arms again and the press lapping up every incendiary word. And then, of course, Bitch Barrister Moncrieff popped up live, giving her silk-bound tuppence-worth of napalm for editorial imbalance. No matter how bad your day is going it can always get worse, Fran reminded herself.

Her phone rang. Caller unknown. 'DS Millhaven.'

'What's this bullshit about a new suspect?' demanded a gruff, angry voice.

Dean Talbot? 'Who is this?'

'That cunt, Sinclair, killed my sister. You *told* us he did!'

'Dean –'

'Are you saying you were wrong all along?'

'You can't believe everything you hear in the news.'

'Yes or no? Did Sinclair do it?'

'I've always thought so –'

'But now you're looking at someone else? Who?'

'I can't tell you that.'

'Can't or won't.' He sounded increasingly angry, and much as she disliked him, she sympathized.

'No one takes this more seriously than you, the families and us, Dean, but –'

'Bullshit! You had your chance!' He hung up.

Fran breathed out slowly. That had sounded like a declaration of war. She was about to call Dearing and the guard detail when she noticed a missed call from Stark.

'Everyone in position?'

Harper on the radio for the umpteenth time, urgent, purposeful and bloody annoying. And still pissed off about hearing Stark's news of a lead just *after* his puff-chested press piece, although, so far, he'd not torn Stark off a strip about it. Still saving up, Fran thought.

One by one the various officers arranged around the house of Patrick Burgess confirmed they were as much in position as they'd been for the last hour.

Frustration was showing. It had taken too long to set this all up. The sun had set behind the houses and it was growing darker by the minute – which at least was better for hiding cars full of bored, fidgety coppers.

But there were no lights on or movement inside the unkempt terraced house, rented by Burgess. Harper assured them a search warrant was on the way but Fran doubted it. This was too thin, so far. Burgess wasn't officially a suspect in anything other than keeping bad company, and any judge with an ounce of sense would be playing this one by the book with all the press scrutiny. After all, why would anyone turn up out of the blue and gloat about a heinous crime, having just given his name to two policemen outside the door?

The day off might swing it though. That was Harper's play. They'd tracked Burgess online and spoken with his employer, who told them he'd taken the day off at short notice 'to visit his unwell mother'.

Both driving licence and employer confirmed his current address as this little cul-de-sac outside Teddington. The local force were providing the uniforms but Harper was lording it about the way only he could, putting backs up wherever he went, giving Greenwich a bad name.

'Is he asleep?' asked Hammed, twisting round.

Stark had his head resting against the window, eyes closed.

Fran sighed. 'It's the soldier thing, apparently.' She'd seen him wake screaming, and knew he found sleep hard. But sit him in a car, action pending, and . . .

'*Who begat hate*,' he mumbled with a faint twitch.

'Wonder what *that* means,' said Hammed quietly.

'I prefer to be thankful I don't know,' replied Fran, both true and untrue. People thought coppers loved puzzles, but the only puzzle a *proper* copper liked was a solved one. Puzzles were to be tackled on sight and forced to cough up their secrets. After her older brothers each tired of the inscrutable Rubik's Cube, she'd saved up her pocket money for an instruction booklet, solved it, then hid it from them to stop them messing it up again. A sign of things to come, perhaps. But while she burned to know everything, the contents of Stark's tortured dreams were the kind of thing she'd probably instantly regret unpeeling.

Someone's coming, hissed a voice over the radio.

All eyes watched a figure march up the road with a single bag of shopping.

Wait for my go, said Harper. *And remember, suspect may be in possession of a gun.*

The figure stopped outside the house, fumbling keys out . . .

Fran held her breath until he had his key in the lock and the door open.

All units, GO GO GO!

29

'He's going to press a complaint,' said Fran, as unhelpfully as she could.

Harper ground his teeth, staring through the one-way glass at the unhappy figure sitting in Interview One.

Burgess had panicked as men with torches came shouting out of the darkness towards him, thrown his shopping bag at them and reached into his jacket – at which point the uniforms had wisely hesitated and Harper had tackled him to the ground like a charging bull; literally dumb as an ox. You couldn't fault his bravery. Only his discretion, motivation and sense.

Unfortunately, Burgess, whilst definitely the man in the driver's licence and online images, was not the man who'd visited Sinclair in prison and hospital – more pudgy than stocky, lacking the full beard and glasses and, it turned out, much of a sense of humour.

That left the uncomfortable truth; that someone had stolen or duplicated this man's driver's licence, a fact supported by his insistence that following the theft of his wallet a year earlier, he had been the subject of protracted identity theft issues after the emptying of his accounts and credit card fraud, and was still fighting to regain his money and credit rating. One of a number of contributory factors to his current humour failure.

It was a common enough action among the criminal fraternity – to follow someone who looked enough like you and purloin their ID. That wasn't going to stop the press pouncing on this latest 'police failure', or this Burgess pressing a complaint.

'Perhaps if we'd gone in softer ... ?' Fran twisted the knife. *Groombridge would've*, she didn't quite add.

She braced herself for the explosion ... but instead, Harper let out a long sigh. 'Yeah. I fucked up. Trying too hard as usual.'

If he'd sprouted glowing golden wings and floated up into the sky amid a choir of angels Fran would hardly have been more astonished. He turned his face towards her with a look she'd never seen before – not quite humility, but closer than she'd ever thought possible. 'Look, maybe you don't trust me, but this is bigger than that. I'm going to need your help if we all want to get through this shiny, without letting Sinclair screw us again, or Brass hang us out to dry.'

We? Us? Who did he think he was kidding? The more shiny they came out of this the better chance he'd have of keeping Groombridge's office. And if they didn't, he'd reap whatever reward DAC Stevens had dangled – some cushy post, or even a prime DI slot in Lewisham MIT after a forced merger. If Sinclair's bottom-feeding legal team weren't behind the latest press leaks then Stevens was, with Harper his inside source. 'This isn't about shine. It's about finding the truth.'

'It's about *both*.' He sighed, frustrated. 'I'll stay here, try smoothing things over. I need you and the others upstairs looking for the arsehole using this poor sod's name.'

Fran frowned at the camera still and photofit. 'Can't shake the feeling these look familiar ...'

Harper made a face. 'They always do.'

Fran stared at them again, but nothing came. Just another fleeting ghost of suspects past.

Stark knocked hard to be heard over the thumping music within. He'd tried the bell but couldn't hear if it worked.

When no one answered he started using the base of his fist instead of his knuckles and kept going until the music inside dimmed sufficiently for voices to be heard within, swearing, before it opened.

'The fuck?' a two-syllable welcome from a two-syllable face. Tall, handsome in a lean, sweaty way.

Stark recognized him instantly; lead groper of the gang of lads surrounding Pensol in the club three nights ago. Despite his intervention, she'd gone back for more. The recognition appeared to be one-way, so Stark started with a smile. 'Hi. Sorry to bother, but my friend has lost her phone and purse and thinks she might've left them here.' The smile didn't seem to help.

'You what?' frowned the man.

Stark started again, without the smile. 'Pretty girl. Annie? Five-five, short blonde hair.'

'I don't know what the fuck you're on about.' The man sneered dismissively, closing the door. Or trying to. He looked at Stark's solid shoe, wedged in the gap.

It had been a long day getting nowhere and a lot of people had wasted an evening chasing his mis-lead. The Patrick Burgess they were after was a ghost. The real one they'd inconvenienced on his own doorstep was probably still chewing over their apologies. The press already had a report of a failed raid to add to their relentless speculations about the case, and him. Harper was doing a strange impression of a half-decent copper, which had Fran edging round him like a cat trying to work out a puppy. Hobson and his Tower Hamlets team were running out of known associates to rattle and no connection had been drawn between their dead car thief and the Talbot brothers, or indeed anyone else on the endless list of people who'd love Sinclair harmed. Groombridge was adrift in shark-infested waters, Cox had dropped by to show his support, twice, which was unsettling at best, and DAC Stevens had been on the news declaring that Greenwich Police had all due resources at their fingertips – in other words, just beyond grasp.

And he'd been sent home to sleep by Harper. So he was doing the only useful thing he could think of that didn't involve thinking about Kelly. 'Let me put it another way,' he said, holding up his warrant card. 'The phone I'm looking for was last traced to this address. The girl it belongs to is a fellow police officer. And if you don't hand it and her purse over in the next ten seconds my colleagues in the patrol car over there and every copper within three miles of here is going to kick their way in here and start using words like invalid consent by reason of intoxication under the 1956 Sexual Offences Act . . .'

It was clear from the sudden further dimming of the music inside that the man's friends had heard some of Stark's declaration. Judging from his dilated pupils there was a good chance there were also substances inside they'd not want found.

'Yeah.' The man gulped, now with a rather different look on his face. 'Wait, yeah. I know who you mean. I think she left her purse.'

'And her phone,' said Stark, loud enough to be heard inside.

There was a burst of hissed whispers and scraping furniture, and possibly the sound of someone falling over something in haste, before the man was handed something which he in turn offered to Stark. Pensol's sequined clutch bag, unclasped. Stark checked the contents. Phone, keys, driving licence, bank cards. No cash. No condoms. 'Is this everything? Because if she tells me it's not . . .'

'*I think these were* . . .' hissed a voice inside, passing the man something, which he handed Stark with some trepidation.

Small. Cotton. Love hearts.

He saw the look on Stark's face. 'Look, nothing happened, man. *Seriously.* She fell asleep on the loo. When we tried waking her up she got all hissy and bailed, left her shit. I was going to find her, drop all this back, you know . . .'

'Yeah, I can see how you got right on that.'

'Nothing happened, Bro –'

'*I'm not your bro,*' growled Stark, shoving the door hard into the man, sending both inward, the latter falling backwards over his own feet, with three anxious faces looking on. 'Any brother of *mine* would've escorted a drunk girl home, not groped her uninvited or taken her back to theirs with three mates for *God knows what*!' The man looked fit to piss himself, scrambling away from Stark's sudden fury, the mates in question backing away too.

'*Shit,*' hissed one of the lackeys, 'that's the nutcase from the club that fucked up that massive bouncer!'

Stark's eyes narrowed. 'I didn't fuck him up. I just encouraged him to pause for thought. Much like I'm doing now. But if any of you ever so much as look at my friend again, I'm going to come back here show you what fucked up *really* looks like. *Clear?*'

At this point Stark noticed the door was half off its hinges with the force of his entry. A suitable emblem for his own mental state. It was evident from their faces that this, and his message, were entirely clear. His work here was done.

'You should've let me handle that,' suggested Ptolemy, as Stark climbed into the back seat.

Peters withheld her opinion. Both had witnessed Stark's off-duty approach first-hand in the past, however righteous, and neither quite knew what to say about it. She glanced at the clutch bag instead. 'Everything there?'

'Hopefully.' Hopefully the cash was spent and the condoms lost, and not the other way around.

'So, where now?'

'Her place, for clothes, et cetera. Closer to your area of expertise, I'd say, and I could use the back-up with her flatmate. She doubts my motivation.'

'For how many nights?' asked Peters. For someone who had done everything in her power to fix Pensol up with Stark, she managed to pack an undue level of disapproval into that question.

Stark sighed. Losing his temper always left him feeling drained afterwards; among other things. 'As many as she needs.'

30

Pensol was asleep on the sofa when he eventually got home, shortly after midnight. If there'd been any press outside, they'd given it up for the night. He'd kept the lock oiled after Kelly moved in. Police hours required stealth to avoid disturbing loved ones, but there was little need for that tonight.

A washed-up plate and cutlery sat in the drainer, which was good, but an empty bottle of white wine stood on the coffee table, which was less so. A gentle shake established she was out cold. He considered moving her to the bed, but the sofa was comfortable and he was tired. He found a second blanket and draped it over her instead, leaving her clutch bag and the suitcase her flatmate had packed beside her.

Something from his earlier dream in the car came to him, an echo of the nightmare he'd woken from that morning. *Begat?* He found the copy of Ted Hughes' *Crow: From the Life and Songs of the Crow* that he'd read during his convalescence and soon found the poem in question, but as a guide to unravelling portents it proved little help.

He was just wondering what to eat, when the phone vibrated. His heart sank, half-expecting Kelly. It was the next worst thing. 'Sarge.'

'Where are you?' demanded Fran.

Stark sighed, closing the fridge and resting his forehead against its cool door. 'Home.'

She paused, perhaps put off by his failure to play the usual game. 'Alone?'

'I have a guest. They're sleeping.'

'Well, I'm sure she won't miss you then. I'm texting you an address. Meet me there. We've got another victim.'

'I should've had him pick me up,' muttered Fran.

Marcus pulled the handbrake, having parked a suitable distance from the blue lights to avoid detection. 'He's not an idiot.'

'That's my point. He'll wonder how I got here.'

'I understand your point,' replied Marcus, with the polite calm that so infuriated her. 'I should imagine, however, that it has been quite some time since he started wondering why you insist on keeping up this charade.'

Fran clicked her tongue, determined to believe Stark wasn't on to them for as long as possible. 'I knew it was a mistake to meet at yours. Why do these things always happen at night?'

Marcus considered this for a moment. 'We could discuss post-daylight inhibition reduction, the likelihood that even murderers have day jobs and the fact that darkness is the ideal time to dispose of bodies . . .'

And interrupt hard-working coppers' already limited personal lives, thought Fran bitterly.

'But really I just think God has an odd dislike of detectives and pathologists,' concluded Marcus, without rancour.

'You don't believe in God any more than I do,' Fran countered.

'Perhaps that's why he or she dislikes us,' said Marcus, climbing out of the car and fetching his bag from the back.

Kidbrooke Green Park was, as a description, a bit of a stretch. A small area of patchy grass with down-at-heel basketball or tennis courts missing their nets, isolated amid the urban sprawl. A tired spot for desperate mums to bring screaming toddlers, listless teenagers to smoke and God knows what else, and dog owners to allow their little parasites to piss and shit. A patrol car sat across the entrance, lights on. On the far side, a path into the cluster of trees closed off with police tape. And between the two, Sergeant Clark, with one of last year's rookies. He nodded to the two newcomers with the straightest face Fran had ever seen. 'What've you got, Tony?'

The straight face winced. 'Nothing good.' He tilted his head to the rookie, who held out his phone with a photo on the screen.

Oh God, no.

Fran wasn't even sure if she'd said it aloud.

How could this be possible?

A girl. Early twenties; slim and pretty, before the beating – and dead. Grey electrical cable round her neck. Wrapped in plastic and dumped. 'Drugged, raped, strangled, cleaned with bleach,' she breathed. So much like the others that Fran almost felt she knew her already . . .

'Too soon to tell anything like that,' said Clark, a tiny bit sharply.

No. He was right. Bad procedure. Bad form in front of the rookie. 'SOCO?'

'Held up at a fatal RTA in Beckenham – no ETA yet.'

Fran cursed silently. 'We need to start working this. Who found the body?'

'Local dog walker. Let his hound off the lead to do its business and followed when it didn't respond to call. I'm afraid the poor girl may have a bite mark or two, to add insult to . . . you know.'

'ID?'

'Nothing.'

A set of headlights turned their heads. Fran hoped desperately for SOCO, but it was Stark.

He got out, walking towards them with his cane, looking comically sinister against the flashing blue lights. 'Tony. Ed.' He nodded to the uniforms. Trust him to know the rookie's name. 'Marcus. Sarge.'

He knows, thought Fran, cursing Marcus.

'Bit quiet,' commented Stark, meaning the place should be crawling with white overalls.

'Too quiet,' said Fran, handing him the rookie's phone.

Stark was an intensely private person, full of secrets and bound emotions. But sometimes the dam creaked. Pain from his war wounds, obviously. A deep and troubling sadness too, she often thought, and loneliness. But most often, when something really showed, it was as

if frost formed on him, set his features in ice. She'd learned to inter-
pret this most often as anger.

Now, his face hardened with interstellar cold.

Fran stared. 'What?'

'*Shit*,' he breathed.

'You know her?'

'So do you.' Stark shook his head in disbelief.

'What . . . ? Who is it?'

Stark felt in his pocket, pulled out a business card and handed it
to her.

On the front, a name. On the reverse, handwritten, a mobile number, and – *Call me x*.

PART 2

31

Emily Thornton. Twenty-four. Dangling jewel in Sinclair's team of legal winnets.

Someone had reached into the heart of this terrible mess and stolen her away, right under their noses. The implications were immediate and horrific; leaving, among all the unknowns, one certainty . . .

. . . It could not have been Julian Sinclair.

'CCTV will back us up,' said Dearing, letting a yawn slip – another uniform pulling back-to-back shifts to keep the thin blue line from snapping. A replacement rookie hovered behind him. 'He hasn't left this room.'

Of course he hadn't. His hospital room was air-conditioned with sealed windows and two police on guard, never less than one with rest breaks. Wishing it was Sinclair wouldn't make it so. This was a devil they *didn't* know, worse on every level. This sunk their whole case. And as soon as the press caught wind, the shit really would hit the fan.

Someone *else* had taken Emily; beaten her, raped her, strangled her with cable, cleaned her with chemicals, wrapped her in translucent blue plastic and dumped her in the bushes of Kidbrooke Green Park. That put Sinclair's own theory front and centre: The mysterious man who'd visited him in prison and hospital, the man passing himself off as Patrick Burgess, who had met Emily that very morning – moved now from person of interest to prime suspect.

And the next logical question – was he the killer all along?

Would retesting the lost DNA swab have confirmed the original findings or contradicted them?

Was Sinclair innocent after all?

Was the Greenwich Strangler still out there?

Dearing glanced at the door. 'You going in?'

'Not without his lawyer present.'

'What's going on out there?' said a peevish voice, the door opening to reveal Sinclair, blinking in the corridor light with a sour expression. 'What next – deafening death-metal music and psychedelic strobes?'

'We've got an orange boiler suit in just your size,' replied Dearing smoothly.

Sinclair ignored him, peering past, still blinking. 'Joe . . . ? What's going on?'

'Nothing that can't wait until morning. I'm sorry if we disturbed you.'

'Something obviously *couldn't* wait, so now I'm *doubly* disturbed.'

Dearing muttered some form of agreement, which Sinclair pretended not to hear. 'You might as well tell me.'

'It's not appropriate for us to speak without your legal representation.'

'I won't tell if you don't.'

Until I hear it all on TV, thought Stark. 'That's not how this works.'

Sinclair rolled his eyes. 'Look, between you, cold mountain and the boy, that more or less makes three of you to witness that I give you express permission to tell me what the fuck's going on, without my lawyers present. Plus that,' he pointed to the security camera. Video only, but a form of corroboration.

Dearing shrugged at Stark. The rookie did a decent impression of wallpaper. Stark sighed. 'All right, but if the press get one whiff of this before the family are notified, we'll know it came from you.'

'I won't tell a soul, I swear.'

'Okay. Then I'm sorry to inform you that around midnight the body of a young woman was found murdered, in a manner not dissimilar to the victims of the Greenwich Strangler.'

Sinclair blinked, confused. 'Well, I'm truly sorry to hear that, but surely this just proves everything I've said.'

'Perhaps. But the reason I'm *sorry* to inform you is that this victim was Emily Thornton.'

'Emily . . . ? The paralegal?'

'So it appears.'

Sinclair looked shocked. 'But . . . wait . . .' He frowned, then looked cross. 'And the first thing you did was race over here to check if it was me?' He interrogated them both with his eyes, growing visibly angrier. 'I'm right, aren't I? You haven't even told her family yet, but here you are; *accusing*.'

'It's just routine –'

'Like hell it is,' snapped Sinclair. 'It's *Burgess*. He met Emily this morning, if he wasn't already stalking her. Don't you see, he's *taunting* us . . . ?' He stared searchingly at Stark. 'But you don't care, do you? You've made up your mind, just like the rest? I thought you were better than this, than them. I thought *you* at least might understand what I've been through, what it's like to have your world ripped open for spectacle – but I suppose it's different for the famous gladiator than it is for the poor Christian thrown to the lions!'

'I assure you –'

'This is my *life*!' spat Sinclair furiously, almost tearful again. He seemed to race through emotions without control, more indicative of an injured mind than the controlling cool of the psychopath Fran insisted lurked inside. 'Don't you *understand*?' he wailed. 'You get to go home at night. Where can *I* go? You stole my life. You've snatched me up, bound me, ruined me, and you're still trying to throttle the life from me with your relentless persecution. You're no better than *him*. You're worse. At least the Strangler is honest about what he does!'

A ward sister came scurrying to chastise them for disturbing other patients at four in the morning, but Sinclair had already retreated into his private room with a slammed door, leaving them to face her ire.

32

'Right,' said Harper, to kick off the 07:00 meeting, those just arrived looking bleary, those up all night looking worse after hours with SOCO on site or setting up the preliminary investigation here.

He held up a morning tabloid, Stark's face on the front next to Sinclair's, followed by another, and another. The straplines – *SAVE AND PROTECT? – STARK JUSTICE – STARK v STRANGLER*. Variations on yesterday's theme, of course. They didn't even know about Emily Thornton yet. 'Time to put distractions aside,' said Harper, eyeing Stark as he dropped them collectively into the bin.

'Karen Gillespie, Magda Janowski, Teresa Leman, Paige Talbot, Leah Willoughby, Sara Brompton,' he said slowly, pointing to each photo on the hastily rearranged board and the corresponding positions where each victim was found marked on the big wall map. 'And now, Emily Thornton. Uniform are sat outside her flat. No sign of disturbance, so I'll get keys off the family. I'm told the pathologist has promised preliminary results this morning?'

Fran nodded, straight-faced. If Harper guessed about her and Marcus, she'd never hear the end of it. Stark still found it amusing that his earliest instinct about the pair had proved correct. Anything that warmed the heart after a long, cold night was welcome.

Harper stared at his team, tiredness and frustration hovering like a dark cloud. 'I hate to say it, but we have to go right back to the beginning. Patterns, timings, sightings, descriptions of people that didn't match Sinclair but might match this shit,' he tapped the CCTV images and photofit. All images of the *real* Patrick Burgess had been removed after the man himself was transported home full of tea, chocolate biscuits and the humble apologies of Her Majesty's metropolitan constabulary. 'But first and foremost – find out who he is and feel his collar.'

Newspaper theatrics aside, Stark found himself nodding, as were others. If it were anyone else, one would have to admit that something had changed in Harper since his last brief, despotic reign. Last time he'd strutted in like a prize cock, demanding to be called Guv'nor before he'd earned it. But his hectoring and bullying seemed, this time, to have given way to sober resolve. There was a vast distance between demanding respect and commanding it. It required a different way of seeing, of being. If Harper could make that shift, however belatedly, he might become a man worth following. He wouldn't be the first. Every green lieutenant fresh from Sandhurst required moulding by their NCOs. It was the ones set in bad ways that made every soldier's life a misery.

The big DI moved to the other board – the shooting and attempted kidnapping of Julian Sinclair – and ran through it all from the top. 'We don't have the manpower for running these as separate lines. I'll be asking for more today. But for now, we need to stagger. Fran, Joe, you've done two nights in a row. Go get some sleep if you can, get back here this afternoon to take over.'

Stark glanced at Fran and saw no resistance. Perhaps it was just that Harper was right, but more likely she was simply too tired.

Harper watched them both go with a satisfied smile. Taking orders *and* getting out of his way. Next thing you know, with a huge stroke of luck, he'd wrap this whole thing up while they slept.

But first things first, a man's job needed doing.

He dealt out his orders to the rest and set off.

His BMW may not be brand new, but it was big, powerful and just about the only place he could light up a cigarette without anyone bitching at him or guilt-tripping him with dirty looks. The radio was playing old rock songs and he cranked up the volume to a bit of Hendrix – 'Crosstown Traffic'. Cracking the window, dragging deep lungfuls of blissful nicotine, he hit the blue lights, driving fast, almost laughing aloud at the childish thrill of it. Life offered too few chances to kick back, to do what you felt like and be damned, to be a man.

The sun was breaking through irregular clouds and he donned his shades, grinning. Maybe, just maybe, everything was turning around for him, getting back on track.

Glancing at the address scribbled on the scrap of paper, he felt his way west, threading through the maze of streets and only resorting to the map printout as he neared his destination. Satnav was for wimps. City cops found their way.

There was a uniform car parked nearby but they'd waited for him as ordered. The Family Liaison Officer greeted him without a smile.

There were two cars in the drive and lights on inside. Nice cars, nice drive, nice house. Private education had launched Emily Thornton into a premier law school. A family house on this street cost serious cash. But money couldn't buy happiness. Not after today.

They'd waited till morning. Family Services said it worked better if you caught them together but better still if you didn't wake them. But nothing was going to soften this blow. Harper's primary interest was to make sure the family had been informed so he could release the girl's details to the press and get on.

He strode to the door and knocked.

The FLO stood at his shoulder. Harper tried to recall his name, but if he'd ever known it, it had slipped away. Life was too short. All Harper could recall was that he didn't like the man; thought him a namby-pamby sham of a copper, more interested in making nice than making cases. The man didn't like him either; thought him a callous bastard, more interested in nailing culprits than serving victims. Both had said as much to each other's faces once, in a heated exchange. At least he'd had the balls to say it. Harper felt some sympathy for the loser. How frustrating must it be to loiter around misery, offering up endless cups of tea and empty assurances while real coppers did the actual police work?

Harper wasn't callous. Nailing culprits *was* serving victims. And he would never leave this terrible task to some limp-rag FLO, like some detectives. This was part of a DI's duty, to look a family in the eyes, break the bad news.

He rehearsed his words once more in his head, just like the training course – touchy-feely crap. There was no good way of doing this. The words, however compassionate, would alter this family's life irrevocably. Family services thought it was better for them to do it. Perhaps they were right. But a DI's power came with responsibility. It wasn't enough to be *sorry for their loss*, as if that mattered. They needed someone to promise retribution, to take up their white-hot grief and hammer it into the sword of justice.

Movement inside. The door opened on a chain. A woman in her late fifties, seeing uniforms in the street, sensing trouble. 'Mrs Thornton?'

'Yes?'

Harper introduced himself. 'May we come inside?'

'Why? What's . . .' But the list of terrible possibilities spun in her eyes like the wheels of a one-armed-bandit, and shuddered to a terrible jackpot. '*Emily* . . .'

She read enough in his blank expression to know she was right in the worst possible way, and let out a low, keening wail, collapsing in despair as her husband came running to the door.

33

'You look tired,' said Marcus, glancing up from his work.

'Just what every woman yearns to hear.' Affectionate concern hardly excused such a lack of chivalry.

'Sorry; you're in the wrong place for chocolates and flowers.' She could always tell if he was smiling beneath his surgical mask. He wasn't now.

He was right on all counts, of course. But Fran was as unlikely to nip home for a nap as Harper was to sprout those golden wings. The mortuary was a cold place for compliments and flirtation. The corpse on the slab between them would silence Gelos. The fact that she knew the name of the Greek god of laughter was, like so many things, Stark's fault, who said such things aloud as if it wasn't weird.

Emily Thornton's laughter had been silenced.

The photograph they'd lifted from the lawyer's website did little justice to the fine-featured young woman in person, and little would offer justice for the state of her now. The universe had blessed her mightily, only to curse her brutally.

Fran shivered involuntarily, but if Marcus noticed he said nothing.

Calloused though she might be, she doubted she would ever develop immunity to the indignity of this terrible place. The thought of ending up here, laid out on the altar of forensic science, naked and cold beneath this seamless harshness of lights, subject to microscopic inspection and invasion, gave her the heebie-jeebies. She hid it, of course. Professional detachment. Doubly so with Marcus. He took it in his stride, but this was his domain and she had never interrogated his untroubled demeanour or how he maintained it. He was here to provide her with facts. She was here to see for herself, needing those shivers from time to time, to feel the horror, to feed and stoke her indignation and never let its embers die down, ever.

That was why she'd started spending more time here. More than she'd done in her last job in Croydon. Nothing at all to do with Marcus. Not initially. Anyone who said otherwise was risking a slap. Not that anyone knew about her and Marcus. Except perhaps Stark. Marcus was right, Stark didn't miss much. Worst of all, he would piously say nothing until eventually the waiting burst the confession out of her. Not that she'd seek relationship advice from someone whose track record was shaping up to be even more pot-holed than hers.

Marcus busied himself scraping beneath fingernails for evidence, finger by finger, meticulously sealing each swab into individual screw-lid pots and labelling them, and Fran imagined some future dinner party guest asking how they'd met. Thankfully this line of work didn't get you invited to dinner parties either.

As a beautiful young lawyer, a lifetime of chic dinners had beckoned this poor girl – all gone now. Taken. Fran shivered again, blaming it on the unnatural cold of the morgue and covering it up with closer inspection of the bruising and abrasions on the upper thighs and knees, and around the mouth and cheeks – similar to injuries found on all the victims, bar Paige. Leah had described being tied forwards over a table, gagged with a hard ball held in place with straps around her head, assumed to be a gimp-style sadomasochistic ball-gag; another recognizable MO, another tie between the killings by Sinclair and this one that couldn't be him. A copycat was her best hope. The other option was Sinclair's innocence, and she wasn't ready to believe that yet. 'Bite marks?' she asked, pointing to the impressions in one leg.

'Not our killer's, unhelpfully. *Canis lupus familiaris* – or domestic dog to you and me. More of a test nip. Probably didn't like the reek of bleach.'

'What's this?' she asked, pointing at the vivid blue staining around the girl's groin.

'Toilet cleaner, if I had to guess.'

Inside and out. Fran shivered. 'Different from the others.'

Marcus nodded. 'The rest of her looks to have been cleaned with regular bleach, though; like the others.'

Maybe the toilet cleaner was just there, handy with its upturned spout, thought Fran with another shiver. 'This looks worse, though.' The terminally attractive paralegal's face and body were peppered with bruises, and there was a swollen cut across one cheek. And of course, her neck.

'Indeed,' nodded Marcus. 'Rob, give us a hand flipping her over.' Marcus's assistant materialized and did the honours.

Fran's flinch at the dead-meat manhandling was nothing to that on seeing the poor girl's back.

There was a lone motorbike paparazzi staked outside Stark's building, hoping for a better shot than those camped outside the station. At a glance, it might even have been the one from outside Leah's flat. If Stark's charm offensive hadn't worked first time another confrontation might only make matters worse, so he parked round the back, ducked in through the communal cycle store and let himself silently into his flat. Pensol was still deep in sleep, somewhere peaceful, from her stillness. She looked like an angel, gracing an ugly world.

He ghosted past into the bathroom, resisting the burning desire to collect a triple whisky on the way. The sun and yardarm were far from acquainted and he had to be back in the office in a few hours. The Full English breakfast from the local cafe had provided fuel but little comfort, and sat now in his stomach like a mother's disapproval.

Stark leant against the wall of his shower, desperate to feel clean, but stinging with the blood and dust that scalding water could never wash away. His hands shook, with weariness but mostly anger, the sheer effort of holding it in hour after hour. He'd come a long way in controlling it with Doc Hazel's help but today . . . today . . . when all you could do was screw your eyes shut and wait . . .

Faces flashed.

Karen Gillespie, Magda Janowski, Teresa Leman, Paige Talbot, Leah Willoughby, Sara Brompton . . . Emily Thornton . . . Marianne Pensol . . . Kelly Jones . . . smiling . . . *laughing, weeping, dying . . . burning . . . His peeling hands itched with fresh flame, his missing finger throbbing his whole arm with agony . . . blood and smoke, choking, hissing in his ears . . . Faces in the flames, screaming . . .*

NO! He screamed, inside, in silence, tearing himself from the waking dream, that old world of pain, and back into this one, hardly less horrific.

He'd read the victim files a dozen times, stared at the photos of cold corpses marked with the pain they'd endured, with a kind of bafflement that lent detachment of sorts. But if meeting Leah Willoughby, seeing the damage and pain she *still* endured, had lit a righteous rage in him, then this had poured fuel on that fire. He, more than most, knew how hard it was to comprehend death where just hours, minutes, seconds earlier, life had shone. But Emily had smiled at him, *hoped* at him . . . Who would take that and crush it? What husk of a human assumed that right? He also knew better than many that any person subject to duty, passion or terror could take up arms. War made killers and victims of all. Even criminals, the ones he'd known, had motive, greed, desperation. But this . . . paint it any way you like; talk about power, hatred, psychopathy . . . this was simply monstrous.

No wonder Fran was obsessed. The team. Even Harper had every right. Humanity gave you the right.

And there it was again, like a tsunami . . . Stark ground his teeth, clenching his whole body against the bucking fury, the all-consuming need to lash out, pound his fists bloody against the tiles, smash his way out of the shower and tear everything down. He knew this feeling. Knew its disproportion and futility. Its logic too – to destroy as much as necessary of things that were repairable or replaceable, to avoid unleashing on people, even bad people. Doc Hazel worried at his turning it inward, but what was the point of letting it out?

He thrust the lever to cold instead, letting the icy accusation turn him blue and chattering even while the rage burned inside.

He opened his eyes to drive out Emily's smile, and found himself wiping water from the glass screen to stare at the mirrored bathroom cabinet instead – all but seeing the packets of OxyContin inside. Whisky was impossible, but you could function on Oxy. He had before. How long now, without? Two years? How much suppressible pain instead endured? How many times had he come close? How many more could he risk? They needed to go. What started out as defiance had extended into morbid experiment, a dare, where to fail was to fall. But throwing them away now would signal retreat. Defeat. Unconscionable betrayal. Survivors stood on the backs of the fallen. The anger was nothing to the guilt.

Emily's fate wasn't his fault, any more than fallen comrades, any more than Kelly's heartbreak, Fran's frustration or Hazel's concern. But they suffered while he survived. Hazel and he would never see eye to eye on this. She labelled it subjective toxicity – the fear of hurting those too close, withdrawing further and further. To assume responsibility for all around you was illogical, she insisted; but not to do so was *inhuman*. And once you let that slide, what were you? Anger was a natural reaction to guilt, she said. But it was the *only* response to injustice.

So . . . No retreat. No defeat. Not today. Not with a monster to cage.

Not so long ago, his willingness for this job had remained a wavering thing. Leaving the Territorial Army behind left little outlet for the frustrations of day-job policing. Enforced convalescence had made him yearn for re-occupation, but what had really changed in him was the decision on some basic level to embrace the rage, turn it inward and use it.

Shivering, he wrapped a towel round his waist and tiptoed into the bedroom, pulled on some boxers and stared at the bed, wondering whether to bother. With so much in his head, the effort of sleep seemed daunting.

'*You found it!*'

Pensol appeared at the doorway, dressed in a pair of his old army baggies and T-shirt, checking through her clutch bag in relief. 'How did –?'

The question died on her lips as her mouth fell open, her eyes widening with horror.

34

'*Oh my God*,' she breathed softly.

Stark froze in her searchlight stare, bare but for boxers, fighting the urge to cringe and cover up, the self-consciousness he'd felt exposing his scarred body to Kelly that first time returned in force. But there was little point turning away, no good side to show. He'd gotten himself back into reasonable shape, but the surface . . .

She might have averted her eyes, but perhaps she couldn't. Or wouldn't. She was a very different person to the shy young woman she'd been, stealing glances and giggling with her peers. Different from casual one-off tumbles in semi-darkness. And very different from Kelly – who he still needed to call back . . .

'I had no idea . . .' Her face shone with stinging sympathy as she padded towards him across the carpet, Stark wishing the floor would open up and swallow him. 'You . . . you *poor boy*,' she choked, one hand over her mouth, tears glistening in her eyes. She slowly circled to his left, eyes running over the countless shrapnel and surgical scars that peppered him, gasping when she saw the mess of his back where the bullet had exploded out through his shoulder blade, and all the surgical incisions surrounding it.

She paused to peer at the old tiger tattoo atop his left arm, slashed through by a diagonal shrapnel scar, and frowned at the crow on his right – fresh ink, redness not long receded.

When she'd completed her circuit, tears ran down both cheeks. 'I had no idea.' Her hand rose unconsciously to lightly touch the entry scar on his chest but he flinched involuntarily and she jerked her hand back as if stung, looking into his eyes, fearful she'd hurt him.

He often stared at it in the mirror himself but he could rarely bring himself to touch it. It wasn't sensitive, as such, but consciously touching it sometimes triggered memories more vivid than plain recollection. It was odd that this only seemed to apply to where this bullet had struck. Perhaps it was because the other scars were shrapnel, random blast damage. Even the much more recent bullet through his leg had been more accident than design, whereas the bullet through his chest was aimed, deliberate. Or perhaps because it ended his fight, brought him face-to-face with death. Kelly had quickly learned to keep her kisses away from this one mark. She had both soothed *and* stung.

Pensol was blinking back more tears. Her hands rose and he flinched again, but looking up she gently traced the scar down his right temple, knowing now what his visible wounds left unseen. 'We all look at you and gossip like star-struck schoolgirls, but we didn't know, none of us knew . . . what you'd *given*.' Stark had to force himself not to recoil again. She could not know how such words freshened his wounds. 'How do you do it?' she asked. 'How do you carry on?'

He looked at her, wondering where to begin or how honest to be. 'By taking a long, hard look at the alternative.' She absorbed this bluntness with worrying solemnity, causing him to wonder how close to the precipice she'd drifted herself. 'By accepting there can be better days ahead.'

She looked away as if ashamed, looking instead at his leg; the freshest wound, sharing a birthday with hers. Lifting the hem of the T-shirt, she looked at her own scars, comparing. 'I . . . I hate looking at it.'

'It's healing well. Give it a year. They get easier to live with as they fade.'

'It makes me feel ugly.' Her hand covered her mouth again as she realized how that must make him feel. 'I'm sorry . . .'

'They're part of us now,' he replied honestly, trying to reassure her with a smile. He'd had longer, worked harder and needed help to get this far. 'But you are just as exquisite as before, if not more so. Flawlessness isn't the same as beauty, and a scar taken in service is a badge of honour. There is nothing, *nothing* ugly about that or you.'

Tears rolled forth once more, unheeded as she stared into his eyes for reassurance, and perhaps something else. She tilted her head up, inviting. 'Just once,' she breathed. 'Please. Just to know I kissed you once.'

A TV-ad fantasy, peddling temptation in pyjamas and the life-style of your dreams. All you had to do was buy the aftershave, kiss the girl and forget your old life. Only this TV was cracked. She was too lovely for him to trust his motivation or restraint, and too damaged for him to trust hers. But sometimes, when the hurts were counted, the kiss of life was all there was left.

Polite, confident and bland ... straight out of the Groombridge handbook, thought Harper. He'd been criticized for grandstanding in the run-up to the disastrous shootings. He'd learned a number of harsh lessons that day. He wouldn't screw up this time, not on this grand stage.

The steps of New Scotland Yard itself with twice as many TV trucks, including American channels.

'But are you saying there's no connection to any other crimes?'

He suppressed a smile as he picked out the wizened old harridan from the *Greenwich Crier*, still first with her hand up like the parochial class swot, even among the assembled great and good of the national networks, God bless her. 'As I said,' he nodded sagely, 'all I can confirm at this time is that the body of a twenty-four-year-old woman was found in the early hours of this morning on Kidbrooke Green Park and a murder investigation is underway. Immediate family have been informed but I'm not yet at liberty to release the victim's name.'

He saw eyes roll in his audience and silently cursed the family. There was a sister, off blowing Daddy's money on an exotic gap year and irritatingly yet to stray within range of a cell-phone tower. The family didn't want her finding out about Emily's death on social media the next time she went to upload her latest barrage of auto-tweaked Instagram selfies – leaving Harper fuming. And much as he'd like to, he couldn't make the connection public before the post-mortem without opening himself to the accusation of drawing a line to Sinclair and the sudden minor gap in his legal team. What was given could be taken away. He needed Emily's pretty face on screens next to his ASAP to cash in on this chance in case it evaporated in one of Stevens' Machiavellian moves or National Crime swooped in on some pretext. But in the meantime, he could make the most of what he couldn't say . . . 'You will understand that the early hours of any investigation as serious as this one merit considerable delicacy. More information will be made available in due course as operational considerations allow.'

But do keep asking, he thought, scanning the crowd, picking out the hot blonde from yesterday near the back, crimson lips pursed in thought as she checked her phone. His eyes paused also on a cute young redhead near the front, hoping she'd raise a hand to beg his beneficence. She didn't. Perhaps too junior. Perhaps he should introduce himself . . .

Not that he'd ever cheat on Jessica, not again, and especially not with a *reporter*, but the eye could enjoy candy the mouth declined. Flirtation was in his nature. Jess understood that. It had worked on her after all. She had a beautiful laugh. He missed it. Perhaps he should take her out to dinner this weekend; that overpriced Michelin star place she used to love, where he'd taken her back in those early dates when he was pulling out all the stops to impress. He felt himself sigh. It was hard to go out now. The laughter came less easily since her sobriety ruled out wine with the meal. Perhaps a movie instead . . . ?

'Has there been an arrest?' asked the blonde suddenly. 'Scarlet Jennings, Capital-Cast. Reports are circulating that a man named Patrick Burgess was arrested in a raid last night, but released . . . ?'

Where the bloody hell had she got that name? 'A man was briefly detained, but quickly discounted from our investigations and released –'

'Are there any similarities at all between this killing and those of the Greenwich Strangler?' interrupted the *Crier*.

He smiled inside, remembering what a pain in the arse the old witch had been in the past. 'It's far too early to indulge in speculation.'

'Given the age and gender of the victim, the location of the body, the recent release of Julian Sinclair and rumours about a new suspect, I should think it a rather obvious line of enquiry. The vulnerable young women of this borough deserve to know whether they can walk the streets in safety.'

Several of the other journos had closed in to enjoy the spectacle and, if possible, feed on the scraps. The *Crier* had been a thorn in the side throughout the original case and they were obviously determined to stir up another frenzy. First to nickname the killer, they'd never let it drop. But it had been DCI Groombridge facing the lions then. This lot would learn that DI Harper brought a whip and a chair to this circus ring, but right now he was more than happy to see their hungry eyes. 'As I said, you should respect the sensitivity and integrity of this investigation and resist inciting hysteria before the facts are confirmed.'

35

Indulge in speculation . . . Resist inciting hysteria . . .

Groombridge sighed. The news would be repeating it all day and the anchor was even now pointedly indulging in hysterical speculation with a reporter outside Scotland Yard. *Before the facts are confirmed . . .*

Harper was cleverer than most people credited. But stoking press flames was a dangerous game, even for the best of reasons, which didn't include self-aggrandisement.

'You're not listening,' said his union lawyer, an earnest young woman facing stacked odds.

'I was listening intently,' he replied, turning back from the wall-mounted TV. 'Just not to you. Sorry.'

'You're not taking this seriously enough.'

He smiled apologetically. 'Perhaps not.' The IPCC panel had kept them waiting for nearly thirty minutes so far. A preliminary hearing, nothing official; just a chance for him to state his position for the record – considerably worse, as the implications of last night's killing filtered up the food chain. Greater weight would be given to the suggestion that he'd pursued and persecuted the wrong man all along. There was blood in the water and Bosch and Moncrieff were out there, circling. This felt less like the quiet before the storm and more like the sea sucking the beach dry to feed the approaching tsunami.

'Do you know something I don't?' she asked.

'Nothing pertinent.'

'Then why aren't you worried?'

'About the ignominious ending of my career and reputation?

About the disastrous impact on my talented and dedicated team? Why would I be worried?'

She considered him a moment. 'Why aren't you worried *outwardly*?'

Because I've stood over corpses, stared down killers and inflicted the worst possible news on loved ones too many times, thought Groombridge. 'I've learned life's too short.'

She frowned, but any expounding on her displeasure was prevented by the materialization of an officious-looking male PA hovering with a paint-thin, impatient smile. 'The panel will see you now.'

'You didn't kiss her?' Dr Hazel McDonald rubbed her eyes and glanced at the clock. There was a patient outside her door, and a full list beyond. A psychotherapist's work was never done.

'No.'

'But you wanted to.'

'And more.'

'And she wanted you to?'

'Yes.'

'Then why didn't you?'

'You know why.' Stark's voice had that edge of impatience he got whenever she paused to unpick.

'I know why it might not have been a good idea, but was that why you didn't?'

'Yes.'

'And how did she take it?' Rejection was a powerful issue for someone in this girl's state.

'She cried. But she was already crying. I hugged her till she stopped and then put a brew on. She thanked me before I left.'

'You left?'

'Back to work.'

'You ran away.'

'She seemed okay by then, happier.'

'And more stable?'

'Such things are hard to judge from the outside, I'm told,' he replied pointedly.

Indeed, but he would never have left her if he'd had the least doubt, and he knew the signs. 'And she thanked you, for . . . ?'

'The hug, the brew, the clothes, her purse and phone . . . ?'

'And for not kissing her?'

'Who knows?'

'And how do you feel about not kissing her?'

'Like one of those guys that finish last.'

'A nice guy?'

'And a berk.'

'But still a nice guy.'

'A beautiful girl just stood in my bedroom and asked me to kiss her, and I didn't.'

'And she thanked you.'

'Whoopee.'

Hazel sighed. 'You see? This is why phone sessions don't work.' God knows he gave little away in person, but over the phone she stood next to no chance. His recent string of one-night forays could be looked on in different ways – a young man enjoying harmless sexual freedom. A bad man, taking. A good man trying to slip the shackles of duty and honour, pain and sorrow, if only for a few hours, if only with willing fellow fugitives.

'You said to call in emergencies.'

'To arrange a session, not conduct one.' Though if this was what it took . . . she was at least relieved he felt willing.

'Define emergency.'

'Don't be awkward.'

'You don't have an opening today. But I need to talk.'

Indeed. But he was still holding something back. It wasn't just that she sensed it, more that he always did. He couldn't give details, but the case on the news sounded bad. His profession was both crutch and irritant. 'You know that when people open up about "a *friend*" in difficulties, they're often talking about themselves.'

'She needs help.'

'Has she asked for it?'

'Not verbally. That's why *I* need *your* help.'

One reason among many. 'You're asking how to broach a difficult subject without harm? Where do I start . . . ?'

'Short answer.'

'It depends,' she replied with brevity, drawing a precious chuckle from him.

When she'd first met him, he'd walled denial and anger behind caustic wit and impatience. The first classic stages of grief – begun with the death of his father, accelerated by war and exploded into a downward spiral in his final, fateful day in Helmand nearly three years ago. More than one knife-edge moment later, he'd scraped himself bloody along the bottom of the depression curve until another fateful day three months ago. If being blown up and shot had triggered his decline, being beaten and shot had somehow signalled its end. He'd hit bottom and bounced – in those final moments, choosing life over death, and to finally confess his fear of the darkness within. She'd suggested he see it as the first step in renewal. He agreed to try. Acceptance being the final stage. She could kiss him now for that chuckle alone, given where he'd been. Such small gains were the triumphs that made it all worthwhile. 'Isn't the army way just to say things straight out?'

'Blunt force isn't always the best approach. The army knows that as well as you.'

'She's come to you for help.'

'I know.'

'But you feel what – underqualified?' A straight jab. Their best sessions often felt like sparring. He needed to feel she'd earned any concession she drew from him. Little victories.

'What – I'm fixed so I can fix her?' he scoffed.

'You've changed, therefore she can. It's a process, remember. You're further along the curve than her, that's all.'

'You think she came to me because she wants me to confront her? Show her the way?'

'Or she just wants you to kiss her.'

Another blessed chuckle. But it was a serious point too. Stark was handsome, charming and aloof in the sexiest way. Hazel had seen the photos in his medical files – seen the cost unflinching duty had written into him. Now Marianne Pensol had too. The crush the poor girl might have had on him before her own world exploded could be an altogether different beast now. Would she look on Stark as a kindred spirit? A saviour? Thank God he hadn't kissed her. Or more. A dove shouldn't fly at the sun. Though, in some ways, Hazel felt truly sorry for the dove, to see the sun and never reach it. 'I have an idea, but I don't think you'll like it.'

She told him, and he didn't like it. 'I'll think about it,' he said. 'But I don't think there'll be time, with work as it is.'

'Is this an emergency or isn't it?'

He sighed.

'You know,' she hazarded, 'when people talk about a *real* friend in difficulties, they're often *avoiding* talking about themselves.'

He took a few seconds to respond. 'You've seen the news?'

'The girl in Kidbrooke?'

'She gave me her number, yesterday.'

'*You knew her?*'

'I didn't really get the chance.'

Even so, the heart of Stark's pain centred on failing to protect those around him, starting aged eleven with his father. 'Is that something you want to talk about?'

'Not before I slam the cell door on the fucker who killed her.' You didn't need to be a shrink to hear his anger seething, even over the phone. Anger was an earlier stage of grief, but with Stark it had lodged deep – compressed. He'd described the fury within him as a monster, prowling the darkness just beyond the inconstant light of the campfire. He struggled to differentiate it from the worst creatures he might encounter through work – more murders came from a snapping of restraint than from cold calculation. But she'd seen his anger erupt, fearful and wild, and seen him drive it back into the dark. He might never be free of it; he might direct it into work, but still he lived in daily fear of the dimming of the light. 'I'm sorry,' he sighed. 'I'm tired.'

'Just work, or trouble sleeping?'

'Troubled, asleep and awake.'

He explained.

The crow again. Of all the imaginings of his injured mind, his feathered totem interested Hazel particularly. As many times as it had featured in the accusational horrors of his nightmares, it had seemingly manifested in waking flashbacks and moments of disassociation as some obscure portent or warning. He'd shown her his new tattoo. Somehow the artist had captured both the light and dark in haunting beauty. 'Death, stalking you?'

'Mocking. Warning. Who can tell. But I've been getting the creeps again too.'

'Being watched?'

'And followed. Even when I'm not.'

'Sometimes you are? Paparazzi?'

'Yes, but it started before that.' She listened to his explanation, trying to keep up and pick out the triggers, impressed that it was flowing from him rather than having to be drawn. 'And it feels so real.'

'More phantom finger than flashback or waking dream.' All equally real in the experience.

'I suppose.'

'Like the crow?'

'No, that's more . . . *hyper*-real.'

'And you're worried this all represents a relapse?'

'I'm worried I might jump some poor sod for walking too close behind me.'

'Given your current pressures, perhaps this is just your way of processing natural anxiety.'

'My condition makes natural dangerous.'

'You never really leave war behind . . .' A common sentiment with combat PTSD. One they'd never agreed on. He felt it anchored him to darkness. She felt it tempered his resolve.

'I'm sure it doesn't say anything in all those professional texts on your shelves about taking the piss.'

'I haven't read a page,' she lied. It wasn't the first time they'd played out this joke. A lazy diversion by his standards. There was something else going on here . . . 'You know,' she said, 'when people suddenly talk openly about themselves, it's often what they're *not* saying that most piques my interest.'

'I liked it better when you played clueless,' he said, referring to the early days when she'd had to sneak around his conceited omniscience.

'So . . . ?'

'You've got patients waiting.'

'Think of it as triage.' Hazel glanced again at the clock. Silence was ever loaded with Stark. She could hear him breathing, thinking, deciding whether to unload. 'Joe?'

He let out an even longer sigh. 'Kelly called.'

36

'Seriously . . . Doesn't this look like someone we know?' said Fran, staring at the assorted images of the man passing himself off as Patrick Burgess, refusing to dwell on the fact that his face was now central on the incident board with Sinclair moved to the edge.

Stark shrugged. 'Not that I know.'

Fran was good with faces and still couldn't make a connection, yet it nagged at her like déjà vu, unsure if the memory was real or illusion given substance by repetition. She clicked her tongue in irritation. 'Who were you talking with so intently in your car?'

'Careers advice helpline.'

A slap-down lie. Something serious then, as his body language had suggested. He looked about as tired as she felt, but she didn't ask why he was back so quickly, looking more pensive than ever. He was even less likely to follow Harper's edict than she was. Who could sleep with a serial killer on the loose? And the latest victim had slipped Stark her number hours earlier. Perhaps he'd been on with his smug-faced shrink. The way things were going, Fran might enjoy some quiet time in a padded cell, so long as she could skip the confessional bullshit.

Marcus had run her through his preliminary report and sent her away before beginning the full post-mortem. She summarized it for the team now, watching the familiarity sink their hopes.

Cause of death, strangulation, unless alternate indications emerged. Blood was being tested for Rohypnol or other indicators. Extensive bruising pre-mortem. Sexual intercourse, both vaginal and anal, with tearing, suggesting force. Wrists and ankles bound with smooth cord, possibly the same electrical cable found round her neck. Probably tied over something hard like a table, like the others. Body cleaned with powerful bleach externally and toilet-bleach internally. SOCO had found little initial evidence at scene, indicating this all happened elsewhere, but wider searches were being conducted in daylight. The blue polythene sheet was a different grade to the other killings, but so had been that around Paige Talbot, and if the killer had lain dormant for two years a fresh start with fresh supplies was hardly surprising.

'I thought I sent you two home,' said Harper, announcing himself with dry irritation, reportedly still pissed off after checking with the FLO that Emily's sister still hadn't responded to the mother's texts.

Fran explained her forensic diversion – enough to send her straight back to work after a shower and change of clothing, still sickened by the sight of Emily Thornton's whipped bloody.

Stark explained nothing, earning a frown from Harper but nothing more.

'So, same MO,' said Harper needlessly.

'In most ways,' agreed Fran. 'But not all . . .' She used the assembled magnets to fix a series of new photos to the board, as the team crowded round for a closer look.

Hammed winced. Williams muttered darkly under his breath. Dixon turned away, and for once, Fran couldn't blame him.

All the victims except Paige had suffered bruising across their backs, buttocks and hamstrings. inflicted with some form of smooth whip, possibly a plastic cane or more electrical cable. Punishments, the profiler had suggested, or just plain sadism – fatuous tit. Emily Thornton was something different. More extensive and considerably more brutal, the skin broken in criss-crossing lines.

'I'm betting the profiler would use words like *hate-fuelled* and *frenzied*,' said Fran. Harper wasn't the only one to take notice. Any deviation put them closer to the copycat theory and further from the you've-wasted-two-years-persecuting-the-wrong-man theory.

'And *escalation*,' added Stark, ever determined to consider the gloomier option. Victim number six, Sara Brompton, had suffered significantly worse than the others. Punishment for her lookalike,

Leah Willoughby's escape. Who was to say this wasn't further punishment? Sinclair hadn't done this. But if he was innocent of all, then why had the killings stopped with his arrest and begun again now? Had Emily Thornton suffered the pent-up fury of the killer's two-year abstinence?

Harper clearly didn't like that line of thought any better than she did.

'Time of death hard to pinpoint, not knowing the temperature of wherever she was killed, or when she was moved,' Fran added. 'But she left work at six-thirty and was found around eleven-thirty. Anything on traffic?'

'Nothing helpful and everything but,' replied Williams, who'd been scanning footage. 'There's a secluded footpath looping around the back, linking underneath the A2 to a number of routes, Kidbrooke Station and the Ferrier Estate, but any of those would be a long way to carry a body from somewhere you could park out of sight. If this happened elsewhere and the killer brought the body by vehicle, the most practical entrance is Nelson Mandela Road off Rochester Way. Nearest traffic cameras are on the pedestrian crossing traffic lights where Rochester Way flies over the A2, here . . .' He pointed on the full wall map. 'The A2 has plate-recognition cameras, so you'd be mad to come that way and we'd need a plate to look for, of course. There's a set of speed cameras on Rochester Way here to the east and another pedestrian crossing with cameras further on, but there are numerous routes in avoiding all these.' The usual metadata, a haystack made of needles, any one of which may or may not be suspect.

'Stay on it,' said Harper. 'Any update on timeline?'

Dixon stood and cleared his throat. 'Emily left work in College Way at six-thirty p.m. and walked to the Maze Hill station. We have her boarding the train at six-forty and disembarking two stops later at Charlton, three streets from her home. Then nothing. Uniform report no signs of a break-in at her flat from outside, and neighbours report no disturbance.'

'Time we had a look for ourselves,' said Fran. 'How we doing on access?'

'The parents coughed up,' said Harper, holding up a set of keys as if this was some hard-won concession he was ready to play down should his colleagues burst into spontaneous applause. As if he'd not imposed himself on the bereaved family in the moment of their utmost grief only to sit on the bloody keys for two hours while he played Billy-Big-Bollocks on TV, waddling around in shoes he'd never fill.

'Right . . .' He levered his useless bulk from the desk he'd been leaning against to address his latest captive audience with his best grave expression. 'We have to agree this wasn't Julian Sinclair.' He paused for effect. 'Some people are gonna suggest the rest weren't either. Which means we need to show Leah Willoughby our photofit and photos of the shit posing as Patrick Burgess. Fran?'

'She's going to tell us to fuck off again.'

'And your skin's too thin?'

Fran had known this was coming the second she saw poor Emily Thornton's plastic-wrapped corpse. 'Stark should go.'

'She told us both to fuck off,' said Stark. 'Not sure my first charm offensive left the right impression.'

'I'll go with him,' said Hammed. Never one for volunteering, he met Fran's surprised face with a shrug. 'I never met her last time. She might not get hissy with me.'

'Fine,' said Fran, at the same moment Harper said 'Good.' They exchanged glances, both acknowledging that Fran had spoken out of turn, though hers contained rather more irony.

'Okay then,' Harper jangled the keys at Fran. 'Seeing as you're allergic to sleep, you get the victim's flat.'

37

Flashes erupted in Stark's face as he manoeuvred out of the car park – paparazzi calling out his name, shouting questions, one stepping in front of the car, camera raised.

Stark revved the engine hard to signal his intent and the photographer moved aside just in time as the car slid out on to Royal Hill and away.

'Arseholes,' said Hammed, glancing back, but thereafter lapsed into silence. Least loquacious of the DCs, he habitually let Williams and Dixon lead social conversations, happier to chip in a quip as and when. Without the other two here, tension soon tinged the quiet, but Stark had too many worries queuing up to set that near the front, not least his face all over the papers again. He had to concentrate anyway. Not on driving, but on not driving like he was still in Helmand, like every snarl-up was a potential ambush, like every parked car was a bomb. Being the driver was better, he'd eventually had to admit to Fran, but without a reliable passenger on threat assessment he still felt exposed. So he concentrated, or tried to, on the conversation with Hazel replaying in his head as they so often did, and the elephant in the telephonic consulting room – Kelly. If he left it much longer she'd call first.

And Pensol. So much for no retreat. It felt topsy-turvy to flee your *own* flat with polite excuses, but what was one more misdeed among the rest?

Perhaps it was because his concentration was all over the place that he found himself clocking the motorcyclist tucked three cars back, who'd made the same last few turns. Black helmet and jacket, but Stark couldn't make out if it was the pap from outside both Leah's flat and his.

Slowing, he filtered to turn left at the next lights, surreptitiously watching the bike in the mirrors do the same.

'Short cut?' asked Hammed, as the satnav suggested a U-turn to get back on course.

'Detour.' They came up to another set of lights and filtered to turn right. The bike did likewise. When the lights turned green he brought the car up to the line and braked, ignoring the horns of protest from the vehicles behind him.'

'Everything all right?'

'Dandy.'

'Your counter-espionage skills?' Hammed asked wryly, checking his wing mirror.

'Just a precaution.'

'Press, you think?'

'Wouldn't be the first time.'

'Got the plate?'

'It's a bike.' Plates on the back only.

He waited through amber then flicked on the concealed lights and siren and pulled away just as the lights turned red, cutting right across oncoming cars. Protesting horns followed them up the street from the ensuing gridlock. The trapped bike did not. Stark killed the lights and rejoined the route and Hammed gave a small huff, probably thinking the whole episode had been in his head.

Perhaps it had. There was no paparazzi outside Leah's flat when they arrived, but if it had been the same biker he could probably guess their destination.

An urban fox had met its end beneath uncaring wheels in the street outside. Black wings clattered as a crow hopped to a standstill on the pavement, eyeing the carrion, weighing the odds of darting between the traffic to snatch a morsel. People walked past, seemingly oblivious, and Hammed was busy checking his phone, offering Stark no reassurance that he wasn't just hallucinating.

As predicted, their welcome wasn't warm. 'I told you to fuck off.'

'And I told you that if you wanted justice you'd have to help,' replied Stark, holding up the photofit to the lens.

There was a brief pause. 'Is that your "new suspect"?' An audible sneer.

'You tell me.'

'Where's Fran?'

'Looking for this guy.'

'Wasting her time, like you.'

'Then this won't take long, and we can get back on the right track.'

After several seconds, the intercom buzzed.

Fran stared disconsolately at the text message conversation on her phone as Williams pulled the car out of the station car park, ignoring the paparazzi and their notable disinterest in *her* compared to the frenzy she'd observed from the window as Stark had left the station.

How did it go? she'd asked.

Like carefully explaining all the workings of a suit of armour so they know where to stab you, Groombridge had replied.

Fran cursed silently. No one had put more into nailing the killer than Groombridge. He should be leading the charge now, not facing one.

Wish I could swap places with you, she texted back, then felt foolish. They neither of them had much tolerance for open sentimentality. To make it worse, she realized, she meant it. He was worth ten of her. Not that she'd have any more idea than him what to do in civvy street.

Her first childhood career choices had been to become a unicorn, or a dragon. Never a princess. After that, a professional goalkeeper, just to show her dad and four brothers that if they would only let her play in goal she was going to be the best goalie in history – until she realized goalies had to be tall and athletic and weren't allowed to kick everyone else in the shins. As a teenager she'd mostly just wanted to be someone other than herself.

Then, after a couple of years of discovering that regular jobs, like most fashions, didn't really fit her, she saw the recruitment poster. The Met's early attempts at inclusivity. Black and Asian female police constables, wide smiles, helpfully pointing directions for an elderly couple on the street, some inane strapline. Her grandfather had been in the police in Barbados. She'd forgotten. Memories of the old man with the world's widest grin, bouncing her on his knee, had brought tears to her eyes. He'd died before they could afford another family flight.

All it took to set her heart irrevocably on the police was her father's disapproval. Wily sod. How he'd laughed when she eventually realized he'd played her. His welcome into seventies white Britain had put paid to his own thoughts of following in his father's footsteps and none of her brothers had shown any inclination. His smile at her passing out ceremony shone with pride, his own mischievous father's smile glinting through like the Caribbean sun off the shining sea.

Of course, the women in the poster were actors or models, the real Met police proved somewhat less gender- or colour-blind and Fran never did find much patience in herself for smiling at the public. But she was part of the mix now, resolutely sat on the scales to counterbalance all the bullshit and prejudice.

So do I, replied Groombridge. He didn't use a wink-face emoji.

Fran tucked the phone away, staring out of the window at the stained city and mottled sky.

'Good to have the old gang back together,' said Williams, meaning Harper. By way of conversational openers he was over-fond of lighting her fuse and standing back.

'Sod off.'

It was all right for Williams and the others. Harper liked to be liked, never more so than by his subordinates – one of the lads, standing his round, holding court – in other words just being a crashing bore. But Fran he saw as a rival, and Stark he saw as a threat – both of them capable of exposing his deficiencies. Groombridge too, though the DCI had never offered him anything but support. And all that was before his role in the shootings. The old gang . . .

Williams chuckled. 'What doesn't kill us . . .'

Fran huffed irritably. 'Will damn well regret it.'

'You won't get me to change my statement.' Leah eyed Hammed with suspicion as she handed out mugs of insipid tea, short on sugar and care.

Stark sipped his all the same. A brew was a brew. And if the locals served you slop for a laugh, at least they weren't shooting at you. 'We just need you to take a good look.'

'And say what? That I was wrong? The only mistake I made was trusting you lot.' She took the identikit and stared at it. 'Not him.' Stark showed her the stills from the hospital and prison CCTV cameras. 'These the best you've got?'

'For now.'

Leah was clearly underwhelmed. 'Still not him.'

'Sure?'

'It was Julian Sinclair. I'll never forget that face.'

'None of us will,' replied Stark kindly. 'But the defence said that was because he was all over the news, that you imprinted on his face after the fact.'

'That I made it all up for my fifteen minutes of fame,' sneered Leah. 'I know what that bitch said. Did I make up these?' She lifted her top to show them her back, and the whip scars. Not as savage as Emily's injuries, but still . . .

'You said he wore a mask,' Hammed chipped in.

'For the camera – while he was beating and raping me,' she replied, the jagged edge in her voice, glinting. 'The rest of the time he swanned around unmasked. He was going to kill me after.'

Leah had always maintained her attacker had filmed his assaults. But no camera equipment or footage had ever been found or showed up online in the darker areas of the web, as far as anyone knew, at least. Sinclair's computers and home had been torn apart for them – email, phone, internet providers – warrants had been awarded and enacted to the frustration of all, and with the eventual conviction now quashed they'd not get such licence again.

Stark noted Leah's trembling hands, and the defiance with which she clenched and hid them. The way her eyes darted, jumping at a door slamming out in the common stairwell, her pre-emptive distrust and reactionary aggression – all reinforcing the impression formed on his last visit. His combat PTSD treatment was funded under the NHS, and the powers that be would hardly dare not live up to their obligations under the Military Covenant where he was concerned, for all their failings of others. But who was helping this girl? Victim support only worked if you asked for it, and Leah was hiding herself away in bitterness. With the case tearing open old wounds, she might spiral into self-destruction . . .

He tucked the images away. 'Thank you, Leah. I'm very sorry we had to bother you with this. Is there anything we can do for you before we go?'

'Like what?' she mocked. 'Stop barking up wrong trees, lock up Julian Sinclair and throw away the key. That's all you can do for me, short of letting whoever shot him finish the job.' Her eyes narrowed. 'Don't you pity me. Don't you *fucking* dare,' she shot to her feet. 'Go! Fuck off out of my flat!' she hissed, wiping furiously at unwanted tears. 'I don't need you! I don't want your help! You're *fuck-all* use, the both of you, *all of you*! Go on, *FUCK OFF!*'

Emily Thornton had lived in a nice street in a nice terrace split into upstairs and downstairs flats, each far more than Fran could afford.

'I always say we're in the wrong game, Sarge,' commented Williams.

'You don't get this kind of money being a paralegal,' Fran replied. 'You get to be a paralegal because you've got this kind of money behind you.'

'Bank of Mum and Dad,' Williams nodded, fitting the key to the outer door. 'Poor sods.'

A middle-aged, upper-middle-class woman in active-wear and expensive, spotless trainers frowned at the uniformed officers and cars soiling her street as she unloaded bags-for-life from her Range Rover, wondering if she was safe in her bed, or whether something distasteful was occurring that might impact negatively on property prices. The kind of things that slunk in if you let people divide up the houses into flats to be peddled to riff-raff.

Fran stared at her until she turned sniffily away, clicking a key over her shoulder to command the boot lid to bow itself closed while she nipped inside to change for competitive salad ordering in the latest darling-little-bistro with her gal-pals.

If there was an opposite to rose-tinted spectacles, that's what Fran had on today.

On Emily's side of the street, where the hoi polloi made do in over-priced sub-divisions, the common lobby was neat and tastefully plain, with few of the usual scuffmarks or footprints you saw in areas with shared cleaning responsibilities. Williams fitted the next key. 'Got the code?'

Fran held up the four-digit code, provided by the mum and dad.

But the intruder alarm didn't trigger.

A powerful wave of bleach assaulted their noses. The tasteful furnishings were awry. There was blood on the carpet and wall. And it got much worse from there in . . .

The snooty cow across the road was going to dine out on poor-me anecdotes for years.

38

'You can't save them all, you know?' Hammed's first words since they left. No wry aside about how well that had gone or banter about wit and charm. 'I saw that look in your eye.'

Stark scanned his mirrors but there was no sign of the biker-pap. 'What look?'

'Like you can fix everything.'

Like he was fixed, changed, further around the curve. Or round the bend. The saviour complex Doc Hazel too frequently alluded to. 'She needs to know help is available.'

'We're here to catch criminals, not sweep up wreckage,' replied Hammed matter-of-factly, eyes fixed outside the window.

In Stark's view, sifting the wreckage for what could be saved was *everyone*'s department. You help where you can, otherwise what was the point? But it was easier to let the topic lapse.

He couldn't help wondering if this conversation was a sign of a deeper resentment than he'd previously recognized. If Hammed distrusted Stark's past actions and motives, his thoughts on Stark's possible promotion to sergeant might be festering. His was the only signature missing from the office get-well card delivered to Stark's hospital room. Stark had put that down to Hammed missing the bloody conclusion of the last big case due to his mother's sudden passing, but perhaps it was more significant. Perhaps Harper's poison had seeped in his ear?

Another saddening worry for Stark's list, to be addressed when and if the dust and ash ever settled around him.

*

Shut two strange cats in a confined space and you'd get somewhere close to the silent tension in this car, thought Fran, as she sat with Harper outside Emily Thornton's flat, waiting for SOCO to clear them for re-entry.

As soon as he heard what they'd found he'd jumped in his dick-head Beamer to come see for himself. Pointless. She'd sent Williams back to the station to balance things out. They needed legwork more than Harper's inspector-level eyes on the crime scene.

She'd have done the same, of course, but that wasn't the point. Groombridge wouldn't've.

At least no press seemed to have followed him.

It was the same car he'd had as a sergeant, unnecessarily big, over-powered, tidy but ageing, paint starting to fade, leather seats showing wear; an almost laughable reflection of its owner. He could afford to upgrade now but he liked his things. It also stank; obvious epicentre of the cigarette funk that followed him around. She wondered if he'd spark up now – his car, his rules – but he didn't. She rarely saw him smoke – he wasn't a fag-break lead-swinger like some. He got his fix on the move. Perhaps he thought that didn't count. He and his wife had both quit when they were trying for a baby, he'd let slip once.

With lamentable results all round.

Fran was more likely to take up smoking than have babies. She'd nephews and nieces aplenty and if her biological clock ever started ticking she probably wouldn't have time to notice. She'd seen too many female colleagues park promising careers for lives riven with chaos and impediments, seen the attempt, successful or otherwise, put cracks in previously strong relationships and heard of some unfortunate few, like Harper's wife, for whom the ticking clock ended with an implosion.

'How's your revision going?' he asked, a cross between thinking of something to say and fishing for information. If she made inspector they'd be back on parity and he'd have to stop the lording prick rou-tine and, with any luck, piss off back to the provinces.

'I doubt I'll sit the test,' she replied. 'What with all this.'

'Oh.' No protest that she must. He never had been a great liar. Perhaps another reason his wife's train left the tracks – on top of his many personality defects. Fran didn't know which had triggered the poor woman's tailspin into booze and husband battery – failure to conceive or his clumsily disguised infidelity. Or both.

Hard to picture a bloke like Harper letting his slip of a wife hit him. Far easier the other way around. Had he soaked it all up out of love or guilt, or both? How were they even still together? How much forgiveness could a marriage withstand? Rumour had it, his main reason for leaving Greenwich had been to relocate his wife into a new rehab centre, and not just embarrassment at failing the Inspectors' Exam first time round. But at the end of the day, he was just another alpha-male arsehole who couldn't keep it in his pants, and Fran would've buried the hatchet in his balls.

A white-clad SOCO waved at them from the pop-up transition tent and watched them pull on disposables – one cool, tall and weathered; the other short and embarrassed. Overalls made Fran look squashed. They already had her shoes. She'd always kept spares in her car, before it'd been shot up. She really must get back on to Central Procurement. Williams had cheerfully swapped into *his* spares, waving her goodbye as she stood in oversized blue SOCO wellingtons grinding her teeth.

'Ready.' Senior Crime Scene Manager, Geoff Culpepper, beckoned them inside.

Fran had read the story of what happened here in seconds but let Culpepper spell it out for the hard of thinking to her left.

The victim had opened the door to her attacker. The lazy explanation was that she'd known them, but it could be any of a dozen others: Delivery for signature. Have you seen my cat? Would you like a quote for repairing those slipped roofing tiles you hadn't noticed? Once the door was open, a shove, a threat or a weapon might be all it took to gain entry and elicit silent capitulation.

After that Emily had been bent forward over her own kitchen table and tied there with grey electrical cable and her clothes cut off her with kitchen scissors, all littering the floor, and then . . .

The un-twisted cables lay at the foot of each table leg. How she must have struggled against them . . .

There was a straight length on the floor nearby, about a metre long, with traces of blood. The whip.

'Son of a bitch,' breathed Harper, narrow-eyed above his mask. You could accuse him of many things, but not heartlessness.

Afterwards the killer had dragged the body into the bath for cleaning. There were plastic bottles on the floor. Domestic bleach. And toilet duck, with its handy curved spout, blue drips staining the white floor tiles . . .

Fran only just made it outside and beyond the cordon before throwing up in the gutter, retching till her stomach ached and her head spun, spitting the last and gulping in air like some green-gilled rookie. All these years . . . countless crime scenes, never once till now. Somehow seeing the poor girl laid out beneath Marcus's ministrations, beyond pain, was less horrifying than seeing exactly how she suffered before; how they'd all suffered . . . Her stomach lurched again.

She shook her head, swallowing the nausea, furious. Horror clouded the mind, and that could not be afforded.

At least the snooty cow wasn't across the street to see this. Or the team.

'You okay?'

Harper. Of course. A new well of humiliation opened beneath her. 'Stomach bug.'

He fished out a packet of cigarettes and lit up, inhaling deeply and blowing out with visible satisfaction. 'I won't tell anyone.'

Fran suppressed a curse, forcing her mind on to something else.

So much about this was like before, but much was not. None of the other victims had been assaulted in their homes. They'd never found out where the crimes were committed. The toilet cleaner was new, and the savagery of the whipping. Signs of expediency, desperation perhaps. A creature didn't alter habits without reason.

Questions. But the biggest – 'Why move the body?'

39

'Why move the body?' asked Stark, staring at the map where Williams had just flagged Emily Thornton's flat. It was some distance from where she'd been found.

'Ritual? Routine?'

'Risky,' Stark added. There was no sense to it. The previous killings had taken place somewhere unknown. The killer's secret place; somewhere to be preserved, perhaps, sacred, or more likely cleaned, purged even; dump the remains elsewhere, remove the evidence. But this killing was in the victim's home. The only thing that needed removing was the killer and any trace of themselves. 'They left the bleach, electrical cables, cut clothing and the blood – why not just leave her there too?'

'Perhaps he gets a kick out of leaving them for someone else to find. "Look what I did." '

'Like a cat leaving a dead bird for you,' said Hammed, joining them.

Dixon stayed at his desk, away from the boards. 'A copycat,' he said.

'Indeed,' Stark nodded. 'But who's copying who? And why? Misdirection?'

'Your fan club's going to climb up here if Owen doesn't give them something soon,' said Hammed, jerking his thumb to the window and the gauntlet-run of press hounds baying below.

Stark flagged the fan-club comment and Hammed's use of Harper's first name for later consideration, postponed for now by Gwen's name on his buzzing phone forcing him to step away. 'You wait months for a reporter to call, then twice in twenty-four hours.'

'I'm amazed you haven't been bombarded.'

'I only share this number with my special friends. I don't suppose you've been following me again? Or do you have people for that, now you're a new media star?'

'No. Why, has someone else?'

'No comment.'

'Of course.'

'Everything okay?' he asked.

'Me?'

'Well, we definitely agreed I wouldn't be talking about me, so I can only assume you're calling with exciting news of your own.'

'If only.'

'Oh well . . . good talking to you then.'

'Why hasn't the new victim been named and is her murder connected with the Greenwich Strangler case or not?'

He had to admire her audacity. 'On the record or off?'

'You're going to tell me to piss off either way, right?'

'In as many words.'

'There's a genuine public interest here. You of all people know duty and honour aren't the same thing as blind adherence to the rules.'

A good shot, but the police used the press when necessary and the moment that got turned around, rot set in. 'Some rules are better than others.'

'And who decides that?'

'In my case, the chain of command.'

'Maybe, but *quis custodiet ipsos custodes*, Joe.'

Who guards the guards? 'You're quoting Juvenal at me?'

'Someone in your lot is already leaking to my lot.'

'Wouldn't be the first time.'

She huffed in irritation. 'If you change your mind, call me – *before* you call your shrink.'

Stark stared at the call-ended icon, but her 'guards' challenge lingered as he thought of Harper squatting in Groombridge's office, with DAC Stevens pulling his strings.

*

'Women trouble?'

Fran turned to see who Williams was addressing. She could've guessed. Stark looked as close to sheepish as a wolf might get. Whatever was going on, she added it to her current list of grievances.

'You do get a lot of calls that you have to take outside,' commented Dixon, grinning at Stark.

'Or calls you don't take,' smirked Hammed. 'Treat them mean . . .'

Williams made an *ignore-him* face. 'What's her name?'

'Whose name?' asked Harper, striding in and immediately latching on to Stark's discomfort.

'I'm not sure he keeps all their names in his head,' chuckled Hammed.

'Oh, right,' Harper smirked. 'You really should try. Girls like that sort of thing.'

'I'll bear that in mind should the need ever arise,' Stark replied dryly.

'If you're all done,' Fran interjected, 'perhaps we could focus on finding the shit that did this to Emily Thornton?'

The level of contrition varied, with Dixon at one end and Harper at the other. Did none of them realize what was at stake, with Groombridge out there somewhere being hauled over hot coals?

'Quite right,' nodded Harper, spoiling her moment of righteous superiority. 'Have you downloaded those photos yet?'

Fran held up the SOCO memory stick of photos from Emily's flat. There was no body in them, but plenty of horror. She handed it to Dixon all the same.

A run-through with commentary had the desired effect – both sobering and galvanizing.

She already had uniform going door-to-door and scouring the local area for CCTV, and the traffic team were on it too. It was legwork time again. And they now had three incident boards set up in the office, with desks of the officers they should have, but didn't, stacked against a wall.

Afterwards, Fran knocked on Harper's door. 'We need more warm bodies.' And no more cold ones.

'I've already asked. Seems like no one's keen to lend crew to a sinking ship.'

'Even lukewarms?' The usual suspects of lazy or thick DCs other boroughs were only too happy to loan out. A case with this much media attention should guarantee additional staff, but the man responsible for signing off on that was, of course, DAC Stevens – all the resource they *didn't* need.

'Even DI Graham's playing hard to get.'

Shit. Even their own station's main CID team across the hall? Groombridge had friends to call on and favours he might've called in. Harper had neither. This IPCC witch-hunt could hardly have been timed to hurt more.

'Boss,' called Dixon, holding his desk phone. 'Incident line has a sports shopkeeper on saying he sold three plain white hockey masks like the ones on the news to some bloke a fortnight ago.' Dixon knew better than to waste her time and quickly recognized her *and?* face. 'Says that he tried to sell him more hockey stuff but he wasn't interested. And he didn't look like a sportsman.'

'Description . . . ?'

'IC1, twenties to forties,' confirmed Dixon.

'That it?' A white guy of indeterminate age. Fran blew out a sigh. 'Right, well you'd better show him pictures of the Talbot brothers, and Damien Castor,' she said, glancing at the car thief's bloodied face on the board. 'One of him *alive*.'

Harper nodded absently and retreated into his office to play at being Groombridge while spinning in the chair he didn't deserve.

A couple of dragging hours later, Fran retreated to the canteen in search of caffeine, and hope.

'No reinforcements, I assume?' asked Stark, appearing at her elbow like some damn ninja-ghost.

Fran irritably licked scalding coffee from her fingers. 'Detective Inspector Harper is having trouble attracting volunteers.' He nodded, unsurprised, but didn't depart or apologize. 'Something else?' Another nod. She knew that look now. 'Something I'm not going to like?' she sighed. 'Something personal and important?' A category

Stark reserved for things he refused to explain but expected her to put up with.

'Sort of.'

'Don't tell me it *is* women trouble, because unless you've come to your senses about Kelly, I'm not interested.'

His fleeting look of discomfort was like an unexpected glint of gold in the rock face. Fran grinned. '*You have?*'

He gave that deliciously pained expression saved for moments when he'd let slip something he instantly regretted. 'She called. Wants to meet up. To talk.'

'About?'

'Didn't say.'

'And you didn't ask?' Fran rolled her eyes. '*Men.* So you're seeing her tonight?'

A shake of the head. 'That's personal and *unimportant.*'

'I beg to differ. So when *are* you seeing her?'

'I haven't called her back yet.'

'You're avoiding?'

'That's one way of looking at it.'

'Name another.'

'Standing still in the minefield.'

'Waiting for what?' scoffed Fran.

'An alternative.'

'*Typical.* Give the man a hail of bullets to run towards . . . But an emotional decision to make and he's paralysed.'

Stark offered only a small facial shrug.

Fran expressed her disgust, though far from love's fearless heroine herself. 'Okay, we'll circle back to Kelly. So what, then – shrink?'

'Not exactly.' His explanation was as candid as it proved annoying, leaving her, as it did, with no reasonable grounds for objection. 'You really are a glutton. Go on then, piss off.'

Stark had barely gone when Harper bustled out of his office. 'Mother*fucker*! You seeing this?' He held up his phone. Capital-Cast six o'clock news – a blonde in red lipstick and coat reporting in front of a residential police cordon. A photo in the corner of the screen, a victim named in the scrolling strapline.

'... and given Emily Thornton's direct connection to the *still-hospitalized* Julian Sinclair,' expounded the reporter, 'the obvious question is – does this further underscore Greenwich Police Station's failure to find the Greenwich Strangler?'

'How the fuck did they get this?' growled Harper, staring round the office. 'Where's Stark?'

40

'I can't do this.'

There was a level of dread in Pensol's voice that, to be frank, Stark shared. 'It can help.' As police counsellors would have suggested to her at the time, *but not if you're unready.* Probably a bad time to confess this was Hazel's idea, not his. Unlike Leah Willoughby, Pensol didn't seem a danger to herself as much as her liver and dignity, but then he wasn't the best judge of extreme behaviour.

'I won't know what to say.'

'Everyone else feels that way. But you don't have to put in to get out. Not until you're ready. I'm not promising anything, but the first step is the hardest and only you can make it.' *And God help you, the road might get smoother but it never ends.* That realization took longer and hit harder. 'And I'll hold your hand if you like.'

He'd meant it figuratively, but her hand crept over the handbrake to grip his. She was trying not to cry. Perhaps this had been a mistake. Maybe she just wasn't ready.

You can't save them all. Hammed's words mocked him.

But you had to try. Even if it meant taking time out from trying to stop a serial killer. As Harper had said to the press, Stark's role was hardly so significant he couldn't be spared a few hours to help elsewhere. Not that the press cared for reason. He was certain at least one bike had tried following him from the station scrum, and he'd had to direct Pensol out the back way from his flats to meet him.

'I . . . haven't said thank you,' she said quietly, wiping away a tear, fighting for control, looking for anything else to think about. 'For taking me in. And that night in the club, getting me home safe, and not . . . you know.'

Perhaps she thought it odd – to wake undressed in bed, twice now, unmolested – perhaps thinking he found her unattractive, given his refusal to even kiss her just hours ago. 'No need.'

'I slapped you, I think. I'm sorry.'

'You're not the first.'

'I remember being angry . . . With everybody, everything. Nothing made sense.'

Stark just nodded. Wishful drinking was a refuge he was familiar with, when wishful thinking felt senseless.

'Callie said she gave you a hard time in the morning.'

'Good friends are protective.'

She nodded, looking at him. 'Why don't you use your first name?'

A direct question. A good way of avoiding one's own thoughts. 'Habit.'

'Why did you stop?'

'School, police, army; I've been Stark for so long . . . Maybe it's a uniform thing.'

Her gaze drifted to the world outside the car, with its gloomy clouds and fading light. It was starting to rain, and the windows were steaming up. 'I think I'm done with uniforms.'

'That would be the Met's loss.' In his experience it was easier to remove uniforms physically than mentally, but she'd have to decide that for herself.

'Joseph's a nice name.'

'My mum calls me Joseph when I've been bad.'

'You haven't a bad bone in your body.'

Plenty of broken ones though. His shoulder blade was a patchwork and the titanium plate and screws in his pelvis had increased his mineral worth, if not his self-worth. 'Nobody's perfect.'

She looked down, perhaps taking this as a rebuke. 'Can I call you Joe? Stark seems . . .'

'A bit stark?'

A crooked smile. 'Impersonal, I suppose.'

'Sure.' He had, after all, undressed her twice in a matter of days, and she had inspected him in turn. 'If I can call you Annie?'

'I prefer Marianne.' She sighed, as if being called Annie by some had irked her for years. She'd not told her flatmate or her mentors, Ptolemy or Peters, but she'd told him.

'Noted.'

'Why a tiger and a crow?'

His tattoos. Stark fought the instinct to deflect. Personal questions brought out the fight or flight in him, but evidently she needed intimacy in this moment, perhaps just to give her courage. 'Princess of Wales's Royal Regiment – nickname, the Tigers,' he explained. Too good not to get inked, several of the lads had insisted, celebrating surviving basic training, and the younger Stark had thought, why not? A decision of innocence. Of hubris. He could barely remember making it now, nor relate to that boy and his blind optimism.

'And the crow?'

That was an altogether different decision, by an altogether different man. A re-balancing. And one he wasn't ready to share.

She sensed his hesitation and apologized.

'No, I'm sorry. Some things are harder than others.' Given what he was asking her to do this evening, that seemed a lousy cop-out.

She squeezed his hand. 'Sod it; let's go in.'

Opening the car doors into the cold drizzle was like letting the world back in, popping their misty bubble of quiet reflection and discomfort.

There was a little poster, hand-written and cheaply photocopied on to cheerful orange paper beside the uninspiring portico through which they entered the shabby civic building. Following ambiguous signs along poorly lit corridors, downstairs to the basement level and through some battered doors, they emerged into the kind of utilitarian, civil-service-chic space that can only ever have been spawned into existence in seventies Britain.

Several people gathered around a foldout table, tipping tap-water from plastic jugs into disposable cups, exchanging forced-sounding pleasantries, palpable tension in the air. A crowd too big for comfort, too small for hiding.

Pensol froze. 'Oh God, I ... I can't ... How ... ?'

'With honesty and courage, as little or as much as you like, as often as you can, or nothing. No one will judge you here. All these people have trauma to work through and one thing in common – they could use a little help.' And it was as jumbled a collection of specimens as you could imagine – so far removed from the assembly of damaged squaddies Stark remembered that it was quite shocking.

What he *didn't* tell her was that he'd never found group therapy useful in the least. His insular nature left him weak in this situation, but the army had forced it on him. Those first sessions in Headley Court Defence Medical Rehabilitation Centre still stung in his memory – his crushing anger at the sheer rudeness of those that spoke up; that did 'share'. He still despised that word. A problem *shared* was a problem more than one person then *had*. Saying as much hadn't earned him extra rations or friends among the other broken inmates, outwardly jovial and determined, inwardly bitter and frightened. He'd eventually 'engaged' because that's what they insisted you had to do to 'get well' and it seemed to help the others, but Group was agony for him. Pensol would have to decide that for herself too. He'd only truly confronted his own need much, much later, one-on-one with Hazel, through her patience and cunning, and even that still felt like pulling his own teeth.

The good doctor herself spotted them both now and beckoned with a smile, greeting a few others as the group took a chair each from the stacks and shuffled into the obligatory circle of pain, as exposing as it was clichéd.

Stark felt as trapped as Pensol looked.

Hazel introduced herself, welcomed and thanked them all, listed the limited rules – that they were here for each other and that all said here was in strict confidence and support – and invited contribution.

No one moved. In Stark's experience no one ever wanted to go first, but that was the army. He'd thought here, among civilians, there would be some fanatic to the process twitching in their seat to open up. Prejudice, of course. He glanced at Pensol. She was trembling.

You won't like it.

Hazel's words, never more correct. He'd run towards enemy fire because someone had to and he knew how; but this twisted his stomach ... But he wasn't here for him. Out there in the world the case ground on without him causing widespread harm, but in here was someone he might actually help. So he raised an arm and forced his grimace into a poorly executed smile.

'Hi, everyone. My name is Joe. And I have Post-Traumatic Stress Disorder.'

'Are you supposed to be in here?' asked Fran under her breath, joining him at the incident board with pictures of Emily Thornton on it.

Groombridge knew who it was because the name was written in Williams' neat capitals on the whiteboard in blue marker. This was his first chance to add a face to the name. A whole day wasted, churning over old ground, confronted with case notes scribbled by himself and others up to two years ago, invited to admit or deny, reveal or refute, defend himself and his team against the wildest accusations. All nice and friendly, behind closed doors, just an exploration ...

He might now forever associate their insipid coffee and cheap biscuits with a swelling weariness, frustration and indignation.

'Guv?'

'I'm not,' he replied. Bad enough having to sneak into his own station without the press seeing him. Williams and Hammed kept their eyes down to avoid contradicting him. Harper's overbearing voice could be heard through the door to his office, *his* bloody office, on the phone. 'Stark about?'

'Important personal errand, Guv.'

'Ah,' Groombridge smiled, knowing her feelings on the matter.

'You need him?'

He'd been hoping to catch them both together. He didn't have many more cards to play. 'How are you getting on with Owen?'

'I'm not sure you want me to answer that, Guv.'

No, he wasn't sure himself.

Seeing his attention return to the boards, Fran glanced around again. 'Want me to fill you in?' she asked, in a conspiratorial manner that might be laughable under other circumstances.

A nod.

She ran through the three boards one by one – the late Miss Thornton, the original Strangler case and the attempted kidnap and shooting of Julian Sinclair. This whole thing felt circular, a web of hate with Julian Sinclair sat in the centre, smiling like a Cheshire spider with snake eyes.

'Nothing from the door-to-door in Emily's street, or private CCTV?'

Fran shook her head.

'And the press leak?'

'I think Owen suspects Stark.'

Does he? wondered Groombridge. One could only hope the lawyer, Bosch, wasn't so much of a bottom-feeder as to leak his own god-daughter's name before her sister had been informed, but Moncrieff or Sinclair himself remained the least awful source. The next being some low-ranking police insider with an axe to grind or pocket to fill, and the worst, someone higher . . . 'The hockey masks?'

'John door-stepped the shopkeeper. They were paid for in cash and the in-store CCTV has long since overwritten itself. Photos of the Talbot brothers and their poker-pals drew a blank, and Tower Hamlets' dead car thief, Castor, was only a "maybe".'

'And nothing yet linking Castor to our patch anyway, or the Talbots,' said Groombridge, blowing out a sigh. Maybe he just supplied the van, guns and masks, but if somehow it turned out the three masked men weren't the Talbot brothers at all, that left them even further adrift.

'Sir?' Harper entered, with a faintly accusatory expression. 'You can't be here.'

'Just passing through.' Groombridge turned to the team. 'Keep up the good work, everyone.'

'How'd it go with the Brass numpties?' asked Williams, rarely wary of the direct approach.

'Nothing for you to worry about.' Groombridge smiled his best reassuring smile. 'Keep your heads in the game.'

'There you are,' said a brusque voice, the implication being that Groombridge was where he shouldn't be, though Superintendent Cox was too old-school to reprimand an officer in front of his subordinates.

'Just reassuring the troops, sir.'

'Yes, yes; we could all use a little, I'm sure.' Cox puffed out his moustache, seemingly ruffled. 'But in the meantime, I just heard Sinclair's lawyer, Bosch, is kicking up a stink, saying we should face corporate manslaughter charges for causing the death of his god-daughter, Emily Thornton, and others, by negligently prosecuting Sinclair thereby allowing the real killer free rein.'

41

'Suffer from . . .' said Hazel conversationally, stacking the last chair. Stark sighed. Saying you *had* PTSD wasn't enough, you had to admit you were *suffering*. He looked tired. 'I'm proud of you.'

'I wasn't here for me.'

'Were you not?'

'We're not on the clock, Doc.'

'It says I have the room for another two minutes.'

'Save it for Marianne.'

Hazel gestured to the empty hall. The girl had gone to freshen up. She'd not spoken a word, but that was to be expected. She'd just listened and cried. 'Will you bring her again?'

And would he speak again? For most patients, engagement was cause to rejoice, but with Stark she knew the sheer exposure cost him more pain than gain. He was almost vibrating with it, and anger, too entwined to separate. You had to look so hard to see it. The latest murder victim, the one he knew . . . And now Marianne . . . two more cuts. Fresh guilt to tear at him, and undermine his fragile new beginning.

'I'll offer.'

She nodded. 'You help where you can.' His own words. Soldiers did what needed doing and left the cost for later.

'You still think I have a saviour complex?' he asked.

'I've never called it that.'

'What *would* you call it?'

'Goodness.' Though in his case, it was a form of absolute humanity exacerbated by impossible decisions and moral injury; and like all things absolute – awful. Stark's danger was not pulling people into his lifeboat till he sank, but throwing himself out to make space.

'You're full of shit.'

'I could be in lucrative private practice and spend half my time on ski slopes or beaches,' she said, gesturing at the room again. 'So maybe you're asking the wrong person.'

He granted a concessionary nod. 'Fools together.'

'You didn't say she was quite so pretty.'

He huffed a chuckle, smiling ruefully. 'Karma mocks me.'

But when would he stop punishing *himself*? 'And Kelly?'

His smile turned to a sigh. 'We've not spoken again.'

'So you'll grasp nettles to help others but not yourself?'

'How would seeing Kelly help either of us?'

'How will you know until you do?'

Kelly was the first great love of his life and he'd pushed her away for her own safety. Time soothed and new loves struck – a hard truth, learned only through experience. Stark, she suspected, had extrapolated it, and was applying the principle to Kelly but not himself – attacking his own emotional rehabilitation as he had the physical, with impatience and a string of symptomatic one-night-stands, and little hope if any for full recovery.

So here he was again, torn between horror and hope. Between the dark and the light.

He nodded at the clock. 'Time's up, Doc.'

They said nothing walking to the car. There had been too many words already.

Pensol had earned her rations and kip.

Perhaps he had too, for his sins.

His knuckles were white – gripping the wheel like he was riding a rollercoaster rather than navigating sedately over Shooters Hill.

Pensol glanced his way. 'You okay?'

Before he could lie, his phone startled them both through the car speakers. The guy in the car pool had connected it up and Stark hadn't yet worked out how to stop it. 'Is this where you ask me where I am and how soon I can get back in?' he answered, assuming Fran.

'Not exactly.'

Kelly. *Shit!*

'Joe?'

'Kelly. Hang on, I'm driving. Can I call you back?'

'You haven't so far.'

'No. Sorry. It's been –'

'Frantic at work,' she completed the sentence. 'When is it not?

Stark winced. 'Yeah, sorry –' A glance found Pensol still staring out the window, trying not to intrude. 'Look, I really can't talk now, I'm not alone in the car.'

A long pause, and probably a silent sigh. 'Okay. Call me later.' And she was gone.

Stark slowly let out the breath he was holding.

Silence returned to the car with added awkwardness, but as they neared home Pensol broke it. 'Do you need me out of the flat? Am I . . . in the way?'

Stark replayed the phone conversation in his head and realized he'd used Kelly's name, common knowledge to the station's wagging chins. 'Not at all, honestly. Unless you want to go?'

'Do you want me to?'

'I want you to do what's best for you.'

'Honestly?'

'Honestly. You're welcome as long as you need.' Plus it was 9 p.m. and he was too tired and hungry for a tedious detour.

She looked thoughtful. 'Why is it hard?'

'Going home?' Stark's mother asked him the same thing – after he moved to London, and every time he'd been forced back home since by injury or the press. 'Sometimes a change of location can ease embedded thoughts and habits, or at least avoid them for a while.'

She nodded. 'Okay. Another night then, if you're sure.'

'I am. Three conditions though,' he smiled. 'Fish, chips and cold beers.'

'You've got to be kidding me.'

'Do I ever sound like I'm kidding you?' replied Fran.

All the more reason I should turn my phone off when I'm off duty, thought Stark, staring at the two chilled beers he'd just de-capped. Not to mention the smell of steaming-hot battered cod and chips emanating from the paper wrapping and the pretty girl on his sofa to share them with, albeit platonically. All more appealing than a night guarding Julian Sinclair. 'This is a job for close protection, not investigation.'

'And you're too important for babysitting?'

'Seventeen hours ago he was all hissy, thinking I was accusing him of killing Emily. Why's he asking for me?'

'Well, I doubt it's to apologize.'

'So we're pandering to his ego?'

'You think I *like* it?' she snapped, audibly smouldering.

'There's press outside my flat. It's only a matter of time before they realize I have a back way in. They'll be at the hospital too.'

'Use your ninja skills.'

'Since when did we start letting suspects dictate terms?' Stark stoked, for the hell of it.

'Since the IPCC put the Guv'nor under the sodding spotlight.'

'All the more reason not to hand Sinclair a victory.'

'Stop trying to wind me up. This came down from *above*,' spat Fran, meaning from Stevens via Harper. 'Julian *shithead* Sinclair won't let anyone else near him.'

'So of course you haven't asked CO19 to watch over the safe-house just to spite him.'

'Of course I have. Now, you've had your important personal time. Get your arse in.'

Stevens and Sinclair – their own personal axis of evil-mindedness. Well, they could both sodding wait. 'You know that thing that winds you up, when I get ready quicker than you think reasonable . . . ?'

'Everything you do is unreasonable and winds me up.'

'Well tonight, I'm finishing my dinner first.'

42

'You're a cautious man,' commented Sinclair, at Stark's detours and double-backs.

Their charge remained surly from their encounter in the early hours, though sadly not enough to ask for someone else. Nevertheless, Stark was leaving nothing to chance, following counter-surveillance precautions, before, during and after extraction, slipping Sinclair out of the hospital via a connected drop-in clinic while Dearing's rookie ran interference out front with the ARV boys, blue lights flashing. Emily's name and connection to Sinclair had detonated another explosion in press interest. The hospital bigwigs wanted Sinclair gone, and too many people still wanted to hospitalize him further, or worse, to simply turn him loose. When offered transfer under wraps to a Met safe house he'd demanded Stark, and either someone up-chain was so keen to keep Sinclair from the press that they capitulated, or that person was DAC Stevens and this little sideshow had already been leaked. 'When need arises.'

Sinclair was also alluding to the fact that Stark had made him sit in the passenger seat, with the giant Sergeant Dearing wedged in the back. It might seem unorthodox, but Stark considered it imprudent to let a suspected strangler sit behind him as he drove, and anyone ambushing them for their VIP would be in for a sizeable surprise if they went for the man in the back. Sinclair glanced sideways at Stark's terse response. 'Good to see a friendly face, at least,' he said sarcastically, lowering his voice to a conspiratorial whisper pitched to be overheard. *'That one doesn't like me.'*

'We're not here to like you,' replied Stark. A cheap shot. Fatigue and irritation at being plucked from R&R for tedious guard duty.

'Good job too,' muttered Dearing, whose inestimable patience was seemingly reaching its limits too.

'Said the sergeant who let an armed serial killer breeze into my hospital room unchallenged,' riposted Sinclair.

'Said the man who invited him, and let him walk out without alerting us.'

'You'd rather I let him kill me, kill *you*, shoot up a hospital?'

'I'd have taken my chances, and we had armed officers outside,' countered Dearing. 'But now another girl is dead.'

'And that's on me too, is it?' snapped Sinclair, rounding on him. 'Did I slip past you? Did you and your under-aged newbie slip off into the toilets for a bit of on-the-job training?' Dearing had no answer, and Sinclair settled back into his seat with a huff of satisfaction. 'I didn't kill her. I didn't kill any of them.'

'Doesn't make you any more likeable,' growled Dearing.

'They teach that diplomacy in police school?' Sinclair shot Stark a cross glance. 'And what about in the SAS, Mr Strong and Silent? You going to let him talk to me like that?'

'He outranks me,' replied Stark evenly. 'And I was never in the SAS.'

'Oh yes . . . Sorry, I forgot. You didn't make the cut.'

Stark didn't rise to the bait. Such things were not discussed. In the wake of the shootings, some tabloid hack had got wind of it. Another news cycle – more talking heads and Regiment-turned-novelist experts, suppositions and exaggerations. His subsequent refusal to discuss it during his interview with Gwen had only made it worse. Skin-deep media outrage at his special forces rejection after collapsing with malaria during the final test was offensive. You made selection or better luck next time, if there was one.

Sinclair didn't mention the malaria. 'You've gone backwards since then,' he mused instead. 'Weren't you a sergeant in the army, or was it only *acting*? Happy as a *grunt*.'

'Gleaming.' Sinclair could think what he liked. Of the growing regrets in Stark's life, serving in the ranks rather than command was not one. It might have been different. He had good university offers, in English, but his applications were never more than an exercise in self-knowledge. His father's death and lack of life insurance had long ago plunged the family into penury and put paid to such aspirations. If Sinclair had signed up, his first in economics would've funnelled him straight into officer training, emerging Stark's superior, and he knew it. Classic narcissist – one moment craving sympathy, the next belittling for dominance – just as Fran described. Or just a scared and put-upon creature, curled inside his coat of spines. There was little doubt he remained in danger, and he knew it. Behind passive-aggression lay a man denuded by prison and visibly jumpy, reminding Stark that he wasn't the only one to catch a bullet recently.

'I'm sorry. That was cheap,' Sinclair sighed, seeming to deflate, rubbing his eyes. 'I'm sorry about this morning, too. I was exhausted. I shouldn't have snapped. It's just . . . hard. Two years in prison terrified of another beating or being stabbed, and then I get out . . . Bad enough the world sniping at you from all directions, but I never thought I'd face real bullets. I know you understand, so I apologize.'

'Police officers develop thick skins, Mr Sinclair.'

'Soldiers too, I expect.' When Stark didn't answer, he stared disconsolately outside. 'I used to have family, friends, a future. For so long, all I could focus on was proving my innocence, being *free*. I thought that would be it. That this nightmare would end.'

Welcome to the club, thought Stark uncharitably. 'Life doesn't work like that.'

Sinclair glanced at him. 'No, I suppose not.' He sighed again. 'Does it get to you, the notoriety?'

'If you let it,' replied Stark. 'But they mostly say *nice* things about *me*,' he added, paraphrasing Leah Willoughby.

Sinclair nodded at that. 'Even so, perhaps we're more alike than you'll admit.'

I only share *willing* female company, thought Stark, but said nothing. Little point adding to Sinclair's litigious grievance, giving the snake what he wanted. *If* Fran was right.

'Do you carry a weapon, Joe?'

Detective Constable or *Officer* to you. 'I prefer a disarming smile, these days.'

Sinclair seemed disappointed. 'I would've thought a man of your skills would carry a gun.'

'Perhaps your majesty would prefer an armoured car and SWAT team?' muttered Dearing.

Sinclair ignored him again, bored of the old toy, testing the new, perhaps. 'You're a private man too, I think.'

Stark focused on the road and his mirrors. 'If you say so.'

'I was too. Before all this.'

'You preferred to avoid detection?' muttered Dearing.

Sinclair wrinkled his face in disgust. 'You can't *still* think I'm guilty?'

Dearing didn't reply. Emily's murder shook such convictions. Fran remained certain. But Stark had seen enough indiscriminate horror and ambiguity to lean more towards abductive reasoning than deductive; Occam's razor over Sherlock Holmes; thus: When you've eliminated the impossible, whatever is left, however improbable, is mostly likely true, based on the evidence available and the quality of your investigation, and should be presented thus to a fair and impartial jury to deliberate. Not as pithily quotable as Conan Doyle. 'Right now, we're just here to stop anyone taking another potshot at you.'

That closed the conversation for a few minutes, before the silence got the better of Sinclair again. 'I thought about joining the army.'

'Fascinating.'

Stark's disinterest owed more to his concentration on the outside of the car than the conversation within but seemed to irk Sinclair anyway. 'You think you have something I don't?'

Empathy? Restraint? Remorse? mused Stark, but again, the thought felt more like irritation than conviction, and not a little hypocritical. If this man really was innocent, he'd every right to bitterness. 'I don't know you.'

Sinclair didn't take the hint to change subjects. 'I'd have been good at it, I think.'

'A natural born killer?' suggested Dearing from the back.

Sinclair shook his head. 'Clear-sighted. Someone who can see what needs doing and won't hesitate.'

'And that's you?' Stark watched a van in the mirror turn off into a side road. His eyes were tired. Busy night streets could make it easier to ditch a tail, but harder to spot one.

'That's the nature of *my* job, too, or was . . .' Sinclair shifted in his seat, checking the wing mirror, nerves showing. This whole conversation felt like a mask for his fear, and perhaps loneliness. 'The press called me a vulture, profiting off my clients' misfortunes. But my job was to help them see clearly, make the hard decisions to survive.'

'Or pick over the corpse.'

'Make the most of bad situations. Creative destruction. It's a harsh world.'

Stark could hardly disagree. But there seemed nothing the press liked better than to vilify a suspect, trawling their past for any hint of darkness – and God help anyone cursed with an ugly face or crazy hair or even just caught on camera with a momentary sinister expression. One such image of Sinclair had become a staple of every news feature, alongside his smarmy good looks, flash lifestyle and business dealings. Prosecution by press; verdict by vox pop.

Sinclair mistook his silence. 'You think you're better than me.'

'At being human,' muttered Dearing.

Sinclair clicked his tongue, staring out the window as if he meant to pretend Dearing no longer existed. 'I'd have it in me, I think, to kill. Not what you're thinking,' he added before Dearing could scoff, 'not like the Strangler. God knows I've had too long to think about what it must take for someone to do what he did to those poor girls. What must've snapped. How that differs from killing in the name of duty or justice. Whether there might be a monster in us all.'

Stark glanced at Sinclair, wondering what really was going on in his head. He'd sat with tribal elders, interpreters and members of the Afghan National Army, all the while knowing they might be Red dressed as Blue or Green. Vigilance and suspicion were as necessary as they were, for the most part, unfair.

Dearing merely huffed, not buying a word.

'Perhaps Sergeant Dearing is a family man,' postulated Sinclair for the jury. 'Perhaps he has a beautiful wife and children. Perhaps he'd snap my neck like a twig if he thought I'd hurt them . . .'

'Damn right I would,' admitted Dearing, husband and father to two girls.

Sinclair nodded. 'And you, Joe? What creature did war let slip in you?'

Pray you never find out, thought Stark. The willingness to kill was a nebulous thing. Under sufficient stress, most may indeed have it. Only in the action itself would a soldier, armed with training, clarity of purpose and legitimate justification, confirm if they did or not. But there was a word for people who needed no inducement and the military did its best to screen out psychopaths – or at least steer them towards special forces selection . . .

Sinclair nodded at his silence. 'A natural born killer.'

Many times over, agreed Stark silently. Justified or otherwise by duty or right; a twisted amalgam of ice-cold logic and burning fury. A psychopath in all but conscience.

'You'd be a worthy adversary,' said Sinclair. '*Hypothetically* speaking. I didn't hurt those girls, whatever Sergeant Sunshine back there thinks, or Groombridge, Harper and Millhaven, the press and families or any of them. But whoever the Greenwich Strangler *really* is, they must be licking their lips to be up against the famous, formidable Joseph Stark, VC.'

'You talk too much,' announced Dearing, giving voice to Stark's own sentiment.

They pulled up outside the safe house, one of a small number the Met kept hidden for such eventualities. Parked opposite, an unmarked car containing armed officers. Need to know, and Sinclair didn't, though the fools could've made some effort to be less conspicuous. Stark was just glad there was no sign of press or betrayal.

43

'He's demanding what?'

'That CO19 withdraw,' said Stark, voice crackled with poor mobile reception. 'They stood out like a sore thumb. He's complaining that we've undermined his safety by bringing them into the loop.'

Fran closed her eyes. Minimum circle in the know, the lawyers had demanded. 'But now they *do* know, surely he's better off with them outside than gone?'

'I doubt this is about logic any more than it's about safety.'

Bloody gun-boys, thought Fran unfairly. All they had to do was sit in a car without being spotted . . . 'I'll get them to swap cars and come back.'

'He said that's what you'd try,' said Stark.

Fran cursed. 'Then I'll fill the sodding street with uniform cars!'

'Suits me. I can piss off home.'

'*Oh* no . . . You're in this for the long haul.' Harper's orders, but Stark didn't need to know that.

'Just so long as I get the first sleep rotation,' he replied, yawning.

For him to admit weariness spoke volumes. 'Sergeant Dearing outranks you.'

'I'll arm-wrestle him for it.'

Fran wouldn't mind seeing that, though if Dearing didn't win in the first few seconds they'd probably be locked immobile while seasons rolled by. 'Just make sure one of you stays awake.'

'To threats without or within?'

'Both.'

'Perhaps I should just handcuff the chatty wanker to a radiator?' he said, another yawn setting her off.

'Bosch and Moncrieff would *love* that. Getting to you, is he? Even Dearing would look the other way . . .' Fran grinned into the phone.

'That works both ways, though,' replied Stark. Alone with two police officers, Sinclair could throw himself down the stairs and scream police brutality. 'He's already asking for his phone back to call his lawyers.'

'And you said no.'

'Safe-house rules. I said he could use the landline but he doesn't trust us not to eavesdrop. He asked to use *my* phone.'

Fran chuckled. 'Because you're best buds now.'

'We'll have to work something out or it'll come back to bite us.'

'And in the meantime he can bite *me*. He wanted protection. And don't let your guard down. He can't be trusted.'

'Agreed, but . . .'

'But what?'

'I don't know,' Stark sounded thoughtful. 'He's erratic, scared. I know he's in danger either way, but . . . If this is all an act, it's a good one.'

Fran didn't like the way this was going. 'Don't let doubt creep in.'

'And you're not?'

'No,' she lied.

'He didn't kill Emily Thornton.'

'But he *did* kill the others.' Fran cursed inside at the growing hollowness of her confidence. If the original forensics *were* contaminated, before being lost, this whole case was built on shifting sands of circumstance and dislike. 'Just . . . don't turn your back. Any sign of press?'

'Not so far.'

'Stay awake then.'

'I ever say how much I hate you?'

'Yes. But we've worse enemies in higher places.' DAC Stevens could still blow this wide open.

Stark huffed. 'Not much we can do about that.'

※

Watching the firearms officers start their car up and drive away felt uncomfortably like watching your Chinook clatter back towards base leaving you deep in bandit country.

Stark left Sinclair to enjoy the view alone, half-smiling as if reducing his own safety was a personal victory. Wrongful conviction might make a man paranoid. So could being shot. And if any trust had been seeded in the drive here, CO19 had blown it. He glanced at Stark. 'I'll see if they try again.'

'I told them,' replied Stark. 'Come away from the window.'

'You'd like that, I'll bet,' muttered Sinclair, still peering out for trickery.

Stark settled into the dusty armchair. 'I find myself indifferent.'

Sinclair glanced at him, displeased. 'You think this is a joke?'

'The men in that car were here to protect you.'

'Says you . . . But someone leaked my release from Her Majesty's spiteful incarceration, and the second I stepped outside someone tried to kill me.'

Stark shrugged, what little energy had sustained him through the drive fading fast, and with it his tolerance for conversation. 'Rather you than me.'

'Says the man who stood between me and the gun.'

'I've had more time to think about it since.'

Dearing chuckled, a deep rumble in his chest, but Sinclair shook his head, amused. 'No, you'd do it again in a heartbeat. You can't help yourself.'

'Let's hope we don't find out,' yawned Stark, resting his head back and closing his eyes.

Sinclair said nothing for a few moments, perhaps waiting to see if Stark really would drop off. 'How do you stand it?'

Stark blew out a sigh. 'Stand what?'

'Them,' said Sinclair, voice tinged with disdain. 'Millhaven, Harper, all your little police pals, him . . .' he said, nodding at Dearing. 'The sheep?'

Dearing rolled his eyes, set three mugs of tea down on the table and settled on to the sofa to the protest of old springs.

'Is that what you think of the world?' asked Stark, struck by Sinclair's tone. 'Sheep and wolves?'

'There's all sorts of predators.'

'Like you?'

'Like us?'

'It's dangerous to think yourself above others.'

'And what's danger, to a *tiger* like you?'

Sinclair had done his homework, but Stark refused to bite. Just when he was thinking he saw a softer side, the man started talking of predators and prey. Not a unique worldview but one Stark tended to distrust. Sharks, tigers, wolves . . . As if man were not the fiercest creature *and* the most compassionate.

'And what does that make you?' scoffed Dearing. Sipping his tea. 'A Komodo dragon, poisoning victims with your foul bite and devouring them after they drop?'

Sinclair glared at him. 'If you believe the lies.'

Stark shrugged. 'We try not to.'

Sinclair's frustration hardly softened, and he returned to staring out the window, rolling his injured shoulder with a wince.

Stark recognized the signs from his own struggles, and those of fellow recoverers in Headley Court – pain, exhaustion, frustration, mood swings, paranoia. Fran was determined to attach a different label. Stark almost envied her. She'd come under fire too, seen death swoop down and snatch another before her eyes and pause to look her way, but she'd shown not the slightest sign of lingering effect, beyond making her marginally more cross with the world than she generally was already.

Dearing switched on the TV. The news was on. Emily Thornton and Sinclair. Muttering a curse, he flicked through channels, but police budgets didn't stretch to satellite subscription. Finding nothing better to his liking, he left it on some wildlife documentary.

Not tigers or crows, at least, thought Stark.

Finally at rest, his hands were trembling again.

Sleep held little offer of relief, but he was too tired to hold night at bay.

The next thing he heard was a loud crash, shaking the fabric of the house, shouting and a gunshot.

44

He was on his feet in a heartbeat.

Alone in the flickering blue of the mute TV. Reality or nightmare.

Commotion from the hallway. Shouting.

The door opened.

Shadow up the wall like spreading black wings . . .

A silhouetted figure in blue overalls and ski mask, raising a weapon. Desert Eagle.

Stark stepped inside range, gripping the arm as he rolled sideways. Gunshot, blinding, deafening. Twisting. A curse, bone-crack, and a clatter as the gun skidded across the bullet-torn carpet, choking dust rising from every surface from the concussion, mixing with the gun smoke. Stark continued his spin, pulling, sending his opponent across the room, crashing over the armchair with a yell of pain and surprise.

Another man in the doorway.

Element of surprise gone.

A knife.

Stark gripped the weapon arm but the man was ready, wrestling.

Stark glimpsed a large boot on the floor. Dearing's. Toes down. Prone. Still.

And shouting from the stairs, swearing, two figures struggling past the doorway – one in blue overalls, one not.

Stark's opponent took advantage of his distraction to force him backward, but he twisted with the momentum, sending the man falling towards the upended armchair – dragging Stark with him.

The next few seconds were pure melee, as the first man joined the kicking and punching while Stark concentrated only on twisting the arm until the knife dropped. The TV toppled and smashed, plunging the room into near darkness.

Three men, fighting on the floor in the gloom in a room containing at least one gun and one knife. Sub-optimal odds. Stark needed to act quickly to even them. Free now to retaliate, he set about it. Pure offensive.

His elbow made contact with a face, eliciting a scream and reduction in incoming blows. One guy tried to scramble up, but a well-timed kick sent him torpedoing head first into the old fireplace with a crash and cry.

Stark was on his feet.

One opponent lay still. Stark put the boot into the other, hard.

Moments later he had two men out cold and both gun and knife kicked far under the sofa.

Only then did he hear the silence.

The hallway was empty aside from the unmoving form of Sergeant Dearing, face bloodied. Stark called out for Sinclair, kneeling beside Dearing to check him over.

Outside in the street, tyres squealed away.

'How goeth the good fight?' asked Marcus pleasantly, setting out two glasses and pulling a bottle of Chardonnay from his fridge. You could say this about Marcus, he never let work frustrate humour. Crap days, he insisted, should be left at the door. The very antithesis of her, but his flat, his rules.

'Just pour the wine,' replied Fran, dumping her keys and phone on his kitchen worktop and taking off her coat.

First it was spare toothbrushes, and somehow since, they'd started leaving spare clothes in each other's flats. Neither of them seemed likely cohabitants, but there was something of Limbo about their current arrangements. Or perhaps she was just looking for grey lining to a silver cloud.

The day had been long and frustrating, and desperately sad. Another young woman brutally murdered, killer or killers roaming free, and Sinclair rubbing their noses in it. Scouring surrounding traffic cameras and CCTV had provided over six hundred vehicles in the vicinity of Emily Thornton's home in the hour before midnight, and thousands in the hours before that, none of which had so far flagged up on any cross-referencing. None of the houses on Nelson Mandela Road had private CCTV, and without anything to narrow the timing, they had nowhere to start. An old pale blue Hyundai had been caught on the nearby speed camera doing over sixty in a thirty zone at 23:43 hours. The nineteen-year-old driver's parents were unimpressed but unsurprised, saying he'd gone off the rails since moving into a house-share with mates a few months earlier. The idiot's mobile wasn't answering. Though as leads went, a reckless teenage speeder didn't exactly fit the profile.

Fingerprints from the murder scene had already been matched to family and friends, none of whom seemed likely candidates. Preliminary forensics might find more, but nothing had turned up so far. They were no nearer to finding the mysterious man who'd passed himself off as Patrick Burgess to meet Sinclair in prison and hospital, and no connection had yet been made to anyone matching his description from the original case files.

Having failed to draw any links between the murder of their car thief and the Talbot brothers, or indeed anyone on their irreducible list of suspects in the attempted assassination of Julian Sinclair, the matching bullets were now being discussed as possible coincidence through the usual high-speed peddling of hot guns.

Steam was beginning to come out of Harper's ears, but at least he wasn't taking it out on subordinates. Yet. It was a good thing Stark had been out of the way most of the day.

'I believe your phone is looking to end its misery,' remarked Marcus.

Fran had put it on silent as she left the office, but it was madly crabbing towards the counter edge on vibrate.

45

'Did you get the number plate?'

Stark shook his head. He'd only caught a glimpse of the departing van, as he ran out into the street.

'But a light-coloured cargo van?' asked Constable Barclay.

'Probably white. I didn't see enough of it for the make.' He'd reported all this with his initial call but Barclay had always been unsure around Stark, and the last time they'd spoken the poor lad had received a curt introduction to emergency field medicine under fire, elbow-deep in blood.

'Keep still,' muttered the paramedic, tying off the last stitch closing the two-inch cut on Stark's right forearm that he must have taken from the knife.

Stark huffed at yet another of the world's little repetitions. 'You're gonna get cut.'

'What?'

'Just something I'd forgotten I once said.' Another bloody shirt for the bin.

The paramedic added the dressing and bandage without further comment.

All in all, he'd come through relatively unscathed. It could have been worse. He glanced over to where Dearing was being treated. Stark had rolled his massive weight into the recovery position then monitored his breathing, but he'd not come round until the paramedics were working on him. Now he was trying to wave them away, insisting he'd had worse playing rugby, still swaying and slurring. The assailants had fired into the ceiling to obtain his compliance, then pistol-whipped him to ensure it. Like it or not, he was in a for a long night of concussion observation.

Stark shivered. It was cold out in the street and the ambulance blanket wasn't thick enough. Shock too, most likely. The paramedic shifted focus to Stark's knuckles, now both bruised and split, applying bandage and cold-packs and offering advice Stark wasn't listening to.

His mind was elsewhere.

On how lucky Dearing was to be alive.

And on Sinclair, and where the third assailant had taken him.

Blake Talbot.

Elder brothers, Dean and Troy, were recovering from concussions of their own, predictably tight-lipped and handcuffed to their trolleys in separate ambulances with a uniform constable each to accompany them. The paramedics had treated them like any other patient, but the coppers were not so polite. Sergeant Dearing was a popular figure.

He stared at the bandages, trying to recall the feeling of punching, feeling it slip away like a morphine high, leaving only aching incomprehension and the urge to go over to those ambulances and show Dean and Troy the true outcome of letting grief bleed into rage . . .

'Seriously, I can't even trust you with babysitting . . . ?' demanded an all too familiar voice. Fran, stepping into the light with Williams on her shoulder and all concern hidden behind exasperation.

Fran's night was going from bad to worse. 'You said it was dark.'

'Yes.'

The ambulance ride to the hospital had been a barrel of laughs. Stark usually became monosyllabic under questioning, but this was his version of shock – a deep, cold fury at the world and his inability to right it.

'So how can you be sure?' she asked, clinging at straws.

He raised his eyebrows, just short of a withering look. He knew his guns, as SOCO would doubtless confirm.

'All right, an IMI Desert Eagle. Not the Glock from the prison,'

Fran conceded. Trust Dean to pack a penis extension of a gun. 'I suppose Blake might've had the Glock. If they had an ounce of brains they'd have recycled it straight back on to the hot gun merry-go-round the moment they got home from the prison.' In which case they wouldn't catch a sniff of it again until NABIS linked it to another bullet in yet another, wholly unrelated crime. 'Or at least have dumped it after shooting their car thief mate in Tower Hamlets.'

Stark said nothing.

'How the hell did they find the safe house, though?' mused Fran to fill the silence. 'Or the prison.' She stared through the door Vista-matic at Dean Talbot, bloodied, bruised and handcuffed to his hospital bed, broken trigger finger splinted and bandaged. Troy was in the room opposite, stitches in his temple and chin from a headlong plunge into the fireplace, among other injuries. Both under guard. Both milking it and claiming concussion so they couldn't be questioned until a consultant ruled them fit, when Fran needed *answers*. 'Did you have to hit them quite so hard?'

'I believe I used proportionate force, yes, Sarge,' Stark snapped.

Fran hid her shock. Needling him was amongst her favourite pastimes, but he usually riposted with humour, however acerbic. He stared at the floor, jaw muscles clenching – like a man grimly clasping a pin-less grenade. He'd incapacitated two armed men and still blamed himself for letting a third escape with the prize. Dearing might've died, and somewhere out there in the dark, a member of the Talbot family finally had Paige's suspected killer at their mercy. Fran thought she should feel more ambivalent about that, but she didn't. She was steaming too. Maybe Sinclair deserved whatever he was getting right now, but that didn't make it right. The law was the law. And there remained a growing possibility that he deserved nothing but an apology and compensation. The very thought made her queasy, but she couldn't continue denying it.

Two in the morning; her brain hardly knew whether it was coming or going and her stomach lurched between calls to be filled and warning against any such action. 'Tell me you at least called Kelly.'

Stark stared at the ceiling, not quite rolling his eyes but certainly wishing for alternative company. 'Must've slipped my mind.'

'Useless,' she said despairingly. 'Well, I suppose we'd better get on with the paperwork.'

'Oh good,' Stark replied darkly. 'There was me worrying I'd have to go back to sleep.'

46

Groombridge stifled a yawn. Others had missed their beds last night, but Fran's update in the early hours had left him sleepless in his. And with this morning's terse summoning from on high, one of the more obvious implications of last night's disaster seemed about to befall them.

'Heads might roll,' muttered Cox, 'whether Sinclair turns up dead or alive.'

'One head, perhaps,' replied Groombridge. Every inch of him, to his copper core, itched to be at the hospital wringing the truth out of Dean and Troy Talbot. Leaving it to Owen was agony.

'I won't let that happen.'

'With the greatest respect, sir, I think you'll be hard pressed to prevent it.'

Cox's moustache rolled, chewing over this bitter truth. As soon as this hit the media there would be no stopping it. The snatching of Sinclair from their so-called safe house was the final nail in the coffin. Dead or alive, harmed or claiming harm, Sinclair or his lawyers, or even just Stevens and the IPCC, would make sure the shit hit the fan – having already stood Groombridge firmly in front of it.

Oh for a blindfold.

'They didn't say what they wanted?' asked Cox, again, clutching at straws.

'There can't be much doubt.' The Independent Police Complaints Commission didn't demand an 8:00 a.m. meeting to chat about the weather.

Cox's moustache set about rolling again. 'And how do we think they found out so quickly?' he mused. Meaning, who tipped them off. Sinclair's sharks, or Harper via his puppet-master, Stevens. 'Right,' he said, glancing again at the clock. 'I suppose we'd better get going then.'

Shadow wings up the wall, circling gracefully over the baking red sand crater, circling, growing, stooping.

Looking up into the desert eagle's glare as it bore down, smoke still rising from the pitiless black eye in the triangular anodized barrel, staring in endless, unblinking judgement.

STAAARK – the diving screech and flash of black wings – mobbing, mercilessly – deflecting the silver raptor in a vicious persecution of razor-beaked punches, kicks and elbow strikes and the joyous, burning, righteous thrill of violence . . . Singing its ode to death in mocking caws . . . *Staaark* . . . *Stark* . . .

'DC Stark . . .'

Shadow across his face, talons biting into his shoulder . . . Stark gripped the claw, ready to twist and snap –

'– *the fuck!*' yelped his assailant . . .

Dearing's rookie, bent double in a wristlock, eyes wide with fear.

Stark let go as if he'd been electrocuted, shuddering and blinking, heart and breath catching in his chest, croaking the kind of mumbled auto-apology given to the air after glancing shoulders with someone passing in a crowd.

The rookie backed away, rubbing his arm.

'I'm sorry,' Stark tried again, shielding his eyes in the over-lit room. 'I was . . . dreaming.'

'No kidding . . .' The rookie's mouth formed a smile his eyes couldn't match. Another tale added to the canon of Stark mythology to exercise wagging tongues and wariness back in the station.

'Never rouse a twitching tiger,' said Fran, eyeing Stark thoughtfully from the doorway.

Wincing, Stark creaked upright like his body was full of sharpened bones. He'd been lucky to escape without a bullet in the face or a knife in the guts, but that came at a price. Scrunching his face, he felt at the tenderness down one cheekbone and jaw, and the small cut on his brow. He checked the wall clock. Five hours? He barely remembered settling into the chair in the nurses' staff room, after insisting Fran nap in the only free on-call room. 'Did I miss the show?'

'Waiting on the lawyer,' replied Fran. 'Canny shites waited for the court-appointed loser to show up only to reject them and call their own.'

'Their own?'

Fran shrugged with a cynical expression. 'Who knew? Repeat-business rates, I guess. He's conspiring with his scumbag clients as we speak.' She looked at the rookie, frozen between them like either might explode. 'Fetch us some coffee, would you? Two sugars, there's a good lad.'

Whether she meant it as any form of kindness, he departed at the speed of relief.

'Nice kid,' she commented. 'Needs toughening up, though I'm not sure nearly breaking his arm was called for. How often *do* you thrash around in your sleep like that?'

'Too often,' replied Stark without thinking, still breathing deeply and rubbing his face to dispel the drowse.

She stared for a second, probably wondering about the impact of such nocturnal disturbances on whoever might share his nights, current or past. At some point today, he'd have to call Kelly back. 'Right . . . well, no sign of the van, Blake or Sinclair. Dean and Troy must be finished concocting their lies with the shark. Rise and shine, soldier.'

47

'Harpy and Millstone ...' drawled Dean. 'The old team back together.' As a taunt, it lacked both originality and conviction. He was in the shit and he knew it, in breach of his parole licence and, barring legal escapology, heading back to prison – it was just a question of how long for.

Derek Stubbs, the Talbot's 'family lawyer', was every bit the laughably clichéd slimeball Fran expected. The perfect accompaniment to Dean's sneering silences and mocking ripostes. Both knew the script, even at this time of the morning. It spoke volumes that the lawyer was willing to turn out this early on short notice.

A senior nurse was present too; concussion being to doctors as whiplash was to motor insurers. As it was, they'd had to lug the recording equipment up from the hospital's police suite to the ward's isolation rooms.

'We have you for possession of an unlicensed weapon and illegal discharge of same,' said Harper.

'You won't find my client's prints on that gun,' said Stubbs. Dean had been wearing mechanic's gloves, essentially just a thicker version of nitrile gloves worn by police and forensics.

'Might find his DNA on it, though, unless he was unusually careful. And discharge residue on his glove and overalls,' added Harper, pleased with himself.

'My client was fighting for his life with a man who pointed a gun at him. The gun went off. You will, I feel certain, find powder residue on the *assailant*'s hands.'

'The assailant?'

'Whoever brought the gun.'

'You think my officer brought the gun?' scoffed Harper.

'You've done just about everything else to protect that sick fuck,' spat Dean.

'What my client means,' hurried the lawyer to prevent any further ad-libs from Dean, 'is that he entered the house unarmed.'

Harper smiled. 'Well, putting that preposterous lie aside for a moment, let's focus on the word *entered*. You *entered* the house by smashing the door in, pointed the gun you claim you didn't bring in the face of a police officer, fired into the ceiling to scare him and then viciously assaulted him.'

'If anyone has been viciously assaulted here, it's my clients,' replied Stubbs evenly. 'And if that man was a police officer, he didn't make himself known.'

'I wonder who your clients expected to find upon breaking into a police safe house, if not policemen,' mused Harper. Fran had to admit, he was getting better at this. Of course, it helped to hold most of the cards in this game. 'One thing is certain, your *clients* are lucky that one officer had a thick skull and the other knows how to defend himself, or your clients might both be facing murder charges.'

'My clients knocked peaceably on that door to request a conversation with the man still suspected of killing their sister. They wanted closure, nothing more.'

'You don't knock on a door with a sledgehammer, or come peaceably in ski masks.'

'The door must have been damaged during your officers' unprovoked assault, for which compensation will be claimed. The sledgehammer, like the gun and knife, must have been at the property already.'

'And the ski masks?'

'Strange the things the police keep in their safe houses. Perhaps for moving people around incognito.'

'We didn't mention any knife,' said Fran.

'But my clients did,' countered Stubbs, with barely a pause. 'Having been threatened with one.'

'Your clients, and you, are full of shit,' said Harper, starting to lose patience.

'How did you find the house?' asked Fran, keen to move on past gloating to extracting actual information.

Stubbs and Dean exchanged glances. This was the obvious question and doubtless already rehearsed.

Dean shrugged. 'Followed you from the hospital.'

'Really?' Stark had insisted that was unlikely. 'What route did you follow?' asked Fran.

Dean shrugged again. 'We just followed.'

'So you were waiting outside the front of the hospital?'

They didn't fall for it. 'Let's just say we had the exits covered.'

'And which one did Julian Sinclair leave by?'

'It's a bit of a blur,' replied Dean, pointing to his bandaged head. 'Since your boy gave me this concussion.'

'Where has your brother taken Julian Sinclair?' demanded Harper.

'Troy's in the other room. Blake wasn't there.'

Harper laughed. 'Then who was the third man – Father Christmas?'

'What third man? Your officers can't count.'

Harper just shook his head in disbelief. 'Where has Blake taken Sinclair?'

'Blake is probably at home jerking off to porn as usual,' replied Dean, a faint smile leaching through. 'Perhaps Sinclair has finally realized what he is, and gone off to hang himself.'

Shit, thought Fran. Was that their plan? 'If Sinclair is harmed, or worse, it gets added to your charges under Joint Enterprise.' Assuming Blake's brothers had foreknowledge of his intentions – which was often harder to prove than you'd think. 'You'll go down for murder after all.'

'Where are they?' growled Harper, cool never far from lost.

'I'm sorry, I'd love to help you good officers of the law,' replied Dean, holding a hand to his head in exaggerated pain, looking to the silent nurse in the corner. 'But I just can't seem to think straight with this dizziness and pain.'

It's over, thought Groombridge.

The order for Cox's attendance was ominous enough, but the

second that DAC Stevens filed in with the IPCC panel, Groombridge knew hope was gone.

His union lawyer casually leaned into his ear and whispered, 'Friend or foe?'

Groombridge sighed. 'The latter in the former's colours.' A divisional commander's presence here was to stick up for his junior officers, in theory. The half-smile on Stevens' face confirmed otherwise. There was no way now that Groombridge was walking out of this room with his warrant card. But for the first time, he felt serious concern for Cox's career.

The Super was the figurehead. He sat above Greenwich's territorial and investigative branches. His involvement in any particular case was tertiary. There was no way he should be tainted by any of this, but the look on Stevens' face said he'd find a way to reap the maximum damage – *his shock and disappointment at the obvious failures beneath him . . . How he'd never before had cause to doubt their absolute integrity and good judgement, which only served to make this devastating litany of lapses all the more lamentable . . . How he'd always advocate clemency, and allowing his officers time to right their ship and make amends, but though it grieved him to the bone, the inescapable spotlight of the media on his mess of a case left him with no mitigation to offer . . .* Et cetera, et cetera . . .

Cox's grave expression confirmed Groombridge's every fear. His battle face; no bull or bluster. People mistook Cox for a buffoon but cornered, he'd come out fighting.

This was about to get ugly.

Stark watched the monitors as Troy was wheeled in on the same chair, still warm from his brother's backside.

It was hard to escape the feeling that this was a waste of time, and exactly what the Talbots wanted. Dixon and Hammed had been sent to question the matriarch, Rhonda, God help them. If she came out from behind her oxygen mask it would only be to spit bile. Far from the sharpest hammer in the Talbot toolbox, and less intimidating than his older brother, Troy was kept on a tighter leash by the lawyer.

Harper had fun with every cheap shot, but the lawyer deflected the questions with even more ease the second time round. Troy looked more worried than his brother, having fewer convictions and no time served. But they still couldn't get to him.

'Tell me about the Tower Hamlets connection,' asked Harper. Troy looked blank. Not a stretch for him. 'The van. Where did you get the van?'

'What van?'

Harper nodded. 'The little Dispatch, the bigger cargo van, either.'

There had been debate about where or when to mention the ballistics link to the murdered car-thief, Castor. Much as Harper wanted to pile on all available pressure, particularly on Tweedle-Dum Troy, finding Sinclair had to remain the priority, and the certainty of a murder charge coming their way regardless would make both brothers even *less* likely to volunteer Blake's location.

Troy folded his arms in silence, but Stark saw no flicker of recognition from either man. Either Tower Hamlets hadn't come up in their pre-match-conflab or Troy was better at poker than his mates had suggested. Or maybe his brothers had procured both vans without him.

Harper returned to Sinclair and Blake, plugging away on the topic with as little success as he'd enjoyed with the eldest brother. Getting nowhere, he tried his cheapest shot. 'Were you planning to bugger him?'

'What?' replied Troy, speaking for more or less the first time.

'Sinclair. Were you thinking of forcing him to receive anal sex?'

'What the fuck?' Troy looked appalled.

'There have been rumours about your sexual proclivities.'

'Fucking *lies*!'

Harper shrugged. 'Perhaps it would be fitting. Let him know how it feels. Do him like he did Paige . . .'

'You're sick!'

'Would you all have had a go, or just you? Take a selfie, raping the shit who raped your sister? Or would that be weird, like incest by proxy? What do you think, Troy?'

'Fuck you.'

'Why didn't you get a gun, Troy? Dean has his Desert Eagle and Blake gets a Glock, but you get a knife?'

'As already stated,' intervened the lawyer, 'Blake wasn't there –'

'I think he *was*. Didn't they trust you with a piece, Troy? Poor dumb Troy. What else didn't they trust you with? I bet they didn't even tell you the address of the safe house.'

The lawyer, Stubbs, placed a hand on Troy's arm to silence him.

'They didn't, did they?' scoffed Harper. 'Just sat you in the back with your little knife. You're a follower, Troy. Dean and Blake are the leaders. Did they tell you the plan? Did they even bother telling you where they planned to take Sinclair?'

Troy just shook his head, refusing to bite.

'It doesn't matter,' said Harper. 'No jury is going to believe Dean and Blake planned this without you. You're all going down under Joint Enterprise just the same. That's breaking and entering, firearms, knife, assault with a deadly weapon, grievous bodily harm and kidnapping – that's fifteen plus even before whatever your baby brother does to Sinclair while you sit there covering for him. If Blake kills him, you're all looking at life. Unless you tell us where Blake went and we get Sinclair back in one piece. It's your one bargaining chip and your only hope of breathing free air before you're too old to care.'

Troy was shifting in his seat, looking to his lawyer for comfort.

'Not to mention your idiot attempt at the prison,' added Fran. 'That's attempted murder right there . . .'

'That wasn't us,' blurted out Troy. 'Tell them,' he urged his lawyer. 'That was nuffin to do with us! They got nothing!'

'As my client says,' added Stubbs, 'you have nothing linking him or his brothers to that unfortunate incident.'

'Three men then, three men now – same target, same motive,' said Fran. 'If you have your client's best interests at heart, you should urge him to cut the crap before misguided fraternal loyalty lands him inside for life.'

It was clear from his face that Troy was scared.

Harper sat back. 'Last chance, Troy.'

48

'Worth a try, I suppose,' muttered Fran.

Sweating confessions out of hardened criminals like Dean was like breaking rocks, hard enough without a lawyer covering cracks. Troy was more squidgy than hard, but even he knew enough to keep his cakehole closed for once. He and Dean were looking at serious jail time, but somewhere out there their baby brother was doing a number on Julian Sinclair, and right now, that seemed more important to them.

Her phone rang and she pulled it out, expecting and almost dreading it would be Groombridge when she had no good news to offer. If Groombridge had been in the mire before, this shitstorm must surely have drawn up every possible lifeline. He might be prepared to go quietly for the good of the team, but the injustice of that was more than Fran could swallow.

But it wasn't him. 'Hobson? I hope you're calling with good news?'

'And a good morning to you,' replied the Tower Hamlets DS.

'Sorry. Long night.' She gave him the short version.

'*Okay* . . . Well, this is just another heads-up, for what it's worth. My DI is calling yours, but I thought you'd want this first-hand.'

'Please tell me you've got something linking Damien Castor to the Talbot bothers so I can march back in and slap them round the face with it.'

'No. But we found some more bullets from the gun that killed our Castor and wounded your Sinclair.'

'Where?'

'Crispy remains of a John Doe found in the boot of a burnt-out, stolen Ford Focus four days ago.'

'Friday?' The day Sinclair was shot outside the prison.

'Evening.'

'But *before* we found Castor.'

'Castor's state of decay puts it around the same time. Uniform thought it was just a typical TWOC-dump till it cooled down and SOCO popped the boot. Then it took the pathologist to spot the bullet holes. John Doe. Burnt. No prints, no links. Lucky we've got ballistics *this* quickly. I'm sending you the file. No sign of the gun itself. But this is where it gets interesting . . . He died with a broken nose and trigger finger.'

'Shit.'

'If this guy was your prison shooter, maybe Castor was there too. Feels like someone cleaning up after. Still fancy the Talbots?'

'Can't think of anyone likelier.'

'That's not the same.'

'No,' she admitted.

'Well, with the bullets link our DCI signed off on expedited DNA testing. We should have the results in a few hours.'

'Okay . . .' Fran sighed. As soon as they got an ID, she was going to have to spend more time shut in a room with the Harper charade, listening to Dean and Troy's smirking denials. As usual, a fresh angle too often just showed you a different puzzle. 'You know, my DCI always says a case is never closed till you know what really happened.'

'Hmm,' mused Hobson. 'I'm not sure we ever find out half the time.'

'I think that's probably what he means.'

They shared a moment of silent sergeant solidarity.

She'd barely hung up when it rang again, and this time it *was* Groombridge – with the worst news.

'Did you hear me?' he asked.

The blood was rushing through Fran's ears. She wanted to sit down, but she wanted to pace, run, kick the shit out of something or someone. It sounded noisy where he was, but he was keeping his voice even, though he must be screaming inside. 'Yes, Guv.'

'The Super's still on a tightrope, so don't go rocking the boat.

You can trust him, Fran. I know you've never really got on, but he'll always be more copper than brass.'

'If you say so.'

'It's a miracle the case hasn't been handed to National Crime. Stevens hasn't got everything he wants so far, so keep a level head. You know who you can trust and how to play the rest. You're *ready*. I have to go . . .'

'Guv?' But he was gone, suspended pending firing squad, leaving her alone as Stark would put it, behind enemy lines.

49

'I will read a short statement,' declared Harper, 'but there will be no time for questions.'

He surveyed his audience with that familiar mix of pride and impatience.

I'm in charge now, he wanted to say; Mike's news still swirling in his head. Suspended, pending full IPCC enquiry. That could take months, years even, with a career in tatters whatever the result. Sacrificed on the altar of blame, by DAC Stevens no doubt. Harper wouldn't make the same mistake. This was his time to shine.

'Around midnight last night, Julian Sinclair was forcibly abducted from police protection by three or more armed men.' Hands shot up and questions were fired amid a broadside of flashbulbs. Harper smiled inside, holding up a patrician hand and raising his voice over the mob. 'Two officers were injured and one remains in hospital, though his injuries are not considered life-threatening. Obviously we are investigating the likelihood that the abduction was carried out by the same individuals responsible for the previous attempt outside Her Majesty's Prison Belmarsh on Friday morning, but evidence is still being gathered. I can confirm that two men were arrested at the scene. The whereabouts of Julian Sinclair and whoever took him remain unknown. I have nothing further at this time.'

Harper snapped his folder shut and turned away from the barrage of questions, calls following him all the way back into the station.

'Chins up, you lot,' said Groombridge, entering at a brisk walk. 'You've all heard my news now, yes?'

Their faces said they had, and the significance was clearly not lost on anyone. Rumour had hit the online outlets with suspicious speed – DAC Stevens' doing, most likely. Williams and Hammed looked angry and Dixon crestfallen. Harper was covering his desolation admirably. 'It changes nothing. Do your jobs and let the rest take care of itself. No corners cut. Owen, this is your show, but keep Inspector Cartwright sweet – we're relying on uniform to find Sinclair before Blake Talbot strings him up.'

'If he hasn't already,' replied Harper unhelpfully.

'Fran, Joe, with me.'

They followed him out into the corridor and he wasted no breath on preamble. 'Your exams Thursday . . . I've spoken with Superintendent Cox and agreed that both of you *will attend*, no matter what. He will escort you there himself if necessary. Is that clear?'

Swallowed protests. Reluctant nods.

'Fran, you get to stay if you want, but get the roster sorted so neither of you are on tomorrow night. I expect you to turn up to your exams *rested*.' He stared hard until she nodded again. 'Here . . .' He handed her a small box of assorted chocolates. 'I've been saving this for a special occasion. Open it when you're alone or this lot'll pinch all the good ones.' She returned his knowing look.

'Right, Joe, you get to give me a hand with my boxes and drop me off on your way home.' Officers on suspension gave up all their police equipment, car included. Stevens had been clear that all such stipulations were to be observed. Groombridge had been blessed with a work car for the best part of two decades. For the near future, Alison's little Honda would have to serve them both.

'Home, Guv?'

'To bed.'

'We've all missed sleep,' said Stark, glancing at Fran as a case in point. He happened to catch her stifling a yawn and she glared at him. But his protest lacked conviction. Everyone was running on fumes, but the dullness in his eyes said Stark was running on empty and failing to mask the effects of a beating.

'Not all of us fought twelve rounds in the process. This mess isn't going away quickly. If you can't sleep, at least get yourself cleaned up and have a decent meal. Fran needs to start rotating her people and you of all people know that. But an early night tomorrow for *both* of you, regardless. These exams are *important*.' More than ever, now succession planning had somewhat moved up his agenda.

'What the hell are you doing here?'

Groombridge was getting used to that voice and that tone. 'On my way out, sir,' he said, turning to his accuser. 'Just getting a hand with my belongings.'

'Nothing case related,' said Stevens. 'You're done here. Take one file or case note from this building and I'll have you arrested. And that goes for your minions here,' he said unpleasantly. 'If they or any of your colleagues are found communicating with you it will be assumed that you're conspiring to misdirect an IPCC investigation, for which consequences will be dire – is that clear?'

'Crystal, sir,' replied Stark, all but standing to attention.

'That goes for all of us, sir,' added Fran, following suit.

Stevens eyed them both with suspicion but no foundation for rebuke. Groombridge might never have been prouder. 'Don't think for a second that the buck stops with your DCI here. I have a list of everyone who knew about Sinclair's relocation, and an even smaller list of everyone who knew the safe-house location. The two of you are on both.'

Groombridge felt his face darken. 'With respect, sir, my team is entirely beyond suspicion.'

'Really? And beyond reproach? asked Stevens. 'You've already bet your career on that and almost certainly lost. No one is above suspicion. And they're *your* team no longer. Go home, before I have you escorted from the building.'

'Sir.'

Stevens stalked away to inflict what damage he could elsewhere.

Groombridge saw Fran was close to one of her eruptions and Stark's jaw was clenching dangerously. 'Suck it up, you two,' he said under his breath. 'Don't give him the satisfaction. This is a setback, not defeat.'

'Why are we even fighting?' asked Fran. 'What the hell is that man's problem?'

'Ambition. Entitlement. Sociopathy; to name but a few.'

'All slap and no tickle,' said Maggie, appearing behind them, face suggesting she could summon no more damning summary of a man. 'You leaving?'

'Something like that.' Groombridge felt sure she'd heard the news.

'Well, don't take the front door. There's a bit of impromptu theatrics taking place on the doorstep.'

'As you've just witnessed,' stated Moncrieff, 'we've tried to get some answers but yet again "*no one is available*".'

'Because Owen's got just enough sense to decline your poison invitation,' muttered Fran as they watched on the screen in Maggie's office.

'Once again, police protection proves itself the exact opposite,' continued Moncrieff to camera. 'Beaten repeatedly in prison, shot on release, now kidnapped, and the police still deny conspiracy.'

'Two officers were allegedly injured,' said the blonde reporter, in her trademark red.

'Says who?' countered Moncrieff dismissively. 'Show me the medical records and I'll believe it.'

'She's a peach, that one,' said Maggie.

'That reporter's not much better,' said Fran. 'She was the one mouthing off behind us while numpty here was storming the clocktower. Scarlet Jennings. I never forget a face I come that close to feeding a microphone.'

'Hmm,' mused Groombridge, deep in thought.

'Julian Sinclair is in mortal danger, thanks to police incompetence, laziness and lies.' Moncrieff appeared to be getting unusually animated, radiating heat instead of her usual iciness. 'His kidnappers' motivation can only be misguided vigilante vengeance, thanks *again* to police incompetence, laziness and lies. When will they realize they can't hide the truth any more and admit their hateful campaign against Julian is utterly baseless, so whoever's taken him knows they have the wrong man?'

'I can see how much this matters to you,' said Jennings, with affected empathy.

'Injustice should matter to us all,' declared Moncrieff, with such conviction that Fran almost spat at the monitor.

50

Groombridge leant his head against the rest and blew out a sigh.

Nothing had passed their lips since Stark helped load his meagre belongings into the car and they ran the gauntlet of camera flashes and shouts out into the start-stop mid-morning traffic. Their silent procession from the station had drawn several sideways stares from the uniformed officers on the ground floor, bad news being the only thing in the universe travelling quicker than light. God knew what he was feeling right now. He'd walked the thin blue line almost as long as Stark had walked this earth and this was his thanks . . . The best man in the force, crucified for doing his job with diligence and expertise. Stark had witnessed the world's unfairness in love and war, but the police was supposed to be where that all stopped, where justice shone its light . . .

Not to mention the impact on the team, the investigation. Stark felt sick. If Fran was the beating heart of Greenwich MIT, Groombridge was the brain. Without him they were systemically futile. In this analogy Fran would diagnose Harper as cancer. Even if that proved half unfair, how would the Greenwich Strangler be apprehended now? The truth revealed? Justice served? Rhonda Talbot would almost certainly now lose her remaining offspring to prison and breathe her last before they breathed free air. And they were no closer to justice for all the other victims. Tragedy compounded. How would the universe ever be righted from all this crushing wrong?

'You look tired, Joe.'

'Perk of the job.'

'Isn't it just . . .'

There was more than a touch of déjà vu to this exchange, and all the hallmarks of an opening gambit. 'Something I can do for you, Guv?'

A glance found Groombridge fixing him with the penetrating stare he saved for career criminals, and Stark. 'What gave me away?'

'The half-empty boxes.' As soon as Groombridge handed Stark a filing box to carry down to the car, the meagre weight of it had confirmed his suspicions. The DCI could get a lift home from anyone in the station, or even a cab. Previous experience made Stark wary of being singled out as chauffeur.

'Bit obvious, I suppose,' Groombridge nodded. 'Okay. DI Harper . . . Do you trust him?'

'Should I?'

'Personally, probably not.'

Stark huffed faint amusement. 'And professionally?'

'I think that depends.' Groombridge sighed. 'I think the copper inside him will drive him to chase this case to the ends of the earth.'

'Without fear or favour?' A paranoid ego in the pocket of a malignant power.

'I suppose that's the question.' About as far as Groombridge might ever go to bad-mouthing a once-trusted colleague.

'You want me to keep an eye on him?'

Groombridge's face pinched with discomfort. 'There are wider agendas in play. Just keep your wits about you and a level head.'

'I don't think it's me you should worry about, Guv.'

Groombridge sighed. Asking Fran to keep calm and carry on was always more in hope than expectation. 'Keep an eye on her too, where you can.'

Stark nodded. 'And you?'

Groombridge gave a rueful smile. 'I'm sure Deputy Assistant Commissioner Stevens would be delighted to hear I'll be catching up on some gardening.'

And he'd be a fool to believe it, thought Stark. 'Was that it?'

'Just be wary. Stick with Fran. Anything you would ask or tell me, tell her.'

Stark nodded. 'And don't tell anyone about the chocolates.' If the

231

confectionery in that box didn't include a clean burner phone, he'd eat a chocolate hat.

It was Groombridge's turn to huff, neither confirming nor denying. Back-channel deniability. 'When all else fails, chocolates cover a lot of sins.'

'Guv . . .' Stark hesitated, but this might be his last chance to ask the advice of his most trusted guide. 'I don't know what to make of Sinclair. I can't decide. After everything that's happened . . .'

'What does your gut tell you?"

'That's just it. I can't tell. Something about him turns my stomach, I get why Fran's sure it's him.'

'Not just Fran,' Groombridge reminded him with a sigh at the potential size of their collective mistake.

'But . . .' Stark explained his suspicions that Sinclair was suffering from early symptoms of PTSD. 'There's too many signs to ignore. I can't help wondering if he's more victim of events than architect. And if he didn't kill Emily . . .'

'We're all thinking the same thing. Even Fran, though she'd sooner cut out her tongue than say so. It's hard to maintain detachment in this game. Ours is to reason why, what, where, when and who.'

Stark nodded, un-reassured. The problem with seeking wisdom was the wise knew to caveat all advice and throw out platitudes and aphorisms like anti-missile chaff.

He dropped Groombridge off, with awkward farewells. It was impossible not to grind one's teeth in frustration.

His phone rang.

This time he checked the ID.

He considered leaving it to voicemail but this wasn't going away, and he'd seen enough retreat for one day. 'Kelly'.

'You didn't call back.'

'No. Sorry.'

'Frantic at work.'

'You could say.'

'So can you talk now?'

Stark took a deep breath and let it out silently. 'Yeah. Sure. When did you say you were off?'

'You don't forget information, Joe. You don't forget anything.'

He winced. He only got away with playing for time when she let him, and he'd already stretched her patience. 'Saturday.'

'I wanted to see you *before* I go, Joe.'

'I know.' His mind was racing. *This is a setback, not defeat ...* The Guvnor's humbling courage left him ashamed. 'How about tonight?' the words were out of his mouth. No taking them back. Instinct bypassing reason; a need to know what she had to say. A decision, perhaps ... Another turning point in his war. Victory or surrender.

'Tonight?' said Kelly, surprised. 'Yeah, sure, that would be perfect. What time can you make?'

'Eight? Work willing.'

'Perfect. At the Princess. See you there. Thanks, Joe, *really.*'

'Okay. Tonight then. I'll text if something goes wrong.' Or I come to my senses, he thought.

'Tonight.' She rang off before he could backtrack any further.

Stark let out a breath, wondering if he'd be able to go with Sinclair still missing, and what selfish hopes might be confronted if he did.

He stared at his bandaged hands, suddenly feeling every ache and pain creep out from hiding.

51

Marianne didn't hear the key in the lock or the door open, but some shift in air pressure alerted her to Stark's return. She looked over from the homes-in-the-sun show she was using to numb her mind, and saw him quietly place his keys in the little wooden bowl on the end of the kitchen counter. Everything in its place.

There was an order to all he did, the way he moved, the way he spoke. Combined with his looks, scars and mythology, it had rendered her all but speechless during their earliest interactions. Waking to find herself existing in his space, worrying about making mess, causing disorder, had been daunting to say the least, but had quickly become comforting – being without all the things that cluttered her own life. Perhaps that was why he lived this way.

His brief speech at the therapy group had been revelatory, inspiring and heart-breaking, much like the man. And yet, much like him, it had left more questions than it answered.

What trauma she'd endured, she saw reflected in him a thousand-fold.

It was shaming, now, to recall her schoolgirl crush on him, to think how easy it had been to romanticize his past, to long to explore his hidden depths. To glimpse them now, un-rose-tinted, was to be overwhelmed with sadness. A light-swallowing abyss of grief and pain, over-bridged with towering courage. Now, she *adored* him. As one might love the sun on one's face and the sound of a sea-lashed shore, the rage of the waves against indomitable rock. Existing in his world was all one could wish for. He made yours better. But it was dangerous to linger. He was intangible, unknowable, reassuring and far beyond her reach. And the fact that he saw it too, that he'd not kissed her when she was there for the taking, resigned to his loneliness rather than drawing another close, was perhaps the most heart-rending aspect of all.

And now he was hurt.

'Joe? *What happened?*' Both hands were bandaged, his face bruised and cut, his movements stiff.

He looked at her with a tired smile. 'Long story. Fancy a brew?'

'Let me make it. You sit down.' He smiled thanks but didn't move away while she put the kettle on, holding on to the kitchen counter as if reluctant to move for the pain.

The hiss of the kettle rose to fill the silence and she felt his eyes on her as she readied two mugs. She wished she'd dried her hair properly and put on nicer clothes and a bit of make-up. Or at least put less water in.

After an age, the kettle reached its crescendo with a cheerless ping and subsided.

'The crow . . .' he said quietly.

Looking round, she found a fixed expression on his face, the same she'd seen as he held up a hand to speak in group therapy. She waited for him to continue; worried that if she spoke it would deflect him. The tattoo was recent. Since they'd both been shot. Marianne could still picture it clearly. A fine artist. The crow itself, beak open, cawing or snapping, wings arched back open, clawed foot reaching forward, was at once fearful and beautiful.

'It . . . represents a decision I made. A turning point of sorts.' A sigh escaped him, like steam. 'I see it sometimes. Or half-think I do. Some cultures consider them a portent of death, but sometimes it feels more like a warning, like it's watching over me.'

'Like a spirit-guide, or guardian angel?'

'More like a haunting. Ghost of deeds past, present and future.' He shook his head with a wry expression. 'Hallucination. Tricks of an injured mind. Life after death, of sorts.'

Was he trembling? With exhaustion? Or effort? 'Thank you.' She forced a smile, not sure why he'd told her or really what he'd meant, but knowing it was important. 'For telling me.'

He nodded, and then limped to the sofa as she set about the tea. When she turned around with two steaming mugs, he was asleep. Marianne sat down, watching him, and let herself quietly cry.

Fran opened the box of chocolates, helped herself to a dark caramel, then lifted the top tray out to explore beneath. The bottom tray contained a chocolate selection outer with a cheap mobile phone centre.

There was no note. Only hope.

Like most detectives, Groombridge had never bothered with a personal mobile phone, and he'd had to hand over his work one. Back channels – recourse of the covert competent when the idiots take over. A quick investigation found it to be programmed with a single number, un-named. This burner's twin. Making sure it was on silent, she replaced it and ate another choccy while ruminating on events.

Chocolate aside; terrible . . .

A convicted killer, released, shot, suing, and now kidnapped by the grieving brother of his youngest victim. Or an innocent man, with a legitimate grudge and sharp lawyers. A copycat murderer, or worse the killer all along, as-yet unknown and free to kill again any time they chose. Groombridge sacrificed on the altar of arse-covering. Harper in charge, to add twisted piquancy.

The world carried on outside like there was nothing wrong, while in this tiny cubicle Fran wanted to cry, kick and scream. But before she could do any of that, she suddenly spun round and threw up down the pan, retching to empty, spitting, flushing the fetid mess away, wishing she could do the same with this godforsaken situation. Investigative brilliance aside, a large part of Groombridge's effort was spent sheltering the team from up-chain shit-rain. Now she had Harper, Stevens' shit *funnel*. It was hard to see how things could get any worse but she hardly dared think that, for certainty that they instantly would.

Groombridge's advice on the end of a burner offered only thin hope, but it was all she had. Optimism, as a rule, hurt her head, but all of this – DAC Stevens, Harper, the IPCC, the rabid press and her crippling guilt – might all go away if she could just lay hands on

Emily Thornton's killer. And they had him on camera, albeit disguised. He'd strolled past two police guards to visit Sinclair, allegedly to *taunt* him.

A phone ring startled her, but it was her regular mobile and the office number. 'Yep.'

'Where are you, boss?' Hammed's voice, urgent.

Fran looked around at the toilet cubicle, wondering if somehow it might have absorbed some of the rage and frustration she'd retreated there to overcome. 'Why?'

'They've found it, boss – the Talbots' van. White Volkswagen Transporter. And you'll never guess who was inside.'

52

The first responders had turned off the engine but the corrugated plastic hose from the exhaust pipe to the driver's window had long since done the trick. Even with the doors now flung wide, fumes still hung in the air of the dank railway arch like a malignant mist.

Carbon monoxide poisoning.

Worse ways to go.

The littering of lager cans and bottle of vodka suggested self-anaesthesia.

Classic suicide.

Fran shook her head.

A person could be forced to drink themselves stupid, especially at gunpoint. And after that, the rest was easy to stage.

There was something almost comically clichéd about where the van had been found. Driving railways into the heart of Victorian London and across the river had left the city criss-crossed with miles of raised tracks supported on soot-blackened brick arches, quickly occupied by light industry, car mechanics, storage, contraband, stolen vehicles and, all too often, dead bodies. Fran could hardly think of a place more archetypal to the Talbot brothers.

A local had mistaken the fumes leaking out above the rotten, paint-peeled door for smoke, heard an engine running inside and called the fire brigade.

The photographer strobed away while the pathologist was inbound, they were told. She hoped it would be Marcus. She could really use a dose of Marcus right now, even if she couldn't bury her face in his shoulder and cry this mess away. His presence was calming. Her emotions still seemed all over the place and, between the stomach bug and cloying fumes, she could hardly look at the corpse. She'd be damned if she'd puke again.

She forced herself to stare at the poison-pink face.

How had things got this fucked up?

Harper was pacing up and down outside, on his phone. Reporting upwards. More shit for his puppet-master, Stevens, to fling at them. Another press shitstorm to follow. Julian Sinclair in the wind, God knows where, and Blake Talbot dead in a van.

'Is it true?'

'No comment,' replied Stark automatically, rubbing sleep from his eyes.

'If it is, you can't hope to keep it under wraps, and if it's not, just say so,' pressed Gwen, down the line.

'Did I mention this call woke me from a deep sleep?' Stark yawned.

'Because you were there last night, when Sinclair was taken? Tell me you weren't one of the officers injured?'

'Would you settle for no comment?'

'Shit. You okay?'

'My shrink might suggest it was too early to tell.'

Gwen sighed. 'Look, the hospital won't admit press, but the Talbots' garage is closed on a weekday and no one I've spoken with knows or will say where they are. I'm not asking for information, just *confirmation*.'

'A fine distinction.'

'Sinclair kidnapped from police protection – *by the Talbot brothers* – puts a serious spin on the scraps DI Harper trotted out. You've already got a leak. I don't want to watch this on someone else's channel later just because you're too inflexible to confirm it now.'

'I'm sorry, but if you want official comment you'll have to speak to my superiors.'

'Like who? DI Harper, who'd rather prance for the cameras? Or DCI Groombridge, who's where exactly?' It sounded like she could guess well enough. 'But I guess we're back at no comment again.' The frustration in her voice was audible. 'Off the record then – do you really think your as-yet-unnamed "other suspect" was behind all the killings?'

'Honestly – and I feel bad this being my only answer – I really don't know what I think.'

The ghost of Blake Talbot cleared his throat and shifted in his seat, staring at the camera and something beyond it. He looked pale and dishevelled on the small screen, with a split lip, bruising and what looked like blood in his hair. The frame stayed steady. The camera was on something stable.

Not ten metres away, one of the crime scene bods was zipping his corpse into a bag.

Connected to the SOCO laptop screen they were watching, via cable into the evidence bag, was the digital video camera found in the Talbots' van. Left for them to find. A serious-looking SOCO techie hovered, watchful, in case they contaminated it, or worse, hit delete.

He cleared his throat again. 'My name is Blake Talbot, and I make this statement of my own free will,' he began croakily, but then took a breath and blew it out forcibly. 'I have not been coerced and what I say is the absolute truth, I swear it on my mother's life.' He stared now into the lens, defiant. Had he any inkling he'd soon be dead?

On his mother's life, thought Fran. The brothers were entirely under the thrall of Rhonda Talbot, even while she clung to life. Was that the threat? Had Sinclair pointed out her vulnerability?

'Me and my brothers tried to kidnap Julian Sinclair,' said Blake, the words edging out uncomfortably, 'so we could force him to confess to killing Paige and the other girls. We took this camera to record his confession. We were willing to do whatever it took to get it. We got the location of the police safe house from an old school mate of Dean's. Danny Lamb. He's a copper in firearms now.'

'*Motherfucker*,' growled Harper, ever keen to overstate his clean-copper credentials.

Blake's breathing was laboured. 'But it all went wrong. And now Sinclair's got away.'

'*Got away,*' scoffed Harper. 'The fucker's right there behind the *camera.*'

'I told him what I did so he'd be scared of me,' said Blake, 'but then he got free and hit me and ran . . . and now someone else knows, there's no going back. The truth is out there . . .' He looked past the camera, to where Fran agreed Sinclair himself was likely standing, probably holding up sodding cue cards and a Glock pistol. 'I'm tired of living a lie. I want to spare my family more pain.'

Yes, that *was* the threat, thought Fran – more pain. Not just himself, his family.

Harper stiffened too.

The silence that followed was bitter and dark, but it seemed obvious to Fran that it had been explained to Blake what would happen if he didn't proceed.

'I confess my sins now entirely of my own volition.'

'Coerced? Volition?' whispered Fran. 'Those aren't his words.'

'You can't see his hands,' said Williams, craning his neck for a better view. 'What is it they say . . . ? We touch our faces six times a minute?'

'He's tied up,' agreed Harper.

'It was all a lie,' said Blake, face sickly, forcing the words out. 'Dean and Troy wanted justice and revenge, but I . . . used them. Because this wasn't the first time I'd asked Danny for a favour.'

'No, you got details of Sinclair's prison release too,' muttered Harper.

'Dean blanked Danny after he joined the filth, of course, but he was still a beat bobby at Royal Hill when Paige went missing, so I asked him for . . . information. He was glad to help. He gave me everything, all the details. He didn't want to tell me the grisly shit, but I made him. Because I needed to know. Because . . .' He faltered, face twisted with a confusion of emotions.

'Shit . . .' breathed Fran. All the details. Names, locations, timing . . . How, where, when and what. How had she missed this? But there was no mistaking where this was going. Firearms Officer Danny Lamb was about to have his feet held to the fire and if he confirmed any of this . . . The taut silence suggested everyone else was thinking the same. After Paige disappeared but before she was found, Blake had gained access to forensic details about how the other victims were taken, treated and disposed of . . .

Blake raised his eyes to the camera, visibly deflating in defeat.

Fran felt the air leave her too. *Person or persons* . . . Bloody *Harper* had been right all along! *Don't say it*, Fran pleaded silently. *Please don't!*

'Because Sinclair didn't kill Paige,' said Blake. 'For all I know, he didn't kill any of them. But I know he didn't kill Paige,' he stared fixedly into the camera, shaking. 'Because I did.'

53

'I never meant to do it,' continued Blake quietly, downcast. 'I never meant to . . .' His face tightened with anger, with frustration. 'She wasn't my *real* sister. Mum pretended, but we all knew. She wasn't adopted or anything. Mum just took the baby when her real mum OD'd. Pretended she was hers. Just said she'd had her at home like she did with me. She always wanted a girl. *Princess Paige.*' He almost spat the last words.

'Mum's lawyer, Stubbs, took care of the rest – birth certificate and all that. He was a . . . friend of the family.' Blake's evident distaste suggested his mother had entertained a few too many 'friends' for his liking. Lawyers weren't the oldest profession.

'There was always a connection with us, Paige and me; different from Dean or Troy. She felt it too. She'd flirt with me to get what she wanted; she could always twist me round her little finger. But if I ever tried to . . . meet her halfway . . . she'd knock me back, say it was wrong; pretend I was out of order. But we both knew it wasn't really. We weren't blood relatives; not close.

'And then she called me, that night, pissed, saying she needs a lift home. I'd just passed my test and Dean had lent me an old banger from the yard. She'd spunked all her money. Nothing left for a cab or night bus and her mates had gone AWOL. And like a tit, I went to pick her up. She was all over the place. All over me. Told me to stop on the way home, so she could piss on the kerb. She put . . . She put her tiny pants in her purse after . . . and she looked at me . . . she knew.' Blake's eyes stared back through the years as if he could see her now, staring back at him, flirtatiously . . . accusingly.

'She started it. She was up for it. But halfway . . . She started saying no. I thought . . . I thought she didn't mean it. And after I . . . I finished, she went *mad*, saying I'd forced her, *raped* her . . . I was just trying to shut her up. She was screaming, trying to get out of the car . . . I just wanted her to be quiet. There were houses all around . . . But . . .'

Tears streaked Blake's face as he lapsed into silence, slumped, the desperate confession seeming to have drained him utterly. Then he slowly brought his hands up to wipe away the tears. His hands weren't bound after all . . . ? 'It was an accident, I swear. I didn't know what to do. Till I remembered Danny, and realized I could pin it all on the Greenwich Strangler. And I did. I had . . . until now.'

The camera stayed on him for several more seconds, before cutting off. The techie stopped the playback to protect them from any button-pressing urges they might suddenly feel.

Fran's only urge was to vomit.

Her head swam with a vision of Paige Talbot, lifeless on the ground . . . victim, not of Julian Sinclair as Fran had been so certain, but her own quasi-*brother* . . .

Poor Paige . . . foolish youth deserved no such punishment. Fran felt tears prickling and blinked them away crossly, furious at her reeling emotions, staring with contempt at Blake's body-bag. Maybe it was all a horrible accident . . . lust, stupidity, panic and fear . . . but nothing excused what he'd done, or letting everyone who'd loved Paige believe she'd suffered even worse, while cheating them of justice all this time.

'Well, that puts a new spin on things,' murmured Williams.

'This is *bullshit*,' Harper spat.

But even he must see the doubt this cast. The anomalies in MO with Paige's body had previously been dismissed as improvisational haste, with a ready-made victim incapacitated through drink. Now they had a plausible alternative – a copycat *via* copper.

'Doesn't feel much like suicide . . .' said Williams.

'But a confession under duress can still be true,' said Fran, as wave after wave of nausea hit her at the thought of what *else* they might've got wrong.

Harper clenched his lantern jaw. 'Where's your boss?' he said to the techie. 'I want forensics all over this. Maybe Sinclair didn't kill Paige Talbot, but he killed the rest, and now he's added Blake to his tally.'

'And how are we going to prove *that*?' asked Fran despairingly. 'Blake kidnapped *him*. We could find his DNA all over this and it'll be argued away as legitimate transfer. And look . . .' She pointed to a box of disposable latex mechanic's gloves, covered in engine oil fingerprints. 'The Talbots thought they were being clever . . . What's the betting we don't find Sinclair's prints on that hose? Or the lager cans and vodka.' No, if Sinclair had done this he'd been as careful as ever. Blake and his video confession, gift-wrapped. Another hole in their case against Sinclair, and a zero added to his compensation claim against them.

No doubt the Talbots had covered their tracks to this place, but they were sloppy. It all might've worked if Stark hadn't whittled their numbers from three to one. Dean and Troy thought they were out for justice, and perhaps they'd finally stumbled into it. Blake's motives were darker. As well as the video camera, he'd brought along the corrugated hose and booze; to force a confession, then kill the confessor to prevent retraction. Two birds, one stone. It wouldn't have been hard to talk Dean and Troy into it. But Sinclair had freed himself and taken Blake by surprise. And as much as this all reeked, any impartial juror would still likely err on the side of suicide.

'No sign of that Glock,' said Williams. The pistol from the prison, and used to permanently silence the car thief, Damien Castor, and the John Doe afterwards – now leaving the disturbing possibility that Sinclair was out there in the wind with intentions unknown *and* a gun. Unless Stark was right and the Glock was long since back on the black market or dumped in the river . . . Who was to say Blake had a gun at all?

An armed response car was already outside Sinclair's flat but there was no sign of him yet, and the nasty thought squatting in the darker recesses of her mind kept whispering . . . Had her impartiality blinded her? Anger was fuel, but not always her friend. Maybe Blake had confessed at the point of a gun, maybe not. Maybe Sinclair had just escaped and this really *was* suicide? Maybe, just maybe, Sinclair really *was* just a victim in all this and she'd been wrong all along. If so, she didn't deserve to become a DI; she wasn't good enough. Harper had seen person or *persons* when she hadn't.

'Fuck,' said Harper, hotly. 'Fuck, fuck, *fuck*!'

Fuck indeed. Fran shivered, placing a hand across her midriff to control a sudden, churning panic, trying to remain outwardly calm when all she wanted to do was cry and let rip.

Harper marched his histrionics outside, yanking out his phone and passing Marcus without a word.

'I arrive at an inauspicious time, I fear,' said Marcus, looking as comedic as ever in his anti-contamination gear, if not as ridiculous as her. She could've kissed him. He sniffed at the fumes in the air. 'Ahh, the deadly pink kiss of carbon monoxide, I understand. Never sure why people think it's an easy way to go. Dying in your sleep isn't quite as gentle if you first have to pass out in a choking panic of foul fumes.'

'Cheery.' Fran pointed towards the lager cans.

Marcus nodded. 'I expect you'd like me to look for anything contradicting this sorry tableau?'

'If it's not too much bother.'

Marcus scrutinized her a moment. 'Are you well, Detective Sergeant? Forgive me for saying so, but you look a little peaky. Perhaps some fresh air . . . ?'

Fran fixed him with a level stare. 'Perhaps a lacy fan and a pink cushion to park my delicate derriere on too?'

Marcus smiled, unfazed. 'I may even have some smelling salts in my valise, for the hysteria.'

Williams winced, studiously averting his eyes and then his whole self towards some distant point of interest.

'Piss, and in case you need directions, off,' replied Fran.

'At, as ever, your service.' Not quite bowing like some little white plastic teddy bear version of Mr Darcy, Marcus pulled up his mask to cover his slappable smile and sauntered off to speak with the Crime Scene Manager.

Fran felt better already. So she called Stark. 'If I can't rest, neither should you.'

'That seems to be a common sentiment today,' he replied wearily.

'Don't tell me you've got company.'

'Was there something I could help you with, Sarge?'

Fran explained.

That seemed to shake him from sloth. 'Tell me we've got eyes on Leah Willoughby?'

'I thought you were Sinclair's new BFF?' she scoffed.

'It hardly matters what I think,' he replied humourlessly. 'He's nursing grudges, either way.'

'Is that an admission of fallibility?'

'To quote my sergeant: "I'm never wrong, only misinformed." '

Fran wasn't sure she'd ever put it so succinctly, but Stark was nothing if not distilled. 'Yet you still think you're the only one round here with a brain?'

'You picked her up?'

'First call I made was get on to Camden to send a car round under blues and twos.'

'Have Blake's family been informed?'

'I'm still staring at his corpse.'

'The way things are leaking, we'd better tell them quickly.'

'Said the soldier with a girl in every press room,' said Fran. His lack of retort was less likely an admission of guilt than just resentment, but she wouldn't apologize for suspicion. It was her job and she was good at it. And it had escaped very few people's notice that Gwen Maddox was a redhead of the hot variety. 'You can't trust her.'

'I can trust her to take no comment for an answer,' he replied. 'Which is why whoever's leaking chose a less scrupulous mouthpiece.'

'We may have found a leak.' Fran explained about Blake's police source.

'But what would Lamb gain by leaking to the press?' mused Stark, sensing her doubts.

'Exactly.'

'While we know a man who might.'

DAC Stevens. Stark didn't have to say it, but he was the obvious suspect – a man never to let the greater good get in the way of personal ambition and grudge. The advent of news-via-social-media had eroded the lofty heights from where broadcast media and print press might still wait for second-source confirmations. Nowadays, all you needed was a few anonymous Twitter accounts to get a story rolling so you could report on what was *'trending online'* instead and leave it to the police to confirm or deny. Why Stark thought Maddox any different was a mystery – as indeed was their association. Her rise from gutter-press-stalker to TV exclusive reeked. Stark, pinned in the spotlight he abhorred, answering or deflecting questions in his inimitable style – a diffident delivery of candid details and personal reticence, as frustrating as it was revealing. Fran had watched it online too many times already – usually after half a bottle of Chardonnay to lubricate a little vocal petulance at how infuriating it was to watch him offer up enlightenments to the public that it had taken her two years to unearth. 'Well, thanks for the tip,' she said peevishly. 'Now if you're quite done cavorting with the press . . .'

'My cavorting days are behind me, Sarge, you know that.'

She hung up, suppressing a smile. He pressed her buttons maddeningly, but as often as not, just when she needed it, including *re-set*.

If there was one thing she hated more than an unsolved crime, over-promoted detective inspectors, upstart detective constables or the press, it was self-doubt . . . and that was why, in general, she'd have no truck with it whatsoever. It was every sergeant's prerogative to remain resolutely suspicious until alternative facts emerged – correct unless misinformed. And she was a *good* sergeant.

Maybe Sinclair hadn't killed Paige Talbot or Emily Thornton, but that didn't mean he'd not done the rest; not yet at any rate. And Leah Willoughby – the one that got away, cheated her attacker, had to be watched, in case he came back to finish what he started.

54

Both Talbot brothers were still under concussion observation at the hospital, and as luck would have it, the lawyer Stubbs was already there.

Troy fell apart at the news; first accusing them of lying about Blake's death, then the manner of it and the confession. Descending into anger, he had to be subdued by the two uniforms and led away, disgorging nothing but abuse.

Dean was a different fish. Harder. More calculated. Prison time had taught him to hold his temper close and make plans. And never to trust the police. Flatly denouncing Blake's 'so-called confession' as a '*filthy* smear', his eyes narrowed at Harper's flat commentary on the apparent suicide. Fran saw the cogs turning. Still on parole, Dean would await trial in prison, and Troy's hopes of bail weren't much better – but there'd be a funeral. Dean and Troy could apply to attend, harbouring thoughts of absconding. Failing that, Sinclair could be hunted by proxy and made to tell the '*truth*' about Paige and Blake. If he ever found himself back in Belmarsh he'd be a sitting duck.

Keeping all such plots behind cold eyes, Dean did at least say enough to confirm that Paige wasn't their sister by blood. He said nothing about Stubbs' involvement, but fixed him with enough of a look to confirm there would be a debt for silence. Stubbs denied all knowledge. Sixteen years was a long time ago to trace the provenance of a dodgy birth certificate and he knew it. One look at Blake's video confession and he'd gleefully claim duress and decry it inadmissible while he dealt with any lingering evidence.

It had been decided to continue withholding any mention of the

Tower Hamlets killings with the John Doe ID pending, and Harper's efforts to elicit some connection to the prison shooting floundered embarrassingly between faux commiseration and toothless toughness. Emerging with nothing, he dismissed the whole thing as a waste of his precious time and sent Fran off alone to tell Rhonda Talbot of her son's death.

Fran could hardly believe she was looking at the same woman.

Stark had described her condition, but it was almost impossible to relate this shrunken husk to the firebrand from the public gallery at Sinclair's trial. Until she spoke. Even if the bile erupted as little more than whispered puffs of condensation inside her oxygen mask, the hate-filled eyes formerly reserved for her daughter's killer now saw only the police that let him walk free. Until Fran's news filled them with horror, denial, tears, and more blame.

Somehow, the stricken silence was worse than the abuse.

Fran gave what little detail she could, unsure how much was going in as Rhonda started emitting a pitiful keening – the agony of a mother's grief for a dead child. Fran thought of the love she felt for her nieces and nephews, but suspected she wasn't halfway there, and was struck with a rare urge to call her own mother. She'd always been a daddy's girl; her mother too frazzled with four older boys to pamper a girl. Her father had found the time by not pulling his weight, but a child doesn't see these things until it's too late. Fran didn't speak to either of them often enough.

The copper inside wanted to ask about Paige's parentage but the woman inside could not. Sentiment, pure and complicated . . .

Rhonda's watery eyes bored into her, searching, and for a second Fran imagined this poor woman, barely a breath from death and at the very apogee of sorrow, somehow sensed Fran's childlessness and dismissed her with a mix of pity and contempt.

Fran needed to get out before she started crying. 'I'm very sorry for your loss.'

She made it outside, the cold air helping her blink away welling tears, unsure quite what had set her off and twice as annoyed for that.

Her phone vibro-shocked her pocket. Hobson.

'Don't tell me. The charcoal in the car was Lord Lucan.'

'Nope,' replied Hobson. 'Nor Shergar the wonder horse. It *was* repeat offender, Istvan Kovacs, Thirty-two, IC1, convictions for theft, robbery, aggravated burglary, GBH and affray, possession of stolen goods, et cetera, et cetera . . . Known associate of Damien Castor, for all the good it did either of them.'

'Links to Julian Sinclair?'

'Nothing so far. No shared prison space with him or Dean Talbot. No links to the Talbots at all on HOLMES.' The Home Office Large Major Enquiry System. 'No links to any victims or families so far.'

'It's got to be more likely that they abetted the Talbots in some way, than they were crap assassins hired by the other bereaved,' Fran insisted.

'Maybe they were hired by the Talbots,' postulated Hobson, 'to keep their own hands clean? Maybe there's a third assassin out there, with or without bullet holes.'

'Maybe.' It sounded far-fetched, but paying others to do their dirty work didn't sound like the Talbots, and killing to cover their tracks seemed extreme even for them. Everything about this case felt extreme, like some pot-boiler thriller, but with all the key exposition pages torn out.

'Either way, the Talbots turned up in person the second time,' Hobson pointed out, upbeat. 'Can't exactly cover their tracks on that.'

Harper ground his teeth, watching the interview playback, fuming at Fran's blunt insistence that they inform Blake's family before hauling Daniel Lamb, Firearms Constable for not much longer, over the coals. Ever jealous of his promotion, her eyes now stabbed with blame for Mike's suspension, as if either were his fault. The difference between them was Fran felt exposed without Mike above her, whereas Harper finally felt free.

But while they'd dithered, the CO19 Chief Inspector had pulled rank and interviewed Lamb without him. Eager to eject his rotten apple without outside interference and in no mood for kid gloves. Leaving Harper to watch it all on repeat.

Harper had applied to CO19, back when it was still called SO19 and he'd been a wet-behind-the-ears constable, but numbers were limited and they were looking for more experienced officers. He'd thought about re-applying later but CID had opened up, offering greater scope for promotion and a better life for him and his beautiful bride. Jessica had always believed in him, eyes shining. Until the baby thing swallowed that light. It wasn't his fault he'd strayed after that. Well, it was but it wasn't. Coming home to see her descending deeper, weeks into months, hardly able to look at him, all light gone. Better she never found out. Especially now she was on the up, sober, steadier, happier. The joy on her face when he'd made Inspector . . . It was like seeing someone back from the dead; you'd never take them for granted again, for all the redheads in the world.

He'd have been a good firearms officer, though. He had the right stuff. Unlike Lamb. The rotten apple caved quickly, confessing to passing the original case details to Blake Talbot in the days between Paige's disappearance and the finding of her corpse, but insisting that it had never before occurred to him that he'd abetted the disposal of a body. In thinking he was helping a friend in pain, he'd effectively opened himself up to an accessory-to-murder charge. That would be a stretch, but it was enough to have him confessing to passing on information about Sinclair more recently. No money had changed hands, he swore, but fear over exposure of his previous indiscretion and the threat of Dean's wrath had been enough to squeeze the safe-house location from him.

His excuses fell on deaf ears. His weakness had placed other coppers in danger. Forgiveness for that was rarer than a hanging judge's mercy, as Harper knew too well.

Grudgingly, he had to admit the chief had done a half-decent job, with a cutting absence of sympathy for his officer's mistakes. The rest would be up to the CPS. But there remained one fly in the ointment . . . Lamb denied leaking information on the prison release.

The Talbots had denied that part too, of course. Criminals only put their hands up when they were red and caught. Confessions rarely fell from their mouths the moment the cuffs closed, like on TV. Copping to the prison incident meant tying themselves to the pistol used, the Glock that also killed Tower Hamlets partners in crime, Castor and Kovacs, and Lamb probably knew that too.

The surviving Talbot brothers would be charged, and their bullshit denials would be laughed out of court. But Harper wanted them for the prison shooting and murders too. Either Lamb told them, or they'd found out some other way or just followed Fran and Stark to Belmarsh.

If the CPS could only be persuaded to charge Dean and Troy Talbot with the shootings, then he could concentrate on Sinclair and his bullshit accomplice, AKA Burgess. Whatever the latter's real name, Harper was sure they were in it together. Perhaps they had been from the start. Maybe that was why the MIT had so much trouble building a case against Sinclair – perhaps he scouted the girls and his accomplice grabbed them . . .

One thing was for sure: he, Detective Inspector Owen Harper, was going to nail them all and come out of this shiny and cash in, whether DAC Stevens got what he wanted out of it or not.

55

'Okay,' said Harper, taking the canteen seat opposite Fran in a funk of cigarette odour. 'It's time we talked.'

Fran looked around slowly. 'I have a carefully cultivated reputation around here for being a moody cow, so if you think cornering me in a public place is going to keep me civil, you might want to rethink your timing.'

'I'm serious. What's it going to take to persuade you I'm on your side?'

'Resignation?'

He wasn't amused. 'Seriously . . . That's your answer?'

'I'm just trying to enjoy a quiet coffee here,' she replied, wondering whether she might get away with 'accidentally' tipping it in his lap five minutes before his next press parade.

The TV in the corner was still alternating between the face of Sinclair, the Talbots and the arches crime scene with accompanying reporter commentary. Not Stark's saintly pal Maddox. The 'less scrupulous' crimson-lipsticked mouthpiece. *'With unnamed sources claiming the two kidnappers in custody are Dean and Troy Talbot, speculation continues online that the body is that of their brother Blake . . . leaving the inevitable question . . . Where is Julian Sinclair?'*

Where indeed? The story had broken twenty minutes ago and grew more rabid by the minute.

Harper glanced at it too, irritation visible, probably still silently blaming Stark. 'And while you're sat here moping, hoping what . . . ?

That some uniform numpty trips over Sinclair's corpse by accident and scoops the glory?'

'*Glory?*'

'You know that's not what I meant,' Harper insisted, but if he'd been trying to light her fuse it was too late to stand back.

'How would finding Julian Sinclair tortured and hung from a tree be glory for anyone? Except your pal Stevens?'

Harper looked confused. 'How would any of this help *him*?'

She shook her head in disbelief. 'Can you really be so thick? Your lord and master will pull whatever shit he can to shut us down and get his gerrymandering power-grab plans back on track.'

'That's crazy. Overseeing the capture of the Strangler will make him look *twice* as good.'

'You just don't get it, do you?' said Fran. 'The difference between you and him is that you still care about looking good when all he cares about is getting ahead.'

'I care about *doing* good.'

Sometimes, Fran conceded, but she didn't say it.

Harper's eyes narrowed crossly. 'So what . . . ? You think he put me here to sabotage the investigation?'

'If the shoe fits.'

He looked incredulous. 'I'm here to help catch a killer.'

'And help yourself in the process. To boost your *ego*.'

'You just accused me of being here to *sabotage* everything.'

'Not through spying,' hissed Fran. 'Just through *incompetence*.'

Harper blinked, anger replaced with shock. 'Is that . . . Is that what you really think of me?'

He looked so hurt she almost recanted, but then she remembered the real leader of this team was sat at home and cussedness prevailed. 'Believe me. If you didn't keep popping up like the proverbial that just won't flush, I'd cheerfully never think of you again.' This might be the career equivalent of climbing a hill in a thunderstorm with a copper umbrella, singing 'All the gods are bastards!' at the top of her lungs, but he'd picked his moment poorly. Pushing her coffee away, she stood to go. 'Hadn't you better run along now?' She jerked her head towards the front window, where the press were gathering outside. 'Your adoring fans await . . .'

'As you're already aware, earlier today the body of a man was found under railway arches in Plumstead,' Harper announced to the massed microphones and cameras blocking the street outside as Stark watched live upstairs, still feeling as responsible for the current mess as he felt useless to resolve it.

'Now that the family have been informed,' Harper gave the mob an admonishing pause, 'we can confirm that the body *is* that of Blake Talbot, brother of the fourth victim in the Greenwich Strangler case and suspect in last night's kidnapping from police protection of Julian Sinclair, former suspect in the Greenwich Strangler case – recently released, conviction quashed. The manner of Blake's death is still being investigated. In answer to speculation, we *can* now confirm that his two brothers, Dean and Troy Talbot, are in custody, pending charges regarding the kidnapping. The whereabouts of Julian Sinclair remain unknown, and we urge him to make contact on the number on-screen, or anyone who may have seen him.'

Gwen was going to be seriously pissed off with him again, thought Stark with a sigh.

'Is he alive?' asked one reporter.

'We've reason to hope so.'

'What about online reports that he's not only alive but armed with a gun?' called out a mellifluous female voice.

Harper tried to hide his shock as the camera switched momentarily to the all-too-familiar platinum blonde in her crimson coat.

'We can't comment on speculation,' he replied curtly. 'But the public are urged not to approach him as he may be in a distressed state and present a danger to himself or others. Further updates will follow as and when . . .'

'What do you say to rumours this investigation may be linked to two fatal shootings in Tower Hamlets?' asked the same voice.

Harper's jaw tightened. If it *was* Stevens leaking all this, it didn't look like his stooge was in on it. 'Investigations are proceeding on a number of fronts, as you would expect.'

'Isn't that usually code for you don't know what's really going on?'

That was just plain rude. Perhaps Stevens' pocket hack was paying for her scoops with targeted agitation. Stark almost laughed at the thought of an embarrassed Harper trying to get approval to investigate *that*. 'On the contrary, it's an assurance that progress is being rapidly made.'

'Again, why are *you* telling us this?' asked the provocateur. 'What of the rumour that DCI Groombridge has not only been removed from the case, but suspended pending dismissal?'

Harper snapped his smart leather folder shut. 'No further questions, thank you.'

No further questions ... If only that were true, thought Stark, clicking again on Blake's confession, hardly more cheering – especially on a third viewing. It reminded him too much of other videos he'd seen. Captured aircrew, kidnapped NGO staff or journalists ... confessing in futile hope beneath jihadi banners. His blood ran cold.

'His hands weren't tied,' said Williams, peering over Stark's shoulder at the completed playback.

'But his ankles and waist could've been.'

'The pathologist didn't find any signs.'

'It's not hard to bind someone without leaving marks.'

Williams glanced at him, perhaps wondering whether he knew that from training or experience. 'He'd been in a fight, though; nasty bang on the head ...'

'Consistent with his prisoner's fight for freedom.'

'Nothing contradictory from SOCO on site,' Williams said. 'Forensics pending.'

'Any prints and DNA will just show Sinclair was there,' Stark predicted.

'No need for bleach.' Williams nodded.

No, thought Stark, just a little clear-sightedness. Someone who saw what needed doing and didn't hesitate. The only time the Strangler had left any forensic evidence had been when Leah Willoughby escaped before he could obliterate it. Assuming that was Sinclair ... Assuming the lost DNA *hadn't* been cross-contaminated as his barrister asserted to trigger the case review. But mistakes *did* happen, and Sinclair wouldn't be the first man locked up for crimes committed by another . . . Fran might burn Stark for heresy, but the fact that Sinclair couldn't have killed Emily, and might well not have killed Paige, floated in the middle of this horror show like an iceberg in the fog, when the last thing they could do was slow down.

'You think he's innocent?' asked Williams, looking to Stark for some kind of lead.

'Not of this,' replied Stark. Staring at the screen.

'Reckon he had a gun on Blake,' said Dixon hopefully. 'The missing Glock.'

'We can reckon all we like, but if it walks like a suicidal duck and quacks like one . . .' Williams sighed – a rare and dismal indicator.

Stark cursed silently. He should've taken more precautions, anticipated that if the Talbots were capable of finding out about the prison release then they might learn the whereabouts of the safe house too. Now Blake was dead and Julian Sinclair was off radar, possibly armed . . . either guilty and monstrous or scared and aggrieved.

He stretched painfully, stifling a yawn. Being woken by his phone, fully dressed beneath a blanket on his sofa, was a common enough occurrence, but looking over to find an elfin blonde insistent on whipping him up hearty brunch while he showered was a welcome addition. A little bunk-time and rations was just what the medic ordered when you'd taken a beating, but it was no miracle panacea. 'What about the Burgess lookalike?'

'Nothing new,' replied Dixon, busy with Hammed rearranging one of the incident boards around a historic mugshot of Blake Talbot.

'And the speeder?' asked Stark, looking at the flash-exposure photo of the blue Hyundai hatchback.

'Delinquent still hasn't made contact. Fran was going to request a phone ping, but what with everything else . . .'

'Your phone's ringing, Joe,' said Hammed, pointing to Stark's desk.

An internal ringtone. Stark reached over the stacked files on his tiny desk. 'DC Stark.'

'Call for you, sweetie,' said Maggie, queen of the control room. 'Says he knows something about last night's kidnapping.'

'Name?'

'Wouldn't say. Called the switchboard, not the hotline. Says he'll only speak to you. Bit peevish. I'm recording the call.'

'Okay, thanks.' The line switched. 'This is DC Stark.'

'What's all this bullshit about being a danger to the public?' demanded an all-too-familiar voice.

56

'Where are you, Julian?' replied Stark, waving for his colleagues to shush. Urgent faces said they'd heard the caller's name.

'Safe. Or so I thought till your Inspector Harper set the world and their slavering dogs on me.'

'Well, perhaps you can come in and set the record straight.'

'You'd all love that, I'm sure.'

'Are you hurt?'

'Not much, no thanks to the police.'

'Tell me where and I'll come and get you.'

A small, bitter laugh. 'No offence, but I think I'm safer if your organization, for want of a better word, doesn't know where I am.'

Hard to argue with that right now. 'We need you to make a statement.'

'I'm not convinced your needs align with mine.'

'We have a duty to protect you.'

'*Duty?* Then how did the Talbots find me?'

'I can't comment on that.'

'How did he die? The one that took me, Blake? Did he kill himself?'

'I can't comment on that either.'

'He was still breathing when I got away. Before you go saying I had anything to do with it.'

But *what* was he breathing when you left, wondered Stark – fresh air or exhaust fumes? 'Why don't you tell me what happened?'

'Someone in your team tried to have me killed; *that's* what happened. You can't fit me up, so you feed me to the wolves.'

'Let's not jump to conclusions.'

'That's all you've *ever* done,' scoffed Sinclair bitterly.

'Not me.'

'You expect me to believe you're better than the rest? Did you even put up a fight last night, or did you just wave them through?'

Sergeant Dearing was still in the hospital, but Stark bit his tongue. Sinclair probably guessed this was being recorded. All this innocent indignation could yet be for the benefit of the tape. 'What is it you want, Julian?'

'The same thing I've always wanted – exoneration.'

'You've had that.'

'I'll never have that,' he complained, 'until your lot accept I'm innocent and tell the world you were wrong about me, wrong all along. Even then I'll never get my life back. You're still telling the world I'm dangerous. You *know* I didn't kill Emily Thornton from my hospital bed. Leah Willoughby and her drink-addled fantasies were utterly dismissed in court. Your so-called forensic evidence mysteriously disappeared before it could be re-tested. There is absolutely nothing real linking me to the other victims ... and Paige Talbot ...'

'What about Paige ... ?' Stark held his breath in the faint hope that Sinclair might let slip knowledge of Blake's video confession.

'*He* killed her. Blake. He told me it was him.'

'And why would he say that?'

'He was going to kill me. He wanted to gloat, or scare me.'

'Rather hard to corroborate, under the circumstances.'

The silence down the line suggested that wasn't the response Sinclair wanted. If he was responsible for Blake's death, he was smart enough to guess the police wouldn't buy suicide – that was just plausible deniability, planting the seed of reasonable doubt. What he'd want, was to know if they bought the confession, and so far that at least hadn't appeared online.

'But something your idiot colleagues might've considered, if they'd not been so busy besmirching me,' said Sinclair coldly.

Hard to argue with that too. Blake's confession might have been made under duress, but there was a ring of truth to it. It seemed an unlikely thing for Sinclair to have thought up unless Blake had indeed confessed it to him in hubris. It was, when it came down to it, hard to argue with anything Julian was saying, and if that left nothing but Stark's faith in Groombridge and Fran, perhaps it was time to shine some uncomfortable light on that too ... 'I wasn't on the case then.'

'But you are now. You know I didn't kill Emily. And I didn't kill Paige. When will you admit I didn't do any of it?'

'When we've reason to believe otherwise.'

'Guilty until I somehow prove my own innocence,' Sinclair said, with audible disdain. 'As ever.'

'We don't decide guilt,' replied Stark. 'We pursue evidence.'

'Or fabricate it.'

Stark wondered if Sinclair was recording this too. He should probably stop talking. 'No. Charges were brought against you in good faith, supported by evidence, resulting in a conviction.' Could Sinclair hear the doubt creeping into his voice?

'Since quashed. And your saintly DCI Groombridge on his way to being sacked. What does that say about the strength of your evidence?'

That the truth is often hard to establish, thought Stark silently, not wishing to read such words back in the papers or a lawsuit. That Julian hadn't killed Emily or Paige. That all they'd ever had on him was circumstantial locations, lost forensics, the addled recollections of a drugged victim and his inherent unlikeability. The gut-churning possibility that they may have ruined the life of an innocent man while the real killer roamed free. Seen thus, Sinclair's unpleasantness might be the only justice in this mess. 'Where are you, Julian? There's still people out there who'd wish you harm.'

'Thanks to you and DI Harper, with your laziness and lies, painting a target on my back because you're too scared to admit you got the wrong man. Are you going to guarantee my safety?' he scoffed. 'Under your protection, I've been falsely accused, my reputation and business destroyed, wrongly imprisoned, shot, kidnapped and you're still making out it's all *my* fault. I'll take my chances alone, thanks.'

'That's a mistake.'

'I don't think so.'

Stark felt the conversation slipping away . . . 'Have you ever met or had contact with anyone called Damien Castor or Istvan Kovacs?'

'No. Why?'

'Are either of those names familiar to you?'

'No,' Sinclair insisted irritably. 'What's this about?'

'I'm not sure yet. Did Blake have a gun?'

'Oh, here we go again. You never *listen*.'

'Only, if we had that gun, we might tie it to your shooting at the prison and the Talbots with it.'

'Surely you can't be in any doubt?' Sinclair jeered. 'You *can* count to three?'

'Evidence lets me sleep easier.'

'I don't know how *any* of you sleep at night.'

'If you do have that gun, or any other, you'd be far safer turning it in.'

'If you didn't shoot me in the process. You'd love to think I have it, wouldn't you? To be able to say I was dangerous after all. You never give up.'

'Like I said, give me reason to. Come in. We'll talk about it, just you and me. Start from the top. Your side of everything.'

'No. I think it's time I made the most of my hard-won freedom, *without* police interference.' The line clicked off.

'Well, he's a barrel of laughs,' announced Maggie's voice. 'Got the number. Mobile. Pinged off a tower near Euston.'

'What do you mean, *gone*?' said Fran, coming to an abrupt stand-still just inside the office, clearly unhappy with whomever she was speaking to on her phone. 'When was she last seen?' She listened intently, displeasure coming to the boil. 'What the *hell* . . . this wasn't a patrol item! We've all got budgets to keep to, but I tend to prioritize the lives of the public above that sort of thing. Leah Willoughby is in clear and present risk of kidnap, torture, rape and death – no, we *do* have a firm suspect, possibly armed with a pistol – yes, of course he's a legitimate suspe—'

263

It wasn't often that someone dared interrupt Fran, but the person on the other end was either foolhardy or senior enough to go toe-to-toe with a stroppy sergeant from outside their borough.

'No, that will *not* be good enough,' said Fran. 'Yes, I can get my inspector to call you, but while we're waiting for that, how about you pull your finger out and scour the streets . . . You utter fucking *twat*!' she finished, evidently having been hung-up on. 'Rats from a sinking bloody ship!' she spat. She looked up, meeting Stark's eyes, her expression as grave as his own must be.

If he'd been wondering how all this could possibly get worse . . . now it seemed Leah Willoughby was missing.

57

'Camden sent a car like I asked and told her about Sinclair, but now they're saying she's gone. They swear they were sat outside but she slipped past them somehow, assuming they didn't nip off for coffee and doughnuts or blithely continue their patrol,' said Fran, evidently disgusted. 'Shat themselves when they realized. Pulled the old suicide threat line to persuade the letting agent to let them in. No signs of disturbance. Her mobile is unreachable.'

'Family?' asked Groombridge. 'Didn't she have a mother somewhere?'

'Died last year,' replied Fran, voice distorted over the background traffic noise. She knew better than to make this call anywhere inside the station. 'Not that they were close. And that was it for family.'

'Friends?'

'None left, as far as I can tell. I've called the few I had noted from the case prep. Leah was so angry after the trial, before it even – those that didn't leave she drove away.'

'Boyfriend?'

'How would we know? And I wouldn't blame Leah if she never let another man near her. Camden say they're checking local pubs and shops, but they're still giving us the runaround ... Her job centre says she misses appointments. Victim Support have never heard from her. The neighbours told Camden that she comes and goes quietly and we're the only visitors they could remember. We can't list her as missing yet, but Owen wants to put out a press statement saying we need to speak with both Leah and Sinclair. You can imagine the chaos that would cause ...'

'Assuming Stevens sanctioned it.'

'What's the betting it's in tonight's news anyway?' said Fran, taking his meaning. Stevens would far rather this come out as an embarrassing leak than a pro-active appeal. 'You think Owen realizes he's providing the water for this leak?'

'What have I taught you about conclusions?' Groombridge chided her.

Fran made a face. 'Reach. Don't leap.'

'I don't believe for a second he'd conspire wittingly.'

'Just wit-*less*-ly,' Fran suggested. 'He'd rather believe it was Stark than DAC Sugar Daddy.'

Groombridge detected a hint of defiance that often suggested she was refusing to feel bad about something. He waited, allowing a pause to lengthen.

'I may have accidentally expressed doubt in his motivations,' she confessed, with a quick summary that doubtless flattered her side of the confrontation.

'That wasn't wise.'

'He tried playing nice. He was lucky I didn't slap him.'

'Your version of keeping a level head.'

'Exactly,' Fran insisted. 'Anyway, he'll find out how much he can trust his lord and master once this is all over.'

Indeed he would. 'You can say it, you know.'

'Say what?'

'That maybe we got this one wrong. That Julian Sinclair could be completely innocent.' Groombridge hung it out there, half hoping for outrage, for affirmation . . .

'It doesn't bear thinking about.'

'Perhaps it's time it did.' Neither of them wanted to believe it, but the job wasn't about what you wanted, it was about truth. 'Maybe the forensics *were* contaminated. It happens. And what have we really got on him beyond a questionable witness and coincidence . . . ?'

'Other than a powerful dislike . . . ?'

'Exactly.'

'I'm disliking a lot of people today,' she replied pointedly. Her version of a sigh.

'And yet you've started calling Owen Harper by his first name?'

'Slip of the tongue,' she countered irritably.

'If you say so. Anyway, Leah could be anywhere, out feeding the ducks, buying groceries or drowning her sorrows in some pub. It's too soon to assume she's been snatched up by Sinclair or anyone else.'

'Too soon,' replied Fran, audibly frustrated. 'It's always too soon until it's too *late*.'

Stark watched Fran yank off her coat crossly, cheeks slightly flushed with cold or anger. No coffee or Danish from her preferred local bakery, she didn't smoke and wasn't likely to have popped outside for a quick chat with the press encampment. A private call then. And there were only two likely people she'd brave the elements for – Marcus and Groombridge – and Marcus made her cheeks flush for different reasons.

'Got any of those chocolates left?' he asked innocently.

'Piss off,' replied Fran, glancing around pointedly.

'Sarge . . .' Dixon waved, hanging up his phone. 'That was the kid with the blue Hyundai caught on the speed camera near where Emily Thornton was dumped. Only he's claiming he sold it a week ago.'

'Likely story,' Williams scoffed disparagingly. 'Do you reckon he's more scared of the points on his licence or that Daddy would stop coughing up for insurance?'

'Who'd he say he sold it to?' asked Fran. 'DVLA still have it registered to him.'

'Just some bloke, through some car sale app. Paid in cash, took the signed V5 Sale Declaration with him saying he'd post it to the DVLA on the kid's behalf.'

'Idiot.' Williams shook his head at the teenager's naivety. 'So he's still liable for any speeding fines, congestion charge, bridge tolls and murders.'

Fran sighed. 'Description?'

'Forty-ish. Brown beard. Baseball cap. That's all he could remember.'

'Could be our mystery prison and hospital visitor,' said Hammed.

'Yeah,' said Williams, 'but what kind of idiot dumps a body in the dark corner of a park and then makes their getaway at conspicuous velocity past a reflective-yellow speed camera?'

Reasonable logic, but Fran generally insisted the world was almost entirely populated by idiots.

'The kind who wants to get caught,' suggested Hammed. 'Serial killer show-off. Sicko getting off on fame . . . Maybe they're fed up with letting Sinclair take all the credit.'

There was a moment of silence. Sinclair hadn't killed Emily. He probably hadn't killed Paige. Now Hammed's words reflected a paradigm-shift to a world where this whole thing – Karen, Magda, Teresa, Leah and Sara – might be the sick actions of person unknown. Just as Harper had said on day one.

Fran nodded reluctantly. 'All right, ask the kid if the buyer called his mobile or emailed. Maybe we can trace them.'

'It was both,' said Dixon, holding up his notepad and rattling off a phone number. 'Pay-as-you-go. Currently switched off. I'll get the networks to notify us if it switches on.'

A burner. The email wasn't promising either. rdh**91@gmail. com. 'Predictably anonymous,' muttered Fran. Emails were much harder to trace; you could set up a new account any day of the week. Bring back the good old days when everyone still used their names in their email address. 'Let's ask Google if they can tell us when and where this email address was set up and used . . .' No one laughed. Silicon Valley giants weren't renowned for revealing their users' private info to law enforcement. Another dead end. 'You passed the Hyundai's details to uniform last night?'

Dixon nodded. 'Nothing so far.'

Which left them exactly nowhere. Fran did her best to inject some urgency, but in truth this was still a tenuous lead at best, like all the others . . .

The phone Sinclair had used to call Stark was also a disposable, registered that morning. They were still trying to trace the point of purchase but that was unlikely. Triangulation put the call from streets near Euston Station but it was switched off now or ditched. Whether or not Sinclair was as clever as he liked to think, he knew the basics. Transport police at Euston were already checking his image against their CCTV. Nearby Kings Cross Station and St Pancras International too. Maybe he was planning a long train journey, one-way. Otherwise, what was he doing so far north, and how had he got there? And how had he paid for the mobile? Cash? The prison said he'd been arrested with a wallet-full, so he'd been released with the same. Maybe he just took a cab? His legal team insisted they knew nothing of his whereabouts, for what their assurances were worth.

Most worrying: Euston wasn't far from Camden, with Leah's flat nestled in its northernmost border with Haringey.

Heads were soon drooping. They needed more hands. Harper had been summoned to Scotland Yard and returned in a sullen mood – the pressure doubtless mounting.

Stark necked the tepid coffee that had appeared beside him some time earlier, yawned and stretched painfully. The various pains of the previous night's fight had taken advantage of his sedentary afternoon to settle in and make themselves uncomfortable.

The previous night's . . .

'*Shit!*' he breathed, pulling out his phone. It was dark outside and . . . after eight. No text. Yet.

Dixon looked quizzical. 'What is it?'

'I was supposed to meet someone.'

'Personal and important, is it?' asked Fran pointedly.

Stark made a face. 'Kelly.'

Fran's arch look disappeared instantly. 'You're supposed to be meeting *Kelly*?'

Stark could only nod.

She should have been pleased but was obviously happy to park that while she subjected him to her very best *men-are-useless* look. 'And you're supposed to be where right now?'

'Princess of Wales.'

Fran stared. 'Well? Go on, then – hop to it. John, give this numpty a lift so the paparazzi don't spot him and tag along. Text her you're on your way. Say it was my fault. No buts . . .' She held up a hand. 'You've looked half-dead all day, you're sod all use for a late night here anyway, and it's rude to keep a girl waiting. Text me after, let me know what she wanted.'

Stark raised an eyebrow.

'In the morning, then?' asked Fran, pushing her luck quite deliberately.

Stark made a face. 'Dream on, Sarge.'

58

One text and thirteen minutes later, Stark entered the pub at a brisk hobble, forty minutes late, far from comfortable with his ejection from the search for Leah, or the impending conversation.

Kelly hadn't responded to the text.

The barmaid looked up and frowned in recognition. Katy, friend and ally to Kelly, waiting to see if he'd behave before deigning to smile. Taking in his bruised face, bandaged hands and limp with a weary expression, she tilted her head, directing Stark's eyes to a table in the far corner where Kelly sat watching him with an expression somewhere between relief and annoyance.

Stark was just glad she was here.

He was both apprehensive and happy to see her, after everything he'd done to hold hope away from him, to hold her away . . .

Perhaps he'd done enough, turned a corner as Doc Hazel insisted. Perhaps his unsteady first steps and bar-stool pick-ups had actually been leading him here.

Kelly smiled. 'Joe . . .' she stood to kiss his cheek. The cool brush of her silken hair, the subtle waft of jasmine perfume, the warmth of her skin exploded into his senses like an IED. 'Thanks for coming.'

He looked into her cornflower-blue eyes, her faint smile, and saw she was nervous too. 'It's good to see you.'

She gestured towards his face and hands. 'Should I ask?'

'Best not.'

'How are you otherwise?' she asked, glancing at the silver leaping-tiger handle of his cane as he hooked it over the adjacent chair and sat opposite her. 'Your leg?'

'Healing.'

She smiled at the one-word dodge, but it faded. 'You look tired.'

He shrugged. 'Work.'

A tight smile said she'd hoped for more but with little optimism. And then, to his dismay, he saw that old flicker of sorrow as her eyes scrutinized him. Like the inverse of falling seamlessly into banter between old friends, she knew him too well to miss the pain he tried to hide and he knew her too well to miss the sadness it caused her. 'I tried to see you, in the hospital.'

'I know. I'm sorry. I wasn't fit to see anyone.' The truth of this didn't make it sound any more satisfactory.

Kelly watched him for a moment more. 'Your mum let me in while you were sleeping.'

That, he hadn't known. 'She never said.'

'I made her promise not to.'

'I don't know what to say.' Or what she could have thought, seeing him, lying there one barely conscious decision from death.

'And then you were gone. Back to Gosport. She tried to persuade me to come down, but . . .'

But he'd made his feelings clear. No wonder his mother had fussed around him quite so crossly. Thank God his sister had already given her two grandkids, or the occasional barbed remark would have been the least of her lashing. 'She didn't mention that either.'

There was a two-thirds-finished pint of Guinness on the table and a half-eaten mezze plate of olives, cheese and prosciutto, their favoured pub nibbles. 'I was hungry,' Kelly explained, 'since you so rudely kept me waiting.'

Stark tried a hangdog smile. 'Fran told me to blame her.'

'Just so long as you don't answer your phone when she calls.' It had been the cause of their first date abandonment in this very pub, and others since. 'Usual?' Kelly asked, glancing at the bar.

'If Katy will serve me.'

'Unlikely, but I'm buying.' Kelly nodded to Katy, green-light to a prearranged plan. 'Have you eaten? Shall I get more nibbles?'

Stark realized he'd not eaten since Pensol had fed him, reminding him that wherever this led, it couldn't be his place – that thought itself filling him with a hollow sense of shame.

'We can order something else?' asked Kelly, sensing something amiss.

'No.' In the world Hazel painted, regret had to be accepted along with everything else, but guilt was hardest of all. 'I'm not sure I'm hungry.'

He'd not meant to say it that way, but she took it negatively. 'I'm sorry. This is –'

But whatever it was, was cut off by his phone. In a strange way, the irony of it, the shared look, helped ease the moment.

'Fran?' asked Kelly wryly.

'Amazingly, no.' Pensol. He left it to voicemail. Now was hardly the time.

'Damsel in distress?'

'Not really.'

'Young, beautiful and besotted, though?' Kelly watched him carefully.

'She's got bigger problems than me.'

'But you're a factor?' Her expression seemed to contain both sarcasm and empathy . . . and possibly jealousy.

'The bullet they pulled from her lung was a greater one, I'd say.'

Her disapproval evaporated. 'One of the officers who was shot, when you were?'

Stark nodded. 'Everything else is just . . . collateral damage.'

'Is that what I am?'

The suddenness of the question brought Stark up short, more than the truth of it. He was saved from answering by the materialization of Katy bearing a frosty pint of lager and a double whisky. 'The good stuff,' she announced, by implication suggesting she'd rather have served him the cheap shit in a dirty glass. 'Another plate?' she asked, never looking at Stark.

Kelly shook her head and Katy withdrew, if watchfully.

'I think that beer got colder on its way from the bar,' said Stark.

'I may have been spotted in here drowning my sorrows a while back.'

There wasn't much to say to that. 'I'm sorry.'

'Are you?'

Another direct question, worthy of an honest answer. 'Yes. I wish I could say I never meant to hurt you, but –'

'You were trying to spare me greater hurt,' Kelly interrupted, making a point. When the moment had come, he'd fumbled his explanation abominably. He was too tired and she was too upset. But she was way too smart to misread his reasoning.

'I was in a bad place.'

'And now?'

And now . . . he wasn't? That would be a lie. The monster within him still prowled the dark. That was what he'd held back from Kelly, the wellspring of all their pain. Was he a fool to hope it would hurt her less a second time around? The nightmares of blood and war came less often these days, the flashbacks hardly ever, but the crow had screeched its warning against hope all the same.

'You haven't touched your drinks,' said Kelly. Nor answered the question, she didn't need to add.

His stomach was twisted in a knot. 'I'm not sure I'm thirsty either.'

'Joe . . .'

'What did you want to talk about?'

'Can't we just enjoy a nice drink together?'

'For old times' sake?' The tiny barb in his voice was meant for him alone, but she heard it all the same. 'I'm sorry. It's just I'm not sure I can enjoy anything without knowing why I'm here. My head doesn't know whether I'm on parade or patrol.'

'And your heart?' Her limitless blue eyes shone like searchlights on his soul, exposing, blinding, mesmerizing.

'My heart says what it always has.'

'What does it say, Joe?' She wanted the words that burned. The words that bind. Three little words. 'Say it, Joe,' she pressed, eyes imploring. 'I need to know.'

Three selfish words.

'Just say it,' she sighed. 'Say you love me. Too much to expose me to the demons you hold inside. Too much to let me help you chase them away. Too much to hold my hand in case it burns me.'

'Why, Kelly? Why now?'

'Because it didn't work,' she stated, suppressed emotion tightening her features. 'It was too late. That thing inside you that has you so scared of what you might do . . . it already tore out my heart.'

Everything he'd feared, he thought miserably. But that didn't mean he was wrong. You couldn't treat a burn without removing the heat.

'Silence . . .' she sighed after several seconds. 'Has nothing changed, Joe?' Frustration. Accusation. That had changed. A few months ago she would have held those in.

'Something has,' he said. 'Or we wouldn't be here.' And there, the barest flinch in her eyes. A truth concealed. And all his fresh hopes, foolish and selfish as they were, dashed upon the rocks of his own stupidity, with this untimely meeting suddenly making the worst kind of sense. 'You're seeing someone.'

59

She *had* called to slap him in the face, after all.

The silence felt like an eternity.

Kelly actually looked guilty, as if she had any cause.

Stark forced what he hoped was a smile, despite the futile self-recriminations inside. 'And you're going on holiday together on Saturday?'

'Yes, but –'

'Let me guess . . . Robert?' Another flinch said he'd guessed correctly. The two-faced Doctor Charming from her work. He'd smiled and shaken Stark's hand, his covetousness ill-concealed. 'Well, he's got what he always wanted.'

'Joe, that's unfair.'

'I'm sorry,' replied Stark with total honesty. He'd never considered Robert a threat, but it should be no great surprise that the good doctor had swooped in to inveigle himself with silken commiserations and honeyed words. Stark had discarded her. Robert would never treat her so.

'It's not –'

'I should go,' he interrupted, standing and retrieving the cane.

'Joe, *no* . . .'

Stark found he could no longer look her in the eye. Not because he blamed her, but because he knew that while this was the best outcome he should hope for, it felt like the worst. 'Thanks for the drinks,' he smiled tightly. 'It was good seeing you again.'

He wanted to say goodbye, or good luck, or that he wished her and her new beau every happiness, but words faltered and his legs carried him away, past the scowling Katy, cleaning a glass like she'd far rather be throwing it at him, out into the night.

He paused, leaning on his cane, catching the breaths choking his chest, fighting the shame. The cool air stung his dry eyes, taunting him to shed tears he'd no right to. He stared up into the starless April sky instead, expecting his own personal rain shower, but perhaps even the sky felt he was beneath its contempt.

Wisps of mist hugged the ground like ghosts from the Black Death plague pits, commonly said to have given Blackheath its name, clawing their way above ground to savour his mood. The tramp across the dark expanse made little impression on his consciousness beyond the plodding cold and vague acceptance that his shoes would need cleaning in the morning. His mind covered many times the distance, zig-zagging between his conversation with Kelly and all the previous ones, had and not had.

Dixon had promised to text him any developments but his phone remained silent. He considered diverting to the station but felt drained, sore, miserable and useless, and if those weren't a good enough reason to go home for curry, beer and a whisky or three, then what was?

When the paranoia struck it almost came as a welcome distraction. The punching, chilling, hyper-alertness; ears and eyes straining for danger without, ignoring all within. Madness masking madness. Behind and to the left, there *was* a figure crossing the heath, stirring eddies in the mist to catch aflame in the distant streetlights, but heading in the opposite direction. Just another poor sod tramping home – hopefully after a less disastrous engagement – and Stark refused to have his wits tricked again by these phantoms of dangers past.

Yet still his skin prickled . . . at something beyond . . . a sound . . . a motorbike idling at the heath edge, rider sat astride, silhouetted and still. No lights on. It was too dark for paparazzi photography. Just another innocent, another phantom. He was so tired of these *imaginings*. Sick to death of this pointless, wearing vigilance. As if his fractured mind didn't have external concerns enough. Grinding his teeth, he accelerated into the rising fog like *Titanic*, heedless of ice. Reaching the far edge of the heath, he hobble-jogged between cars, unable to stop himself checking his six or believing the nothingness he found.

The walking cane took up tutting as he skirted the top of Greenwich Park. The few gates in the high brick wall surrounding it were closed off after dark, though that didn't prevent the odd overnight stabbing inside, as Stark knew from his first case here two years and a lifetime ago. Reaching the south-west corner, he turned north, where a twin row of mist-bound oaks slanted the narrow Chesterfield Walk footpath with eerie shadows.

Stark froze, all but sniffing the air, imagining wisps of breath from behind every tree, cursing himself for paranoia but feeling encircled. He only realized that his hands had gripped his cane, pressed just beneath the tiger handle and twisted when, with a quiet *snick,* the eight-inch steel stiletto slid out of the shaft like a cold-steel snake-hiss in the darkness, waiting . . .

Car lights passed down Crooms Hill, away to his left.

. . . leaving a bike engine, idling with no lights.

Stark turned quickly across the damp grass, determined to confront or dispel this madness. But as he reached the street-lit road, the bike revved and the black shape sped away into the impenetrable murk.

Somewhere above and behind, an abrupt clatter of wings lifted away into the night sky . . .

60

Fran watched the poised figure clip coolly down the stone steps on patent heels, phone pressed to ear, to hover by an expensive black car, pristine and polished all.

The call finished. The phone disappeared into a designer handbag, and the car unlocked itself as the woman reached for the door. Keys were passé for those for whom time was money. People who left work after nine at night because they were billing every second.

'Tell me where he is?' asked Fran, stepping from the shadows.

'*Jeeezus!*' Moncrieff clutched a hand to where her heart might've been, had she possessed one. 'What the *fuck*?'

'Tell me where Julian is.'

The Bitch Barrister collected herself, like cracked ice freezing smooth, looking Fran up and down with a mixture of impatience and disdain. 'Like I told you before, I have no idea where he is, and you'd be the very last people I'd tell if I did.'

'You confess that you'd lie? Deliberately mislead a police investigation?'

Moncrieff's perfect face pinched. 'Don't try to be smart . . .' She eyed Fran's dumpy frame. 'It doesn't fit.'

'You had a plan. Somewhere to tuck him away after your grand prison-release press parade.'

A rare flicker of discomfort told Fran she was right. 'There was no parade, thanks to you. Instead you led him out like a lamb to slaughter. Not once, but twice. You should just be grateful he's alive. You're in enough legal shit already.'

'I'm just a sergeant.' Fran smiled darkly. 'I leave gratitude and legal worries to higher pay grades.'

'You think the buck will stop with them?'

There had been a moment, after the Bitch had eviscerated Leah on the witness stand, and later made Fran herself look a fool, when the corners of Moncrieff's dark lipstick had twitched upwards. Fran had sworn to herself that if she ever saw that smug smile again she'd punch it. It took all her will not to do so now. 'But what's in it for you?' she wondered aloud. 'You've done your job. Or is Bosch cutting you in?'

Moncrieff's eyes flared with indignation. 'Alien as the concept might be to you and your lazy, incompetent, corrupt colleagues, some of us act purely for *justice*.'

'Then take me to him and prove it.'

Another flicker. Concern? Pain?

'You really *don't* know where he is, do you?' For the ice queen to crack like this . . . 'Oh my God,' said Fran slowly, a shocking possibility impacting like a slow-motion slap. That maybe, just maybe, all the Bitch's bluster wasn't just for show. For the first time in this hellish dance, she suspected Moncrieff actually *believed* . . . And with that suspicion came another, more horrifying – that she wasn't in it for the money or prestige at all. Not any more. 'You're in *love* with him.'

The barrister's face froze in shock, as if Fran had reached across the courtroom to tear her wig and gown off, revealing fetish gear beneath. 'How *dare* you?'

'How dare *I*?' spat Fran. 'How dare fucking *I*? Justice, my arse. All this time you've acted like the smartest person in every room, and it turns out you're just a lovesick fool.' She watched Moncrieff flinch. 'The least credible witness in court. I've seen fuckwit doormats lie their arses off to alibi worthless, abusing boyfriends before, but you must surely be the most deranged. Not only isn't he even yours, he's pathologically incapable of love.'

'He's innocent.'

'He's used you. From start to finish. And you've let him.'

'You *know* he didn't kill Emily Thornton, or Paige Talbot –'

'You *have* spoken to him,' said Fran, seizing on the slip. 'Where is he?'

Moncrieff didn't stay rattled for long. 'I don't know what you're talking about.'

Fran was a heartbeat from cuffing the cow and dragging her in for obstruction. But she was right about one thing, the police were in far too much legal shit. 'Maybe you're right. Maybe he's innocent as a new-born. But aren't you legal types supposed to weigh every possibility? What if *I'm* right, and you've freed a monster? God help you when the next girl turns up dead. You better start hoping you're not his type after all.'

Moncrieff slid into her car and revved up the sports-tuned exhaust – no telling if Fran's warnings had pierced her thick hide.

Fran thought about following but doubted her crappy pool car could keep up, and she'd probably made things worse enough for one night.

There was a serenity to Pensol's face in dreamless deep sleep, free of apprehension and doubt. The Pre-Raphaelites would have painted her draped in silk, asleep amid wildflowers – *Innocence In Repose* – not passed out on a sofa with a rough army blanket pulled tight, the silent TV bathing her in unnatural light, a half-empty bottle of cheap blend whisky and a can of Diet Coke.

What was the point of sleep if you had to drink yourself into it? Stark had never reached a conclusion on that one. Were the hours passed worth the sorry awakening? He remembered her earlier call and listened to the voicemail. Semi-coherent apologies – no specifics.

The *Crow* poetry book lay on the table beside the whisky. She must've found it beside his bed. Tough reading on a dark and boozy night.

The sliding door to his little balcony was slightly ajar, letting in the night air. He peered into the street below but saw no one. Perhaps even paps had to sleep.

Closing the door and turning the heating up a couple of degrees, he left Pensol to it, taking the bottle, his muddy shoes and cleaning kit into the bathroom, slipping off his jacket and setting to work, the actions smooth and automatic, freeing his mind to reflect.

But the power to untangle events into manageable threads eluded him. So he remade the bed with clean linen and finally turned to himself; peeling dressings from his hands and arm and showering – doing his best to ignore the unshaven man in the mirror with his battered face and accusing eyes.

'He won't text,' said Marcus, as Fran checked her phone for the third time in the three minutes she'd been home.

She slid it away from her on the kitchen worktop, careful not to look like a child caught red-handed. Marcus wasn't one of those prissy people who thought it rude to check one's phone in company; he just wasn't someone who felt the need to do so himself. He treated his phone as an unavoidable modern contrivance that could allow other people to take up too much of your time if you let them, and was quite fastidious about not answering it unless it happened to be convenient, or it was work.

They'd still be in the pub. Of course she didn't really expect Stark to text. He preferred to torture her.

'If it went well, I'm sure texting you will be the last thing on his mind right now,' Marcus added, careful not to smile at the laddish inference – getting one's end away being the be-all-and-end-all of male existence.

'It's if it went badly that worries me.'

'One more scar will hardly show.'

'One more straw breaks the camel's back,' Fran countered.

'Speaking as a man of science, I'm not sure any camel has ever died of a broken back,' said Marcus, working the stir-fry around the wok.

He had a limited repertoire of quick meals suited to an unhealthy work-life balance, but what he cooked he managed well enough, within the confines of a flat even smaller than hers. The lack of children and her affair hadn't stopped his ex-wife demanding the house. Knowing Marcus, he'd probably accepted a smaller share of the equity than he was due, but that wasn't the sort of thing he would discuss. 'What about a broken heart?'

'They do have sorrowful eyes,' Marcus conceded.

'I should call him.'

'You should not.'

She picked up her phone, regardless, but it rang before she could dial.

The office.

Marcus watched her face as she listened, assessing whether she'd stop to eat or just go.

Finally, out of distractions, Stark opened the bathroom cabinet and stared at the OxyContin for the millionth time. If there was ever a time to kill pain . . . even self-inflicted.

He pulled out the Zopiclone instead. Sleeping pills. Second-to-last resort. What was the point of sleep if you had to *drug* yourself into it? Were the hours deleted worth the foggy-headed awakening?

Popping out two of the innocent-looking pills, he washed them down with a long, burning swig from the bottle.

So be it.

Jamming the screw cap tight, he traipsed into the bedroom, flopping back on to the mattress, fighting off a million thoughts while he waited for the world to fade out.

You *couldn't* leave war behind. But with a little assistance, you might ignore it till dawn.

Unless your sergeant calls . . .

'Seriously,' he sighed. 'You can't wait till morning?'

Fran huffed. 'Where are you?'

'Are we really going to play that game?'

'Cut the crap.'

'I'm at home. Read into that what you will.'

'So it didn't go well?' That wasn't why she called, but she'd ask, if only to wind him up.

'Was there something else you needed, Sarge?'

'I'll only keep asking . . .'

'Good luck with that.'

'I'm drawings conclusions from your sunny tone.'

'This is my default tone for these calls.'

'So I've noticed. But I'm guessing your cool impatience has nothing to do with female company in the shape of Miss Kelly Jones?'

Troubles came in many shapes. Pensol passed out on the sofa. Kelly, somewhere in the arms of Doctor Robert. 'Put it this way . . . You'd better get to the point, because I just took two sleeping pills with a shot and if you need me to go throw them up you should say so quickly.'

61

Harper scowled as Williams took out his noisy phone with a mumbled apology and read a text.

He'd always liked Williams, but found his affable lack of ambition baffling. Williams was good, and Harper needed a reliable bagman. Williams could be a decent DS to Harper's DI, a good man to take along wherever this Faustian pact with DAC Stevens led, but he just wouldn't step up. Career constable. Why on earth would anyone settle for that? Hammed, sat in the back, aspired for more but wasn't sergeant material unless he pulled his socks up sharpish; too much of a clock-watcher. Mummy's boy, waiting for the world to hand him everything on a plate. And Dixon was a limp rag.

Fran had Stark. If they passed their exams. If they sat them. The morning after tomorrow, but with the case as it was ... The next round of tests would be six months away. It was wrong to wish them a setback, but they'd wish him no less. It was a shame; they were good too, but they made themselves impossible to get along with. He'd not helped matters, historically, but he'd tried harder this time and they still stood off. His ears still rang with Fran's words.

They'd never got on, but that wasn't it ... They must know what Groombridge had in his drawer – they'd probably even supplied it. That *damn* photo of him and DAC Stevens. All he'd done was report to a senior officer, as ordered, but now they thought he was Stevens' stooge, leaking, undermining ... And worse than that; interview video had caught him threatening a suspect before the arsehole's subsequent psychotic break and rifle rampage. Fran had been in the firing line and Stark had saved the bloody day, catching a bullet in the process, but not before innocent blood was spilt ... and they both blamed him, he was sure of it now.

He shook himself, letting out an angry breath. None of that mattered, not now. For right or wrong, he was riding the Stevens train – and if it dragged him uphill he'd look back over the heads of everyone here and their petty prejudice with a clear conscience. He stared at his hands; thick and strong, scarred from years of rugby and the usual scrapes, but free of blood – Lady Macbeth be damned. Everything he'd done, he'd done for the job, for the case, for justice and the oath. For career too, of course, but what was wrong with that? The cream had to rise in this sea of shit. He owed it to the force, to himself and to Jess; to be all he could be. He'd crack this case and move on. Move up.

And it was all within reach, because now they had a proper lead ...

Uniform patrol had spotted the pale blue Hyundai hatchback, parked a hundred metres from the house of Richard Hardacre, boyfriend of Karen Gillespie – victim number one in this macabre tale – hub and most vocal cheerleader of the sodding victims' group and the very first suspect, for a short while. But the alibi that seemed to discount him before the second body even dropped had come from his brother, and there was some facial similarity to the bearded man masquerading as Patrick Burgess at the prison and hospital. Fran had been right – he *did* look like someone they knew. The judge had signed the warrant on the spot.

Now they were just waiting for an armed response vehicle, and for Richard Hardacre to show up, resist arrest and break down into a full confession ...

Killed his girlfriend, Karen, got a taste for it and went on to kill Magda Janowski and Teresa Leman, earning the moniker of the Greenwich Strangler. Meanwhile Blake Talbot killed his quasi-sister Paige and dressed it up to blame him. Perturbed, or indifferent, Hardacre slipped up with his next victim, letting Leah Willoughby escape, so hunted down and killed a lookalike replacement, Sara Brompton. Meanwhile the police started looking at Sinclair and the press painted his face all over the news. Leah got it into her addled head it was him that took her, while Hardacre cleverly spun up his pernicious Greenwich Strangler Victims' Group to keep media pressure on the police and ensure Sinclair took the rap. Finally he lay low for two years but couldn't resist visiting his patsy and coming out of retirement to kill Emily Thornton right under their noses, to rub said noses in it while tying the killings directly to Sinclair through Emily. Classic psycho, upping the stakes, showing off. But he'd finally made his mistake, got cocky, because he'd done it believing Sinclair would be out of hospital that day.

And now the car, parked right near his house. Sloppy. Eventually they tire of getting away with it and start to crave the adulation of being caught, being known, becoming famous in their own name; or so the profilers said or didn't say, depending on whichever research they'd read most recently.

All wrapped up on Detective Inspector Owen Harper's watch, relaunching his career.

And ending that of Mike Groombridge. Sinclair – innocent after all, wrongly accused, persecuted, shot and kidnapped . . . Mike was a dead man walking. Time was, that might've caused Harper anguish.

He'd been the exemplary bagman, years of loyalty, and for what . . . ? Mike had been good to him right up until he'd tried for Inspector – since then, he'd done everything possible to undermine him. He'd *used* him, and finally blackmailed him to go. Everyone thought Mike Groombridge was a saint, but he was just like every other archetypal big man, stamping on the fingers of the better man below to stave off his inevitable obsolescence – hardly better than Stevens.

Heads-up, came Fran's voice on the radio. *We've got movement.*

Fran watched the figure walk up to Hardacre's flat . . . and past it . . .

Dixon let out a tense sigh behind her.

Not Hardacre, crackled Harper's voice.

The very words that kept whispering inside Fran's head – *not Hardacre, please not him*. This had to be a Sinclair trick, surely. If this whole thing turned out to be Richard Hardacre, hiding in plain sight all along, mocking them with fake indignation, she'd have to resign. To have been so wrong, for so long . . . They'd had Hardacre in. They'd interviewed him on a body count of one. To have to look Sinclair in the eye now and apologize, to tell Leah that they should've caught this man long before she, Magda, Teresa, Sara and now Emily fell into his clutches . . . before Blake Talbot muddied the waters killing Paige and throwing her into the mix . . . and to be sat here now, unable to face her reflection in the sun-shade mirror, knowing that she almost, *almost* hoped they *weren't* about to find the killer . . .

There'd be nothing else for it. She'd take Richard Hardacre, slam the cell door shut, apologize to Leah and the families, *and* Sinclair . . . she'd wear it all . . . and then resign – or at least drink a vat of Chardonnay, swear and cry at Marcus, and move on to the next case and do it all better next time, and the next, until she could look herself in the eyes again.

Stark re-closed his and rested his head against the window again. He said he'd tickled up the sleeping pills, but perhaps there was still some in his system. Then again, when had any of them last really slept? She felt so tired her insides didn't know which way was up and her eyelids only liked down; and she'd not taken a beating.

'Are you seriously not going to tell us what happened?' she asked to keep him awake, enrolling Dixon without permission.

Stark didn't open his eyes. 'I hadn't planned to.'

'Good news or bad? Surely you can just tell me that.'

'From her perspective or mine?'

'Don't be an arse. Just tell me.'

'She's seeing someone else.'

If Fran had craved distraction, this delivered like a kick in the guts. She might've expected anything else. Kelly loved Stark, really *loved* him. Yes, he'd been a colossal arse, but the idea of her giving her heart to another was . . . 'Seriously?'

'Handsome, besotted, reliable Doctor Robert. They're going away on holiday. I neglected to ask where.'

'And she asked to see you to tell you that?'

'I had it coming.'

'Shit, bad luck, mate,' said Dixon quietly from the back.

And nothing else. *Bad luck, mate.* As if that helped. The males of

288

the species really were useless, acting as if detail was something to be given but never demanded, or coaxed out with sympathy.

'Best forgotten,' replied Stark evenly.

Was he really that much of an idiot? thought Fran despairingly.

A tap on the window made her start. Uniforms, with guns.

A signed warrant and single swing of the ram took care of the door.

Hardacre lived in a narrow three-storey terrace, not yet split into flats like some of its neighbours.

Or had lived.

62

'Suicide?'

'Looks like.'

'Looks like, or is?' Harper's patience was already at the limit. Two hours stuck outside, waiting for SOCO and the pathologist to arrive and ready the scene for the dumb flatfoots. Their sacrosanct forensics 'golden hour' with one-for-bad-luck as usual.

'Can't tell you much more until I dig deeper, so to speak,' said Turner. 'Luckily I've nothing else planned for the night.'

The pathologist had always struck Harper as supercilious. He might seem nice as pie, but you still got the impression he would find you more interesting dead. Harper had seen enough death to find little fear or disgust in it, but the idea of spending your days elbow-deep in cadavers was frankly macabre. He seemed to get on with Fran, which was even weirder, and with Stark, which was another good reason to distrust him.

Harper had ordered the DCs to wait outside. The last thing the packed crime scene needed was Dixon's weak stomach, Hammed's weak mind, Williams' weak commitment or Stark's weakly disguised ego.

Firearms had cut the body down as soon as it was found hanging from an exposed beam in the kitchen, but there were no signs of life.

Richard Hardacre – face bloated and purple from hanging. Neck livid and torn by the rope. Harper could hardly contain his excitement. This could be all the confession he needed. 'Tee-oh-dee?'

Turner consulted his notes. 'Skin temp to ambient puts it around five hours ago, give or take. I'll need to check the thermostat timings and take a rectal temperature to be more certain.'

Harper kept the distaste from his expression. 'So roughly eight p.m. After dark, but people around. We should get started on the door-to-door,' he said to Fran.

'It's midnight,' she replied, ever ready to contradict him. Hissy at this breakthrough on his watch.

'And the street is full of blue lights and radio squawks. The neighbours are probably aching to know what's going on and we need to wrap this up.'

He spotted a petite SOCO watching him, only her pretty eyes showing. He smiled at her, wondering what she looked like without the mask. And indeed, without the rest of the anti-contamination gear. She looked away demurely. Harper thumbed at his wedding ring through his nitrile glove and turned to Culpepper, the Scene of Crime Manager. 'Look for the note. No way this fucker checked out without a farewell.'

'You should see this first.' Culpepper led the way to the hallway where a door stood open on a carpeted stair heading down. 'Mind your step.' Like Harper was some clumsy tit.

He'd have been better saying mind your head. The basement to which the stair led was built to receive coal via the street-level chute and not six-three detective inspectors. Along with all the clutter and boxes stacked against one wall, was a desk with a computer, phone, modem, untidy files and a noticeboard cluttered with pictures of every victim, newspaper reports, Sinclair's trial information, Freedom of Information Requests – all screamingly suspicious, were it not clearly the hub of the Greenwich Strangler Victims' Group.

What *was* suspicious, was the six-foot tall roll of industrial blue translucent polythene propped in the corner next to the large cardboard bobbin of grey electrical cable and a box containing bottles of household bleach, plus the stash of liquid Rohypnol bottles in a plastic bag concealed in a storage box along with an S&M ball-gag – bright pink plastic-ball scored with teeth marks – and a wallet containing a driver's licence and credit cards in the name of Patrick Burgess, the long-suffering victim of identity theft. Hung in the corner was the bulky coat and baseball cap worn by Sinclair's prison and hospital visitor, along with a theatre-grade false beard, glue and wig.

The desk drawer contained a Hyundai branded car key and corresponding DVLA V5 form with one scrawled signature – the foolish teenager.

There was also a long-lensed camera with memory card. One of Culpepper's minions had it plugged into a laptop, scrolling through dozens of photos – of Emily Thornton outside her office, and Leah Willoughby outside her flats . . .

Jackpot.

'Boss.' Another of Culpepper's minions had materialized. 'Just got the blue Hyundai open. Boot's lined with the same polythene,' he said, eyeing the roll in the corner. 'And there's blood.'

Shit, thought Harper. If that was Leah Willoughby's, it was going to take the shine off his triumph.

'No note,' muttered Fran, again, inviting agreement.

'It's not as uncommon as people think,' offered Williams.

'For regular depressives, maybe,' scowled Fran, 'but a serial killer . . . ? They're supposed to be all about showing off.'

'Not always,' countered Williams again, who'd had to spend the most time with the specialist crime profiler during the original investigation after Fran lost patience with the man. He shrugged apologetically to her scowl of disapproval.

'How often do they give in to suicidal remorse?' asked Stark.

Fran threw up her hands, accepting this as vindication for her doubts, but Stark wasn't sure what to believe any more. None of the DCs had been invited inside the crowded crime scene, but what Fran told them sounded fairly conclusive. Harper leant against his car up the street, smoking while talking on his phone – probably reporting directly to Stevens now without even the pretence of having to go through DCI Groombridge or even Superintendent Cox. All the more worrying if Stevens was invested enough to take the call after midnight.

Stark's own phone rang, earning a mixture of disapproval and enquiry from Fran, as if it might be Kelly calling to pile on more soap-opera misery. But it was Gwen.

Stark ignored the eyes on him as he retreated across the street, answering. 'It's a bit late for a social call.'

'The fourth estate must never sleep,' said Gwen. 'Lest the rest of you forget yourselves.'

'And something tells me that you were confident I wasn't sleeping.'

'Someone is, if you don't know what I know.'

'Which is?'

'I'm not sure why I should tell you, since you keep stonewalling me.'

'And yet you called.'

Gwen hesitated just long enough to make her point. 'Okay, just to be clear, this is a free heads-up between friends and trusted professionals, to show you how that works . . .'

'Irony noted. So what is it you know?'

'That exactly twenty-four minutes ago a new blog post appeared on the Greenwich Strangler Victims' Group website.'

Stark frowned. 'Authored by . . . ?'

'Richard Hardacre. It's his blog.'

'Twenty-four minutes ago?' Stark checked his watch, with a nasty feeling where this might be going.

'Midnight exactly,' confirmed Gwen. 'To the second. And something tells me it was a scheduled posting, typed earlier.'

'And what something is that?

'Aside from the cagey tone to your voice right now . . . ? I think I'd better read it to you.'

63

00:00:00 – 6th April

This has to stop. All those girls. Poor Karen. Never willing to go as far as I wanted, to really show me your love, even with the roofie helping. I never meant this all to happen. I had to keep looking, but each time was worse. Magda, Teresa, Leah and Sara. Paige Talbot wasn't me, I swear it. But this has to stop. I tried for two years but it wasn't enough. It was never enough. Emily was a disaster. Julian told me he'd be out of the hospital. I should've waited to be sure. But as soon as I saw her I thought she might be the one. I wanted to help her see, but I don't think she did.

And now Leah. I thought maybe a second chance, finish what I started.

Why can't they understand? I just wanted someone to understand my love, someone worthy.

But there's no one.

I must stop searching. Stop pretending. This is the only way. I'm sorry. I'm so sorry.

Richard

Hardacre's blog post didn't get any better on the umpteenth reading. The Selfie Generation – so self-obsessed, even suicide notes were shared online. Fran hardly knew where to start with that, but this was worse, so much worse. The heartless fuck had used the victims' group to hide his guilt all this time and now used them again to proclaim it.

SOCO had used his thumbprint to unlock his laptop, finding it still logged on to the website, blog scheduled for posting at midnight, ensuring time to complete his final act of murder upon himself without interruption from police or ambulance. Tech had confirmed the email address from the user login: rdh**91@gmail.com. The same email account used by the anonymous purchaser of the Hyundai. Richard Dillon Hardacre, born in 1991 – simple once you saw it, and twice as frustrating. The burner phone used was found in the basement too.

And if Stark's press pal had it, by now the terrible message from beyond the grave was probably tearing through the families' sleep as well.

And still no sign of Leah.

Finish what I started. Ominous words indeed. And worse for being just as Fran had predicted. There could be no doubt now that Leah *had* been taken again, and worse. If she'd lost her life in some sick dungeon only Hardacre knew about, he'd left her there or disposed of her before taking his own life . . . Bodies rarely showed up when you needed them to, whether you were the killer or the police. They might not find her for days, weeks, or ever. Yet Harper strutted round like the prize cock he was, practically dancing.

Fran felt drained, fighting the urge to bury her face in her hands. There was often a deflation after the high of closing a case, nailing the bad guy, but this . . . She could still hardly believe it. Didn't want to. She felt cheated. And worse, *guilty*. If Richard Hardacre was the Strangler, then Julian Sinclair really had been guilty of little more than being peerlessly unlikeable, until perhaps taking matters into his own hands with Blake to prove his innocence. And if he *had* killed Blake Talbot, her misdirected persecution was partly to blame for that too, on top of all the other victims after Karen, while Groombridge paid for her negligence with his career and reputation.

Better that than the killer still be out there, still be Sinclair, he would say, but she'd been so *certain* . . .

If Sinclair had staged Blake's suicide, then why not this . . . ?

But the evidence against Hardacre was damning, as Harper had cheerfully thrown in her face.

He'd sent her to meet the Family Liaison Officer at Hardacre's parental home. Victims' families got an inspector; the killer's had to make do with a sergeant. After one in the morning. This was already too public to wait for daylight. Not the most fun moment of her life, and the worst of theirs – letting the FLO break the terrible news whilst trying to delicately press them for anything they might know about Richard's movements on key dates, or any mention of any old property he might have used to imprison, rape and murder young women, in as many words. There was little point withholding the connection, with the suicide note out there in the ether, but Fran kept facts to the bare minimum. The FLO was brilliant, and would gently keep at it while he took the bereaved couple to formally identify their only son's remains, but they were predictably horrified, numb and dumb, and the agonizing exercise produced nothing that might lead Fran to Leah Willoughby.

The arsehole at Camden was being more forthcoming now, but it was too little, too late. Somewhere out there Leah was either alive and terrified, or dead at peace, and the latter seemed far more likely.

Blood from the car – already confirmed as O-positive, Leah's type, but also Emily Thornton's and 37 per cent of the UK population – was off now for DNA comparison. They still had Leah's on file.

Fran rubbed her eyes. Christ, she was tired. Tired of all this shit and death. If there *was* a god, they'd long abandoned this world, sick of the endless sin. Love outweighed hate, her dad had insisted when her teenaged faith floundered – God was in the love. They didn't discuss such things any more.

'Sarge.' Stark placed a takeaway coffee from the local all-night cafe on her desk with a paper bag that gave off the unmistakable aroma of warm Danish pastry.

'I take it all back about you.'

'Hush, you'll make the other underlings jealous.' His eyes were drawn to the incident board's latest photos of Hardacre dangling in his kitchen and his smile faded. 'Bring back the hangman . . .'

'What?'

'Something Rhonda Talbot said.'

'And you *agree*?' Rhonda might be entitled to that opinion, or the husband of the second victim who'd hung himself in grief, or even Fran herself in anger, but they'd still be wrong.

Stark gave the faintest head shake. 'A society choosing retribution over any hope of rehabilitation or restitution, demeans itself.'

Even if it took the UK until the sixties to work that one out, thought Fran. About the same time it took them to decide that maybe racial discrimination shouldn't be legal either.

'Even in war you target combatants, not prisoners,' added Stark.

And talk about killing like it's normal, thought Fran, suppressing a shiver. 'Blurrier lines, I'd imagine.'

'Fog of war?' He thought for a moment, as if staring back through time. 'No, for me it was . . . clarity. The fog comes after.'

So saying, he placed a plastic bag on Dixon's desk and withdrew greasy paper parcels of cardiac-horror from the local chippy and a pair of energy drinks for them. Whatever got you through the night. She'd sent Williams and Hammed home to rest for the morning session, but there was a limit to how long they could keep this up.

Fran held the coffee under her nose to stave off the wave of vinegar, salt and fishy saturated fat as the boys tucked in with hungry appreciation, if little cheer. A poor victory lap. If the pubs had been open Harper would probably have them all drinking to his achievement, as if the case was closed, as if there wasn't a mountain of paperwork to get through and a young woman still missing, even if presumed dead. Small mercy, he'd buggered off home instead, to get his beauty sleep for the triumphant morning press statement. It made her want to puke.

At least Stark was eating. During previous crises his appetite had gone notably AWOL, along with sleep and good sense. Perhaps this latest thing with Kelly really didn't bother him as much as she thought.

He shared a moment with Dixon and settled at his desk, doing what he always seemed to do when there was nothing to be done; returned to the files. For some reason retreating into cerebral tedium seemed to keep him ticking over when everyone else flagged, as if he found it relaxing – which given the things he'd been through was probably true. He had two modes – asleep or alert. Keeping his mind busy helped – the more mind-numbing the better – or so it seemed. The office equivalent of polishing boots and stripping down a rifle.

Fran almost smiled. But then her eyes returned to the photos.

She pushed the bag of Danish away with a fresh wave of nausea, the smell of pastry and coffee, her go-to culinary indulgence, suddenly turning her stomach. She'd been feeling this way for days now, since Sinclair's impending release. Her body not being able to tell night from day . . . or morning . . .

She sat up straight.

No . . . Surely . . . ?

They'd only been seeing each other a few months and he'd always been a gentleman about precautions. And now she'd started the pill . . .

Perhaps that was it, she thought; a reaction to this particular pill . . . the doc had said to watch for abnormal menstruation and she was due about now, wasn't she? She'd been at her grumpiest best this week, but with good reason. Fran's answer to PMT was to remain irascible every day of the month, but this didn't feel like that anyway. More likely, just her jaded brain reacting to the seriousness of this relationship step.

She shook her head. Wouldn't it just be the last straw . . . ?

Or perhaps, she thought, a way out. Sod the Inspectors' Exam. Sod this poxy job and the likes of Harper and Stevens and all the injustice they represented. Sod all the bodies, blood and bile, late nights and heartache, fast food and bad coffee . . . Pack it all in and raise a kid or two. Loads of women her age started families these days. Thirty-seven. *Shit*. Staring at her crow's feet in the mirror she sometimes wondered where the years were going, while looking at the world she felt a hundred. She'd assumed it was all too late – let the nephews and nieces answer the pang in her heart. But her own child . . . ? And Marcus was a good man . . .

Tick, tick, tick, tick . . . *boom*.

Stark watched a complex sequence of emotions play out on Fran's face, but whatever troubles she was currently wrestling did not appear to invite enquiry. He had issues enough on his own mind and one front and centre bellowing like a drill sergeant.

The thought of Kelly with Doctor Robert Laithwaite made his skin crawl.

He had no right, but it did. Another wound to accept and recover from, some might say self-inflicted, but actually just the same old festering infection of war. Fog, clouding his thoughts when he should really be focusing on finding Leah.

Forcing his mind from personal troubles, he flicked open the old case file he'd been reviewing yesterday . . . or was it the day before? Sinclair's business dealings. While the others picked over the original Hardacre file from his brief stint as suspect and anything from his home that might steer them to Leah's location, Harper had of course suggested Stark finish what he'd been doing first.

Soldiers learned to survive on power naps in quiet corners or stationary vehicles, but his brain was already turning to mush and an hour of this threatened to have him curled under the desk. Not least because it was futile: now it seemed that however unlikely it might have seemed just days ago, Julian Sinclair really was innocent after all.

64

'Someone give me *something*, *please*.' Exhausted frustration had descended on the office. Fran's mind was racing, desperate for anything, any hope of finding Leah alive. The alternative was as unthinkable as her possible – *impossible* – pregnancy.

Stark had his frozen-concentration thing going on but the things he found fascinating too often bored her to tears. No one offered her anything more than apologies, and the object of her irritation didn't even look up. 'Nothing you'd like to share with the class, Joe?'

He didn't sigh or roll his eyes at the interruption, but you could tell he was thinking both. 'Nothing relevant.'

Fran peered over his shoulder. 'Why are you still looking at Sinclair?'

'Orders.'

Harper. Sergeant long enough to know that bypassing Fran to sideline Stark with time-wasting orders was a double snub. 'Didn't we just cut down swinging evidence that we've been wasting our time on Sinclair for *two sodding years*?'

He shrugged and yawned at the same time, rubbing his face. 'I suppose. I've just never known you be so wrong before, not about this sort of thing at least.' There was too much home truth in the first part of that for Fran to enjoy taking umbrage at the second. 'I prefer confessions enunciated clearly into police interview recording equipment.'

'And gift horses with pearly whites,' scoffed Fran, though she agreed completely. 'All right,' she sighed, suspecting she'd regret it. 'What's stirred your pot, anyway?'

'The Fraud Squad report.'

'Seriously? You're going to hit me with number-nerdery at four-thirty in the morning?' Fran found herself stifling a yawn, just in time to un-stifle it with feeling. 'I was bored with all that two years ago.'

'Wasn't it *you* who interrupted *me*?' replied Stark flatly.

Dixon, who'd stopped to listen, wisely ducked his eyes back to his own work.

'Well, you know how much I enjoy your little diversions,' she countered. There was more to say on that matter, but her phone vibrated on her desk. Marcus, the last person she wanted to talk to right now, with notions of pregnancy clouding her every thought. 'Hang on a minute, Marcus,' she answered. 'I may need you to rescue me before Stark bores me to death.' She put her hand over the handset, looking at Stark. 'Skip to the end.'

'The Jersey connection. The property speculation.'

'Not this again.' She rolled her eyes again, but didn't enjoy it as much as usual. She was too tired, and Stark's refusal to roll his own had somehow taken the fun out of it.

'Did they follow up on *all* the properties?'

'Any premises he had access to were searched at the time.' She gave him the look reserved for mortals foolish enough to doubt her powers. 'Not that any of that matters now. We've got our man; Richard *wanker-face* Hardacre, hiding in plain sight with his holier-than-thou song and *bloody* dance this whole time.' She pictured Sinclair's famous smile widening while he waved his damages compensation like a flag for all to see. He'd probably have a ghost-written autobiography on the shelves by summer – *Sinclair: My Harrowing Journey from Persecution to Exoneration* – a heart-rending tale of hardships overcome. 'And somewhere out there, the miserable shit dumped Leah Willoughby – dead or we'd better all damn well hope alive – and wherever it is won't be in those sodding Sinclair files!'

Stark gave a pointed look of agreement, and if she dialled down her glare at all it was only on grounds of exhaustion and the wrong half of her wishing it really was still Sinclair they should be chasing.

'Aren't you forgetting something?' He nodded to her phone.

Shit! 'Marcus,' she said with forced calm. 'Be warned – my time-wasting bar is set pretty high right now.'

'Then I think you'd better get down here.' He sounded serious.

'Hardacre?'

'I've found some disturbing contra-indications.'

Fran sat up, far more interested than she should be. 'Meaning . . . ?'

'Preliminary test shows high levels of Flunitrazepam in his blood – our old friend, Rohypnol – which I'm guessing might just clear your impatience bar.'

Fran harrumphed to maintain the high ground. 'Easing the pain of his own departure? Or Dutch courage? He had enough of the stuff stashed in the basement.' From an American manufacturer, bought illegally online no doubt.

'Maybe, but at these concentrations, balancing on a chair to place his head in a noose might've been tricky. But here's the thing. Fluni-trazepam is fatal in sufficient dose, which, as you say, he had to hand several times over.'

'Why hang yourself when you can just put yourself to sleep?'

'Exactly.'

'Atonement?'

'I suppose.'

'You don't sound convinced.'

'No. Because that's not all.'

65

'His bladder evacuated –'

'Please don't tell me you dragged me down here to tell me a hanged man pissed himself,' interrupted Fran, with more barb than banter.

Marcus sighed. 'Not at all uncommon, you're quite correct, but his urine-stained trousers contained no Flunitrazepam. None at all.'

Fran let her impatience show. 'So?'

'So he pissed himself *before* he drugged and hanged himself,' said Stark.

'Precisely.' Marcus pulled back the sheet covering Hardacre's earthly remains, a grotesquely swollen, discoloured face and neck. 'If you look carefully here . . .' He pointed to Hardacre's left cheek. 'Hanging constricts the blood flow as well as air flow, causing the face to darken, and unlike strangulation, where the pressure is released after death, the hanged man's face remains purple and then of course darkens port-mortem. Making this rather hard to spot, but if you look closer . . .'

'A bruise? Someone hit him?'

'Maybe.'

'Someone assaulting him, or fighting him off?'

'You know I don't like to speculate.'

'But . . . ?'

'People fighting for their lives, fighting someone off, tend to claw as well as punch, and this young man, for everything else he's been through, doesn't have a scratch-mark on him.'

'And *his* fingernails?' asked Stark. 'Was *he* fighting someone off?'

'No foreign skin or blood.'

'But he's dead. So maybe he was taken by surprise, subdued by violence and threat,' mused Fran. 'Sat in the chair, where he wet himself in fear, *before* being forced to drink the Rohypnol.'

'The floor and toppled chair beneath the victim were soaked in urine, but not from the hanging.'

'You're saying this is a fit-up.'

Marcus gave his standard non-committal expression, but looked to Geoff Culpepper, the Senior Crime Scene Manager, whose invitation at this inhospitable hour meant there was more bad news coming.

He held up a photo. The rope, looped over the beam in Hardacre's ceiling. 'There's more abrasion than you might expect – indicating it may have been dragged over the beam under load.'

'So he didn't climb up on the chair, he was hauled up on the rope.' Fran was looking unhappier by the second.

Stark stared at the slab of meat that had been a thorn in Fran's side for two years, and suddenly felt his breath stop.

Marcus noticed. 'Something amiss?'

'Watch tan line on his wrist . . .'

'Thailand for three weeks, two weeks ago,' said Culpepper. 'According to his passport. There's smiling photos on the laptop.'

Fran harrumphed. 'Bastard never missed a chance to plead poverty to *me*.'

'I don't think this is the man who visited Sinclair in prison and hospital.'

Now Fran was staring too. 'Why?'

Stark pointed. 'It's his *right* wrist . . .'

'Ah,' Marcus nodded sagely. 'The sinister hand.'

'Sinister?' asked Fran, with the same impatience she expressed whenever Marcus and Stark drifted into veteran in-speak.

'His medical records should confirm. If not, the family,' said Marcus. 'But watch on the right wrist usually indicates a lefty.'

Stark nodded. 'And the man signing himself into the prison was right-handed.'

'Shit.' Fran's face said it all. 'So he may not even be the accomplice.'

'Which brings us neatly back to you, Geoff,' said Marcus.

Culpepper puffed out his cheeks, opening the file in his hands. 'Well, this is yet to be ratified by a supervisor, but preliminary labs say the blood from the car and saliva on the gag are both Emily Thornton's.'

Fran's expression was mixed. 'Nothing from Leah Willoughby?'

'Not so far. The bolt of polythene found in Hardacre's basement and the back of the car are an identical grade to that Emily Thornton was found in,' Culpepper continued. 'But so far, we've found no fingerprints on it, or the electrical cable, Rohypnol, wallet and cards or the memory stick of photos.'

'Could just be consistent with your average fastidious psycho.'

'Maybe. The car was spotless too. All they've found on the swabs so far is kitchen spray bleach. Same with the negligible hooverings. They found one hair. Short. Blondish. They're still running it.'

'Could be Leah's?'

'Maybe. But . . .' Culpepper made a pained face.

'But it was all a bit easy to find, wasn't it?' said Fran, summarizing everyone's coalescing doubts.

Stark looked at Fran. 'What kind of perp dumps the body and then triggers a speed camera . . .'

'The kind that wants to frame someone else,' she nodded. 'To make sure the car led us to Hardacre, all tied up in a neat little noose.'

Their silence filled the room like a highly sceptical elephant.

Sinclair was still behind bars a week ago, but the car might have been bought for him. All fingers pointed to the mystery visitor – deliverer of another unverifiable confession.

'*Shit*,' said Fran again, with more feeling.

'Yes.' Marcus nodded with sympathy. 'Hard to know how to feel.'

'No, it's not,' said Stark quietly, seeing his feelings mirrored in Fran's eyes. Someone had pulled the sickest joke on them. The cruellest insult to the families. The most cowardly and despicable misdirection.

66

'It's not much to go on,' sighed Groombridge, sitting alone at his kitchen table, streetlight slanting in through the venetian blind, keeping his voice low in the hope that Alice had gone back to sleep upstairs.

'And not much to celebrate, either way,' agreed Fran. There was no triumph in her voice. If Hardacre proved innocent there was still a collar to feel. Sinclair, innocent or otherwise, was still out there, possibly armed. His bearded visitor, guilty or otherwise, remained a mystery and Leah was still missing.

'But enough to cast doubt. What about Blake Talbot?'

'So far nothing to contradict the story – kidnapping, altercation, escape, confession, suicide.'

'So we've two self-murders – one sloppily faked, one carefully faked.'

'Or genuine.'

'But you don't believe that.'

'No.' But there was a quaver of doubt in her voice. Fran hated doubt.

'Conclusions?'

She made a frustrated noise. 'That it's like they were staged by different people. One careful killer, one less so.'

'Sinclair and his mystery visitor,' agreed Groombridge. 'And you don't like that conclusion?'

'It's not that, it's . . .' She yawned. 'It's just that, normally each crime fills in the jigsaw a little, but this . . . the bodies stack up and we just get more confused.'

Groombridge mused for a moment. He could fob her off with one of his standard pep-talk platitudes – *the killer always slips up eventually* – but she was wise to him now and they both knew it wasn't always so. This was new territory anyway, and serial killers were as beyond his understanding as hers, even after two years. 'Probably not a good time to be kicking Moncrieff's nest, then.'

'She had him stashed away but he's skipped, I know it.'

'Doesn't feel like we *know* very much at all. How did Owen take it?'

'I didn't see the point in waking him yet.'

She didn't see the point in him at all, but that wasn't the point. 'He's the SIO, Fran. Like it or not.'

'I'll make sure to update him before his precious press conference,' she added. Vindication wasn't much comfort with a killer still at large, and tempting as it might be, she wouldn't embarrass the Met just to embarrass Owen. This was to be his coronation, but the crown he yearned for dangled just out of reach.

'Owen may let his ambition guide him overly, but he's more copper than you think.'

'Don't tell me to give him a chance,' Fran said bitterly. 'I don't have any other choice.'

'Better pass your exam then.'

'Like all this helps.'

'No excuses. You want to run cases your way – get your pips,' he replied brusquely. 'When is it over . . . ?'

'When we know what happened,' she replied dutifully.

Catching the criminal wasn't, alas, always the same as solving the mystery. 'And no one hates not knowing more than you. That's what it is to be solid copper. You're a good sergeant, Fran. Your troops love you. But you've always been crap at taking direction from above. Time to shake off the shackles. Be the leader. Be the one who finds out what happened.'

He heard her sigh. 'Yes, Guv.'

'Good. Now I'm going back to sleep,' he almost certainly lied. 'Call me when you know.'

He hung up, and smiled. The world would always be rife with sin. But if he could leave one legacy from the tatters of his long service,

Fran and Stark on the side of the angels might just make it all worth it. He crept back into bed.

At least he'd avoided waking Alice.

'Surely if there's any silver lining to suspension,' muttered her quiet voice, 'it's not receiving calls at five a.m.'

'Joe?'

'Hope I'm not waking the fourth estate.'

'Very funny,' replied Gwen, clearly still wide awake and firing on all cylinders. 'And I hope you're not calling to ask me to spike the story, because you're hours late.'

'So I see.'

'You're reading my work. I'm all a-gush.'

'I'm your biggest fan.'

'It's a bit early for a sarcastic call.'

'Justice never sleeps.'

'Perhaps your individual bit doesn't. So what's got you dialling my number?'

'Reciprocity.'

'In the form of . . . ? An update? Cos I could use something meatier to flesh out my copy than old bio notes and quotes from his Strangler blog.'

'A note of caution.'

'Why?'

'Things aren't always what they seem.'

'He posted his confession online.'

'Someone did.'

Gwen absorbed that for a few seconds. 'Can I quote you?'

'No. Nothing's certain.'

'Then why call? Isn't this against your vaunted moral code?'

'Because I owe you one.'

'You owe me *three*.'

'Because you have scruples, then.' Whatever the truth, there'd be egg on faces. Fran had woken Harper with the news and he wanted silence – let the killer think their trick had worked, let them grow in confidence and make mistakes. Fran had protested those mistakes might come at the cost of more young women's lives but her words fell on deaf ears. Such impossible decisions were above Stark's pay grade, but he'd sworn to serve and protect, and the best he could do today was protect Gwen.

'So Sinclair is prime suspect again?'

'I can't say.'

'Do you know where he is?' She had to draw her own conclusion from his silence. 'But you understand casting doubt on Hardacre's guilt casts suspicion back on Sinclair? One question leads to another.'

'It does. But I can't answer.'

'While asking me to swim against the tide. Was Hardacre your so-called new suspect, or are you still looking for someone else?'

'I can't say.'

'But are you looking for a copycat killer for Emily Thornton's murder or one suspect for all?'

'I don't know.'

'Are Dean and Troy Talbot also being charged with shooting Sinclair outside Belmarsh Prison as well as the attempted kidnapping yesterday?'

'I can't say.'

'Was Blake Talbot murdered? No, wait . . . you can't say.'

'Our usual impasse,' agreed Stark. Theirs was a trust born of grief and the fallout of war, and hobbled by integrity at odds. Hardly *cavorting*, as Fran put it, but there was no point trying to explain it to her.

Gwen gave a grunt of dissatisfaction. 'I think I need more coffee.'

As gratitude went, that was probably all he was due. But you had to start somewhere. Stark pocketed his phone, thinking he needed a nap. But at least it was one good deed for the day, for right or wrong. One fixed star above a horizon-less sea of confusion, fear and loathing.

67

'Good morning, everyone,' said Harper, purposeful of stride, sombre and presidential, unfolding his official leather document wallet on the lectern in the grand New Scotland Yard press room for the first time, hiding the bitter disappointment inside.

This was supposed to be his victory lap – killer identified while the solemn search for the missing girl continues. Fran's call had ruined all that.

'You will, I'm sure, already have read or heard of disturbing developments in this fast-moving investigation. Around ten last night the body of a man in his late twenties was found in his property in west Woolwich. The family have been informed and formally identified him as Richard Hardacre, boyfriend of the first victim of the Greenwich Strangler, Karen Gillespie.'

Hands shot up. Harper noted the blonde, Jennings, in her eponymous scarlet among them, but her previous questions had been rather pointed and the cute redhead near the back had her hand raised this time. He smiled inside. He'd throw her a bone. 'You at the back. I'm sorry, I don't know your name.'

'Gwen Maddox; Facts-Feed. Detective Inspector, can you confirm whether the confessional suicide note posted online last night can be taken at face value? In short, is the Greenwich Strangler dead by his own hands, or still at large?'

Harper's face froze. Maddox. He should've recognized her from Stark's endlessly repeated interview – and people accused *him* of grandstanding? And here she was, shooting from the hip . . . ? Bullshit. That question was primed. *Stark*. Despite their differences,

Fran had called to relay the forensics concerns before he made a fool of himself claiming victory. But if Fran knew, Stark knew. Always him ... undermining, silently supercilious, now defying orders and greasing the press. For what ... Money? No. Why did Stark do anything ...? For glory. To shine at the expense of others. *Golden-fucking-balls*. Seditious shit probably had some threesome going with the redhead *and* the blonde! 'That question,' he replied, keeping his voice even, 'is at the very foremost of our current efforts. A post-mortem is underway, but –'

'But Hardacre's death is being treated as suspicious?'

Harper hated being interrupted, particularly in front of the cameras. 'We are, as ever, keeping an open mind until the facts are established. I would encourage you all to do the same.'

'So the women of south London should still fear for their lives?' asked another hack, taking up the theme. The old bat from the *Greenwich Crier*.

'Vigilance is always advisable.' Harper cursed the words as soon as they were out of his mouth.

'But, specifically,' said another, sensing blood in the water. 'What should women look out for?'

'Are you saying Greenwich police cannot keep the streets safe?' stabbed Jennings.

'Is the death of Blake Talbot being treated as suspicious?' asked the redhead, Maddox. 'And have you located Julian Sinclair?'

'And do you still believe him to be armed and dangerous?' Jennings twisted her knife.

This was a fucking *ambush*. Harper slowly closed his leather folder, waiting for silence, cursing Stark, and Fran. Endlessly, the jealous weaklings around him clawed and spat. 'As always, we would ask you to allow the investigation to take its natural course and respect the sensitivities of the bereaved. That's all for now.'

Stark turned away from the canteen television, trying to force the hushed mutterings of the crowded room to the outer edge of his consciousness.

It had been a long night. That made it harder to feel sorry for

Harper, and easier to ignore Kelly's call an hour ago. Perhaps she felt there was something more to say, some explanation she felt he was owed. Too personal to leave a message.

Now she was trying again.

He watched it vibrate on the table until it stopped, and again no voicemail followed.

When it rang again, he snatched it up and walked out into the stairwell, sickening with every step but needing this over; ended. 'Kelly, I'm working. I'm sorry, but this isn't –'

'*Bastard!*'

Shocked, he blinked in silence.

'I've been up half the night going out of my mind,' continued Kelly, voice edged with anger. 'Going over and over it all. Kicking myself. Crying myself stupid. Blaming myself for . . . *everything*. For all that pain in your eyes, *still*, and making it worse. But you wouldn't stay and listen, and you won't answer your mobile and you keep the home phone on silent . . . so I went to the flat . . .'

'You went to the flat?' asked Stark, confusion making him stupid.

'You let me think it was all my fault. I've been tearing my hair out. You made me feel like shit last night, like I'd betrayed you, and then I go round hoping to apologize, to explain, and who answers the intercom but some girl I've woken . . . asking if I like to leave a *message*!'

Pensol. Stark closed his eyes. 'You don't understand –'

'*I* don't understand! *I* don't understand?' said Kelly, anger in her voice he'd never heard before. 'You let me feel ashamed. And all the while you had someone waiting at home. I've been such a *fool*!'

'It's no—'

'How long?' she interrupted again. 'No, it doesn't matter. You should've told me, Joe. You should've just *told* me.'

And with that she was gone.

For good, most likely.

The end.

Death by misunderstanding.

Perhaps, in the end, that was how all relationships finally expired. More grim than fairy tale, hardly to plan and no happily ever after.

But what endings were happy?

'What's up with you?' demanded Fran, head appearing round the door. 'Look like you've seen a ghost.'

Stark took a hard breath. 'Just sharing a joke with the universe, Sarge.'

Fran made the face to show she didn't care, which usually meant she did care but didn't have time or inclination to waste trying to winkle the truth from him right now. 'Whatever. Come on. The lab nerds hit a jackpot, of sorts.'

68

DNA.

Genes may have landed Fran without the classical looks to launch ships or be sacrificed to monsters like the Greenwich Strangler, but oh how she loved the helical stuff.

God bless Rosalind Franklin, Maurice Wilkins, Francis Crick, James Watson and Professor Sir Alec Jeffreys, and God bless Joseph bloody Stark for dropping their names into otherwise-normal conversations so she had to look them up afterward. God bless the Sanger Institute, the Human Genome Project and all nerds everywhere for deoxyribonucleic acid – God's gift to criminal investigation.

Yes, of course there would always be arguments about sample size, contamination and transference. Yes, there would still be cock-ups, like the one that sprang Julian Sinclair, or, depending on your point of view, the one that convicted him. But Fran could forget all that for now, because she had *DNA*.

No sign of Leah Willoughby's so far – good news in a murder investigation was never that different from the other kind, but as long as they hadn't found her there was a chance – but that wasn't what had Fran's heart all aflutter . . .

'Who's this then?' asked Williams, sipping coffee from the travel mug his wife sent him in with most mornings, as everyone crowded round her desk to peer at the face on her screen. Dixon looked like he could use more coffee of his own and Hammed was still pulling off his coat.

'Forget Richard Hardacre,' replied Fran, 'may he rest in whatever corner of afterlife they set aside for the unlikeably righteous – and say hello to the bitter-sweet face of Brian Leech.' Beside the screen, she held up the photo-fit and best camera still from the prison visit. Leech lacked the beard. His hair was short and mousy, not dark brown. But there was a resemblance to Richard Hardacre, and to Patrick Burgess whose stolen ID was used as an alias by the prison/hospital visitor. From their concentration, the team around her saw it too. 'Thirty-eight. History of mental illness including schizophrenia. Cautions for domestic violence and stalking his ex-wife. Narrowly acquitted of sexual assault, two counts, for lack of evidence. Convicted for breaking and entering and making illegal illicit images of another without permission with a spy camera he hid in the bedroom of his neighbour, a young woman of whom he amassed an extensive archive on his computer.

'Peeping Tom,' muttered Williams in disgust.

Fran nodded. 'But get this. He was initially arrested for identity fraud, using stolen credit cards and ID from the woman's boyfriend to buy everything from flash clothes to a shiny new motorbike.'

'Patrick Burgess's identity theft file listed fraudulent purchase of designer clothes and a motorbike,' said Dixon, whose determined emulation of Stark seemed increasingly to include reading things that made Fran sleepy.

'Served the full six years; denied parole. Released five months before the Greenwich Strangler first struck. Then did a second stretch for credit card fraud, served nine months of eighteen, released eight months ago.'

'All during the time the strangler went quiet,' breathed Hammed.

'Who says prison doesn't work?' said Williams. 'Please tell me he was cell-mate to Julian Sinclair.'

Fran shook her head. 'First thing I checked. But the good news is that prison didn't teach Brian Leech, here, not to leave his DNA at a major crime scene,' she said, delivering the *coup-de-grâce*. 'The hair found in the Hyundai.'

'All that effort framing Hardacre, and he gets done by one stray hair?' scoffed Williams. 'Should've stuck to fraud.'

'They all slip up eventually,' said Fran, basking in the welcome relief of having a name and a face, a solid suspect, like the sun burning away the mist of self-doubt. Dearly wishing Groombridge was here to say *I told you so*.

'Do we have an address?' asked Hammed.

The cloud inside the silver lining. 'Whereabouts unknown. Probation service list him off-grid soon after release. Skipped straight from his transition lodgings and hasn't been seen since.'

'Who says probation doesn't work?' muttered Williams, earning murmured affirmations.

'So Sinclair is still in the clear?' asked Hammed, further darkening Fran's sky.

'It's looking increasingly that way,' she admitted.

'Meaning the Guv'nor is still in the shit,' said Williams.

'What's that . . . ?' asked Dixon, pointing to a red flag in Leech's details that Fran hadn't noticed.

She clicked on it. HOLMES had confirmed no known connections to Sinclair, but there was something else. 'Brian Leech shared a prison cell with . . . *Istvan Kovacs*?' she read aloud. The ex-con found burnt and full of bullets from the prison Glock? That didn't make sense. Castor and his pal Kovacs were supposed to be connected to the Talbot brothers, the victims of the Greenwich Strangler, not the Strangler himself, if that's what Leech was.

There was a moment's pause, while those assembled attempted to cast aside all prior assumptions about the attempt on Sinclair's life outside the prison.

'But what would they have to gain?' asked Dixon. 'Taking Sinclair out?'

'No better patsy than a dead patsy?' mused Williams. 'If Leech *is* the Strangler. Willing to use and abuse old prison contacts. Castor and Kovacs were probably expecting less bang, more bucks.'

'So . . . what? The Talbots had nothing to do with the prison?' asked Hammed.

'Maybe *they* got the idea for raiding the safe house from hearing about the prison raid?' suggested Williams, thinking his way through the new paradigm on the hoof, like they all were. 'Sort of offered them three patsies too, if they hadn't run into Joe . . .'

It was only glancing at Stark now that Fran realized he'd contributed nothing throughout. He was instead staring at her screen with the icy look he got when she suspected he was very angry indeed.

'Shit …' he breathed, yanking out his phone and scrolling through photos, until he found what he was looking for. A video; his own voice, giving someone a hard time about a camera … his confrontation with the motorcycle paparazzo outside Leah's flat.

He hit pause and held up the screen. A face, mostly concealed inside a bike helmet, visor up, wisps of facial hair. But it was the eyes … 'Fucker's been watching us this whole time.'

69

The rider's press credentials and bike registration both proved false, predictably. Plates stolen from another bike, press credentials copied from a legitimate set with the photo changed, dead simple with a long lens and a laptop, explained the legitimate owner, if you could call a member of the paparazzi anything of the sort.

The bike itself was a different make and model from the one poor Patrick Burgess had unwittingly paid for, but as Williams pointed out – even a twice-caught loser like Leech learned to cash in hot wheels and buy clean, especially one with connections like Castor and Kovacs.

'Are you seriously expecting me to go back out in front of the cameras and tell the press that two of my so-called-detectives were face-to-face with the killer four days ago,' Harper scowled, 'but Stark told him to *piss off*?'

'I wasn't really thinking the press would be your first concern,' Fran replied tartly.

'Tell *them* that.'

'To be fair, we won't know for sure until we clap hands on him,' Fran insisted. 'But assuming it *was* him, we had no way of knowing.'

Stark remained silent, still furious he hadn't put two and two together. That he'd dismissed it all as *paranoia*.

Harper glowered at him. 'Some consolation that'll be to the families of Emily Thornton, Richard Hardacre and whoever in this world still cares about Leah Willoughby.'

'*I* still care about Leah Willoughby,' Fran bristled.

'Funny, given how much she hates *you*,' scoffed Harper. 'Or is yours more guilty conscience? And in the meantime you're telling me

I've now got more connecting Leech and his dead associates to the prison shooting than I have the Talbots?'

'We certainly don't have the full picture yet.'

'Are you going to hide behind Groombridge-isms? Fat lot of good they've done *him*.' Fran's face stiffened with offence, but Harper had already turned back to Stark. 'And you think he's been following you?'

'Could just be my imagination.' But he didn't think it was. Thinking the killer might have been watching his flat sent shivers down his spine that hadn't eased up until Ptolemy and Peters called back to confirm they'd collected Marianne and taken her home – with no suspect motorbikes in sight.

Harper's expression didn't get any happier. 'Why, though?'

'Curiosity,' said Fran. 'And ego. Just like the profiler said.'

'Fame by association?' Harper feigned disgust. Stress and sleep deprivation had taken their toll on all of them, but his antipathy towards Stark seemed to have ratcheted back up towards the bad old levels.

Stark said nothing. If psychopaths saw people as irrelevancies, threats or treats, having one follow you home wasn't good. His wit and charm offensive outside Leah's flat hadn't prevented a paparazzi exclusive; it had put him in the crosshairs, and that rather put Harper's dislike in the shade.

'Perhaps we should dangle you outside the station as bait,' Fran suggested, but no one laughed.

Harper shook his head, disappointment plain. 'You've got descriptions out?'

'Of course.'

'Then you've done just about all you can do for now,' he said, implying a low opinion of her abilities that set Stark's teeth on edge on her behalf. 'I'll talk to HQ about releasing Leech's name and face to the public. And the bike. But needless to say, I don't want a word of the rest breathed to the press before then.' He looked at Stark as he said this. Stark had recognized Gwen's measured volley in the press interview. Maybe Harper had recalled the connection between her and Stark and was now joining the dots according to his own twisted numbering. Either way, Stark already had worse things to keep him awake.

Four hours later, the map was now marked with dozens of hits: licence plate recognition camera sightings of the bike's fake plates since they were reported stolen six months earlier. The problem being, telling the stolen plates from the replacement ones on the original bike. Each hit had to be cross-checked with corresponding traffic camera footage, recent first, working backwards, but the thief had stolen plates from a bike of identical make and colour, and both riders wore black helmets and clothing, impossible to distinguish at speed. Staring at the search pattern knowing it might be fifty per cent contaminated was dispiriting, but Stark kept at it with Dixon.

'So this thing with Kelly – definitely over?' asked Dixon. His voice was tentative, but he was the only one on the team who cared too much not to ask. Apart from Fran, who'd ask whether she cared or not.

'More over than ever,' Stark replied flatly.

'Hard to compete with a doctor,' Dixon joked in commiseration.

Hard to compete with stable, thought Stark, nodding.

'My mum always said I should try harder at school,' continued Dixon, to plug the silence. 'Hard to know what else I do now. Not many job ads for ex-murder squad constables with two shit A levels.'

Or damaged vererans, thought Stark. 'Who else'll have us?'

Dixon smiled ruefully. 'I think we just summed up police recruitment.'

They pondered this inwardly for a while, wondering how they'd fare in the so-called normal world. Perhaps it wasn't too late for John Dixon. A job that didn't turn his stomach, a chance to meet a girl who didn't walk all over him when he turned up late and apologetic, a chance to be happy.

'Wait a minute,' said Dixon, pointing to the screen. 'Bethnal Road. Speed camera. Unpaid fine. Isn't that just up the road from Leah Willoughby's flat? That was just after the bike's plates were stolen. The real owner contested the fine. Six months ago. Has he been stalking her all this time?'

Stark rubbed at the two-day stubble on his chin. 'But he waited until Sinclair was released before doing anything about it – to frame him some more?'

'He killed Emily Thornton while Sinclair was under guard in hospital.'

'Only after Sinclair told him he was being discharged.'

'And he made a mess with Hardacre,' said Dixon. 'He's not very good at framing people.'

70

HQ ratified Harper's call to release the name and picture of Brian Leech as a person of interest. A slow trickle of possible sightings began to come in and so the shit-sifting began again. Fran hovered between desperation and depression. Whoever the killer really was, Sinclair or Leech, Harper was right about her guilty conscience – the target on Leah's back had been painted there by Fran, and alive or dead, she needed to find her.

What she didn't need was to be sent home by Harper to rest – however much she really did need that. Or for the pharmacy at the end of her road to have run out of sodding pregnancy tests like there'd been some local glut of teenage carelessness when proper grown-up women were going out of their minds with uncertainty.

She tried the Groombridge back-channel burner again and finally got through. He took the increasing likelihood of his ultimate disgrace with typically maddening disregard. 'Good work. Get some rest – you'll need it. I'd say, that's an order, but I find myself short on authority.'

'How have we managed to get everything so wrong?' she asked desperately.

'I'm all out of helpful sayings,' Groombridge admitted. 'But to paraphrase a certain sergeant I know – one can't be wrong before all the facts are in.'

'I could give you some choicer quotes,' Fran suggested.

'Dislike is a powerful motivator, I'm told.'

'Not for sleeping.'

'There I can't help you. This job has too many opportunities for self-recrimination, but no time to indulge them. We follow where the evidence leads, with open eyes and dauntless heart, and cry into our beers after dark. Thus it ever was and shall be. That's the job, take it or leave it.'

'Thanks for the pep talk.'

'Any time.'

She wanted him to tell her what to do, but he was never much for that. Swim or sink, was his preferred teaching method. She wanted him to tell her it would all be all right, but team morale was her job. And now he was gone, and she was alone in the deep end.

Marcus was already asleep as she settled into bed, but a little fidgeting, huffing and puffing soon established a response. 'Can't sleep?' he sighed blearily.

'I should be back at the office.'

'There's little more you could do right now, especially after two nights without sleep.'

Fran glared at the back of his head in curtain-dimmed light. 'I can't switch off.'

'Have you really given it your best attempt, in the solitary minute you've lain here?'

'It's *mid-afternoon*.'

'For people with normal lives.'

Fran snorted in disgust.

Marcus sighed. 'Well, it seems you have two choices. Get up and cook whatever you can find worthy in my fridge, *or* . . .'

'Or what?' she demanded, growing suspicious.

Suspicion was her business. She was good at it and thankfully, as now, often right.

'You're sure?' Stark stared down at the street from the balcony window. He'd checked the perimeter on his way in, more than half hoping Leech was foolish enough to come back.

'No sign,' replied Pensol down the line, checking out her own window at his request. 'You really think it was him?'

'Better safe than sorry.'

'But you think I need to be watchful?'

'At least until we've caught this shit.' Before he's finished with poor Leah and is considering his next target. What else could he say? If his celebrity had put a target on Pensol's back he'd no choice but to burden her with his fear.

She voiced no recrimination. 'Someone did buzz for you this morning. Early. She wouldn't leave a name. She sounded cross. It sounded like . . .'

'I know.' Pensol had a pretty good idea who it had been and why she was cross. 'It's not important. Comms error.'

'Will she call again?'

'I don't think so. But it's for the best.'

'You don't sound happy about that.'

'This is my default setting.'

'I'm sorry . . . if I've messed things up.'

'You haven't. That mess goes back a while.' And continued on. His couldn't help picturing Pensol, now, leaning up to kiss him. The old, young Stark wouldn't have hesitated for a second. How he missed that innocent fool.

'You should rest,' she said. Not just from weariness, but from himself.

At least she didn't suggest he take better care of himself. 'I'll certainly try.'

Stark sat on the edge of the bed trying to summon the will to shower and change.

Exhaustion and repetition taught the seasoned squaddie to shut down when idle, but knowing people were out searching for Leah Willoughby felt like knowing another squad was out on patrol – it squatted in the back of the mind, asleep or awake, often unnoticed until the relief of seeing them return – until it was your turn again.

His mind drifted back to that last night in Helmand, waiting for dawn – stripping and cleaning his weapon, reloading magazines, gear check, radio batteries, GPS, letter to Mum . . . forcing rations down . . .

He lurched awake six hours later to a text from Williams.

Double shout. Get in ASAP.

A thick fog had rolled in as he slept, filling the window with a strange ethereal light to lighten the mood.

Patrol time.

71

Dozens of sightings, most spurious. Harper never had liked hotlines. Trusting success to the idiot public never sat right with him. Tip-offs, rumours and massive wastes of time, and dubious credit if anything came of it. Proper legwork was better. But today, a combination of both dangled a fresh chance to catapult his career.

The first lead had come from an anonymous local claiming he'd seen both bike and biker 'acting suspiciously', possibly with a gun, outside a row of en-bloc garages. Such places usually belonged to a local home or business, but of those answering their doors so far, only three garages had been claimed. An initial Land Registry database search had drawn a blank on the remaining three, and methodically running hundreds of properties could take hours or find nothing if they were owned by someone further afield. Local uniform reported no sights or sounds from within, no sign of criminal entry to excuse a nosy copper widening the hole for a look-see. High-profile cases put everyone on edge and by-the-book. So another wait for a warrant.

But it was the second lead that had set Harper's pulse quickening. Another anonymous sighting, but of a stocky, bearded man driving in and out of a derelict industrial building at night, sometimes in a white van, sometimes in a small blue car, possibly a Hyundai. It had seemed too good to be true, even before DC John Dixon, of all people, pointed out the location was a half-mile from the Vauxhall Pleasure Gardens where Leah had been found after her escape.

Again local uniform reported the site silent and locked up tight. Harper was all for kicking doors in but lacked reasonable cause.

Warrants for both locations were being rushed for judicial signature, but during the delay Deputy Assistant Commissioner and all-round-wanker Stevens had muscled in, bringing CO19 with him and grinding everything to a halt. Now this was a Firearms operation and their chief inspector was playing everything by the book to make up for his earlier rotten apple.

Happy as Harper would be to bypass their circus and get on with it, Firearms at least attracted higher media profile. Just so long as his big moment wasn't swallowed up in some wrongful shooting.

'Right, is everyone clear on approach protocol?' asked the 19 Chief. 'Trojan Team One to Site A, the industrial unit, with DI Harper. Team Two to Site B, the garage lockups, with DS Millhaven. To reiterate: there's every reason to believe a Glock pistol remains in play, so maximum precautions. Clear?' All his little robots confirmed they were clear.

'Very good,' said Stevens. 'Now I'm sure I don't need to remind you all of the vital importance of finding Leah Willoughby alive . . .'

Harper raged inside. Fran's suspicions of how much importance Stevens placed on the exact opposite kept worming their way in. If Leah *was* found alive it might save Greenwich's reputation, but that chance declined with every wasted word, and she was probably dead already. But there was still a collar to be felt, and all hope of snatching glory was disappearing almost as fast as saving the day.

'. . . and on stopping the perpetrator of this horrible pantomime. Take no chances. And good luck.'

'Two-faced snake,' muttered a voice quietly. Harper was astonished to see it was Cox, standing next to him. The Superintendent looked round as if only just realizing Harper was there and puffed his moustache. 'Yes. Well . . . carry on, DI Harper,' he said irritably before departing.

He'd never understood Groombridge's apparent respect for Cox. The blustering old fool was yesterday's man, and Harper's aspirations lay elsewhere now anyway. But he couldn't shake the suspicion that those words had been meant for his ears.

To make matters worse, Stark and Fran had both shown up minutes before the briefing. Tipped off. Williams or Dixon showing where their loyalties lay. Not Hammed who, Harper suspected, rightfully resented Stark's precocity. Well, whatever happened tonight, Harper would make sure Stark was nowhere near it. He wasn't going to play the hero at Harper's expense again.

'Not you, Stark,' said Harper. 'We've too many all-action heroes on this already, and I'm sure Nineteen can do without your giant brain and dodgy hip.'

Fran's mouth fell open.

'Whatever you say, Guv,' Stark said, to douse her fuse. 'I'll man the phones here.' He was sure the phones were every bit as manned as they'd get, but he'd eat all the humble pie Harper could dish out if it just meant they'd all get the fuck on with it instead of wasting even more time here.

'Good,' Harper said. 'Fran, stay close on Site B. Can't have some-one from Nineteen making the arrest without one of us there to share the credit.'

Fran nodded, un-enthused and unconvinced.

Stark's phone gave him the excuse to step away from that unex-ploded ordnance . . . Straight into the path of another.

A text from Kelly.

Joe. I need to see you. Can we meet?

Stark stared in surprise, wondering what on earth remained to be said. What could she want to say or hear? This could be a chance to explain about the girl answering his buzzer, of course, but to what end? *Sorry, really not a good time*, he typed back.

Are you at work?

Yes. Can I call you later?

There was no response from Kelly, and ten minutes crept by with Stark increasingly suspecting he'd caused even further offence. Then . . .

Really need to talk face-to-face. I'm out the front, across the road from the station. Just two minutes, please!

Stark glanced at his watch. The raids were leaving in five minutes. He thought of calling her, but a face-to-face offered less chance for confusion and ambiguity.

Please, Joe! chimed his phone.

Okay, two minutes. Stark's thumb hovered over the send icon, wondering why he was acquiescing. The world seemed determined to challenge his courage and undermine his efforts to balance out past misdeeds.

'Something wrong?' asked Dixon, looking searchingly at him.

'When is there not?' Stark mused quietly.

'Did you see my email? About the undertakers?'

'What?' Stark shook his head, only half-listening. 'No, I haven't . . . Look, sorry, Kelly's outside. I'd better sort it before you lot jolly off.' He hit send, and grabbed his jacket on the way out, heading for the stairs – more painful than the lift, less slow. But as he reached the ground floor he found his path blocked. Harper, alone with DAC Stevens in the lower stairwell, conspiratorial whispers silenced by his approaching footsteps, eyes unwelcoming.

'Stark? Where are you going?' demanded Harper. 'You're on phone duty.'

'Just have to speak to someone. Back in a minute.'

'Who?'

'Just a very quick personal matter, sir.'

'Then I suggest you resolve it in your *personal time*,' chimed Stevens.

Stark kicked himself. He considered just doubling back through the rear exit and around, but his stubbornness got in the way. 'I'm sorry, sir, but this is important and won't take long. I assure you it won't impact on my forty hours,' he added, with no sarcasm necessary. They all knew the creaking crutch of undeclared overtime was the only thing keeping the Met staggering on since the financial crash and crushing boot of anti-Keynesian austerity – doubtless enthusiastically embraced by career-first ambitious dogs like Stevens, licking the hands of power while biting anyone in their way and shitting on the rest. This situation was only sustained because un-trod beats and parked investigations upset coppers more than they troubled slippery politicians, but goodwill had its limits and Stark was letting his show.

The DAC's eyes narrowed. 'Have a care, Constable Stark.'

'I'm sure I don't know what you mean, sir. But if I might just pass, please? The sooner I'm gone the sooner I'm back.'

Harper held out a hand. 'You're not going anywhere unless I say so.'

'Please, sirs, this really can't wait and I'll be back on those phones as ordered before DI Harper and the team leave.'

'Take one step towards those doors and I'll report you for insubordination and dereliction of duty, Constable.'

'Respectfully, sirs, I am entitled to a refreshment break in any work period exceeding five hours, which this will be.'

'Subject to the exigencies of service,' quoted Stevens from the same regulation.

'Which I have clearly stated will not be impacted.'

Both senior officers swelled with indignation.

Harper placed a grip on Stark's upper arm.

Stark's hackles rose. In all but a second, a long career in the police force played out before him, subject to the constant grating of arseholes like these two, and he asked himself whether that normal sort of life he and Dixon had pondered might not be better all round. 'Are you attempting to physically restrain a subordinate in the workplace, sir?' he said darkly.

'What are you going to do, call your union rep?'

'I should warn you, I feel both threatened and fearful.'

Harper's grip tightened, either too stupid or too conscious of his overlord's presence to consider how it had ended the last time he tried laying hands on Stark. 'You think you're so clever, don't you?'

'Remove your hand, please, or I will be forced to defend myself.'

Harper glanced at the DAC, confident Stark wouldn't dare. His grip grew a thrust and snarl. 'Fuck you, Sta—'

Stark gripped the arm, twisted the wrist and shoved. The yielding Jujutsu twist would have been sufficient to control his opponent. Adding the aggressive Wing-Chun shove was simply to shift the obstacle and needn't have hurt, but Harper was a big man and just enough force to move him was enough to make him trip over his own clumsy feet and crash across the floor, grasping his shoulder, gasping like a fish out of water, while Stevens recoiled in fear.

'Do excuse me, sirs,' said Stark, walking past the shocked Stevens and through the double doors.

'*Stark!*' barked Stevens after him. '*You're suspended! Effective immediately! Come back and hand over –*'

The doors closed on his words, and possibly Stark's career, but he was currently too stupid with fury to spare time for feeling stupid. The oblivious desk sergeant wished him a good evening as he passed through the airlock, across reception and out into the night.

He looked for Kelly, but there was a parked van blocking his view of Burney Gardens. Clicking his tongue with irritation, he rounded the vehicle, searching the street-lit shadows, and sensed movement behind him, just before the vicious crack of electricity jolted him from consciousness.

PART 3

72

This is stupid, thought Marianne, for the hundredth time.

No phone number, just an address she'd nosily read on an envelope containing stray mail Stark was collecting to forward on.

Kelly Jones.

Historic figure of envy from Pensol and others.

An old terrace house in Blackheath divided into two flats one above the other. Shared front door that Pensol had been staring at for ten minutes since deciding not to ask the cab to wait.

Light on behind the front room curtains.

This was stupid. She should be locked up safe at home, not out trying to repair the relationship of a man she'd fallen for. Classic avoidance. And worse, to come all this way and stand here too scared to ring the doorbell, uncertain of what to say, only that an explanation was owed. He wasn't falling for her. He didn't even want to kiss her. And whatever their current status, Kelly deserved to know why there was a sleepy woman in Joe's flat that morning. If he could speak his pain and fear to a circle of strangers, Marianne could do this.

Sod it . . . She marched up to the door and pressed the button, hearing a faint ring inside.

Nothing.

'Looking for me?' asked a voice behind her.

A girl: pony-tail Sloane Street shopper with the silver-spoon accent and Prada bag to prove it. Kooky-chic and skinny as . . . too cute to dislike with any heart.

Marianne put on her work smile. 'Kelly, Flat B.'

'I'm A.' The Sloane smiled apologetically. 'No answer . . . ? She's a darling. Probably still at work.'

Marianne tried again, and shrugged.

'Oh well . . .' The Sloane waggled her keys and Pensol stepped aside.

A brief glimpse of a small shared lobby and the Sloane closed the front door with a chirpy farewell.

Marianne stared at it, wondering if she should leave a note.

She didn't have pen and paper and was embarrassed to disturb the Sloane.

Cursing, she turned to leave, but then her eyes fell on a tote hand-bag behind the bins, contents spilling . . .

Now hardly seemed the time to be filling in a disciplinary form, but Harper was fuming far too dangerously not to savour this.

Detective Constable Joseph Stark had disobeyed and violently assaulted a superior officer. Whether or not Stevens had the power to suspend Stark verbally without due process was questionable, but Stark was finished all the same, and it couldn't have happened to a nicer twat. Harper had extended the olive branch, tried to put the past behind them, blame on both sides and all that, and where had magnanimity got him? Stark had been skirting insubordination daily, masking prideful prejudice behind a poker face, hiding behind Fran's skirts as ever and worse . . . briefing the press to embarrass him and now breaking his fucking arm in front of a very senior officer!

Harper flexed his shoulder. Okay, so it wasn't broken, but it hurt. A bit. He might have to see a doctor . . . later, when all this shit was done with, when he had the killer in a cell. Perhaps he'd knock up a sling from the first aid kit for the triumphant press conference, win a little sympathy to go with the glory – the dauntless General, leading his troops from the front . . .

Harper filled in the form on his screen with a twisted smile of glee. Stark had finally made his bed.

He stared at it, wondering if his hasty description of the event was adequate. He would be called on later to elaborate.

So would Stark, of course. A tiny part of Harper could acknowledge that this was a waste of decent material. Goldenballs had a first-rate brain on him, but would always be a first-class pain in the arse. So what if he had a troubled history – who didn't? He wasn't a proper copper and never would be.

'Time to go, sir,' said Dixon round the door.

'Okay.'

'Did you get a chance to read the email I sent you earlier?'

'What?'

'About the undertakers?'

'The thing about Jersey?' Dixon the limp-rag had apparently taken it upon himself to start trawling back through old properties linked to Sinclair, particularly those he'd helped his clients liquefy, and thought he'd found something new; some old undertakers. Harper had lost interest two lines in, but Dixon was hovering like a puppy hoping for a pat on the head for leaving a steaming present on the carpet. 'We looked into all the properties linked to Sinclair two years ago.' Harper had led that line of enquiry with Hammed and didn't take kindly to the suggestion something had been missed.

'But this one was bought up by one of those Jersey property companies, who tried to get planning permission to convert to residential. But the local authority refused on some policy to retain employment premises, so it just got boarded up and sold on to another –'

Harper held up a hand. 'Does any of this have a point?'

'Maybe. It was Joe got me thinking –'

Stark . . . Harper should've bloody known. 'More importantly,' he interrupted again, 'does it tie back to Brian Leech, seeing as that's who we're actually looking for right now?'

'We still need to find Sinclair, though, don't we? And the drawings on the Planning Department portal –'

'Sinclair can stay under whichever shitty rock he's crawled, for now,' said Harper irritably. 'We've wasted quite enough time on him and Joe Stark's wild goose chases.'

'Saddle up, posse,' called a loud voice; one of the swaggering firearms lot. Dixon retreated, leaving Harper staring at the form, cursor still hovering over the send button.

Stark had humiliated him in front of one of the most senior police officers in the land, and Stevens would back Harper's account to the hilt. Unless he didn't. In the cold light of day, Goldenballs Stark was the MET's decorated PR poster boy, and once Stevens had what he wanted . . .

Better to wait till Stevens played his cards, before showing yours. There'd only be one chance to cash in and Harper couldn't afford to find Stark's joker face laughing up at him again.

Crammed with all the usual handbag non-essential essentials, a wad of opened bills still in envelopes, action pending, all addressed to Kelly. No purse or phone, but keys on a Help-For-Heroes keyring – a charity for injured veterans.

Who dropped their handbag without picking it up? Had she been mugged? And if so, where was she . . . ?

One key opened the outer door. Another the inner door to Flat B.

No response to a tentative 'Hello?'

She knew it was wrong, but curiosity drew Marianne up the stairs into Kelly's home, heart aflutter, ears straining for the sound of footsteps, a voice raised in enquiry, in alarm . . .

But the flat was silent.

A mess of eclectic furnishings and decoration, jumbled with clutter, the coffee table sprinkled with more opened mail, poorly refolded Sunday paper supplements and a used coffee mug, a gym bag and at least three discarded tops. Travel memorabilia and photos. A stunning girl with silky brown hair, smiling in various places, with various people . . . instantly recognizable from the online photos of Stark's medal ceremony at Buckingham Palace, glowing beneath a broad-brimmed cream hat, poured into an elegant sky-blue dress that perfectly matched her eyes.

That photo wasn't here.

Not one photo of Joe on display. But they'd be here. Put away. Too painful to look at, too precious to throw away.

Marianne crept into the solitary bedroom, bed barely made, wardrobe door open revealing a tightly packed collection of all the usual, from scruffy to sparkly, a few plastic-wrapped from the cleaners, including, of course, the sky-blue dress. A hatbox wedged atop with a suitcase and other items.

She fought the temptation to investigate every drawer.

The tiny kitchen and bathroom were equally cluttered.

How had someone this messy survived in Stark's world? And how had someone this beautiful ever allowed him to leave hers? No one knew why, though Marianne had now experienced something of how beguilingly precarious his life might really be ... like one of nature's huge stone columns, worn from the promontory mainland, beset by wind, rain and sea; defiant and doomed.

Tears welling, she retreated to the lobby, courage overwhelmed with sudden humiliation and dread.

This was stupid. Kelly would walk in any second, demanding to know who the hell she was, dialling the police, leaving Marianne to explain her foolishness to everyone in the station.

That was one possibility.

The other, given a killer may have been stalking Joe, was altogether more terrifying ...

She was just returning the various lights to off when a creak on the stairs froze her blood.

73

'Did I wake you?'

'I'm suspended, not retired.' Groombridge allowed himself a little bluntness for the fun of it, though Maggie was a long-trusted colleague and vital control-room back channel over recent years, with her finger ever on the station's pulse. He hadn't been sleeping; he'd been pacing his living room like a caged cat, waiting for news.

'And I shouldn't be phoning you, but I am,' she riposted, 'despite Deputy Assistant Commissioner Shifty's edict to the contrary.'

'Duty lies heavy on us all,' replied Groombridge.

'Some more than others.'

'It's too soon for news on the raids. So what illicit knowledge have you to impart on this portentous eve?'

'I'm not sure I've a mind to tell you now.'

'*Maggie* . . .'

'With half the station and the MIT out on their little raids, I wasn't sure what to do . . .'

'Speaking your mind would be a start . . .'

'All right, DCI Grumpy-pants,' she tutted. 'Well, I've got DS Ptolemy here with me. He's had a call from PC Pensol . . .'

Fran gripped the seat in front as they cornered at speed, trying to think about anything else but her stomach. A jolly ride in a cramped minibus, like a perverse seaside trip, wedged in with smelly, over-excited adolescent boys. The bus was central in a convoy of Armed Response Vehicles and struggling to keep up under blues and twos as each armada raced to be first on site, swaying and rattling its human cargo while the radio in front gave a constant chirping of updates. Both cross-border raids, Site A required personnel present from Lewisham and Site B people from Lambeth.

Harper would hardly be her go-to mental topic for making her feel less nauseous, but she'd glimpsed the bull-headed berk holding one arm as if pained, and obviously angry. Her immediate thought had been Stark, who'd put that same arm in a sling two years ago. The latter hadn't come to see them off. Probably sulking over the phones in his own granite fashion, but it wasn't like him.

The prevailing theory was Site A, the industrial unit, was more promising, hence Harper calling dibs. Fran's bus was still very much on edge. She had Williams and Dixon for company, but there was no space for conversation.

Both DCs looked as tired and wired as she felt. She and Dixon had little better to do, but Williams should be at home with his family. Parents needed all the sleep they could get, she understood, trying not to imagine herself in the role. His wife had gone part-time after the first child and, Fran had gleaned from snippets, never recovered in status, income or self-worth. You couldn't work murder cases part-time; *full*-time wasn't enough. What was Fran supposed to do, ask Marcus to park *his* career? A baby really was inconceivable.

Her phone added to the vibrational misery. Groombridge's back-channel burner. Answering it, while trying to hide its obvious non-smartness, she spoke as quietly as the background cacophony allowed. 'It's a bit early for an update.'

'I know that,' replied Groombridge, curtness not lost in the noise. 'Just wondering if Stark is with you?'

Fran frowned, uncertain she'd heard correctly over the din. 'No. He's back at the station. Why?'

'Never mind. Keep me posted.' And he was gone.

Shaking her head, she tucked the phone away as the van lurched around a corner.

Fran didn't get carsick. It wasn't the kind of thing a girl with four older brothers could allow herself. The feeling in her stomach was anticipation, she resolutely told herself, or exhaustion and hunger.

And not a baby. Definitely not that; not now. She could be pregnant tomorrow.

Finally free from the office, racing under blues and twos, Harper felt the thrill of the charge and revelled in it. Yes, CO19 might kick in the doors and Stevens might make a play for the limelight, but Harper would get the credit for this even if he had to do a little press briefing himself. If that hot redhead Maddox was willing to take dictation from Stark, she'd surely beg for the skinny from a bona fide DI.

His phone buzzed to life. Number withheld. He ignored it.

'How long?' he asked, impatient at the slowness of the convoy. The other team would arrive at their site first. Instinct told him his was the more likely chance, but if he was wrong . . . Fran would make the collar and leave him high and dry.

The AFO sergeant in the passenger seat assigned to accompany them pointed wordlessly at the satnav time. Just because his Chief Inspector was running the show he thought he could be rude. That and packing a sidearm.

With a bit of luck Harper would have the last laugh. Finally reap his just deserts. You never knew, he might land a coveted spot on the Flying Squad and a gun of his own.

The phone vibrated again, and paranoia overcame his disdain for people who hid their numbers. 'Who is this?' he barked, holding it to his ear as he drove, enjoying the disapproving glance from the AFO.

'It's Mike.'

'Guv?' he asked, instantly hating his hemispheric brain for coughing up the out-of-date title while half of it drove and the other half tried to guess why Groombridge was calling.

'Is Stark with you?'

Stark? 'Why?'

'It's a simple question, Owen.'

'So was mine. I'm sorry, Mike, but you shouldn't be calling –'

'This isn't about the case,' Groombridge interrupted rudely. 'I just need Stark.'

'I don't know where he is and I don't *care*,' replied Harper coldly. It was up to Stevens to announce Stark's suspension, not his, however tempting. 'Now if you don't mind, I'm kind of busy.' He hung up, rubbed his sore shoulder and cursed.

The satnav said eight minutes.

And if anyone still wanted Stark, they could go find him in hell.

74

Crack-thump.

The supersonic crack of the bullet passing close, followed by the thump of the gunshot itself following behind. The shift in the air and confusion of the ears. Baffling. Removed. Like seeing something inexplicable in the corner of your eye only to turn your head and find nothing, unable to recall what you'd seen or felt, only that it was wrong, terribly wrong.

An age between heartbeats.

The slap in the face, heart-stopping realization ... Bullet ... Passing ... BULLET!

Your brain suddenly cottoning on. Body flinching far too late. Only the luck of the miss keeping you breathing. Such moments, the single scud of the heart, stuck with you years after; rushing back on you now.

Another thump and jolt.

A pothole. Just a ...

Hot air, restricted and stale, fumes, and noise, too harsh for dream ...

Pain ... equals consciousness.

Mouth dry and jaw sore ... a gag – cloth in the mouth held in place with something hard, like cable twisted around the back of the head ...

Hands and ankles tied too.

Cloth bag over his head, making it even harder to breathe.

Ache ... from being hog-tied, but also on left knee, elbow and side of the head – direction of fall after the stun; knocking himself out.

G-force as the vehicle cornered; not fast, but lying on your side, body sliding slightly on the hard floor. A van, hard cargo area overlaid with something crackly – *plastic*.

Like cattle in the abattoir, ready for slaughter.

Stark tried to swallow, but the wet rag in his mouth depressed his tongue and made him gag . . . made his eyes water with the effort of not choking.

Ambushed.

Right outside the station.

And worse . . . Much, much worse . . . Whoever was driving this van had used Kelly's phone to lure him.

He lay still, listening above the poorly sound-proofed diesel engine and suspension clatter. An urban road, slow and irregular; still potholed from winter, the stop-start of late evening traffic and frequent junctions.

Stark's watch was bound behind him but the unconscious part of his fractured brain that perpetually quantified his surroundings started estimating time against speed, while the part that controlled his physical being struggled against his restraints with even less success. Guesstimating how far he'd travelled was futile, not knowing how long he'd been unconscious, but even less use unless he could free himself before they arrived to launch some form of counter-ambush.

Cursing, he let himself roll with the next turn, attempting to at least leave fingerprints on the wall of the van in case this ended as badly as he feared, but the plastic sheet seemed to be wrapped up the sides.

'Quit wriggling or I'll zap you again,' said a voice up front.

Male. London accent. Unfamiliar . . . Not Julian Sinclair.

Stark hoped it was Brian Leech, because that at least meant Fran and the others were out there trying to track him down. Right now that seemed Stark's best hope of freedom, and, gut-wrenchingly, perhaps Kelly's too. He'd considered Pensol a target, but never, in his wildest nightmares, *Kelly.* But if the bike had followed him to their meeting at the pub . . . and the following morning she'd buzzed at his flat . . . And she was in the papers with him when he'd been to the Palace to get his damn medal ... How could he have been so *stupid*!

Perhaps Leech just had her phone. But *perhaps* was thin hope.

The turns were coming closer together, the van closing in on its destination.

75

Fran craned her neck to see the garages, but the fog had folded over the city like a blanket, blurring the landmarks highlighted in the briefing.

It was eerily quiet for London, even nearing the witching hour, with adjacent streets cordoned off with uniform cars. Streetlights lit the diffused world unforgiving amber, punctuated with flashing electric-blue. One or the other might've been her colour, not that she cared much for such things, but together they painted her and the claustrophobic world with the ghoulish shades of bad news. She stamped her cold feet and tried to shrink down even further into the oversize coat the firearms boys had handed out – dark navy-blue with POLICE emblazoned front, back and sides in big reflective yellow font to prevent friendly fire, and give any bad guys a sporting target.

'Try him again,' she muttered at Williams.

'Sarge.' He dialled again, the screen briefly lighting his face like a TV flickering in the front room of a couch potato too lazy to turn on the light or close the curtains. He shuffled his feet, cold or in need of the loo, then hung up. 'Still straight to voicemail.'

'And he didn't say anything else?' she asked for the hundredth time.

'No, Sarge,' replied Dixon miserably.

But something was up. Stark AWOL on some damsel emergency.

No answer on his mobile or the MIT office. The idea of him shirking duty was unthinkable, even for Kelly, and if there was one thing Fran hated more than waiting powerless on a freezing cold street at night, it was not knowing ... something, anything, everything. Whether Leah Willoughby was alive or dead. Whether they'd catch the Greenwich Strangler tonight or never. Whether she was pregnant. Stark's whereabouts ought to be low on her list, but for some reason his unexplained absence had the hairs on her neck standing.

'Right, if he's not manning the phones you'd better hitch a lift back there instead. And if and when he shows his face, slap it for me.'

The radio crackled to life.

Trojan Control Vehicle Bravo to Obs White. Sit rep.

Observer White. No activity.

Control Bravo to Obs Black. Sit rep.

Observer Black. No activity.

Control Bravo to Breach Team White. Sit rep.

Breach Team White. In position. Standing by.

Trojan Control Vehicle Bravo to Breach Team White. Standby, Standby. Go!

Fran held her breath, pulse quickening. Officers on the line. Not her people, but her kind, entering the unknown.

Please, she pleaded to the God she neither believed in nor despised, conspicuous in her life only by his or her absence – *please*, let Leah be in there, alive.

A prayer as forlorn of hope as it was faith.

Down the street there was a muffled crack, followed by raised voices flattened in the fog.

'Stay by your car,' barked the AFO babysitter, showily checking the safety on his MP5 carbine.

Superior little shit. For all his hardware, he was stuck here with them and just as much a spare wheel; an Authorized Firearms Officer, guarding the perimeter while the Specialist Firearms Officers did the glory work storming the castle. Harper was certain which team he'd have been on if he *had* gone down that road.

A scattergun barrage of radio traffic confirmed officers were out there in the mist closing streets and encouraging residents to stay in their homes away from windows while various teams made various approaches. The CO19 Chief and his people were standing round a laptop with a live feed from a thermal camera pointed at the old warehouse building by some luckless fuck in body armour out there in this claustrophobic fog. The image was all blues and greys. No heat sources. But internal rooms or a basement would be invisible.

The usual massive waste of time, as likely to spook a quarry as ensnare them. Just kick in the door and have done. If you think the perp has a gun, take two or three of your own, but all this pussy-footing around . . . 'Health and safety gone mad,' he muttered.

Hammed looked up from his phone. 'Guv?'

Just get on with it, breathed Harper silently. All he could think was that Fran might be in the right place and not him.

Obs Black to Trojan Control Vehicle Alpha, the radio crackled suddenly. *Vehicle approaching from south. Medium van. Please advise. Over.*

Trojan Control Alpha to all units. Fall back from sight. Let vehicle approach.

Obs Red to Trojan Control Alpha. Have vehicle, now approaching Red side. Stopping. One exiting. Over.

Control Alpha to Obs Red. Roger. Eyes on. Keep appraised.

'Right,' muttered the Chief Inspector nearby, rubbing his gloved hands together with anticipatory excitement while his controller called each observation team in turn for a sit rep. 'Let's do this.'

Harper nodded, muttering, 'About *fucking* time.'

76

If there's one thing worse than a punch in the face, it's a punch you can't see coming.

Bell-ringing pain, teeth-rattling ... Stars swirling, like a boat-tossed sea-sickening sky ...

Gasping, inhaling cloth; mouth blocked, nose bloody ... choking ... panicking ... *panicking* ...

NO!

Battling every instinct, screaming inside ... Stark fought for control ... *fight the panic, take control – win!*

He'd experienced waterboarding in SF training, a brutal demonstration of how the strongest could be rendered gibbering by simple application of a plank, rope, cloth and a watering can. Simulated drowning. All the agony of torture with none of the tell-tale marks – the visible kind at least. 'Enhanced Interrogation' at its most plausibly deniable.

Slowly, painfully, he won.

Still tied. Still gagged. Still hooded. No light, little air. Between the jangling of his heartbeats in his ears, gagging breaths, movement around him ...

His attempt to fight back had been as futile as it was brief. The van had made a final few turns and stopped. The driver had got out. Stark had thrashed and banged as hard as he could in the back to attract attention, but the driver climbed back in, repeated his earlier threat, drove forward a few yards as if through a gate and got out again.

When the main side door slid open, Stark had already positioned himself for one good two-footed kick, connecting with a satisfying grunt and the sound of his abductor falling. But then came the retaliatory sucker-punch.

Another exploded now with equally zero warning, and the suffocating panic clamped down all over again, with no chance even to clench his teeth against the following crackle of voltage.

. . . someone in rear, over.

Trojan Control Alpha to Breach Teams. Standby. Go, go go!

Voices erupted somewhere away in the fog, the words lost. On tiptoes, staring into the orange mist, Harper strained his ears for gunshots, but there was just shouting and garbled radio traffic.

Minutes seemed like hours. Then . . .

Breach Red to Trojan Control Alpha. Two suspects restrained.

Breach White to Alpha. Building secured. All clear. No one else home.

Breach Red to Alpha. Suspects are IC3 male and IC1 female. Late teens. Do not match descriptions. Repeat, do not match descriptions. Claim they're a couple.

'*Fuck!*' Harper set off, ignoring the remonstrations of their babysitter. He had to see for himself. And what he found was disaster.

Terrified young lovers looking for a quiet spot to mist up the windows only to find themselves trussed like Christmas turkeys by shouty, armed police.

Harper's hopes had soared, only to crash down in flames.

He almost didn't hear what followed. Calls for scene preservation and SOCO, talk of bleach, blue plastic sheeting and electrical cord . . . All Harper registered was the thumping of his heart and crushing anti-climax.

'Sounds like the right place,' commented Hammed.

Of course this was the place, thought Harper bitterly. Probably where they all died; after God knows what agony, degradation and terror, while we searched just about everywhere else.

Right place. Wrong time.

Another piece in the puzzle wasn't what he needed. He needed a collar. He needed Leah Willoughby, alive or dead, and a culprit, red-handed. Why couldn't they just be here? Why couldn't he catch a *break*?

Turned out it was perfectly possible for fog to form *inside* – if the side in question was in a large, unheated, unused and utterly empty old brick garage, tucked down a forgotten side street on a freakishly cold April night in the middle of a London pea-souper.

SOCO were giving the place a cursory once-over, but if there was any evidence to be found it was fresh as a daisy found pressed in the pages of a thousand-year-old tome in the damp crypt of the world's worst-maintained library. More likely, this was a complete red herring. The press had arrived to rub it in, and some local businessman would probably turn up in the morning demanding compensation for their broken door.

What was the betting Prince Charmless would call any second to tell her he'd slain the dragon and saved the princess?

God, she was tired.

Bloody Marcus.

She tugged off a glove and surreptitiously texted him. *Knackered. Cold. Bored. Hungry. Blame you.*

He texted back in less than a minute. *Poor baby.*

Hate you.

Love you too.

Fran stared at that last. He wasn't allowed to say that. They had a rule. Well, *she* had a rule, which despite being unspoken, he'd observed. Until now.

'Something wrong, Sarge?' asked Williams.

Fran thought about that, but the list was simply too long. 'Sod this, I need some coffee.'

77

Pain brought Stark round. His captor must've taken the time to extend his beating after zapping him. His left eye felt gummy with blood. The gag and hood were still in place. He felt dizzy and nauseous and fought to get a hold of himself again, lest he throw up and choke.

Rotating his head made that more likely, but he needed to find some equilibrium.

It took several seconds to realize he was tied now to a hard chair.

Through the ringing in his ears he thought he heard a voice, or laughter. Then movement towards him and another explosion into his cheek.

It took a minute or more of swallowing the terror to get his breath under control again, and another to regain sufficient grip on gravity to realize he was on his side ... Chair toppled by the blow, head pounding against the floor ...

'That's for making me zap you again,' laughed a voice.

The same voice from the van.

Stark hoped their knuckles hurt.

But there was another sound ... screaming? Weeping? Muffled ... *gagged*. *Kelly*. They were making her watch. But she was *alive*.

He tested his limbs. Wrists bound together behind his back and to the seat ... Each ankle to the respective chair leg. Cables. Probably the grey electrical kind. The chair was metal tubing, plastic seat. Not much give. But the wrists ... Training taught you to flex your wrists as the bindings were tightened, to try and create a modicum of slack;

something to work with. Stark didn't remember being dragged in and tied, but either his addled brain had remembered or his captor wasn't thorough, and that *was* something ... And his legs ... His feet were no longer held against the floor by his weight. If the chair legs ended straight, not bent round in a loop ... he tried sliding his ankles downwards ...

'And this is for *kicking me*!' A boot exploded into his stomach.

No chance to bend with it. Starting winded left nowhere to go, no control to be sought. By the time he was able to try and breathe he was already slipping under. His whole body started racking with the agony of suffocation, but the cloth in his mouth shifted back, stopping all, stars exploding and dimming, spinning away from reach ... He thought he could hear Kelly screaming, but it might have been him, or just the blood pumping uselessly through his ears ... Every cell in his body screaming out for oxygen ... burning with agony, *burning hands, smoke-stung eyes ... trying to keep the wheel straight as the damaged Land Rover screeched and rattled headlong down the narrow Afghan street with bullets and RPG incoming ... trying not to choke on the smell of his burning flesh ... blinking through the blackening smoke ... lungs bursting with the weight of the injured man over his shoulder as he ran ... RPG blasting him sideways ... pinned back to the blood-red earth by the final bullet ... chaos and screaming ...*

Medic!

Stealing dark ... and blinding light ... Detonations. Rotor blades. Suns exploding, falling into the black hole at the centre of everything.

MEDIC!

Rough hands, ripping the choking blood from his mouth ...

Oxygen, flooding, drowning ... infusing him with pain ... so much blessed pain ... Searing into his lungs and brain ...

Shouting ... so much shouting over the din in his ears ...

Shouting.

Shaking.

'... no use to us dead, you *idiot*!'

A blurred silhouette materialized in the glare, rough hands

righting the chair with him in it as each breath dragged in brought the world brighter and the pain with it.

The burning of his hands was more in the wrists. His fingers were sticky – with blood, he guessed. In his suffocating panic he'd wrestled hard. There was some flex there, some slippage . . .

A hand slapped his face.

'Wakey-wakey, soldier boy. It's time for your next fifteen minutes of fame.'

Neck whiplashed, skin stinging, but no longer hooded or gagged, he turned his face slowly back to his abuser. The silhouette blurred through the bloody left eye, swimming into focus with the other . . .

No sign of the straggly hair and beard of his prison and hospital visits – the man crouching before him was gym-fit, clean-shaven with short peroxide hair, but similar enough in features to Richard Hardacre, and only bulky clothing away from Patrick Burgess. He'd clearly abandoned his impersonation of the latter after doing his best to pin everything else on the former. A clumsy ruse, and chilling.

Stark tested his jaw, rolled his tongue around his mouth, collecting the blood, and spat on the floor. 'Brian Leech.'

A flare of panic in the eyes . . . He had to know his name and description were already in the news. Perhaps he thought his new look would hide him.

'We know who you are,' said Stark, keeping his good eye locked on Leech's. 'Every officer in London is looking for you.'

'Who says we're still in London?'

Who indeed. By Stark's estimate they'd zig-zagged roughly six kilometres through urban streets since he first came to, but before that . . .

Leech searched his eyes and smiled. 'You don't have a clue where we are, and neither do your friends.'

'It's only a matter of time.'

'Maybe. But I'll be long gone before anyone finds you here. Or them . . .'

Standing, he gestured across what Stark guessed to be a domestic bedroom, walls, floor and ceiling lined with slabs of interlocking black foam like you'd find on the floor of a gym, itself covered with blue plastic sheeting, taped in place. Soundproofing and forensic containment.

A dungeon.

Aside from a cool-box in one corner, there were just three pieces of furniture. The chair Stark was tied to. Another, to which someone else was bound and gagged with cable and cloth, and a sturdy wooden table – bent and tied over which was a naked, ball-gagged woman.

The seated captive, evidence of violence inflicted upon his face, was Julian Sinclair.

The woman was not Kelly, but Leah Willoughby.

78

'Not who you were expecting?' grinned Leech, pleased with himself.

Leah's face was stained with tears. She shook her head faintly in misery but made no new sound, just staring as if she had so little fight left that seeing her would-be rescuer so soundly subdued could have no impact on her morale. The bright pink ball-gag stretched her mouth painfully wide, the black leather straps holding it firmly in place. If she cried too much and blocked her nose she'd suffocate.

With a cold eye, one might call the dullness to hers fortunate. Drugged, Stark guessed. Though not enough to drift free of her horror. The Rohypnol. There was a sports bottle with a built-in-straw on the table. Post-mortems had found circular bruising and cuts inside some of the victim's mouths, suggesting something small and tubular had been forced in. He'd either spiked their drinks in bars or forced them to drink later. The Strangler liked his victims placid. Small mercy perhaps. A length of grey cable with a knot at one end for grip lay across the table for her eyes to contemplate, the lines across her back indicative of what she'd already endured, having been in Leech's clutches for over a day. Stark's eye was anything but cold.

The sound of a train clattering past right outside gently rattled the room, and it suddenly dawned on Stark where he probably was, pieces falling into place like the tumblers of a lock . . . clicking open.

Camden Uniform hadn't seen Leah leave the building.

In the chair, Julian Sinclair watched. Bound and gagged himself, he seemed almost passive. Whatever countless scenes he might have fantasized about finally proving his innocence to the police, this terrible diorama was never among them. He met Stark's eyes with almost no apparent recognition. The same stupefied, thousand-yard stare Stark had seen on captive combatants – lost in the disbelief as much as the fear. Or perhaps he was drugged too. It made sense.

What *didn't* was how he'd ended up here. Stark's only thought was that poor Emily Thornton had been party to whatever hideaway Sinclair's legal team had prepared for him, and Leech had forced it from her. Stark's jaw clenched. He couldn't help Emily now. But Leah was still alive. And Sinclair. And the countless women out there that needed protection from the real monster in this sick story – and one woman in particular.

As if reading his mind, Leech held up a phone in a battered leatherette case that Stark recognized. 'Wondering how I got this? Wondering where she is? Whether she's *safe*?'

The twisted delight emphasizing the last word made Stark's skin burn. He wanted to tell the creature that he'd kill him, pursue him to the ends of the earth and choke the life from him, but threats were futile, and what he wanted above all was to know, as Leech said, whether Kelly was alive, or whether her bitter association with Stark had come to the bitterest end.

'I'll tell you,' smiled Leech. 'But first you have to tell me something.' He stood, reached into a small holdall on the floor and pulled out a Glock 19. The missing pistol used to shoot Sinclair outside the prison . . . used to kill Leech's unwitting ex-cell-mate accomplice, Istvan Kovacs, and his car thief associate, Damien Castor. And although he not seen it at the time, the stun baton on the table near Leah's face looked a lot like the one used to incapacitate Stark in the prison footage.

He had no time to celebrate these connections. Leech chambered a round and pointed the pistol at Leah, then at Sinclair, then at Leah. 'One lives. One dies. You choose. Now.'

Stark stared back, silent.

'You're thinking they'll both die anyway,' said Leech. 'Maybe you're right. But there's quick ways to die, and there's slow. Mercy is yours to give. One dies now, quick. One dies later, really, *really* slowly. And you get to choose.'

Stark had chosen lives before, down the barrel of a gun. Under fire. Chosen targets, one by one. Life after life. Too many to count. Too many to live with. Relax, breathe, aim, hold, fire. Relax, breathe, aim, hold . . . kill. Enemy combatants. Not this. Not captives. It happened. Everyone knew the accusations, the denials, the trials, the excuses . . . Wounded, dying enemy, finished off by traumatized, angry soldiers. Prisoners tortured for information or sick kicks, sometimes unto death. Moral and legal wrongs, abhorrent on every level, yet all too understandable to any who'd fought past fallen comrades, witnessed the worst atrocities.

But nothing had prepared Stark for this.

'Come on, soldier boy,' said Leech, growing impatient. 'Where's your courage now? Where's the "coolness under fire" bullshit the papers all printed about you? Choose one, and I'll let you see Kelly. Or,' his smile returned, 'choose yourself, and they all get a bit longer. You never know. Maybe your flat-foot friends will find us in time.' He swung the gun towards Stark now. 'Maybe you can save them all, just by saying your own name.'

79

It was just weird.

John Dixon scanned the street.

No way would Joe Stark abandon his post. No matter what was going on with Kelly. Not without a word. Anyone who didn't know him would call that slim justification for pinging a phone location, but none who did.

Stark's phone was on and, according to triangulation, right here outside the station. The desk sergeant said Stark had left through the front lobby and not returned.

The streetlights glinted off the smooth repair patches where bullets had torn into the road surface. Sometimes he stopped and stared at where the blood had been, or up the looming clocktower where Stark had almost died. But there was no blood now, and no Stark.

A car passed and, feeling self-conscious, he pulled out his phone and tried again.

It was only as the car's lights passed that he saw it . . . A faint blue light in the bushes of Burney Gardens opposite. He hung up and it stopped, dialled again and . . .

Jogging across, he found the phone vibrating beneath a bush.

Stark's.

John looked around, confused, and now doubly worried.

Minutes later he was logging into the Station CCTV suite with clumsy haste. The system was sluggish as he fumbled his way to what he needed. There were three cameras out front; one beneath the entrance canopy just above head height, and two higher covering the street each way.

Stark had left just before eleven . . . There . . . At 22:49 the camera showed him leaving the station entrance, leaning on his cane. He looked about and limped across the road behind a van. Then nothing. A minute later the van's lights came on and it pulled away.

Stark was nowhere to be seen.

John played it again.

None of the cameras offered a view through the van, but he had a horrible feeling.

'*John*,' barked Groombridge, startling him as he entered at speed with three people in tow. Sergeant Ptolemy, who'd been kind during John's rookie years, and his constant companion, Constable Peters, who John found intimidatingly female. Plus a pretty blonde in civvies that it took him a moment to recognize as Constable Pensol, the rookie that had caught a bullet in the shootings . . . much shorter hair, leaner and seeming older, as if the bullet had bled the softness from her youth.

'Guv . . . What –'

'Never mind that,' said Groombridge.

'But *Guv* –'

Groombridge ignored him, turning to Pensol. 'Right, show me what you've got.'

'Guv, seriously –' John tried again, but Groombridge held up a hand to silence him.

The girl sat at the machine next to John's, typed in her details, then plugged in a memory stick and called up a video file. 'This is from a house opposite. I didn't have my warrant card with me but her downstairs neighbour helped me sweet-talk the owner, after we scared the life out of each other.' The file was decent quality colour. It angled down over the owner's front door but just caught the footpath across the road between parked vehicles. 'There . . .' she pointed as legs passed and walked up a path, followed by another. 'I was looking for a mugging, but then . . .' One pair of legs backed out, dragging something out of sight behind a *white van*.

'Where is this?' asked John.

Something in his tone must have penetrated their attention.

'Blackheath,' said Pensol, looking at him for the first time, 'Stark's ex –'

'*Kelly*,' John finished the sentence before she could, a different kind of dread overcoming his usual hesitancy in the face of beauty. 'There's something you all should see.'

'Why?'

Leech tilted his head. 'Why what?'

'Why any of this?' asked Stark.

Leech's eyes narrowed, guessing he was just playing for time. 'Because I don't like it when people think they're better than me.'

'Yeah, you must get tired of that,' Stark replied levelly. The little hostage-negotiation training he'd received in Hendon Police Training Centre differed somewhat from army counter-interrogation techniques, but both highlighted the need to stay calm and non-confrontational, to keep your wits about you. Not easy when his wits were screaming to know where Kelly was and how he'd dragged her farther into his dark world than even he had ever feared possible.

Anger flared in Leech's face, then he slowly shook his head and smiled. 'You think I don't know what you're doing?'

'One of us doesn't. You're out of your depth.'

'Really?' Leech indicated the room, and those who were tied up while he had a gun. 'I get her,' he pointed the gun at Leah, who whimpered faintly. 'I make you watch, before I kill you too. Then I put the gun in Julian's mouth and pin the whole thing on him, again.'

'Just like you tried with Richard Hardacre. That took us two hours to figure out.' Never mind the fact they'd mistakenly chased Sinclair for two *years*.

'I'm losing patience,' hissed Leech. 'One of you three dies now. Decide or I'll decide for you.' The look in his eyes seemed deadly serious.

Logic dictated Stark choose Leah. The best chance of any of them surviving this was Stark himself, but should the opportunity come Julian was in better shape to assist than Leah, and it might indeed be merciful to end her suffering quickly now. But this wasn't a numbers game. Stark's chances of getting free remained low. He was in no doubt Leech meant to kill them all, at whatever speed. And the Glock wasn't fitted with a suppressor. If the cavalry were their best hope, perhaps a gunshot might escape this dungeon to speed their arrival. 'Me,' he said quietly. 'Shoot me.'

Leech watched him, like a playground bully after the first punch works too well. 'Say please.'

'Just do it,' said Stark, training abandoned. 'I'm sick of your face. No wonder you don't like women saying no. Have any ever said yes?'

Leech's anger rose again. Clenching his jaw, he stepped to Stark, raised the pistol to his head and pulled the trigger.

The dull click was deafening.

The only other sound in the deadened room was Leah's stifled keening.

Stark opened his eyes to see Leech grinning.

No round. The magazine was empty.

Stark let out the breath he'd held, thinking it his last.

'See,' said a voice behind Leech. 'I told you he'd choose himself.'

80

Still grinning, Leech stood aside. Across the room, Sinclair had both hands free and his gag hanging limp around his neck. Now visible, his hands were encased in black nitrile gloves. And the harm to his face, Stark realized belatedly, wasn't fresh.

Slowly he reached down and untwisted the cables around his legs, then stood and stretched theatrically. 'You really should work on your knots,' he said to Leech, before turning to Stark with a small smile. 'Sur-*prise* . . .'

For the first time, Stark really saw the serpent Fran had always seen. If he'd felt a fool before, he felt the full weight of his stupidity now, cursing himself for slowness of thought and action. Gone was any vestige of the frailty and PTSD he'd thought he recognized. Feigned, just as Fran had warned – for him; his weak spot, his saviour complex. Sinclair suddenly looked lean, alert and quietly pleased with himself. Harper's instincts had been spot on – Leech hadn't been confessing in Sinclair's hospital room; he'd been *conspiring*. All murder enquiries began the same – person or *persons* unknown . . .

Julian Sinclair, Blake Talbot and Brian Leech – *three* killers.

Fran was going to be livid. Pity he might not live to see it. 'Bravo,' he said, hiding his shock. 'Now there's twice the chance they'll track us down.'

Sinclair shook his head, amused. 'Half as much, I'd say, with your ramshackle team out chasing their tails elsewhere. Who do you think called in tonight's anonymous tip-offs? And even if by some miracle they did come knocking here, we're both accomplished at keeping captives quiet and playing innocent to the police, aren't we, Brian?'

Saying this, he popped the lid off the cool-box, pulled out two chilled beers, twisted off the caps, passed one to Leech and took a deep drink of his own.

Stark silently cursed them to choke. 'You've been working together all along?'

'No, Brian joined the party late,' said Sinclair, 'but with quite the entrance.'

'Where's Kelly?'

'All in good time . . .' Sinclair searched his face. 'Aren't you going to say you'll kill me if I've hurt her?'

Stark's fist balled behind him in impotent rage. 'I will.'

'What about her . . . ?' Sinclair nodded to Leah. 'Don't you care about her too? And people say *I'm* the monster.'

'Let her go.'

'Why?' The blunt truth of the question was chilling. Sinclair studied him. 'Even if you were free . . . ? You've killing in you. You've medals to prove it. But always framed in right and wrong – honour and *restraint*.' He shook his head as if diagnosing some pitiable disease. 'Unlike us . . .' he raised his bottle to Leech who grinned and drank deep.

Sinclair put his bottle down to pull a small pistol from the holdall. 'Blake Talbot's,' he explained, noting Stark's interest. 'Some children shouldn't be allowed sharp toys. Came in handy persuading him to have a little booze and snooze in his van.'

So Blake *had* been armed; not with the Glock 19 they'd all hoped would tie the Talbots to the prison and more, but a Glock 26 sub-compact. The little brother's gun to Dean's penis-extension Desert Eagle and dumb Troy's knife. A fraternal pecking order in weaponry. 'You forced his confession. Staged his suicide.'

Sinclair gave a mea-culpa shrug. 'Least I could do after he tried to pass his little mongrel sister off as my handiwork. And this, obvi-ously,' he added, indicating his bruised face. 'I don't take well to insults.' He placed the gun on the table in front of Leah's eyes, indi-cating he'd taken her previous escape as just that. 'What's the matter, Joe? Isn't this what every detective wants? To know exactly what happened?' Now fully unmasked, Sinclair's frown seemed as oil-slick thin as his smile. 'Well, now you get to watch . . .'

Stark nodded, took a deep breath and shouted at the top of his lungs. '*HELP! CALL THE POLICE! HE* –' Leech pulled back an arm and pistol-whipped him across the side of the head, but watching it coming, Stark was able to move with it to ensure the chair toppled once more. Unfortunately, enough of the blow landed to ring his head like a bell, leaving him too stunned to take advantage and try to free his legs, and before he knew it he was upright again, with the gag firmly back in place.

'Well, that was a waste of bloody time,' cursed Fran, clutching her coffee for some kind of warmth.

After the armed officers had demanded their nice thick coats back and faded into the night to defend the capital from unseen terrors, the minibus had eventually crawled back to the station somewhat slower and less charged, leaving her tired and chilled to the bone. Not to mention pissed off that Harper had found a scene of crime, sans criminal or victim. She felt sorry for Hammed, stuck out there with him.

Her coffee was cooling quicker than she was warming, and smelled wrong.

Dixon looked like he'd been mainlining intravenous caffeine here, worrying from one foot to the other as he turned to see them return. Movement through the glass in Harper's office caught Fran's eye and she was astonished to see Groombridge speaking intently into the phone.

'Sarge,' said Dixon gravely. 'Thank God you're back.' He explained quickly and showed them two short videos on his monitor.

Fran stood, flummoxed.

'He get in the van?' asked Williams.

'Inconclusive from these cameras,' replied Dixon. 'But I can't find him on surrounding streets. Cameras on the college might have this angle, but they're closed till morning.'

'Got the van's plates?'

'Fakes. They match a car registered scrapped. But it's the same van in both locations.' Dixon looked about as sick as Fran suddenly felt. 'I followed it across a few cameras before I lost it both times, but I never saw the driver's face.'

'Welcome back,' said Groombridge ironically, standing in the door to his office like he'd never left.

Fran stared back. 'Guv? Should you –'

He held up a hand. 'Let's worry about that later. Our search just widened from Leah to Stark and Kelly as well. Cameras?'

'Nothing on ANPR yet, Guv,' said Dixon, knowing he probably shouldn't be calling him that. 'Ptolemy, Peters and Pensol are already widening the traffic camera search to find the van again.'

'Best go help, then.'

'Guv.' Dixon shot to his feet, taking Hammed with him.

'You lot look like you could use a stiff one,' announced Maggie, the control room matriarch, face taking no real pleasure in the double-entendre. 'Thought you should know, we just took a call for DC Stark, from one Clive Baxter, quite rude, lives in the same block of flats as Leah Willoughby. Said Stark gave him a card, and he'd only speak to him.'

Fran set her nasty coffee down on Dixon's desk. 'He's seen Leah Willoughby?'

'No. But . . .'

81

'Best not rile Brian,' suggested Sinclair helpfully. 'He's still upset about you messing up our plan outside dear old Belmarsh Prison. I should be too, considering you nearly got me killed,' he rolled his shoulder with a wince. 'Your boy-scout intervention spoiled a fun plan.'

He waited expectantly, highlighting Stark's inability to play his part with questions.

'The public clearly needed help seeing me as the victim,' he explained. 'I thought being "kidnapped and tortured" might win them round, pump up the compensation claim and pay the Talbot family back for the hurtful things they said about me. Brian here was only too happy to help, for his own reasons, and his little associates needed the money. They were supposed to rough me up a little, park me in the Talbots' car yard and give you lot an anonymous tip-off, but you ruined that. Though a bullet wound delivered all the media coverage I'd hoped for and more, and I have to say, your name added unexpected celebrity pizzazz. My legal team were salivating. After all, what's freedom without the means to enjoy it?'

So Sinclair had organized the kidnapping attempt through Leech's prison contacts, and the Talbots only copied the idea later. Again, Stark might have taken some satisfaction from knowing the truth, were his chances of sharing it not so dire.

'You did worry poor Brian, though,' Sinclair added. 'He was always supposed to dispose of his accomplices, of course – call it initiation – but if I'd died, or blamed him, he thought I might renege on my side of the bargain to mentor and deliver him to Leah ...

hence his rather panicky visit to my hospital room. I suppose I shouldn't have expected more. His prior escapades *were* all a bit spineless. No offence, Brian.'

Midway necking the last of his beer, Leech swallowed slowly, frown suggesting offence *had* been taken.

'That's why he contacted me,' continued Sinclair, undeterred. 'He'd developed a bit of a thing for Leah from her time in the spotlight, and I thought a visitor might be fun. I expect his schizoid *prancing whore* letter rang some alarm bells with your lot – the world is worryingly full of nutcases. Anyway, as soon as I saw this one's passing resemblance to Richard Hardacre, it dawned on me just how useful he might be, and it wasn't hard to persuade him to up his game.'

Sinclair's tone had completed its drift from collegiate to condescending, and Leech's confusion was quickly turning to anger. He didn't like people thinking they were better than him. Stark was happy to be audience to fatuous gloating if it delayed him being witness to worse, and even more so if it riled Leech to turn on his master with that glass bottle.

Sinclair showed no sign of concern. 'I let him have a practice swing on pretty Emily. I don't normally share my toys but needs must when you need an alibi . . . At least I know she got more or less what I'd have given her. He filmed it for me. I like to savour these things later; keep myself warm at night. She was a trooper, that one. Brian got quite carried away – all that pent-up frustration. Maybe I'll let *you* watch it. Her debut and swan song, combined. The adverts before tonight's main feature.' He pulled a mobile hard-drive from his pocket. 'Bet you wish you knew where I hid this . . . I'd let you watch them *all*, but sadly for you, time is short.'

Sinclair tilted his head. 'Does it hurt – to know what a mess you and your friends made of all this?' he asked, searching Stark's eyes. 'You should've known Paige Talbot was too young . . . And now with her brother's confession, and Emily's tryst with Brian while I was under guard,' Sinclair shook his head smugly, 'if I was ever charged with so much as a parking ticket again my barrister would have a field day. Lovely, savage Miranda . . . so easy to twist her passion to win into devotion. She's a *little* old for my taste, and far too useful, but you can't sit through visits from a hot, power-hungry power-dresser without thinking – why not . . . ?' He paused to consider this. 'Maybe I will come back for her later . . . thank her properly,' he mused, then looked at Stark. 'I've decided to take my show back out on tour. London's become a bit claustrophobic. Now I have Brian's fake-passport contacts, I thought I'd take all the money Bosch wins me and travel the world. So many countries . . . So many pretty girls . . .'

'Some of that cash is for me,' said Leech, reaching one hand to the wall as if steadying himself . . . The empty beer bottle slipped from his hand and bounced on the cushioned floor.

Sinclair's gaze slid to him, like a snake eyeing a mouse, all pretence of warmer interest gone. 'Like I said, I'm not much for sharing. You had your fun with Emily. First dibs on Leah here is all the reward you were ever due, for what that's worth. I mean, look at her. Yesterday's toy – broken and ugly. Why would I, with such shiny new playthings out there? Like the ones you've brought me tonight – the nation's hero and his beloved girlfriend.'

Stark wanted to cry. But far more than that he wanted to break free of these bonds and beat Sinclair to a bloody pulp.

The snake all but licked the air to savour Stark's agony. 'I see, you don't like sharing either.' He looked back at Leech, who was blinking stupidly now, as if struggling to follow. The added reason for Sinclair's tasteless verbosity, Stark realized suddenly – he was waiting for Leech's drugged beer to kick in.

Stark's gagged warning yell was as incoherent as it was futile. Leech was already too far gone, taking vain hope of the black hats killing each other with him.

'You've come to the end of your usefulness, Brian,' Sinclair confirmed. 'All the breadcrumbs lead to you. A stray hair in the Hyundai, Hardacre's house keys hidden in your kitchen. ID-theft evidence and a paper trail to the fake crime-scene the police are raiding right now. Your computer unlocked with months of footage from the spy cameras you installed in Leah's ceiling upstairs, photos of Emily outside her flat and the video you shot inside. The whore letter. Your bike, camera and all the stalking photos I had you take of Joe and his lovely girlfriend . . . And after they're found out there in the cold, I'll make sure the police find your van outside and you in here, having finally "finished what you started" with Leah and sensing the net closing in, taken the coward's way out with the rest of the Rohypnol and *all* the blame with it. While I . . .' he flourished his surgical gloves like joyless jazz-hands, 'was never here.'

He waited for any sign of understanding. 'You're the fall guy, Brian. That's all you've ever been.'

'*You* . . .' Leech blinked, words failing, thoughts failing even as he recognized his betrayal, eyes drooping as he slowly half-sat-half-collapsed to the floor. He raised the Glock at Sinclair and pulled the trigger, frowning in confusion at the three empty hammer-clicks it produced before the weight of it dragged his hand down – their earlier joke on Stark now delivering the second punchline Sinclair had doubtless planned.

He shook his head. 'I suppose if I cared at all, I'd hate stupid people.' Crouching, he inserted the sports bottle straw into Leech's mouth and squeezed. 'Drink, Brian. I'll put the bullets back in for you after.'

Stupefied and suggestible, Leech swallowed, again and again.

His breathing slowed, heavy eyes wandering, perhaps searching for help he knew would not come.

82

The engine roared, the Beamer responding to his every urging like a thoroughbred, racing under blues and twos with an armed unit in tow.

Slamming on the brakes with a curse, Harper slowed just enough to avoid T-boning a taxi through a red light, ducking behind it and racing on. Beside him, Hammed gripped the roof handle and his seat in grim silence between occasional directions. Harper knew what he was doing. He'd done the advance driving course, back in uniform. Years ago, maybe, but it was like riding a bike . . .

Leah Willoughby's flat.

Her neighbour had caught the news on TV and couldn't help thinking their new person of interest looked a bit like the fella that rented the ground-floor flat below Leah Willoughby's six months ago – kept himself to himself apart from the motorbike coming and going all hours and the loud music. And apparently, there was a white van clogging up the rear car park now.

After a day of false dawns, maybe this would be the one. And poor Fran, realizing he was nearest, had done the right thing and called him – handed him a chance of victory for the greater good, doubtless through gritted teeth. The idea that Stark had been kidnapped from right outside the station was frankly ludicrous, but Harper didn't care much either way. Serve him right if he had. Only catching Leech mattered.

He swung the car through a roundabout, trying not to grin. This was what being a copper was all about. The gunning engine and siren were his music, adrenaline and cigarettes his sustenance, and catching Leech red-handed would be his end-of-date sex.

Brian Leech's breathing had slowly subsided until there could be no doubt it had ceased altogether.

Only then did Sinclair cease staring into his eyes. 'Dull,' he said, dissatisfied. 'Not much spark there in the first place. You don't want to dose them too much or you never see it go out. That last, pleading look.' He sighed. 'Still, business before pleasure. Besides ...' He stood slowly, brightening, eyeing Stark. 'My cup runneth over.'

As Leech had slowly expired, Sinclair had calmly explained how he would arrange this tragic tableau mort for the police to find, none of which boded well for Leah.

What the police would find, and when, were very much on Stark's mind too. His bonds and gag remained too secure for hope. Coppers lived with risk. Violence was a constant threat in uniform, in harm's way on the streets of the living, but Stark might have expected to grow soft in the house of the dead, steering an MIT desk and staring down suspects in the safety of the interview room. Subsequent events had proved that wrong, but who would have thought, after three full tours of duty in front-line war zones, he'd face flying bullets in civvy street and then end here? But right now, his foremost questions were the whereabouts and wellbeing of Kelly, Leah's dull whimpering, and how to get free in time to do anything about either.

Sinclair looked at Leah with a weary expression. 'You know, since she escaped I've often thought about finishing what *I* started. That final squeeze. But now we're here, she really just disgusts me too much.'

Taking the sports bottle, he unclipped Leah's gag, forced the straw into her mouth and squeezed. She gagged and choked, perhaps with more fight in her than Leech, but swallowed. 'There,' he said, patting her on the head like a good little doggie and looking to Stark with a conspiratorial whisper. 'Time for the real finale.'

83

The van and bike were both visible through the rear gate. Same false plates. Meaning maybe Stark wasn't just crying into his pint somewhere but really was inside with his abductor, and Harper was almost glad to have two surly Authorized Firearms Officers to hand. His stab vest was of limited comfort facing a killer with a gun. One could fantasize about a hero's funeral, dress uniforms and weeping wife, but a hero's parade appealed more. And the thought of coming to Stark's rescue after all his grandstanding and heroics was hilarious – a delicious cherry of righteous justice on the cake of finding Leah Willoughby and catching the Greenwich Strangler red-handed.

So Hammed took the rear with the stout female AFO while her sergeant stayed with Harper.

'Who is it?'

'Police, Mr Baxter. Detective Inspector Harper,' he said quietly, holding up his ID to the intercom camera. 'You called the station. About your neighbour . . .'

'Didn't call *you*,' said Baxter, sleepy gruffness audible through the tinny door intercom. 'Where's the soldier fella, from the news?'

'Would you rather talk to a detective inspector or a lowly constable?' asked Harper impatiently.

After a few seconds the intercom buzzed and the front door lock clicked open. Harper and the AFO sergeant trod lightly past Flat 1 and upstairs to Flat 6, finding Baxter waiting in his doorway dressed in crumpled pyjamas and worn slippers. 'You didn't waste much time.'

'I've little to waste,' said Harper quietly, indicating that Baxter should lower his voice too.

Baxter grunted. 'Your man said to call if I saw any malingerers.' He huffed. 'See nothing but these days. This country's gone to the dogs.'

'But the guy in Flat One . . . ?' Harper held up his phone with a photo of Brian Leech, wife beater, stalker, illicit sexual snooper, probable sexual predator and now hopefully much more.

'Maybe . . .' mused Baxter, leaning in to peer with bad eyes. 'Got long hair and a beard, but maybe the eyes . . . Seen him flirting with your hussy, Leah Willow-whatsit. Not that she was having any of it. Not good enough for her.'

'Is it him or not?'

Baxter looked flustered, confidence ebbing. It was one thing to call a phone number, another to have a copper at your door at night. 'I dunno . . . I told your people I wasn't sure.'

'Is he in now?'

Baxter shrugged. 'Motorbike's round the back, and that van he just got.'

'And have you seen or heard anyone coming or going, outside?' said Harper leadingly. 'Because that would be *really helpful*.'

Baxter glanced at the heavy breaching ram hanging from Harper's hand and was either just smart enough to read between the lines or mean enough to take pleasure in providing probable cause against a disliked neighbour. 'Yeah. Sounded like a scuffle outside earlier, and maybe some shouting inside after.'

'Thank you, Mr Baxter. Please wait inside, away from doors and windows, until we give the all clear.'

Baxter backed inside, alarmed, closing the door more loudly than Harper would've liked.

He turned to the AFO sergeant. 'That's probable cause.'

'Iffy. We should wait for Specialist.'

Oh, for fuck's sake, fumed Harper. 'Can you hear screaming, Sergeant? Because I could swear I heard something inside that might be screaming.'

The sergeant's stern gaze suggested intransigence, but then he nodded and radioed his colleague outside.

Seconds later they were at the door to Flat 1. The sergeant drew his pistol, un-safed and cocked it and took up a firing position. Heart racing, Harper knocked.

Nothing.

He tried again. Still nothing.

Nodding to the AFO, he hefted the ram, and swung.

The door burst open with a satisfying splintering, as he ducked aside.

No bullets flew out.

'ARMED POLICE ENTERING!' bellowed the sergeant. 'ARMED POLICE!'

The sound of breaking glass somewhere inside, followed by a higher pitched call, 'ARMED POLICE ENTERING!'

In seconds, the two armed officers had met in the hallway, checking room by room, calling 'CLEAR!'

There was a room at the end of the corridor fitted with a security bar and heavy steel padlock.

Taking the ram from Harper, the Sergeant nodded to his colleague to raise her pistol, and took aim.

It took three swings to break in, the female officer charging in first, 'ARMED POL—'

The last syllable died on her lips as she and her colleague froze just inside the door.

84

'Dead,' pronounced the female AFO, feeling for a pulse on the man sat slumped in the corner, chin on chest. From the doorway, Harper could see it was Brian Leech.

The sergeant holstered his pistol and went to the naked girl tied to the table.

Leah Willoughby.

It didn't look good for her either.

'Fuck,' breathed Hammed at Harper's shoulder.

The sergeant feeling for Leah's pulse made a face, shifting his fingers to try again. 'Pulse,' he announced, breathing a sigh. 'Faint.' He looked at the two MIT officers. 'Ambulance. *Now*!'

Hammed just stood there, dumbstruck, until Harper's glare broke the spell and he yanked out his phone.

The sergeant flicked out a Leatherman tool and started snipping Leah's bonds. 'Don't worry, miss,' he said in a calm voice. 'Soon have you wrapped up and feeling better.'

No sign of Stark, or his ex, but who needed cherry when the cake looked this good . . .

There was a sports bottle in Leech's hand. Rohypnol, Harper was willing to bet. He'd finished what he started and called it a day. Catching him alive would've been great – all the publicity of a prosecution and conviction – but this was fine. Capture and conclusion in one. Triumph condensed. Onwards and upwards. 'Got you,' he breathed.

'Don't just stand there,' said the sergeant, 'get a blanket or something. For fuck's sake,' he hissed when Harper didn't react. 'Deb, grab something to get this girl warm.'

Harper blinked back into the present. 'Nothing from the flat. Nothing with the suspect's DNA,' he called after the departing officer.

'Christ,' the sergeant shook his head in disgust. 'Are you worried about convicting a dead man of saving his victim?'

'Ambulance on the way,' said Hammed, reappearing. 'ETA, ten minutes. Camden patrol cars pulling up outside.' He held up two sets of keys in his nitrile-gloved hands. 'One for the bike. One other for the van, I reckon. Gonna check for Stark.'

A minute later the other AFO raced back in with a space blanket from their car.

The sergeant wrapped it around Leah, trying to rouse her, but she was a dead weight, barely breathing. 'Come on now, miss, stay with me. Help's on the way and you're safe now. Stay with me.'

For the second time this night, Stark came to in a moving vehicle.

Sinclair had taken great delight in holding Leech's stun baton on until Stark passed out.

Stark, for his part, enjoyed it less.

But it wasn't a pothole that woke him now. He was in the boot of a car this time, and there was someone protesting strenuously about being underneath him.

Stark caught a familiar scent. Jasmine perfume. *Kelly!* Trying to shout through a gag, wriggling to get free.

Stark was equally limited, but somehow they managed to untangle themselves until they were side by side, more or less facing each other in the near dark. Faint light leached in from the rear-light clusters, but not enough really to see, until the vehicle braked and the light doubled.

Kelly. Alive!

But only for now. And of all the darkest dreams he'd endured, and all the pain he'd feared to inflict on her, he'd never once imagined he would see such fear in her eyes.

It was crushing.

And then it was gone, as the car pulled away again.

The driver was taking it easy, drawing no attention.

Stark twisted and wriggled around to see if he could feel for

Kelly's bonds. She followed his lead, until they managed to face away from each other. His hands found hers, but they were bound tight like his and he couldn't find the cable ends or get enough purchase to untie them. He felt her try his with equally little luck until she gave up, her fingers gripping his, clinging tight.

All he could do was squeeze back, as he felt her body tremble.

All the times he'd sworn to himself that he'd never give her more cause to cry . . .

Stark felt his jaw clench, grinding his teeth. This wasn't it. He wouldn't let it be.

Twisting round again, he tried to manoeuvre his hands to the rear corner, feeling for an edge to the plastic interior. Kelly had no clue what he was doing, but guessing they needed to work together she seemed to move to accommodate him. But he couldn't find what he needed. Twisting upwards, having to put some of his weight back on her, his fingertips found an edge . . . Tracing it round, he found a pressure clip and popped it. There had to be at least one more, but he couldn't find it. Digging his nails into the thin gap, he pulled, but couldn't get enough purchase. His fingers slipped, partially tearing back a nail.

Grunting against the pain, he tried again, and managed to force the end of his left pinky finger into the crack. At the cost of some skin, he managed to force another fingertip in, then another.

He was aware that he was still squeezing the air out of Kelly, and she started to shift in discomfort.

Using his shoulders to shift his weight even more on to her, he felt the plastic give with a crack. One more pull and it came open enough to force his hand in.

Feeling desperately inside, he found the back of the light cluster, fingertip following wires to the metal clips like he'd been taught in advanced SF selection. He found one and squeezed. The clip popped off one side, then the next and his fingertips yanked out the bulb by its wired connector.

Kelly was starting to writhe in panic now. He had just seconds, fingers tearing at anything they could. Tearing out another bulb, he yanked his hand out and rolled off her, hitting his head.

Contorted uncomfortably together, they nonetheless remained still until Kelly's breathing had returned to as close to normal as their predicament allowed.

In the confined scope of prisoner resistance, disabling the rear light of the vehicle counted as a small victory. The chances of a traffic officer happening to see them was small. The chances said copper would bother pulling them over just for that, tiny. But you fought where you could.

From here on up everything must start going his way or Kelly would die.

This journey must be another rebirth. We change, therefore we can, Hazel said. But the process was largely involuntary in Stark's experience. Age, trauma or some road to Damascus revelation – people changed as events led them. Time didn't heal – it just turned wounds into scars. That was the only acceptance he could offer. The past remained unchanged. Steps forward couldn't be retraced, but arms laid down could be taken up. And while there was no Fran or Groombridge to intervene, the policeman could step aside for the soldier behind him.

A monster had reached into his life to snatch a loved one, and Stark would stop at nothing to save her. Here, now, cramped in this prison with the woman he loved, the one person he'd sworn would never see him as he really was, Stark doused the firelight and embraced the darkness within.

85

'No sign of Stark or Kelly,' confirmed Hammed, through Fran's phone on speaker.

Fran felt the air leave her, pain clear on the faces around her. 'Okay, search the flat for anything that might lead us to a fresh location. And the van, check for a satnav.'

'SOCO won't –'

'To *hell* with SOCO. Leech is *dead*. We're not looking for a conviction, we're looking for Stark.'

'Yeah, of course. I'll tell DI Harper.'

He hung up before she could comment on that proposal.

'Okay . . .' She looked at the faces around her in the CCTV suite: Williams, Dixon, and the disconcertingly altered PC Pensol, whose involvement in this was going to rise up Fran's curiosity agenda just as soon as she clapped hands on Stark alive and well. 'We've found the van, but not the two people it was used to abduct. So check every camera between here and Camden. Give me a timeline. Find out where that van deviated one inch from the obvious route. Get patrol cars and Dog Squad checking every scrap of park and wasteland within feasible reach. We don't know why Leech took Stark and Kelly, but it can't be good. Our best hope is he didn't have time to hurt them or worse. Maybe Leech took his own life because he was finished, or maybe because Stark escaped him.'

Groombridge, for all his qualities, was about as tech-savvy as a brick, so just nodded silent approval. Forward movement. Positive message. Leadership. But they both guessed that if Stark *had* escaped, he'd have found a way to get in contact already. The more likely scenario was the worst, and all present knew it.

After a few final turns and bumps, the car stopped. The driver got out, returned, drove them down a short ramp and stopped. The engine cut out. The driver exited again, followed by the sound of moving metal, like a roller shutter.

Stark squeezed Kelly's hand one last time and twisted sideways as much as he could. As the boot lid opened, he kicked it upward, hoping to catch Sinclair in the face, but the lid just swung up and rebounded painfully against his shins.

'Do you really think I'm as stupid as Brian?' asked Sinclair.

This time Stark had just enough time to bite his gag before the cracking baton convulsed him.

Unlike the previous hits it wasn't so prolonged as to force him from consciousness.

Nevertheless, he was utterly limp as he was manhandled out of the car and dumped on the rough concrete floor. Some kind of carport or garage? It was all but dark and his one good eye wasn't working properly.

He was dragged roughly through a doorway across a smooth floor into a dark, cold, echoey space, and tied by the wrists to some chains on the floor. Movement was starting to return to his muscles, but not fast enough to resist.

Sinclair walked back out the way they'd come, presumably to fetch Kelly. Stark tried pulling on the chains, but found the opposite end ascended to some secure fixing overhead and he didn't have the strength to pull himself up.

Instead, he reached his fingers into his back pocket, feeling for the small light bulb he'd secreted there from the car's rear cluster. Shifting carefully, he felt it pop beneath his weight. Feeling again, he was relieved to find a decent shard remained attached to the metal base. Withdrawing it from his pocket with care not to drop it, he slowly manipulated shard to cable. Gripping the base hard in his fingertips, he tried a small experimental sawing action. It took less than half a minute for his fingers and wrist to start aching and he had to rest for fear of dropping his tiny point of hope.

Feeling the cable, it did seem slightly indented, perhaps even slightly rougher, but far from sliced open.

He tried again, and was still trying as he heard Sinclair returning, dragging Kelly. In the dim light leaking in from the garage Stark saw her twisting in resistance while she keened protest through her gag. Sinclair obviously didn't think her worth electrocuting. He dumped her unceremoniously on the ground, and went back to close the door, plunging the room into complete darkness.

Seconds later fluorescent tubes blinked and flickered blindingly to life. Stark forced his gummy eye open, blinking and squinting.

Kelly lay on the floor, staring around in horror. Seeing Sinclair, she crabbed awkwardly away like a sidewinder snake until her back hit a wall. Her fearful eyes darted between Stark and their surroundings, guessing hope was futile but clinging to it regardless.

They were in a windowless room, white tiled walls, grey tiled floor sloping faintly to a stainless-steel grate, so much like an abattoir or butchery that Stark looked up for meat hooks, but the chains he was tied to went up to an electric winch hoist on sliding rails.

On a tripod, stood a video camera with integral spotlight, much like those used by the press, but this footage would be for private consumption. The lens pointed towards a large stainless-steel slab in the centre of the room, like the sacrificial altar in Marcus Turner's temple to forensic pathology.

There was a tall roll of blue polythene and a rack of industrial bleach in five-gallon tubs.

'Alone at last,' announced Sinclair conversationally. 'No police-sheep gambolling to the rescue and no one to avenge you, with Bosch set to sue the life out of them. He was Emily's godfather, did you know? Rather over-fond of her, if you know what I mean.' He smiled. 'Fun to think of him turning all that guilt-ridden grief into enriching me, while I re-watch her final moments on repeat.'

86

'Not that I'm not glad you're here ...' Fran whispered aside to Groombridge, 'but there's still time to pretend you never were.'

Groombridge kept his eyes on the busy team, but shook his head faintly.

He *was* here, in direct contradiction of orders from Deputy Assistant Commissioner Shitbag, and there'd be hell to pay. And she'd cop her share for allowing it. But Stark was missing along with Kelly, and every minute that ticked by seemed torture. If Leech was the Strangler, his suicide boded very badly for them both. They thought they'd lost Stark three months ago and none here could bear the thought of losing him again. Fran would face any HR firing squad before that, and Groombridge was against the wall already.

'Okay,' she nodded. 'Ptolemy says there's more uniforms coming up to help here, but searching traffic cams could take hours. We need to come at this another way.'

Groombridge met her expectant gaze with one of his own. 'I'm not here. So what's your suggestion?'

Fran looked horrified. 'This is no time for your sink-or-swim bullshit.'

'I'd say it was the perfect time.'

'Stark's *life* is on the line.'

'It only works if you're out of your depth,' he said, with calmness he didn't feel. 'Stop flapping your arms like an idiot. You've already started swimming. Keep going.'

'You're being a prick.'

'And you've got limited time before Owen walks back in here and dumps you back in the shallow end, or worse, DAC Stevens to kick us both out.'

She glared at him more fiercely than he'd ever seen before, in a long history and repertoire of glares. The biggest paradigm shift she'd need to make in transitioning to Inspector was to stop looking at him like he knew what to do. To realize, as right now, that he often had no more clue than she did.

'Right,' she seethed. 'Then we need to get everything out on the table.'

Sinclair pressed the button on the hanging remote, watching with interest as the winch whirred to life, dragging the chain upward and Stark with it. With his hands bound behind his back, this could quickly have dislocated both Stark's shoulders, but Sinclair released the button as Stark was balanced up on his knees trying not to tip forward, like a classic stress position, trying to alternate his weight between his shoulders and his kneecaps. Far from helpful as he set about sawing with the broken bulb. So far, he'd cut himself more than the cable.

Sinclair picked up a holdall, stalked to Kelly and crouched. He pulled out a sports bottle like the one left behind with Leech and held it up, showing her the little pistol in his other hand. 'I'm going to remove your gag. You can shout all you want, scream, even – we're in a sound-proof basement and no one will hear. I will, however, hit you really, really hard. You will drink from this bottle.' Kelly shook her head defiantly, but Sinclair was unmoved. 'Don't worry, it's quite dilute. It will make you docile, which will help me, and disengaged, which will help you. You'll thank me, non-verbally at least. Ready?' Gone was all vestige of bonhomie. Sinclair's words were flat statements of reality as he saw it.

Kelly glanced at Stark, seeing him busy. She could buy time at best, and if worst came to worst, she might be spared unnecessary pain. He redoubled his sawing. With a sudden parting, he felt the outer cable sheath split open. Twisting his wrists, the split widened, but the inner wires remained untouched. They had thinner plastic insulation but copper cores, and he wasn't sure how effective the small piece of glass would prove.

She nodded.

Sinclair carefully untwisted the cable binding the cloth in her mouth and removed both.

As Kelly gasped in air, he popped the flip-cap off the straw and held it to her lips.

Hesitantly, she closed her lips around it, sucking in a tentative sip.

'Faster,' said Sinclair, squeezing the bottle, causing her to swallow and choke, coughing. As she stopped he shoved the straw back between her lips and squeezed again. Her cheeks ballooned, and then she spat the huge mouthful right in his face.

Stark was too busy to be proud, feeling the glass cut the insulation on one wire and setting about the copper inside.

Sinclair wiped his dripping face with one gloved hand and slapped Kelly hard across hers.

A fierce growl rumbled in Stark's throat.

Sinclair glanced at him, eyes narrowing, then back at Kelly. Slowly, he closed the cap over the straw. 'Suit yourself. I expect that's enough for forensics to link the *modus operandi*, as Joe's little colleagues like to call it. I could make you drink more. You'll wish you had. So perhaps it's better . . . this way you both get the full show.'

Stark slipped and stabbed his wrist with the glass. The blood wet his fingers and the stub of bulb base slipped from his grip and fell. Instinctively he caught it between his calves, but as he tried to work out how to get it back to his hands it slipped to the floor.

Cursing, he moved to Plan B. With Sinclair still distracted, he'd perched up on his knees, arching his feet up towards his hands. Hell on his kneecaps, it allowed him to test the knotted cable binding his ankles.

It was an expedient twisting, topped with a knot – the cable ends free. Fast but sloppy. His bloody fingertips kept slipping, but for a moment they found real purchase and he felt the knot give. Ignoring the pain, he pulled again and felt the knot slip open, but at the cost of a grunt.

He managed to make his struggling look as futile as possible as Sinclair looked round. 'Jealous? She like you to slap her too?' So saying, he slapped her again even harder, and as she lolled, gasping, whipped something from the bag and rammed it into her mouth, yanking the straps around the back of her head. Another ball gag, in grotesque red.

As her eyes widened in panic, he gripped her viciously by the hair and dragged her towards the slab.

87

Our thoughts are of course with the family and friends of Leah Willoughby at this terrible time. A young woman, who had already endured terrible events, has been tragically lost. Her inexcusable vilification in court and in some areas of the news media has been exposed as lies and prejudice, too late.

And never mind the fact that she took the stand to accuse the wrong man, sending us all down a two-year dead end, thought Harper, deciding to dial down the Leah element of the press conference he was composing in his head as he drove back to the station, having left Hammed at the scene with the SOCO nerds. At least until he knew for sure she'd died.

He took a drag of his cigarette.

Investigations must run their course, he continued, *but with families now informed, we can announce that the prime suspect, Brian Leech, has been found dead by his own hand. We have every reason to believe that he was the Greenwich Strangler all along.*

Our continued apologies are extended to Julian Sinclair, for the wrongful prosecution brought against him – by my predecessors – and to the friends and loved ones of all the victims. At all times the Metropolitan Police Force has acted in good faith and with all possible diligence, pursuing the evidence where it appeared to lead. Sometimes this goes wrong, and a full investigation will now be launched into the decisions taken along the way – again, by my predecessors.

Of course Harper would not be allowed to make any such assertion, but an investigation *would* follow, heads *would* roll, and he would be left standing tall. He'd make sure of it.

The inane radio disk-jockey finished the babbling that had set Harper to daydreaming and finally played a song.

'Don't Stop Me Now', by Queen.

Smiling darkly, he turned it up.

If only he'd found Stark and Kelly too. Alive and well. For all their antipathy, he'd not wish on Stark the fate Leech might have inflicted, and the prospect of having Goldenballs forever in his debt was mouth-watering. But there was a good chance they were dead. And in the meantime, his triumphant press statement would need to include *heartfelt concern for the fate of the nation's hero and his beloved,* missing presumed murdered by the killer Harper had hounded to the end.

And later, the memorial . . .

But right now, he dragged deep on the last of his cigarette, flicked the glowing butt out of the window and sang.

Kelly fought valiantly but with near total futility. Sinclair had strength and brutality and employed both to bend her over the slab, ankles tied to the corner uprights, wrists round the sides to the far ones.

Stark continued to use every distracted moment to work on his ankle bindings, but even with the primary knot now undone, untwisting the rest with bloody fingers was agonizingly slow.

Sinclair fetched a pair of bleach tubs and set them down next to Kelly, then pulled out a large pair of scissors and a small box from his holdall, setting both on the slab before her eyes.

The scissors were probably for cutting off her clothes.

The box contained a dozen condoms.

Tear rolled down her cheeks.

The loathsome snake met Stark's eyes and winked. 'Can't be too careful. After all, I *do* know where she's been.'

The camera was checked and positioned to capture both Kelly and Stark.

Finally, Sinclair pulled out another sports bottle and took a long drink, deep in thought, like an athlete pre-race. Stark would not have been surprised to see him limbering up.

'Not going to ask me why I do it?' he asked, mocking Stark's gag. 'Did my daddy abuse me, whip me with electrical cord? Was I raped at an impressionable age by some hulking electrician who wrapped me up in plastic? Or are both just cheap, handy and ubiquitous?' He sneered.

'To be honest, the whipping was mostly for effect. Part of the disposable smokescreen. I ought to stick with the cable tonight, but I thought it might be more fun to use this.' He reached back into the holdall and produced Stark's walking cane, setting that on the slab for Kelly's eyes too. Leech must have scooped it up as a trophy or a prop for their planned theatrics. What Stark wouldn't give now for its secret blade in his hands.

'The Rohypnol helps with compliance in a city full of eyes and ears, but unlike stupid Brian, I *do* like it when they say no. In fact, the more they whimper the more I enjoy it. That shrink you see on the quiet would try to hang a long Greek label on me, or measure my amygdala. I just think I'm wired more efficiently, like a miracle spark of sentience in a production line of robots.

'You know, I tried scoring myself against the Hare Psychopathy Checklist once, but I just couldn't take it seriously. I mean . . . glibness and grandiosity are just accusations levelled at their betters by the stupid and meek. Everything else was just a tick-list for taking what you deserve. Empathy's only value is in savouring your victories in the eyes of the vanquished, and who likes being bored . . . ? Miranda may be somewhat biased, but she never once suggested I plead insanity. I wonder what you'd score, Joe, if you were really honest.'

Hazel *had* scored Stark once, to counter his concerns. Elements of psychopathy were more prevalent in successful CEOs, politicians, surgeons and soldiers than the general population. Doing what it takes. Decisiveness, fearlessness and mental toughness could equally be framed as impulsivity, emotional detachment and lack of empathy or conscience. He'd scored thirty-six out of forty. Then she'd run it again, asking the same questions with different ethical slants, and he'd scored nine. 'We're all semi-psychopaths,' she suggested, 'separated by circumstance and self-awareness in how we explain our thoughts and actions to ourselves.' Sinclair's dismissive incomprehension pointed to a perfect forty, while delivering whatever conclusions fitted his twisted ideology from Stark's silence now.

'My parents were actually depressingly normal.' He shook his head as if they were the bafflingly broken things. 'For the longest time, I thought myself the only sane person in the asylum, until I realized the walls were just a trick to keep everyone else in.' He smiled. 'I thought about killing them, of course, but they were useful in their little worker-bee way.

'My first was accidental, believe it or not. A Thai prostitute vocally objecting to my attentions in an ugly attempt to extort me. I'd say I remember her fondly, but to be honest I barely recall her at all. Only the feeling, quietening her noise, seeing the light go out. It was . . . satisfying. I couldn't forget that. It was a bit of bother getting rid of her, but I got better each time.' He drew a breath and let it out, as if savouring the memories. 'They say heroin or meth is the closest thing you can come to nirvana, but drugs are so tedious, and the effects diminish with each desperate chase. What I do *never* palls. Ted Bundy said watching women die made him feel more normal.' Sinclair shook his head. 'It makes me feel more *extraordinary*.

'I went back to Thailand three times, and Malaysia twice. One in California. If you're careful, it's not hard, altering your method each time. It's even easier on home turf, establishing that signature MO to focus attention in Greenwich, while getting creative on business trips around the country. Oxford, Birmingham, Manchester, Leeds. *Two* in Jersey. You poor, idiot police with your *jurisdictions*, scurrying around like laughable little ants in a terrarium . . . Kelly here will be my *nineteenth* conquest, not counting Brian and Blake, and I suppose Richard Hardacre and sweet Emily by proxy . . . Collateral sideshows. Expediencies. There've been a few along the way.

'Pity I can't include thick-skulled Sergeant Dearing, though it might have been a bit of a stretch to claim credit. Very pretty wife and blossoming daughters, though. People should be more careful what they post on social media. Maybe I'll plan a little package holiday around them in a year or two. Make him watch, like you. It's good to have things to look forward to.'

His voice never took on the condescension he'd applied to Leech, only a sick version of magnanimity while his eyes searched Stark's for the pain he fed off with each twist of the knife.

Keep talking, arsehole, thought Stark, working the cable behind his back with aching fingers.

'But you . . .' Sinclair took a deep, satisfied breath and let it out slowly. 'You were different. The famous, formidable Joseph Stark, VC,' he licked his lips. 'National treasure and media darling. Too good to be true . . . in the end. It was almost disappointing how easily you fell for my woe-is-me-PTSD act . . .' Saying this, he transformed, visibly shrinking into the traumatized victim he'd used to play on Stark's weak spot, then making an exaggerated pout, wiping fake tears from beneath both eyes with twisting fists, and finally a snake-eyed smile. 'I almost didn't have to remember to yawn.

'Your heroism is your weakness,' he explained, condescendingly. 'But that makes this all the sweeter.' He looked around, breathing in victory, tasting the air. 'Ever think this is where it would all end, Joe?' he asked quietly. 'Abject defeat. The woman you love comprehensively taken before your eyes and the life slowly squeezed out of her.'

Stark suddenly found himself thrashing like a lunatic, straining against his restraints, bellowing dully against his gag. Futile. Furious. Every cell in his body burning to be free, to slay and be done with it.

'*There he is* . . .' leered Sinclair, thrilled. 'The killer inside . . . straining the leash . . .'

He watched intently until Stark eventually subsided, the white-hot anger flaring off to leave nothing better than a puce-faced fool, breathing desperately through his nose while coughing against the cloth in his mouth – more in danger of choking himself than his enemy.

Sinclair nodded slowly. 'I've picked out a nice spot to dump you both. By the time you're found you'll be long cold. The plastic keeps tell-tale bugs at bay. None of your lab rats will be able to tell that the two of you died later than Brian and Leah. I'll move on, leaving the Greenwich Strangler behind with Brian's name attached, but I'll always know ... And when they talk endlessly about his final fatal fixation with the nation's hero and his beautiful lover ... I'm mean, call me selfish, but imagine the pleasure I'll take knowing all that fame is secretly mine, just for me.' He held up the hard drive – his personal horror library – and plugged it into the camera, ready to record. 'My crowning achievement, for me alone to savour ... over and over.'

88

It seemed Sinclair's thumbscrew monologue was coming to an end. Desperate to delay what came next, Stark made speaking noises into his gag.

Sinclair stopped what he was doing with an exaggerated sigh and pressed the button to lift Stark a couple of inches higher so his knees came off the ground and he had to tense his arm muscles to stop his weight tearing his shoulders. Carefully, he removed Stark's gag.

'Why?' gasped Stark.

'I've said why.'

Stark shook his head. 'Why *her*?'

Sinclair frowned. 'Is this a trick question?'

'We broke up. Ages ago.'

Sinclair nodded. 'That explains the shameless little blonde flaunting herself on the balcony of your flat. But not why you met Kelly here for a drink last night.' He half-smiled, confirming that he'd been watching all this time through his accomplice-turned-patsy, Leech. Stalking by proxy probably gave him an even greater sense of power. And all this time Stark's very paranoia had been his blind spot, the sickest mind trick of all. 'And I have to say it doesn't explain this,' Sinclair continued, retrieving something from his holdall . . . Kelly's purse.

Unclasping it, he withdrew something and held it up.

A photo.

Stark and Kelly, smiling in the sunshine in Greenwich Park, taken by a passing stranger who'd spotted them taking a selfie on Kelly's phone. She'd loved it so much she'd printed it to carry in her purse. Perhaps she'd forgotten to take it out. Perhaps not. Right now, he dearly wished she had.

Sinclair saw his dismay, slowly ripped the image in two and ground the pieces beneath his heel. 'One hero, two whores. Perhaps I should've taken them both and made you choose one to live.' Sinclair looked wistful. 'Not to worry. Maybe I'll come back for the spare too. Constable Pensol. Quite altered from her own little burst of fame, but still *delectable*.'

Bad guys in stories always wore evil grins, but in Stark's experience true evil didn't grin, it looked blankly through you like you didn't matter. Weaklings sought affirmation, but the only person Sinclair was smiling for was himself. The rest of the world existed to him only as a source of entertainment. People were just *things*, to play with and break, reinforcing his own omnipotence.

He roughly forced Stark's gag back in and lowered him back to his knees, blessedly slightly more than he'd raised him. Stark was only a twist or two from freeing his feet, but his hands had to be the priority. Feeling the broken bulb beneath his shin, he strained to reach it with his fingers, but could not, cursing silently.

Then he remembered the stab he'd felt as he first broke the bulb. His fingers now reached his back pocket. Feeling inside, he found the remains of the glass, and one curved shard. Carefully, he pulled it out and worked it into position to renew his efforts on the cable.

'Right,' Sinclair nodded, standing, flexing his injured shoulder while drawing in another deep breath of satisfaction and letting it out. 'All good things . . .'

Taking up the scissors, he set about Kelly's clothing, cutting up the back of each denim leg and joining the two so he could tug them free. Kelly thrashed to no avail. Next, Sinclair cut her top. A purple long-sleeve Stark recalled her trying on for his opinion after a hasty shopping trip. He'd told her everything looked good on her and she'd tutted at his uselessness.

The lingerie now exposed had also been cat-walked for his edification, briefly, Stark recalled well with utter dismay. And there was nothing he could do to stop this sick debasement.

With his habitual care, Sinclair now stripped off his own clothing, placing each article into a black bin bag, never letting his clothing or skin touch his environment, grimacing at the medical dressing taped over his trapezius muscle from the passing bullet.

Finally, he reached for the condoms.

394

89

Stark did the one thing he could do, he turned his head away.

'No,' said Sinclair. 'You have to watch.'

Swearing, he stalked to Stark and grasped his face, but a faint sound filtered into the room, like the creak of a heating pipe.

Sinclair froze, listening.

Time was up. All plans and hopes forgotten. Act now or die. *Act now or lose.*

Feeling the glass biting into his fingers, Stark sawed frantically. Sinclair took his action for more futile struggling and shushed him, trying to listen. When Stark ignored him, he reached for the pistol and pointed it at him, staring away into the dark corners. 'Be *quiet.*'

The wetness made it impossible to tell if any progress was being made, and then made the shard slip from his grasp. With bloodied fingers he thought he could feel frayed points from the wires but none seemed to have parted yet, so he switched his attention back to his ankles, tearing at the final twists.'

'I said be *quiet!*' Sinclair thrust the gun threateningly, inches from Stark's face. Looking upwards while trying to listen.

A better chance might not come.

Stark's feet came free. He wasn't sure he could trust them but had no choice. Hopping from knees to feet, sidestepping the pistol, he leapt as high as he could to kick Sinclair in the face. Hearing the chains, Sinclair turned, deflecting some of the blow, but staggering backwards and tumbling over the slab to the floor beyond, dropping the gun along the way.

Stark came down awkwardly, overbalancing sideways, half pulled by the chain into an uncontrolled twist, yanking hard on his right shoulder and leaving him facing downward, arms still behind him, gasping.

So far so mediocre. He was still tied by his wrists and if Sinclair wasn't incapacitated . . .

Twisting awkwardly until he could stand, he tucked his bound wrists beneath his backside and drop-sat with his full weight, yanking stationary inches above the ground with a grim pain in both wrists and shoulders but no notable effect on the cable.

There were sounds of Sinclair stirring . . .

Cursing, Stark struggled up and tried again.

This time he was sure he felt a wire part, but was equally sure it could just be wishful thinking and that Sinclair was getting up . . . No time to stand again; instead he pulled with his arms and all his might, twisting, muscles burning, skin tearing.

With a jerk, another wire parted, then the last, and Stark dropped on the floor with a suppressed grunt.

For a moment he couldn't move. The strain through his shoulders had left his left arm all but numb, but his right hand desperately yanked the cable free of the chain.

Sinclair's hand appeared on the far side of the slab.

Kelly screamed through her gag, arching away from him as much as her bonds allowed.

Sinclair pulled himself up.

Stark scrambled to the dropped gun and rolled to his feet, flicking off the safety, only to find his target all but obscured.

Sinclair was crouched behind Kelly, hand pulling her head back by the hair, a knife at her throat.

The small blade glinted in the harsh lighting.

At that moment the door to the garage splintered inward.

'ARMED POLICE! ARMED POLICE!' Two officers crabbed in, MP5 assault rifles raised. 'DROP YOUR WEAPONS!'

Weapons, plural. One of the officers was aiming at Sinclair, the other at Stark. But while Sinclair was crouched behind a steel slab with nothing exposed but part of his head and the arm holding a blade to Kelly's neck, Stark was standing in the open like a sitting duck.

Sinclair looked shocked, but more excited than scared. 'You first, I think.'

'*Drop the knife!*' barked one officer.

'*And you,*' barked the other at Stark, '*drop the gun!*''

No one moved.

'Best do as they say, Joe,' called Sinclair, half a grin visible.

'*Drop your weapons or we WILL shoot you.*''

'Drop yours or she dies,' replied Sinclair calmly. There was no clear shot on him and he guessed it.

'*Final warning!*'

Sinclair laughed. 'You took the words right out of my mouth.'

Again, no one moved.

'It's over, Julian,' called a familiar voice.

'*Well* ... if it isn't suspended-pending-dismissal DCI Groombridge,' crowed Sinclair. 'With DS Millhaven at heel like the faithful unthinking bitch. And *look*, Joe, your bit on the side made it to the party after all ... just in time for the climax.'

Stark stole a glance, shocked. Pensol, in a stab vest like the others – Dixon, Williams, Ptolemy and Peters. How they'd all come to be here was beyond him. For now all he could do was look into Kelly's cornflower-blue eyes, ringed red with tears, filled with fear, pleading ... and wish she'd swallowed the Rohypnol and been spared all this horror – or even more, that they had never met.

'Lower your weapons,' Sinclair said coldly. 'I won't ask again.'

It was the sudden coolness in his voice that tore Stark's gaze from Kelly.

Sinclair stared back at him.

Stark recalled the video of the suicide bomber he been shown over and over in training, eyes frozen with murderous intent, and the times he'd seen that look for real, like the eyes of a shark – entirely blank, even as it thrashed, jaws maniacally tearing – even as it smiled.

Slowly, Stark lowered his pistol. 'Do as he says,' he called to the armed officers. 'Lower your weapons.'

But they weren't here to take orders from him. He may be a police officer but he was not authorized to brandish a firearm. 'You first. Place your pistol on the floor and kick it our way.'

Sinclair stared at Stark and smiled, in victory, daring Stark to give in, to drop his gun or resist and be shot.

Kelly saw it too, her eyes pleading with him.

'Do it, Joe,' called Groombridge.

Sinclair laughed. 'Listen to the man, Joe. It's over. You lose.'

For a second the blade drifted away from Kelly's skin.

Stark nodded, took a step right and raised his pistol.

90

Gunshots echoed deafeningly in the tiled space.

A spent cartridge bounced across the floor like a little bell.

Smoke billowed in the percussion wave and snaked up from the gun barrel.

Blood ran down between Sinclair's eyes.

The knife clattered on the slab as all motor function ceased and his body gave in to gravity, crumpling to the floor.

Stark waited for the same to happen to him, for that sense of utter wrongness and detached, meaningless pain. But nothing came. One shot only, echoed.

'GUN DOWN NOW!' screamed the nearest AFO.

Stark stepped towards Sinclair, ready to add two in the chest, but they weren't needed. The spark was extinguished. No chance to look his enemy in the eyes and see the sickening hypocrite with not one ounce of mercy in his hollow soul beg for quarter. No chance to spit in his face. Anger had been the commonest driver in Stark's combat experience, but the fury that boiled up in him now twisted with a new and incandescent hatred.

His finger tightened on the trigger, ready to empty the magazine regardless.

'DON'T DO IT!' shouted the AFO, somewhere beyond Stark's caring, too far away to see Sinclair was already dead.

'Stark!' barked Groombridge, though he barely heard him.

'Joe!' pleaded another, Pensol, voice struck with dread. More blood to haunt her. On Sinclair's hands. On Stark's . . .

Only Kelly's muffled shouting somehow broke through, dragging his eyes from the object of his detestation.

Her look of abject shock tore into him ... *and he was in the dim concrete room in Helmand, the mother cradling her boy – seeing only the western devil with his gun* ... shaking her head ... tears rolling from horror-struck eyes, pleading with him to stop. Here, now, she had the humanity he'd long abandoned to war – and Sinclair had tried to extinguish her goodness.

He closed his eyes to shut her out ... To shut them all out.

'GUN DOWN!'

Stark looked round. Both MP5s were trained on him now. Both AFOs ready to shoot him dead if he made one more wrong move. The cavalry, as ever, sounding bugles over the hill after the infantry have bled to standstill.

But he was a soldier no longer.

A killer, complete.

Slowly, his finger eased off the trigger.

He carefully un-cocked his pistol, flicked the safety and placed it on the ground for the Scene of Crime team. Because that's what this was now.

A huge exhalation escaped Kelly's nose, followed by sobbing, then choking. Stark unclipped the gag so her vomit could escape.

'*Step away, kneel and interlock your fingers behind your head,*' barked the AFO sergeant as his colleague made safe the pistol.

Stark ignored him and set about untying Kelly.

In seconds others were helping, the AFOs shoved aside.

When she'd finished retching he slid Kelly gently down to sit with their backs to the slab, hugging her tightly. 'It's okay, Kelly, it's okay. It's over. No one can hurt you now, I swear. It's over.'

Someone wrapped a blanket around her shoulders. Stark heard the word ambulance, and Groombridge and Fran remonstrating hotly with the AFOs, who clearly thought Stark should be in cuffs.

Sinclair had bet on Stark's 'honour and restraint', in that last gleeful smile. He'd have cut Kelly's throat, dropped the blade and stepped back arms raised, believing neither Stark nor the AFOs would shoot an unarmed man presenting no further danger. He might have been right about the AFOs but Stark would have killed him for sure, soldier and copper forgotten, only the darkness left. So of the likeliest endings, Stark had chosen. A risky shot between two unconscionable downsides. Others would have to decide if he was right.

He felt nothing but numb cold now. Not even weariness. Fury and hatred were vanity. Slaying the monster without only fed that within, but what was another life to his tally – another piece of his soul? Blood, fear and death begat *themselves*.

He stared at the corpse, fixing it in his mind.

'Ambulance five minutes out,' said Dixon, kneeling before him. 'Are you hurt, Joe?'

Stark had no explicable answer. All he could do was hold Kelly's trembling shoulders. 'Leah Willoughby?'

'Found. By Harper. Rushed to hospital. Not promising, last I heard.'

'How'd you find them?'

'The neighbour, Baxter.'

'How'd you find us?'

'The undertakers ... Remember. *Your* idea. Follow the money, find the property. It was hiding in the failed fraud investigation files all along.'

Stark hadn't dared hope John would make the connection. He wanted to smile in thanks. He managed a nod.

Dixon tried to look encouraging. 'You're both safe now.'

Safe. As if there was any such place ...

'Trust you not to wait,' said Fran, appearing above him.

Stark could only manage a facial shrug. 'You didn't RSVP.'

'You left the address off the invite.'

Dixon glanced at Sinclair, steeling himself. 'The real Greenwich Strangler, after all.' He blew out a sigh. 'Guess his barrister won't be getting him off this time.' The question hidden inside – *You didn't fancy trying to take him alive?*

Stark held Kelly's shaking form, staring at the blood pooling out across the tiles from the back of Sinclair's head, dead eyes staring up at the ceiling. 'Fuck him.'

Dixon nodded slowly, then tried a smile. 'DI Harper will be

disappointed. He's halfway round his victory lap getting ready to tell the world it was Leech.'

Stark really didn't care.

Kelly's trembling had slowly subsided. Now her sobbing returned with vigour.

That was good. That was a start. The letting go.

His own body was rigid as stone in the crushing cold of orbit. Perhaps it would burn back to Earth eventually. Perhaps it would be better if it never did.

Epilogue
91

'Isn't this usually the other way around?' asked Stark, alluding to the times Kelly had stood beside *his* hospital bed.

Kelly smiled. 'It's still two-one.'

'Let's leave it at worst out of three.'

She took in his battered face and stiff movement with her physical therapist eyes. 'You look worse than me.'

'Superficial.'

She let that pass. 'Where have you been? I thought you'd be here when I woke?'

It burned that he'd not been. 'I had questions to answer.' And many more to follow. Any Authorized Firearms Officer responsible for a fatal shooting was automatically suspended pending enquiry, and Stark wasn't authorized. Stevens now had two sticks to beat him with. But none of that mattered.

Kelly nodded. Even now, her concern was for him, though she'd just endured ample demonstration that threats against him put his loved ones in collateral danger. It was over, now, this time; but it would never be over.

'My mum's on her way,' she said quietly. 'I don't know what to tell her.'

'Tell her everything. She never liked me anyway.'

'She *adored* you.'

'She watched me making you unhappy.'

Kelly blinked at his uncommon bluntness. Her mum had never said anything, but Stark knew he was right. 'Is this what it's like, Joe? In your world.'

She meant in his head, and what it would always be like. Stark wished he had a way of sugar-coating it but could only shrug.

Kelly looked appalled. 'It's not *fair*, Joe . . . You've spent all this time trying to re-learn how to live a normal life . . .'

She looked like she might cry, and he wasn't sure he could bear that. 'If I've learnt anything,' he forced a smile, 'it's to take each new normal as it comes.'

Kelly shook her head with a sad sigh and gestured to the visitor's chair. 'Can you stay a while?'

He sat, and she held out her hand for his.

Her grip was tight. The initial crying had just been the beginning. Stark knew that well. He hoped her path back to the light would be swift and conclusive. His own had lost ground last night. One rebirth too many. But now was not the time to address that. He'd already texted Hazel, asking her to drop by and see Kelly. Everything else could wait.

The numbness had faded, leaving him sore and too tired even for regret.

He wanted to get out of these clothes and shower and eat and sleep and get on with trying to pretend none of this had happened – that Kelly hadn't come within a blade's edge of paying for his sins with her life.

She ran her thumb over the bandages on his wrist, ripped raw from the bonds. One pain lost among many, he could hardly feel them at all. Her eyes lingered on his hands. 'Thank you,' she said, squeezing even tighter. Tears twinkled in the corner of her eyes.

'You wouldn't have been near any of this, were it not for me.'

She shook her head. 'This isn't your fault, Joe, you know that.' Stark nodded but she wasn't fooled. 'When will you learn the evils of the world are not your responsibility?'

'When the world stops directing evil at the people I love.'

She blinked again, then took a deep breath and sighed. 'I love you too, Joe.'

An old argument. A familiar tone. It was just as over as before this terror, almost certainly more so. Love might survive seeing the other person willingly kill, but not untarnished, and theirs was a long and winding road already. Sadness felt as meaningless now as anger, hate, love or hope. He was just relieved she was able to look on his face without recoiling.

She had finally seen what he really was. If she could still say she loved him after that, then that was a victory. As ever, bitter-sweet.

All those unspoken words seemed to fill her eyes now, surely drawing the same conclusion. 'Joe . . .'

'Kelly!' Robert rushed into the room.

Stark relinquished Kelly's hand and stood, backing away. Robert seized it in his and kissed her, pouring his concern over her like a waterfall, words gushing from him. No wonder Kelly liked him, after Stark. What might he think of Kelly still carrying a photo of her and Stark in her purse? Well, it was gone now, and Kelly was crying, and smiling. The happy ending. The cosy diorama.

The blithe optimism of the scene stung.

No doubt Robert would have words for him too, and questions. If the man was half as generous with his bad opinion as he seemed with his good, then Stark didn't care to stick around to hear it. Silently, he backed out and left them to their world, retreating into the shadows of his.

Kelly accepted Robert's fawning concern, wincing at the pain of his embrace and consequent apologies.

When she managed to look up, Joe was gone.

Last night she had finally seen the monster that terrified him, the darkness he caged inside himself and which caged him in turn. When fear would paralyse most and despair take the rest, he'd reached inside for something more. Combining the fury he dreaded with the indomitable courage he denied, he had done what he had to. And in the terrifying aftershock, consumed with rage, radiating the fearsome joy of righteous destruction, he'd looked her in the eye and packed it all away.

But the bleakness that replaced it was enough to make her weep.

She had finally seen the one thing he most feared showing her – exactly what he was capable of. In this, as in so many things, he was the strongest man she knew. But whether, having shown her his darkest side, he would ever forgive himself, was another matter. Before Robert's untimely arrival, he'd hardly been able to tolerate her gaze. While the events of last night might haunt her for weeks, months or years, she knew that sharing this last of himself with her might haunt Joe forever.

And now he was gone. Again.

She'd missed her chance. In the pub, yesterday – to tell him she was standing at a crossroads looking back. And now – to tell him she'd seen past all his fears to the light at the centre of his darkness.

A blonde girl had helped her to the ambulance, whispering about the sleepy girl's voice answering Joe's door buzzer that morning, a lifetime ago. Joe's wounded colleague, finding sanctuary, a friend-in-need, nothing more. Such a pretty girl, with something similar in her eyes to Joe's. Kelly could only cry more in response. And now Robert's arrival had cut off her apology, and any chance of more, perhaps forever.

Missed chances.

Love flew or fell on timing.

She'd stumbled across a star lying broken in the sand and held the pieces to her heart until it burned. And now, as finally its fusion had begun to re-forge him, she must endure seeing his glow recede into the void, leaving only the memory of heat, of churning fire in the vast, cold vacuum – brightest star in a sky of lesser objects.

'Don't ever do this to me again,' complained Robert, still holding her hand too tight.

She looked at his handsome face, creased with sincere concern, and forced a smile.

He let out an exaggerated sigh of relief as if all the pressure of the world had been on his shoulders tonight, and not the man who'd just stepped out of his way. 'I love you.' He beamed. 'There . . . I've said it. Kelly Jones, I *love* you.'

Good-looking, kind, generous, funny, demonstrative and emotionally available . . . What more could a girl wish for?

Kelly nodded and sighed, forcing another smile and wiping at her tears. 'I know.'

92

. . . Thanks to the hard work, dedication and team effort in coordin-
ation of a complex, wide-ranging and fast-moving investigation,
with national and international importance . . .

Led by *me*.

Harper stared at his reflection on the mirror, adjusting his arm in
the sling, unsure if it was the right look or not.

Stevens was waiting outside, ready to introduce him to the eager
press. Ready to usurp credit where he could for his own ends.

Harper glanced down at the leather folder open on the vanity unit
with his notes.

Inside too, a plain manila envelope found on his desk containing
print-outs of news stories involving the Met police, insightful and
cutting, often quoting sources close to investigations – all by Scarlet
Jennings, the peroxide reporter with a penchant for red and tripping
up detective inspectors with insider info. The earliest cutting was
highlighted, three years old – an exclusive interview with newly
minted Deputy Assistant Commissioner Stevens, discussing police
reform and consolidation, while diffidently playing down 'rumours'
of his being tipped as a future Police Commissioner.

The envelope also contained a photo. *The* photo – of Harper
handing case information to Stevens prior to the recent shootings.
There was a Post-it-note stuck on it, with what looked like Groombridge's handwriting.

The only copy.
Always ask – who stands to gain what?

Good *bloody* question, thought Harper bitterly.

The evidence against Leech appeared incontrovertible, and easily enough to pin him as the Strangler and the prison shooter, until Fran spoilt the party with her news of Sinclair – caught red-handed and shot dead by Golden-*fucking*-balls Stark of all people, after apparently confessing everything from Leech to Leah. And half the bloody station there, while Harper stood over a cooling decoy halfway across town.

Two burner phones had been found in the car, Leech's prints on one, Sinclair's on the other, each logging calls to the other. Doubtless how they'd communicated from prison too. And most damning – a hard drive containing the worst of all horrors – snuff movies. Harper had turned away, doubting his eyeballs would ever feel clean again. Some poor sod in forensics would have to use 'distinguishing features' to identify the gimp-masked killer as Sinclair.

Sinclair was the Greenwich Strangler, Leech his puppet accomplice – just as Harper had called it after Sinclair's laughable claims about his so-called visitor. And while he may have missed out on the final collar, the whole case was solved with Harper at the helm – *Senior Investigating Officer* – not Fran or Mike.

But sat there, right at the centre of it like a stubborn stain, Joseph Stark.

Always, *always, bloody Stark.*

Suspended, officially now – standard procedure, pending a shooting enquiry. Brass would try to keep that quiet, but Goldenballs would be straight on the phone to his redhead reporter, and doubtless walk free unpunished, the nation's hero – again.

Maybe Stevens really *was* the leak, but Stark would still be all over the news. Either way, Harper would make damn sure neither of them screwed him over. He had a meeting with National Crime later. Stark's statement included Sinclair confessing to stranglings far beyond Greenwich, even overseas. Harper could find himself working with Interpol – maybe even swing a posting – take Jess to live in Lyon; she loved France.

That should all be worth lead item on today's news and tomorrow's front page, but instead it would be Stark's face. Well, two could play that game. If Julian Sinclair had planned to use Stark's fame as a springboard for his own ego, Harper could do the same for his career. The smug prick could hog all the credit he wanted, and Harper would be there in every spotlight.

Stevens would probably do likewise. Harper would save his disciplinary report against Stark for now, and get busy expanding on the contents of this envelope on Stevens. Insurance.

In the meantime, this was it. Finally, his moment of triumph, and to hell with Stark, Fran, Groombridge and Stevens.

He took off the sling and checked his reflection with a smile. Robust leader trumped wounded warrior in the long run, every time.

Onwards and upwards and never look back.

'You okay, Guv?' Dixon had done admirably well to keep questions to himself this long.

'Peachy.' Groombridge continued to stare out the car window at the front of his fog-shrouded little house, where Alice would still be sleeping. Somehow that was enough – to keep the best part of his heart here, oblivious to all the horror and hurt.

'But you're not suspended any more?'

'Unofficially.' DAC Stevens knew which way the wind blew.

'Brass playing the "we were right all along" card?'

Groombridge almost smiled. It was easy to forget Dixon had a half-decent brain behind his meekness, without which last night might have turned out very differently. 'Something like that.' Though it must stick in Stevens' throat, he thought with little satisfaction.

'We got the bastard – that's what counts.'

Groombridge nodded. 'We did.'

Right in front of their eyes. In all his years of dead bodies, he'd never witnessed the moment of death. Neither had Dixon, who seemed to be coping surprisingly well.

Sinclair dead. Brian Leech dead. Leah Willoughby barely surviving a lethal dose through the protracted efforts of the paramedics.

She was stable now. How she would be long-term was less certain. Perhaps she would recall nothing beyond her abduction, but perhaps not remembering was worse. They hardly needed her testimony this time either way.

Case closed.

DAC Stevens insinuating himself into the glory. Harper too, seizing his moment in the limelight.

Groombridge actually felt sorry for him. His career would get the boost he craved, but knowing he owed much of it to Stark might eat away at him for years.

There was no way to keep Stark's name out of it, or Kelly's. The press would lap it up – the nation coming within a blade's edge of losing their hero and his beloved. The only thing they could hope to hold back was Stark being the shooter. The standard enquiry into police shootings typically anonymized the officers in question. Officer A in this case wasn't authorized, but there was enough grey there to smudge the truth, for now. Unless Stevens leaked it.

Stark needed more fame like a bigger target painted on his back. How many deaths had he seen, or inflicted, God help him? Groombridge burned to question him further, but there were investigative walls between them now. They were all witnesses, to the kind of man he really was.

What a world.

'Perhaps I'm just tired,' he mused quietly.

'Guv?'

'Never mind.'

On news of his suspension, Stark had just chuckled darkly, saying he already *was*. Harper hadn't mentioned the altercation, but Stevens . . .

Groombridge and Cox were old men in this game, but Stark was the future. He had to be. Leaving Groombridge with no choice but to resort to the leverage he'd been unearthing. So a copy of the news printouts he'd left Owen was also on its way to Stark's press pal, Gwen Maddox.

After her string of scoops, Scarlet Jennings was getting more time in front of the cameras. Groombridge could hardly request warrants to go digging for any financial link, and Stevens' shiny yacht predated the possible connection. Yet it had provided one loose edge by which the truth might be unpeeled – Stevens' pride and joy, pictured in full sail so prominently on the yacht club website, of which he was of course Commodore. And buried among Scarlet's broad and calculated social media output, a selfie of her at sea with the Needles coastline beyond – and a familiar sliver of sail and partial sail-number. Money wasn't the only form of mutual back-scratching, and what self-respecting marriage-cheat needed traceable short hotel stays when he owned a boat with a nice comfy bed to put the seal on the oldest form of reciprocity. And they might've remained discreet, had their misdeeds not sat a twenty-year detective on his arse at home with their knives in his back and a team to protect.

Groombridge might have tried passing this upstairs, but ammunition gifted to rivals might be used to keep Stevens in his place rather than oust him. If the threat he posed to Greenwich and the wider Met was to be mitigated, the ordnance had to be delivered from without. And if Maddox couldn't join the ugly picture from those dots she wasn't worthy of the trust Stark seemed to place in her.

Like so much in this life, only time might tell if this was the right course of action. Whether or not mud stuck to Stevens, the Met's reputation would be tarnished yet again.

Groombridge took a deep breath and blew out a long sigh. 'Right,' he said, opening the door. 'Usual time tomorrow.'

'You coming to bed or not?'

Marcus, propped blearily in the doorway to his bedroom.

He'd not been on call last night. Fran had crept in, so as not to wake him. She'd made it as far as the kitchenette, staring out the window at the mist curling around nearby buildings as if trying to claw them away into the elsewhere, leaving Fran alone in a shrinking bubble.

Receiving no answer, he joined her, glancing without comment at the large glass of Chardonnay in her hand with the sun hardly up, let alone over the yardarm.

She barely recalled pouring it. She'd not taken a sip.

'How'd it go?'

Fran thought about that. 'Sinclair and his accomplice guilty and dead. Leah Willoughby alive.' DAC Stevens and Harper triumphant, she continued in the discomfort of her own thoughts. Groombridge's career still uncertain, Stark's hanging by a thread and no one allowed to speak with him even after he'd given his statement to the police shootings investigator from Legal Services. So many questions to be answered, and Fran too tired to force their asking. For now, at least.

Harper hadn't even had the decency to look smug.

Miranda Moncrieff had shown up, bristling and demanding information, and left pale as a ghost after being informed that the man she'd invested time, energy and misplaced love into freeing was not only guilty as sin, but had spelt out his true and terrifying intentions towards her before his death. Much as she wanted to, Fran couldn't seem to take a pleasure in that either. 'Expect to see Stark's face in the news.' At least it might steal some of Harper's thunder.

Marcus nodded, the way men did when they didn't realize they were supposed to be saying something . . . anything . . . 'Will they let you sit the exam in a few days' time, under the circumstances?'

The Inspectors' Exam. Due to begin in . . . four hours. She sighed. Well, she'd wanted an excuse . . . Groombridge could hardly complain. 'They're every six months.'

And what use was she anyhow? Sinclair had run rings round her. Had her doubting her very core. While Harper, of all people, had been right about multiple killers – thrusting out his lantern jaw now for the TV cameras, reaping every ounce of glory, turning her stomach.

And that wasn't the only thing.

Three different test kits from an all-night pharmacy, all positive. What on earth was she supposed to think about that? At *her* age, with *her* job; with a man she hardly knew? How on earth was she even going to tell him?

All she could think of was the desolation in Rhonda Talbot's eyes . . . To give birth was to grow an extra heart in the chest of another, to square your capacity for love while doubling the risk – that if one heart were to die, out there in the world beyond your protection, both would. The world she inhabited, the horrors she witnessed, made her tremble at the very prospect.

Marcus pursed his lips, nodding without understanding. 'I'll put the kettle on then.'

Fran's gaze slid from the all-enveloping mist to the wine in her hand, slowly tipping it down the sink with a sigh.

93

Managing to avoid any press staking out the hospital and the curious glances and verbal probes from the taxi driver, Stark felt grateful for the thick fog enveloping the drive home. His one concession to the wider world had been a quick call to tip off Gwen with the little information he could, off the record. They'd all find out about Stark and Kelly soon enough, and Gwen could be trusted not to turn the opening salvo into a sensationalist broadside.

Closing the door to his flat, he closed his eyes and drank in the silence.

Home. Where else was there left?

A note on the counter, from yesterday, with the spare key.

Thank you for everything. M x

The place felt suddenly empty without her. As it had after Kelly.

Drink deep from the well of victory, soldier, and quit your whining, as his colour sergeant would have said. The killers were all dead. Kelly was safe. Harper was welcome to the credit. Groombridge would survive. Fran would steam. The rest would do just fine.

Stark's teetering career was out of his hands for now. Stevens seemed to be holding off on turning his unofficial suspension into a formal report, waiting to see which way the wind blew, but he still needed someone to vent his frustration upon. Legal Services had taken Stark's warrant card for the shooting. Suspended, pending enquiry. Something else for Harper to smile about.

'Best all round if you're out of the picture for a while,' the Legal Services inspector had suggested.

Stark could hardly disagree.

'This might not help your medal chances, I'm afraid,' she'd added.

The George Cross had slipped way down his list of concerns in the last week. 'Silver lining,' he'd said, earning a look of deep curiosity from her.

'Of course,' she'd added casually, as she stood to go. 'Being suspended on full pay does not disqualify you from sitting your Sergeants' Exam this morning, if you'd a mind.'

Stark hadn't given it a moment's thought. Perhaps Fran would still sit hers, keep part of Groombridge's succession plan alive at least. He thought of Pensol's words – about being done with uniforms. What would she think after last night, or think of him? Later, once he could think straight, he might ask her *not* to give up, to complete her two years' probation and apply for Trainee Detective. If Fran was Groombridge's legacy, perhaps Pensol might be his. That would be something at least.

Seeing his copy of *Crow*, open face down on the coffee table where she'd left it, he picked it up and flicked to the poem called 'Lineage' and the words that had been haunting him awake and asleep, warning him to question the origins of all . . .

> *In the beginning was Scream*
> *Who begat Blood*
> *Who begat Eye*
> *Who begat Fear*

Taking from his pocket the two halves of the photo he'd retrieved from the floor of the undertakers – he and Kelly ripped apart and ground beneath the heel of fate – he tucked them into the book, closed it and slid it into its slot on the bookcase. Kelly would hardly want them back. In two days' time she'd fly away somewhere warm with nice-guy Robert and start putting all this and Stark behind her. Safe beyond the minefield for good.

Best all round.

Stark could see no other future worth the worry. Six days since

414

Fran's call kicked this whole mess off – and on the seventh the wicked might rest.

So many parts of him hurt and his eyes begged to close, but sleep held little prospect of respite from the sadness and horror. The Oxy and sleeping pills sang siren from the bathroom cabinet, calling beguilingly towards painlessness and time deleted, but some enemies needed to be faced head on.

'Who begat hope,' he sighed, bone-weary, reaching past the cheap stuff for the Royal Lochnagar Selected Reserve Highland Single Malt, and a glass.

Acknowledgements

The book before you is much changed from its brimming first draft but, I hope, the better for it. For this I owe immeasurable thanks to my editors, Rowland, Ariel and Ruth, for their patience and clear-sightedness, to my agent, Andrew, for level-headed support and my copy-editor, Sarah, for her collegiate engagement and fine-tooth comb. Thanks also to fellow crime author, ex-soldier and ex-cop, Matt Johnson, for help with the police radio-traffic lingo and for your service.

Thank you *all who serve* – for your selflessness and inspiration.

My heartfelt appreciation must also go to all the wonderful readers who contacted me with thrilling plaudits for *If I Should Die* and *Between the Crosses* and requests for me to hurry up with more. Sorry it took so long. Thanks, likewise, to all you tireless book reviewers, bloggers and those of you generous enough to offer kind book-club or purchase reviews online. As the saying goes – *Feed an Author, leave a review!*

A shout-out to all publishers, booksellers and libraries in these challenging times – keep the faith.

Of course, the most gratitude goes ever to the beating heart of me – my beloved wife, sons, parents, siblings, in-laws and all my family and friends – for your love and support, and for allowing me time away in other parts of my brain. And to my late mother-in-law, Jen, the kindest and most generous of human beings – ever missed.